Alexandra Kollontai was born in 1872 into an aristocratic liberal family. At the age of twenty she married Vladimir Kollontai by whom she had one son. Early in her life she became involved in radical circles, and the conflicts this created caused her, when she was only twenty-six, to leave her beloved son and husband for a life of independent political action.

By 1917 she was on the Central Committee of the Bolshevik Party. One of the few to welcome Lenin from exile at the Finland Station, she became Commissar of Social Welfare – the only woman in Lenin's 1917 government.

Her political and personal life were always stormy. Differences with Lenin forced her to leave the government in 1918. Her two great loves, the revolutionaries Dybenko and Shlyapnikov, both perished in the 30s. Kollontai herself spent the remainder of her life in a succession of diplomatic posts in Scandinavia and Mexico, virtually a political exile.

In her numerous books, pamphlets and speeches, Kollontai expounded innovatory theories about the role of women and the importance of sexual and personal relationships in a revolutionary society. She died in Russia in 1952, unaware that her ideas were to gain her international recognition from a new generation.

Love of Worker Bees

ALEXANDRA KOLLONTAI

Translated by
Cathy Porter

Afterword by
Sheila Rowbotham

CASSANDRA EDITIONS
ACADEMY
PRESS
LIMITED
CHICAGO
1978

Cassandra Editions 1978

Translation copyright © 1977 Cathy Porter

ISBN 0-89733-001-3 paper

ISBN 0-89733-002-1 cloth

Contents

Other books by Alexandra Kollontai in English translation

Autobiography of a Sexually Emancipated Woman, London 1972
Sexual Relations and the Class Struggle and *Love and the New Morality*,
London 1972
Communism and the Family, London 1971, 1973
Women Workers' Struggle for their Rights, London 1971, 1973
The Workers' Opposition, Solidarity Pamphlet No. 7 1962
International Woman's Day, London 1972
Alexandra Kollontai: Selected Writings, edited with commentaries
by Alix Holt, London 1977

Love of Worker Bees has never before been published in
English in its complete form. 'Vasilisa Malygina' was
published in New York in 1927 under the title *Red Love*
and in England in 1931 under the title *Free Love*.

Introduction

For many people who know something of Alexandra Kollontai's political writings but are not aware that she wrote any fiction, this novel and the two short stories will be a revelation. In them, she gives us an extraordinarily vivid picture of people's everyday lives, during and after the Bolshevik revolution, and describes, as few other writers of her time were able to, the passions and fears of men and women whose private and most intimate sexual relationships were being so publicly discussed and questioned at that time.

She wrote *Love of Worker Bees* to reach as wide an audience as possible, to make it accessible to large numbers of women who might not otherwise read, and who might find in it a reflection of their lives and experiences. Short sentences and a simple vocabulary, although certainly making it accessible to Kollontai's contemporaries, do not necessarily make for easy reading fifty years later. And so I have sometimes lengthened and elided sentences and occasionally expanded vocabulary a little, as confident as any translator ever can be that the situations she is writing about do not lose too much of their atmosphere in the process.

Alexandra Kollontai was born Alexandra Mikhailovna Domontovich. the daughter of a wealthy former General in the Tsar's army, a fairly liberal, widely read man. Her mother, energetic and resourceful, was the daughter of a simple Finnish wood-merchant. She brought to this love match a son and two daughters from a previous, arranged marriage. When the Domontovich's first daughter, Alexandra, was born she immediately became the family favourite.

But she grew up a solitary child, neglected by her mother who was constantly preoccupied with running the family estates in Finland and St Petersburg, as well as by her father who was absorbed in the melancholy task of assessing Russia's military failures in the Balkans. The family divided their time between

7

their homes in the capital and in Finland and from her earliest years Alexandra immersed herself in her parents' libraries, reading all the novels and literary and political journals that she could find.

When she was sixteen, she furiously opposed her parents' plans to bring her out into the St Petersburg marriage market, and wanted passionately to leave home and study abroad. Instead, she started writing stories and studying more systematically.

Regular visitors to the Domontovich home at this time were the Kollontais, Ukrainian relatives of the General. With their son Vladimir, an impoverished and elegant young captain, Alexandra embarked on a romantic friendship which her parents' disapproval did nothing to discourage. Two years later she threatened to leave home if her parents did not give their consent to the marriage, and it was finally decided that a conventional marriage, however unsuitable, would be far preferable for their beautiful daughter than a life of precarious independence.

Vladimir, who was now rising in the bureaucracy as a factory inspector, was a man of apparently limited imagination but unlimited devotion to his young wife. Not long after her marriage and the birth of her son, Misha, Alexandra was privately referring to Vladimir as 'her tyrant'. It was when the claims of her adored husband and son overwhelmed her, and led to her first, terrifying 'revolt against love's tyranny' that she began in earnest to write short stories. She wrote not merely to keep alive natural passions stifled by domestic tedium, but also to jolt other women out of their docility and encourage them to assert themselves against the traditional claims of love and marriage.

The stories were never published, and she realized she had been putting her ideas into a literary mould that was no longer capable of containing them. Infinitely more painfully, she was learning to question whether patterns of domination and dependence between men and women could ever be truly transformed within marriage.

1896 was the year she described as the turning-point in her life. It was the year of her first major political disagreement with Vladimir, with whom she had witnessed, for the first time in her life, the appalling realities of workers' existence in a large textile factory. Disgusted by Vladimir's bland assurances about the need for minor improvements in working conditions, it was chiefly her rage at this which led her to seek out members of the Marxist Union of Struggle for the Working Class; this group had formed in the previous year to unite the various Marxist discussion groups in the capital, and was led, as she put it, 'by a man named Lenin'.

By now Marxism was beginning to have more than a merely emotional resonance for her, and she was instinctively drawn to the circles of the revolutionary St Petersburg intelligentsia. For them, too, 1896 was a turning-point, and the year of the Union's greatest propaganda success, as the capital was swept by a wave of strikes. Participating in these strikes were large numbers of women who downed tools in the textile factories in common protest with the men. It was largely from her contact with these women that Alexandra eventually derived the strength to leave her husband, taking her son Misha with her, in order to study the situation in Russia and to participate politically in the events of the period.

Many years later, in her *Autobiography of a Sexually Emancipated Woman*, she described this sad choice as prompted by the 'eternal defensive war against the encroachment of men on our individuality, a struggle revolving around the problem: work, or marriage and love'. Some twenty years later, when she wrote *Love of Worker Bees*, the choice remained an equally painful one for her women characters. The novel and the stories, which derive so much of their honesty from her own experiences, urge women to draw their strength from each other, even if necessary, at the terrible cost of breaking with loved husbands and families. She was always to keep Vladimir's surname in affectionate memory of him and as a reminder of the importance of her years with him.

In her early eager studies of Marxism she had been deeply conscious of the interests and needs of women, but unlike many women of her class, her studies of Marxism and her friends amongst the women factory workers helped her always to locate women firmly in their class first, and then to define the *specific* areas in which they had to fight for their freedom.

Russian women had experienced the first conflict between a feminist and a socialist interpretation of their oppression in the last few years of the nineteenth century. The feminists regarded women's oppression as the primary oppression, regardless of the part women played in the economy; they rejected any analysis of women's special role in the class struggle, and they fought for equalities which would affect only their particular privileged interests in patriarchal Russia.

This was the generation of Olga Sergeevna's mother in 'Three Generations', and of Kollontai's own mother, women of Populist sympathies who did charity work for the peasants, demanded their right to education, and struggled to love and marry the man of their choice.

The socialist women, militant factory workers and women like Olga Sergeevna, found their inspiration in the women revolutionaries of the People's Will Party, and they allied themselves with the larger Marxist revolutionary movement, which regarded the liberation of women as an essential factor in the liberation of the entire oppressed working class.

Out of these two contrary tendencies the powerful women's movement of the twentieth century was born, bursting into industrial militancy in the 1905 revolution, and firmly inscribing itself in the history of the February and October revolutions of 1917. Vasilisa Malygina, and Olga Sergeevna's daughter, Zhenya, are both daughters of this movement, both of them 'new women' of the type Kollontai has described elsewhere in her writings. It was in part the first conflict between her personal and political life which enabled Kollontai to begin her exploration of the special ways women interact with their class.

After leaving Vladimir in 1898 and entrusting her son to her parents' care, she set off with a close friend for Zürich. There she hoped to study with some of Europe's finest Marxist economists, and to rediscover the atmosphere of political optimism which Russian women students had brought to that city in the 1870s. But the journey was a disappointment, and finding little in common with her professor, she turned instead to the writings of Karl Kautsky and Rosa Luxembourg.

Returning to Russia, she moved in with her parents and happily re-established contact with her son. She found now that the Social Democrats in the capital were sharply divided between those insisting on the need for a strong centralized party in order to lead the workers to a proletarian revolution, and those who believed that the workers themselves could gradually achieve their goals through trade-union activities. (The young Olga Sergeevna in 'Three Generations' found these 'revisionists' extremely distasteful when she stayed with M.) These opposing views eventually resulted in the Bolshevik–Menshevik split.

Kollontai was also struck by the discovery that women in the factories were now playing an important role in industrial negotiations, and were beginning to voice independent demands for equal pay and maternity leave. But these women had little organized support outside the factories. It was the professional women who were organized into feminist groups, demanding the vote and access to the professions, and it was the revolution of 1905 which brought to a head Kollontai's ideological clash with these feminist groups, and also made clear to her how loath the Bolsheviks were to endorse the actions of militant women.

When on 9 January 1905 a huge crowd of workers bearing ikons and led by a priest, humbly carried to the Tsar their petition for a constitutional government, Bolsheviks and Mensheviks helplessly tried to intervene and then watched in horror as soldiers hacked down this peaceful ragged demonstration in what came to be known as 'Bloody Sunday'. '1905 saw me on the streets,' wrote Alexandra, who took issue with both Bolsheviks and Mensheviks by unequivocally supporting every attempt by the workers to strike and demonstrate.

Shattered by the atrocious events of Bloody Sunday, she then witnessed the ensuing wave of mass strikes throughout Russia. She was now convinced that women workers must be recruited and mobilized for industrial action; the liberal feminist Union of Women's Equality must be transformed into the 'first organization to adopt any political platform'. In order to encourage factory women to discuss their problems with each other at work and at home, she organized a large women's club in the capital. Realizing that, but for this club, vast numbers of women militants might otherwise be attracted to the Menshevik-supported women's groups, the Bolsheviks supported the club.

In 1908, when feminist groups began making tentative and rather unconvincing gestures towards women factory workers, whose support they wanted for a conference, Kollontai decided to exploit the occasion to mobilize women workers. She wanted them to make radical demands for full economic and sexual equality. She wrote pamphlets, conferred endlessly with women workers, and was inspired to start work on her next book, *The Social Basis of the Women's Question.*

But by now her political activities were attracting the interest of the police, and she was forced to move out of her parents' home so as not to jeopardize them and her son by her 'illegal' actions. Largely because of her activities, the conference was stopped by the police before it had properly begun. Leaving her son behind again, she fled the country and went to Germany.

During her nine years of exile in Europe and America, she

acquired a deep and lasting distrust for the generally reformist policies of the various European social democratic parties; as the realities of a European war grew closer, she devoted most of her time to delivering impassioned speeches against conscription. The outbreak of World War I decided her eventually to join the Bolsheviks in calling for an end to the war and for the re-formation of the International.

Her life in exile ended abruptly with the February Revolution in 1917. A couple of months later she met Lenin and thirty other political émigrés off the train which had guaranteed their safe passage across enemy territory and brought them triumphantly to the Finland station. She waited as Lenin made his celebrated speech to the crowd of 800 people who had come to greet them and then left with him and several other Bolsheviks for the Party's headquarters, where members were given their agitational and propaganda tasks.

Alexandra Kollontai had proved herself a passionate and persuasive speaker while in Europe. She was now entrusted with the crucially important job of addressing the hundreds of sailors on the battleships stationed near the capital. Amongst these men was Pavel Dybenko, President of the Baltic Fleet Central Committee of the Party, and she and Dybenko fell in love. It was thanks to the passion which infused their speeches that Kerensky lost virtually all support amongst the sailors.

But the army too was crumbling, as all along the Western Front thousands of soldiers deserted their posts and joined the Bolsheviks in demanding an end to the war. In October a group of military delegates to Kerensky's Assembly refused obedience to the General Staff and claimed allegiance to the Bolsheviks, whereupon Kerensky left the capital, ostensibly in the deluded hope of rallying front-line troops to march on the capital. On 25 October, Bolshevik soldiers seized the Winter Palace in his absence, and installed the new Bolshevik government. It was as commissar for Public Welfare in this government that Kollontai faced some of the enormous tasks confronting the administration of ravaged, war-torn Russia.

With the ending of the imperialist war by the treaty of Brest-Litovsk, the Bolsheviks then had to deal with the civil war, which threatened to disrupt the new government. The policies of War Communism needed to meet the emergency of the civil war, posed grave economic and political dangers for the future of the revolution; securing a grain surplus in conditions of scarcity produced particular problems, not least of which were profiteering and bureaucracy, against which Lenin so constantly inveighed. Paralysing inflation – prices were rising by something like $1\frac{1}{2}$ million per cent – meant that money was being replaced by increasingly arbitrary criteria of value, and 'wages in kind' were too imprecise to give any guidelines for the future communist economy.

There were some women, however, many of them as young as Zhenya in 'Three Generations', who profited from the universal conscription of labour imposed by the emergency. For them, this first liberating experience of working actively for the revolution, the collective living quarters and the communal crêches and canteens – however squalid and overcrowded – provided a rough-and-ready model for a genuinely collective and communist society.

Later attempts at collective living, such as Vasilisa Malygina tried to encourage in her communal house, took much of their inspiration from this period. Zhenya herself emerged from the civil war as a committed Party worker, with the courage and energy to believe that this model of collective living *could* be realized. But if Zhenya's attitudes and her spontaneous adolescent sexuality were considered repellent by her mother (and by Kollontai's critics, who wilfully identified Zhenya's attitudes with those of her author), it should also be remembered that Zhenya's experiences were by no means typical of the women of that period.

By the end of the civil war, women still put their faith in the Party's intentions to integrate them into the skilled labour force and to socialize housework, moves that had been postponed during the civil war. But this faith helped to conceal the many unprotected areas in women's lives which exposed them all too easily to the insidious attitudes and policies of the past. For all over the new socialist republic, families, couples, young men and women alternately challenged and defended the old accepted notions about monogamy, 'women's work', and women's new role in the economy. Inevitably there lingered on many powerful prejudices against women, which even the most fundamental legislation redefining family and sexual attitudes could not hope to eradicate.

During the early period of the revolution, Lenin had been eager to answer all problems of cultural, economic and administrative life with a series of decrees, one of the first being the revolutionary new marriage law.

Kollontai realized, however, that the chaotic state machinery inherited by the Bolsheviks would ensure that these measures were more powerful as a means of propaganda than as an administrative reality; their important function was to tell the people the nature of the new Party, and how it intended to accomplish its aims. The marriage law, however comprehensive, could actually promise no more than a *programme* for the activities required to bring about the liberation of Soviet women, a framework within which each woman could struggle to improve her position at work and in the family.

Kollontai also realized that there could be no genuinely revolutionary changes in family and sexual relationships until workers' demands were located firmly at the point of production, and workers' demands for increasing trade union control over industry had been fully discussed. It had been in the mutual association and collective discipline of trade union activity that militant women workers in the revolution of 1905 had come to an increasingly confident awareness of their needs, and had developed as revolutionary fighters, demanding their place in the Bolshevik Party and helping to bring that Party to power.

Unless the essential power of the working class was based in the unions, they reasoned, large sections of less organized workers, including many novice women workers who had learnt to identify with the Party, would be forced off the stage and would then merely delegate to their Party the immense task of building a new society. It was these ideas which drew Kollontai to the Workers' Opposition group, which clashed with Lenin and the Party majority over the introduction of the New Economic Policy.

As early as 1918, in the midst of the civil war, the debate about the running of the railways had thrown up the crucial controversy of 'one-man management' of industry. Trotsky, seconded by Lenin, proposed that specialists and technicians be given considerable autonomous control over sophisticated technical and industrial processes.

For many workers, this appeared to be in such flagrant contradiction of earlier Bolshevik promises of workers' control that demoralization set in amongst active sections of the working class. It was trade unionists like Alexander Shlyapnikov, President of the All-Russian Metalworkers' Union, who gave momentum to the Workers' Opposition group. Alexandra Kollontai embarked on a love affair with Shlyapnikov and it was to her that this group turned when drafting the theses of the Workers' Opposition.

The Party leaders clearly intended to abandon many of the policies of War Communism as soon as the emergency would permit, and a few months after the end of the civil war Trotsky proposed introducing a grain tax and restoring the market as a means of distribution. These proposals were introduced a few months later – literally within weeks of the civil war victory and the withdrawal of the imperialist troops – as the New Economic Policy (NEP).

Lenin was to admit frankly that the NEP was in many ways a retreat from the principles of the revolution, and a tactical means of easing contradictions in the economy, whose only real solution could lie in an international proletarian revolution. To operate profitably now, at a time when prices were so high, meant an inevitable growth in unemployment, which was at around one million throughout the 20s.

Inevitably, too, large numbers of new unskilled workers were recently urbanized peasants and women, who had thus gained jobs only to lose them again. Peasants returned to the countryside, large numbers of women were deprived of their jobs, and much existing provision for collectivized housework and childcare disappeared. But there were more insidious, psychological pressures other than purely economic ones which urged women back to the confines of housework and monogamous marriage, as we see very clearly in *Love of Worker Bees*. For the truly desperate women, with no family or husband to support them, there were always the streets and plenty of 'nepmen' with money in their pockets wanting to escape from their wives for a while.

The Workers' Opposition foresaw many of the horrors that accompanied the NEP. When their proposals were discussed and defeated at the 10th Party congress in 1921 their faction was banned and many of its members subsequently expelled from the Party. The following year, Kollontai applied for a modest posting in Russia to Stalin, then acting Party secretary. She found herself appointed as a member of the Soviet trade delegation to Oslo. 1922 was the first year of her 'honorary exile', and from that year until her death in 1952 the chilly diplomatic world kept her far from the questions she had never stopped asking in her own country.

In *Love of Worker Bees* the revolution is given flesh and blood, in all its ambiguities. It is in the sexual feeling of the women that

Kollantai reveals so movingly their struggles and weaknesses, their capacity to love and their confusions about their new freedom. Their moods and feelings are veiled with none of the Victorian discretion that marked such radical precursors as Chernyshevsky. In a generally neglected passage, Lenin laments the absence of 'dreamers in our movement'. In *Love of Worker Bees* Kollontai is voicing the dreams, the fears and the fragile confusions of women involved in the process of changing their lives.

When it came out in 1923, as part of the series *Revolution in Feelings and Morality, Love of Worker Bees* was generally regarded as unwholesomely preoccupied with sexual matters. Nine years later it was being solemnly invoked as a model of 'petit-bourgeois debauchery', a judgement which ensured it never reached the audience for which it was intended and which leaves us wondering what exactly was considered so offensive about the stories. For despite the joyful and obsessional aspects of the sexual relationships which she describes, and the importance granted to people's sexuality, there is sometimes a sanctimonious sentimentality which creeps into the descriptions of her women characters at their moments of greatest crisis and tension, which suggests that Kollontai was writing about deep and unresolved emotional problems.

Later readers may be irritated by the prolonged refusal of these women to accept anything which might disrupt the happiness they sought with their husbands and lovers, and Kollontai frequently describes physical passion as a sort of defence against the harshly rational demands of independence. It is when their sexual attachment to their lovers finally threatens to lead these women into isolation and an anxious inactivity that they find the courage to define their own real needs.

Olga Sergeevna, Vasilisa Malygina and the narrator of 'Sisters' have all met and grown to love their lovers at the time of their greatest fulfilment, just before the revolution – there seems every prospect that these relationships will continue happily as long as they can continue working together politically. In the long periods of separation and loneliness during the civil war, the women are comforted by the knowledge that they will soon be reunited with their lovers.

In 'Vasilisa Malygina', in which Kollontai shows these conflicts in greatest depth, Vasilisa, separated from her lover Volodya, tries to create an extended collective family life for herself and her neighbours in her communal house. But her hopes for this do not diminish her feelings of isolation and extreme sexual loneliness, and it is these feelings which prevent her from honestly facing the course of her life as Volodya's wife. When she is eventually re-united with him, it is entirely on his terms, as his wife, in his house, dressed in the clothes he buys for her.

Vladimir's large chilly house takes her far from her home town, far from the warm squalor of her communal house; her dislike of the lavish contents of the house immediately establishes Vasya's first feelings of isolation from her husband. For he has created this house for her, as a place of luxury and ease in which she can desultorily act the housewife, manage his servants (as he manages his workers) and generally give meaning to his life in the outside world, the world of business newly created by the NEP.

A sanctuary for him, a prison for her, this house becomes the focus of all her submerged feelings of anxiety about her inactive and dependent life, and the only place she can express herself and her feelings for Vladimir. As she withdraws from all Party activity, her energies are slowly undermined by her conflicting needs to support her wayward husband in his disagreements with the Party and her own feelings as a loyal communist.

Vasilisa frequently falls ill in this deathly atmosphere, and as an invalid she can allow Vladimir to coddle her and give in to her feelings of helplessness. But it is the dead weight of this depressing house and the paralyzing effect it has on Vasilisa that give so much vividness to the descriptions of her ventures into the outside world. The garden outside the house, its smells, its trees and birds are a constant source of happiness to her.

In Vasilisa's contacts with the local Party workers, Kollontai gives brilliantly detailed observations of life in provincial Russia in the 20s – there is Vasilisa's friend, the likeable cadre, who is enthusiastically 'purging' the local Party; the inexperienced young Party bureaucrat tying himself up in his own red tape; the office filled with people who have little in common apart from the tedious wait to see the Party secretary . . . And in the house itself an important role is played by Vladimir's servant, an old peasant woman with whom Vasilisa strikes up an uneasy friendship – we may find it as incomprehensible as she does that the new NEP busi-nessmen have servants, as well as many other material privileges. It is the vividness that Kollontai brings to Vasilisa's existence out-side Vladimir's sphere of influence that reassures us of her final liberation, her ability to understand and exist independently in her society.

'Three Generations' gives a historical perspective to many of the problems Vasilisa shares with her contemporaries. While clarifying the ways in which these three generations of women differ in their attitudes and expectations, Kollontai's own sensitive attitude to them suggests how much grandmother, mother and daughter actually had in common. Olga Sergeevna has absorbed from her mother the old Populist ideals of self-sufficiency, the responsibilities that must go with the struggle to love and marry freely. She breaks with many of these ideals when she joins the Bolsheviks some time before the 1905 revolution, only to find that the demands of political work put an intolerable strain on her relationship with men and with her small daughter Zhenya, who is adopted by her mother while she earns a living. It is only after the revolution that she is finally able to establish a stable relationship with the man she works with, and to re-establish contact with her now twenty-year-old daughter. But her new confidence is abruptly shattered when she discovers that Zhenya has not only been sleeping with her husband, but with several other men too, claiming that her enjoyment of sex in no way interferes with her Party work.

Kollontai does not claim to know whether Zenya's youthful promiscuity really represents the sexual revolution she has envisaged, whether the chaos of post-revolutionary Russia has created a new generation of people incapable of deep and lasting sexual relationships, or whether Olga Sergeevna has for too long separated questions of sexual liberation from the liberation written into her programme for the socialist future.

In the final story, the narrator of 'Sisters' shares many of the feelings of slow demoralization suffered by Vasilisa Malygina. Her exasperation with her husband, who succumbs to all the profligate pleasures of 'nepman' social life, comes to a head when their child dies. Shortly afterwards she loses her job; her life now revolves around the long lonely evenings waiting for her husband's drunken return, the hurried distrustful attempts to tell him something of her misery, her fear of his violence, and her pathetic attempts to find some comfort in his lovemaking.

When he brings a prostitute to the house she is too paralyzed to know how to respond, and it is only when she is able to talk to this woman and find out how similar their lives really are that she can face the prospect of leaving her husband. Unlike the anarchic 'freedom' of the 'nepman', to whom the revolution has apparently granted nothing but the dubious freedom to sell his labour at a high price, and exercise his power over his wife, his mistress and his servants, we are confident that her liberation, like Vasilisa Malygina's, despite its terrible and bewildering costs, is a genuine and hopeful one.

Alexandra Kollontai's writings on the transformation of the family and the conflicts between passion and work are of extraordinary inspirational and historical value for women today. Concrete political demands for the liberation of Russia's women are combined in her writings with a vision of a 'fundamental restructuring of the psyche' under full communism; an imaginative assessment of women's evolving needs.

This tension guided her lifelong search for synthesis, a tension which underlay the numerous crises of her personal and political life. She describes a future when people's loyalty would be to the collective family rather than the disintegrating nuclear family, and men and women, freed from the 'grim fortress' of marriage, which in an alienated society was all that protected them from isolation and loneliness, would be able to come together freely, driven by 'mutual attraction, love, infatuation or passion'.

The socialist revolution could not hope automatically to loosen the intricate threads which bound women to their roles through the centuries in feudal Russia. According to her, the revolution had *actively* to encourage women to discuss openly the problems they experienced at work and in the home. Throughout her life, through the experiences of three revolutions, she saw the family clinging grimly to the old culture and fortifying itself against the chaos of revolution, famine and civil war to emerge in the 20s as a place of retreat from the revolution.

In her writings before the revolution on the organization of women workers, and the communist family they were fighting for, this distrust of the tenacity and tyranny of the family (whose basic features seemed to her to *transcend* the war between the classes) emerges. She revealed her ideas in her frequently utopian predictions on the future of the family under full communism, and they strike us particularly sharply now that we have to balance the future of her 'utopia' against the actual possibilities of our own lives.

For although there are now immense new possibilities open to us in a world of advanced technology – deciding whether we have children or not, what kind of work we do, and whom we relate to and love – her predictions still hold true for many aspects of our lives. It is because women need to understand the countless ways they have been conditioned by centuries of oppression that they will find Alexandra Kollontai's writings so relevant.

When we demand that family and sexual conflicts, which have for so long been submerged both by the socialist movement and by society in general, be integrated into our vision for a better society, we may ask ourselves how far such issues were ever truly explored in Russia after the Bolshevik revolution.

Part of the process whereby women are rediscovering themselves is in disentangling the complexities of our family lives, in learning how we resemble and differ from each other, and the way in which we have been conditioned and contained. Novels and art reflect many of the tensions between what we feel to be necessary and what is possible in our lives. Set against the world inhabited by the women characters of Kollontai's fiction is always a better world which they are in the process of creating.

Vasilisa Malygina

★ I ★

Vasilisa Malygina was a working girl of twenty-eight, employed in a knitter's workshop. She was a real city girl, thin and under-nourished looking, with curly hair that had been cropped after a typhus attack. In her plain Russian blouse and with her flat chest you might, from a distance, have taken her for a boy.

She wasn't exactly pretty, but she did have the most wonderful, perceptive brown eyes : just to look into those tender eyes of hers made people feel more cheerful.

Vasilisa was a communist, and had joined the Bolsheviks when war had broken out. She loathed the war, and while everyone else was busily making up garments to send to the front, frantically working overtime for Russia's victory, Vasilisa obstinately argued with them. War was a bloody business, she said – who needed it? It was nothing but a burden to people. And for all those young soldiers going off like lambs to the slaughter it was an outright tragedy!

Whenever she came across groups of soldiers in the street, marching in military formation, she'd turn her back on them. How *could* they march along so jauntily, singing and yelling at the top of their voices, going off to their deaths as though off on holiday! It wasn't as if they *had* to go, they could easily have refused. If they'd just said we're not going off to be killed or to kill other people like us there wouldn't have been a war at all.

Vasilisa was well read; her father was a typesetter and he'd taught her to read early. She loved Tolstoy, especially his folk-tales.

She was the only pacifist in the workshop, and would have lost her job if they hadn't needed workers so badly. As it was, the fore-man just gave her a good talking to. Everyone soon knew about her pacifist views, and she was nicknamed the 'Tolstoyan'. All the other women at work tended to keep their distance from her, for hadn't she renounced her country and betrayed Russia? 'A lost cause!' they sighed whenever her name was mentioned.

It wasn't long before her reputation reached the ears of the local Bolshevik organizer, who sought her out. He soon realized that this girl was reliable, sure of her opinions and well suited to Party work. So Vasilisa was gradually drawn towards the Bolsheviks. Not all at once, of course, not by any means. At first she had argued with the committee members, asking question after question, and invariably storming out of meetings in a rage. But eventually she began to understand their position more clearly, and in the end it was she who suggested that she start working properly for them. That was how Vasilisa became a Bolshevik.

She proved herself to be a passionate and assertive public speaker. She was never at a loss for words and could debate skilfully with Mensheviks and Socialist Revolutionaries alike. The other women at work were shy and tongue-tied, but not Vasilisa; she always spoke up when she had to, and she talked sense too. In no time at all she had gained the respect of her Party comrades, who decided to adopt her as their candidate in the town Duma during Kerensky's provisional government.

This made the women workers very proud of her, and from then on, whatever she said was law for them. She got on well with the more conservative women too. And even if she did shout at them and cajole them, they felt that she knew best, for hadn't she been working in a factory ever since she was a young girl.

She felt if *she* didn't try and understand their needs, nobody would! However, it was not so easy to make her Party comrades see reason about these women. 'You should drop them,' they'd tell her. 'We've got more important things to be thinking about now.' This attitude would utterly infuriate Vasilisa, who would lash out at her Party friends, confront the Party secretary, and insist on her demands being met. Why should women's matters be considered any less important than other things? Women had always been treated like that! It wasn't surprising they were so conservative! How could you ever hope to have a successful revolution without enlisting women? They were crucial. 'Winning over the women, that's half the battle,' was what Vasilisa always said.

She knew what she wanted, and she stuck by it. In 1918 she was a real Bolshevik fighter. Over the years so many people had lost heart, stayed at home, given up. But she was always at work, making speeches, debating, organizing, generally getting things done – she was absolutely indefatigable. It was hard to imagine where she got so much energy, she was so pale and skinny. People always responded to those wonderful eyes of hers though, warm, brown and attentive.

One day a letter arrived for her at her small garret. This was the letter she'd been longing for, a letter from her darling husband and friend from whom she's been separated for so many lonely months. Not, of course, that there was anything to be done about it, what with the civil war and then the industrial Front, for which the Party mobilized all its members.

Vasilisa knew that the revolution was not a game and that everyone had to make sacrifices. That was why she'd lived on her own all those months, away from her husband; that was her sacrifice to the revolution. When they'd been flung to opposite ends of Russia her women friends tried to reassure her by saying 'It will all be for the best, you'll see. This way he'll go on loving you longer and you won't grow bored with him.' They might well have been right, but she didn't care; she was still utterly wretched without him and missed him constantly.

True, she actually had very little time to herself, and was busy from morning until late at night with her work for the Party and the local soviet, one job just piling on top of another. And vital and fascinating work it was too. But nevertheless, when the day was over and she returned to her little room – her garret, as they would have called it in her parents' village – a chill wind would freeze her heart and she longed for her husband. She would sit down to her tea, immersed in gloomy thoughts. Nobody really needed her, she had no real friends, no proper goal to work for. Did other people care about her? Because if they did, she received precious little sign of it from them.

She had been particularly depressed recently because an important project of hers – her communal house – had just been wrecked, and now everyone was going around insulting and criticizing each other. Nobody seemed to realize how important it was to try and live collectively now; or could it be that they just weren't capable of it? The people in the house had insulted her, begrudging her her extra rations as a privileged worker. 'To hell with my rations!' she'd said. 'I can manage quite well without them!' Eventually her Party comrades had calmed her but by then her head had been literally spinning with exhaustion and frustration.

That was how her winter had passed. She would often sit in

her room at night, leaning her elbows on the table, nibbling on a fruit drop to save sugar, and thinking over the day's tribulations. She felt there was no hope for the revolution, nothing but an endless series of frustrations, backbiting and losing battles.

If only her Volodya had been there she could have poured out her troubles to him and he would have embraced and caressed her. She could remember times when he'd said, 'What are you fretting about now, Vasya? Whenever I see you out there in front of other people you look such a tough little thing! "I'm not afraid of anything!" you say. But just look at you now, all huddled up like a ruffled sparrow under the eaves!' Then he'd catch her up in his strong arms and carry her round the room, soothing her like a baby. The very thought made Vasya's heart ache with joy and love for her sweet handsome husband who loved her, who loved her so very much. . . .

Whenever Vasya's thoughts turned to him she felt even more dismal and things would seem even bleaker in her lonely attic. But as she cleared up the tea things she reproached herself, what more did she want out of life? Nothing but pleasure? Did she really want her Volodechka constantly by her side, when she had work she loved and the respect of her friends? The revolution isn't a holiday, she'd remind herself sternly, everyone has to make some sacrifices, so aren't you really asking rather a lot, Vasilisa Dementevna? Remember, it's everything for the collective now, everything for the revolution.

She tried to recall how the furore over the communal house had started. This house had nothing to do with her general work for the Party and the soviet. She had long ago decided to set up a model house filled with a genuinely communist spirit. Not just some sort of dormitory where people lived their private lives and went their own ways – that kind of scheme invariably fostered resentment and bad feeling, for people who lived like that would think only of their own needs and wouldn't live collectively. It was something quite different that Vasilisa had in mind.

She'd patiently set about organizing the house, one step at a time. And what setbacks she'd suffered! Twice the house had been taken away from her, but she had been ready to do battle with anyone, and had finally succeeded in getting her own way. So the house was set up with its communal kitchen, its laundry, its crêche and its dining room. This dining room was Vasilisa's pride and joy, and well it might be, with its curtains in the windows

24

and its potted geraniums. There was a library too, which was used as a meeting room.

To begin with, everything went wonderfully well. The women living there would shower her with kisses, calling her their 'little treasure'. 'You're our guardian angel!' they'd say. 'We're so happy here, and it's all thanks to you!' But then imperceptibly things started to go wrong.

People began quibbling with the rules. There really seemed to be no way to make people clean up after them, and there was constant bickering in the kitchen over the washing-up. The laundry was always being flooded and people had trouble pumping out the water. As one argument followed another and quarrelling and confusion reigned, Vasilisa became the target of everyone's resentment – as though she was the housekeeper and wasn't seeing to things properly! She'd been reduced to imposing fines, which had made the lodgers furious. Some of them had moved out, and more arguments and disagreements followed.

When this confusion was it its worst, a particularly malicious couple called the Feodoseevs decided to really stir up trouble. They found fault with everything, they nagged, they harangued, first it was one thing, then another – there was simply no pleasing them! They had some authority in the house as they'd been amongst the first to move in there; consequently many people tended to regard them as proprietors and followed their example. But as for what they wanted and what was bothering them, there was no way of really knowing! All Vasilisa knew was that they were the bane of her life, and each day they managed to provoke another unpleasant incident.

Vasilisa finally almost broke down and sobbed, she was so tired and angry. But seeing that the whole thing might quite easily fall to pieces, she decided to make a new rule; everything was to be paid for cash down – water, electricity, rates, taxes, everything. She'd then worn herself out seeing to all these new arrangements, but nothing came of them. What could you do if nobody had enough money? The new economy was all very well, but you couldn't get far if you didn't have money!

She was absolutely determined, however, to go on fighting for her precious house – she couldn't bear to see it collapse, and besides, she wasn't the sort to let go of something once she'd committed herself to it. So she'd gone to Moscow, spent several days knocking on office doors, talking to the bosses, and managing to make out a good case for the house. Eventually they were so impressed by her accounts of it that she was given a subsidy for repairs, which meant that she could claim a household allowance.

She'd returned home beaming with pleasure, only to be confronted by the spiteful Feodoseevs, who met her with a dour look. They seemed to suggest by their sullen malevolence that she'd betrayed them in some way by pleading for the house. It was then that they'd started up a new line of attack, putting out scandalous rumours that Vasilisa had been rigging the household accounts to put a bit by for herself! She could hardly bear to think of all the things they'd made her endure!

She badly needed a close friend with whom to talk things over, and it was then that she'd decided to write to Vladimir asking him to come. But he'd written back explaining that he too had important work to attend to which he just couldn't leave. He'd been promoted to a new job and had to straighten out the finances of the firm where he'd previously been employed as a clerk. That winter had been one long uphill struggle for him too, apparently, and he simply couldn't tear himself away at this point; the firm depended on him.

So Vasilisa had to bear the whole squalid business on her own. And what hurt her most about it was that it was the workers, her friends and allies, who were the cause of everything. If they'd been bourgeois anti-communists she wouldn't have cared nearly so much!

Mercifully, however, the house committee supported her throughout. They hadn't let her bring the case to court but decided that the committee members themselves should sort the whole thing out for her. They'd concluded that it was a clear case of slander, based on nothing but malice and ignorance. But just when they were about to evict the Feodoseevs, the couple had admitted their guilt, pleading for Vasilisa's forgiveness and assuring her how much they'd always respected her. Vasilisa's victory brought her no joy, for she was worn out, worried sick, and hadn't the strength to rejoice.

After all that she'd fallen ill, and although she went back to work almost immediately she felt by then as though something had died inside her. She no longer loved her house – she'd suffered too much for it. It was as if her own child had been sullied in some way, and memories of her own childhood had come back. She remembered her little brother Kolka showing her a sweet, and when she reached out for it he'd laugh spitefully and say,

26

'Look at me! I'm going to spoil your sweet for you!' Then he'd spit on it and give it to her, saying, 'Here you are, Vasilisa, you can eat your sweet now, it's delicious!'

And Vasilisa would turn away from him sobbing, 'Horrible boy! Why did you do that!'

That was how she'd felt about the house. She just didn't want to be responsible for it any more. She'd go on serving on the house committee, but she couldn't devote herself fully to it now – it could go to rack and ruin for all she cared! Towards the residents she felt nothing but a deep coldness; for hadn't they joined the Feodoseevs in atacking her? She began more and more to keep her distance from people. Before, she'd always been so sympathetic to people's problems, but after everything she'd been through she wanted nothing more than to be left alone, in peace. She was very tired . . .

Now the long winter was over. The sun shone, the sparrows chirped under the eaves in the morning, and Vasilisa smiled as she remembered her darling Volodechka calling her his ruffled sparrow. And with the spring, even though her anaemia had got worse and her lungs troubled her, she felt the stirrings of new energy.

Through the window she could see the sky swirling with soft clouds, and the roof of the old ancestral mansion which now housed the Palace of Motherhood. In the garden the buds were just beginning to swell; and her heart was filled with spring. How cold it had been that winter! How alone she'd felt, with all her lonely struggles and anxieties. Today was like a holiday from all that. Nothing in the world could go wrong today, for today she'd had a letter from her lover, her darling Volodya! And what a letter too!

Please Vasya, don't torment me any more, because I can't put up with much more of this. You're always promising to come and see me, but then you keep putting it off. If only you knew how unhappy you were making me! So, my little fighter's been scrapping with everyone again, has she? There have been rumours about you even here, you know! Some people say you've even been in the newspapers! Now that you've won your victory, surely you can spare the time to visit your Volodka, who loves you so very much and longs to see you. You'll be amazed how grandly we'll be living from now on. I've got my

own horse and cow, and there's always a car at my disposal.
We've got a servant too, so you won't have to worry about the
housework and you'll be able to put your feet up. Spring is well
and truly here and the apple-trees are covered in blossom.
Do you realize we haven't spent one spring together yet? Our
life together should be one long spring, shouldn't it, my darling!

I really need you especially badly now. I'm in a bit of trouble
with the Party committee. They've made some allegations
against me, bringing up my anarchism again. I've told you about
Savelev. Well, this whole thing has started because of him.
Please, Vasya, you must help me clear this whole business up.
I'm sick and tired of these petty squabbles. They make life
impossible! It'll be hard for them to criticize me, because I work
well, but I do need you all the same. I kiss your brown eyes.
I shall always love you,

always, your Volodya

Vasilisa sat lost in thought, staring out of the window at the sky
and the clouds, smiling to herself as she thought about this wonderful letter. Volodya meant everything to her, and he loved her so
much! His letter lay on her lap, and she stroked it as though it
were his head, forgetting the sky, the roof, the clouds, seeing only
her beautiful Volodya with his subtle laughing eyes . . .

Her heart ached with love for him. How had she managed
without him all winter? It was seven months since she'd last seen
him. The fact that she hadn't been continually thinking about him
made her feel completely wretched. She'd had so many worries and
miseries of her own that winter, she simply hadn't had the time.
She'd managed to push her love for Volodya, her loneliness without him, into the recesses of her heart, and there her love had
remained, sure and immutable. Now at last she'd won all her
battles and rescued her precious brainchild, her communal house,
from all those wretched troublemakers. And she could think about
her love again.

Remembering him now, she could almost sense his presence
there beside her, and it was a sweet feeling. But she was also
conscious of the burden this kind of love imposed – and that it
had to be like this. For she was always anxious about what might
be happening to him. He had no sense of discipline – Vasilisa was
forced to admit that people were right in criticizing his anarchic
ways. He detested having to carry out Party decisions, he just had

to have his own way. But then on the other hand, when it came to work, there were few people to match him, and as for business, he excelled at that.

Living apart, they had not got in the way of each other's work. This arrangement had suited Vasya quite well – if there was work to be done she wanted to be able to give all her attention to it, whereas if Volodya was there she knew she'd want to be with him, and then he'd neglect *his* work too. 'Work before everything,' he'd said, 'but there's our love too, and that's almost as important, isn't it, Vasya?' And she'd agreed. She felt the same way, happy and confident that they weren't just man and wife but real comrades too.

Now he was begging her to come, as a friend might ask another, begging her to help him with his problem. She read the letter through once more – and then slowly doubts started trickling into her mind. If this matter had anything at all to do with Savelev, it was bad news indeed, for this Savelev was a speculator and a thoroughly unscrupulous character. Really, Volodya should know better than to associate with a man like that! As a director, Volodya should be completely above suspicion, and have nothing to do with such shady types. But then he'd always been far too trusting. It was just like him to take pity on Savelev and speak up for him.

But it was simply inexcusable to take pity on people like that – people who helped themselves to public money should be punished for it. Volodya had a kind heart, but people couldn't be expected to realize that, and they would obviously interpret Volodya's 'friendship' with Savelev quite differently. Also, Volodya had a lot of enemies; once he lost his temper there was no controlling him. What if there was a repetition of that incident three years ago, when they'd brought a case against him? Vasilisa knew only too well from her own painful experience how easy it was to ruin someone's reputation . . .

Now it was Volodya who was in trouble. She must go immediately, to help and support him, and make those local people feel thoroughly ashamed of themselves. She felt like leaving on the spot. What did she care about the house now? She suspected it was too late for her to rescue it properly anyway, and it could collapse in ruins for all she cared. Officially, of course, she'd won, but actually it was the Feodoseevs who'd come out on top.

She sighed, went to the window and looked down into the yard.

She stood there a while, silently saying goodbye to the house, with a grave expression on her face. Then her cheeks began to flush and she felt a sense of overwhelming happiness. 'Volodechka! Soon I'll be seeing my Volodya again! Oh my darling, I'm on my way!'

★ II ★

Vasilisa sat in her railway carriage; she'd been travelling for two days already, but another twenty-four hours lay ahead of her. It felt very strange to be travelling equipped for the journey like a 'lady'. Vladimir had sent her the money for the journey (it seemed he could afford anything these days), and had told her to buy a ticket for a sleeper. He'd also sent her a length of material to make herself a nice dress; from now on, as the wife of a director, she would have to be 'properly dressed', he told her.

Vasilisa couldn't help laughing when she remembered how one of Vladimir's colleagues had appeared at her door one day with the money, and the material. He'd unpacked it and gravely praised its quality, just like a salesman. Vasilisa had laughed and teased the fellow about it, but he obviously saw nothing to laugh about; the article, he solemnly informed her, was truly of the finest quality. After that, she'd held her tongue, although she couldn't for the life of her understand these new executive types, nor how you were supposed to behave towards them.

When he'd left, Vasya had stood turning over the material in her hands. She wasn't accustomed to giving much thought to clothes and fashions, but here was Volodya telling her she mustn't let him down! There was nothing for it, she'd just have to get herself a smart dress, the kind of fashionable get-up that women were wearing nowadays.

She'd gone off to see her dressmaker friend and explained the whole situation to her. 'Please, Grusha, make me something as up-to-date and fashionable as possible,' she begged, and Grusha had brought out the fashion magazines a friend had brought from Moscow the previous autumn. She'd been making dresses from them all winter, and people had liked them.

Grusha spent a long time leafing through the magazines, and eventually spotted a dress. 'Look, Vasya, this is just the thing for you! As you're so skinny, this will do wonders for you, it'll make your hips look wider and the front here is gathered so as to hide your small bosom. I'm going to make you a dress your husband will be proud of!'

'That's perfect, Grusha dear,' Vasya had said. They'd bargained over the price, kissed one another goodbye, and Vasilisa had left well pleased. It was just as well there were dressmakers around – she wouldn't have been able to design or make a dress to save her life! Volodya, now, he was different, he was an expert on women's fashions. When he'd been in America he'd worked for various women's fashion stores and picked up quite a bit of information on the subject. Nowadays such accomplishments were coming in useful, and the new 'red merchants' had to keep up with these things. After all, women's frippery was a commodity too!

Vasilisa was sitting on her own near the window of the sleeper. Her travelling companion was a raucous, heavily perfumed nepwoman, decked out in rustling silk and jangling ear-rings. She was at that moment visiting the people in the next compartment, and she and her admirers could be heard shouting and laughing together.

With Vasilisa, however, she'd been extremely aloof, pursing her lips primly as she said, 'Excuse me, dear, but you're sitting on my shawl, you'll crumple it,' or 'Would you mind just stepping out into the corridor for a moment, dear, while I make myself up for the night?' This overperfumed woman behaved as though she owned the compartment, and was only tolerating Vasilisa there out of the goodness of her heart. Vasilisa greatly disliked being called 'dear', but she didn't want to get involved in an argument – she'd better try and get on with people now, she told herself, instead of arguing with them all the time!

Evening approached and spread its long grey-blue shadows across the spring fields. The setting sun hung like a great red ball over the purple line of the distant forests. Rooks flew up from the fields and wheeled in the sky. And ahead stretched the telegraph wires, broken at intervals by poles . . .

This twilight induced in Vasilisa an unaccountable feeling of brooding melancholy, not sadness really so much as a deep longing for something she couldn't describe. In the last few days she'd been feeling so recklessly cheerful, hastily winding up her work and making all her preparations for the journey. Everybody had been so sorry to see her leave, so sad to think they might never see her again. Even the Feodoseev woman had come out to see her, kissing her and stammering out her apologies. Vasilisa had found all this deeply embarrassing; it wasn't hatred she felt for the woman so much as utter contempt – for her and for people like her.

Then her friends had taken her to the station, and had even postponed a house meeting so as to be able to see her off. The Party committee had been there too, as well as the children from the communal house, carrying the paper flowers they'd made for her. It was only then that Vasilisa realized that she hadn't sacrificed her energy and her health for nothing; she could see that the seeds of communal living had been implanted in these people, and something was bound to come of it. As the train moved off and they all stood waving their hats at her, the tears suddenly welled into her eyes and she felt wretched to be leaving such dear friends behind.

But then the town had moved out of sight, and soon copses and suburban villages were flashing past the window; in no time at all the communal house had vanished from her mind, along with the joys and miseries of that winter, and her thoughts raced ahead, outstripping the train, in her eagerness to see her darling Volodechka. She willed the train to hurry, she willed it to speed her loving heart to its destination . . .

So where had these melancholy thoughts sprung from suddenly? Her heart felt as though clamped with cold steel and the tears came to her eyes. Maybe it was because a part of her life was slipping away, just like those stretches of fields outside the window with their spring growth of soft, amber-coloured grass. One field after another passed before her eyes, fields she'd never see again . . . She cried a little, quietly and unobtrusively; then, wiping away the tears she immediately felt better, as though they'd dissolved the icy knot of anxiety in her heart.

The lights went on in the compartment, the curtains were drawn by the attendant, and the atmosphere suddenly became friendly and intimate. She was conscious again that two nights from now she would see Volodya, kiss him again – his voice sprang to life in her memory, his warm mouth, his strong arms. A sweet drowsy languor ran through her body. She began smiling to herself, and if it hadn't been for the nepwoman fidgeting in front of the mirror she would have burst out singing for sheer joy.

The nepwoman left, slamming the door behind her. Stupid

woman! Vasilisa closed her eyes and began thinking about Vladimir again, going over episodes in their love affair. They'd been in love now for five years. Five years! It seemed as though they'd only met yesterday! But then she couldn't imagine a time when Volodya hadn't been her lover and friend. She settled down more comfortably in the corner seat, and, tucking her legs under her, closed her eyes. The carriage rocked gently, lulling her to sleep, but her thoughts ran on. She recalled how they'd met for the first time . . .

It was at a meeting, just before that unforgettable October. What inspiring days those had been! They'd been a mere handful of Bolsheviks, but to make up for it they worked doubly hard. The Mensheviks and the disruptive Socialist Revolutionaries had been in control at that time, persecuting the Bolsheviks, even beating them up, saying they were 'German spies', or 'traitors to their country'! Yet every day the Bolsheviks had increased their number.

Nobody ever quite knew what would happen next, but the Bolsheviks were determined on one thing – to achieve peace, and to oust the 'patriotic traitors' who wanted to continue the war. That much had been clear and that much they'd fought for, with energy and passion. Confident and uncompromising, their eyes shone with a determination which needed no words: we may die, they said, but give in, never! Nobody gave any thought for themselves – this wasn't the time for personal problems!

Much had been written about Vasilisa in the Socialist Revolutionary and Menshevik newspapers – a lot of stupid lies which were part of a general attempt to discredit the Bolsheviks. Let them babble on until they were blue in the face, she'd thought at the time, it all served the Bolshevik purpose in the end! People were anyway coming more and more to believe that the Bolsheviks were right.

'You might have some consideration for me,' her old mother had sobbed. 'Joining up with the Bolsheviks like that, you've disgraced your family and betrayed your country!'

To avoid domestic scenes like this, Vasilisa had moved in with a friend. There her mother's tears no longer affected her, and she had gradually broken away from her family. As though driven by some overwhelming force, she had become completely obsessed with her work for the Bolsheviks. Even if it destroyed her, she was determined to go on arguing, struggling, fighting.

The skirmishes became more explosive, the atmosphere increasingly charged. As news came through from 'Peter' [Petrograd] of the decisions of the congresses, of Trotsky's speeches and of the summons to the Petrograd Soviet, a storm seemed inevitable – and it was then that she'd met Vladimir.

It was at a meeting held in a packed hall, people standing on the window sills, sitting on the floor, in the gangways – almost impossible to breathe. Vasilisa couldn't now remember what the meeting had been about, but in her mind's eye she could still see the platform quite clearly. She remembered that it had been the first time a Bolshevik had been elected president. The committee also consisted entirely of Bolsheviks and left Socialist Revolutionaries – and then there'd been one well-known anarchist from a co-operative; people always referred to him as the 'American'. That was Vladimir.

It was the first time she'd seen him, although she'd heard a lot about him. Some rhapsodized about him : 'What a man,' they said. 'He certainly knows how to make people listen to him.' Other people criticized his brashness. But he had the support of the co-operative bakers and a group of industrial employees, and together they were a militant bunch, a force to be reckoned with.

The Bolsheviks had been delighted when Vladimir had outbid the Mensheviks, but angry when he'd opposed them. They hadn't been able to make out where he stood. The secretary of the Bolshevik group disliked him. 'It's best to steer clear of allies like that. He's just a muddled thinker.'

But Stepan Alexeevich, one of the oldest and most respected Bolsheviks in town, had laughed. 'Wait a while, don't rush him, and he'll make an excellent Bolshevik in time. He's a go-ahead young fellow. Just let him work all those confused American ideas out of his system.'

Vasilisa hadn't paid much attention to all this. She really couldn't be bothered to keep up with all these people who suddenly came into the limelight.

She'd arrived late and breathless at the meeting, where she was due to speak on the brick-building industry. Those days had anyway been one long meeting, for she was a popular public speaker – people listened to her and liked her. They liked the fact that a woman was speaking publicly, and a working woman at that. Vasilisa always spoke to the point; she didn't mince words, and

34

had developed her own, very original, style of speaking. So she always spoke to packed halls.

She'd gone straight to the rostrum when she arrived. Comrade Yurochkin (who was killed shortly afterwards at the Front) had tugged her arm. 'We've won! The Bolsheviks have been voted on to the rostrum, along with the two left Socialist Revolutionaries and the "American", and he's as good as a Bolshevik. He's just about to speak now.'

Vasilisa glanced at the 'American', and for some reason had been surprised. So this was what an anarchist looked like! She would have taken him for one of the gentry, with his starched collar and tie, his neatly combed and parted hair! He was handsome, with extraordinarily long eyelashes. When it was his turn to speak he stepped forward, putting his hand to his mouth as he cleared his throat.

'Just like the gentry,' Vasilisa decided, smiling for some reason. His voice was pleasant and persuasive, and he spoke entertainingly, at some length. He made Vasya laugh, and when he'd finished she clapped and bravoed with the rest of the audience. As he returned to the table on the rostrum he inadvertently brushed against Vasya and turned to apologize. Vasya found herself blushing, and blushing made her even more embarrassed. How maddening! But the anarchist sat down at the table without even noticing her, and, carelessly leaning his elbow on the back of the chair, lit a cigarette. The chairman leaned over, pointing to his cigarette, and indicating that people generally didn't smoke there. Vladimir merely shrugged and went on smoking, as if to say, Your rules don't concern me. He inhaled twice, and when the president was preoccupied with another matter, threw the cigarette on the floor.

Vasya remembered it all. She had pulled a face at him, but he'd taken no notice. He'd only looked at her when her turn came to speak. That night she'd spoken particularly well, and, although she was standing with her back to Vladimir she could sense that he was looking at her. She deliberately overpraised the Bolsheviks and lashed out at the Mensheviks, the Socialist Revolutionaries and the anarchists – although at the time she didn't really know much about the anarchists. She only knew she wanted to rile the 'American' for putting on those gentlemanly airs.

At that time she had long hair which she wore in a plait round her head. In the middle of the speech her plait slipped down on to her shoulder. As she spoke she became more and more excited, forgetting herself completely and not noticing the pins falling out of her hair. When the plait got in her way, she felt uncomfortable and tossed it back. What she didn't realize was that the plait had utterly bewitched Vladimir.

'I couldn't see you properly when I was listening to your speech, but when your plait fell on to your shoulder I suddenly realized you weren't just a public speaker, you were Vasya the rebel – and a woman! And such a comical woman at that, getting all flustered and putting such a brave face on it, waving your arms and cursing the anarchists, while all the time your plait was coming undone and snakes of hair were rippling down your back like threads of gold. That was when I swore I'd get to know you properly.'

It was later that Vladimir had told her this, after they had already become lovers.

When she'd finished her speech she hastily began plaiting up her hair again. Korochkin picked up the pins for her.

'Thanks, my friend,' she said, feeling rather awkward, with everyone looking at her.

She was afraid to look at the 'American' but she knew he must have noticed; he must think her completely ridiculous. This idea enraged her for some reason, and she felt furious with him. What did she care about this man?

The meeting was over; people got up to leave. Suddenly the 'American' was standing in front of her.

'Allow me to introduce myself,' he said, and told her his name and why he was there.

They shook hands, and he congratulated Vasya on her speech. Vasya blushed again, and they began talking and arguing, she supporting the Bolsheviks and he the anarchists. They moved out of the crowded hall onto the street where it was drizzling and windy. A cab was waiting for him from the co-operative, and Vladimir offered to take Vasilisa home. She agreed and they got in. The cab was narrow and they sat in silence huddled close together under its low roof.

Now Vasilia and Vladimir stopped talking and arguing; they were calm and quiet. It didn't occur to either of them that they might be falling in love. The horse trotted along, its hooves splashing through the puddles, and they began to chat about trifles, about the rain, about the next day's conference at the co-operative on the soap-making industry. They were both feeling extraordinarily happy.

When they finally arrived at Vasya's house and it was time to say goodbye, both knew they were sorry that the journey had passed so quickly, but neither of them said anything.

'I hope your feet didn't get wet?' Vladimir said solicitously.

'My feet?' Vasya said, surprised and delighted.

It was the first time in her life that someone had actually thought of her, worried about her like that. She began to laugh, showing her white teeth, and Vladimir longed then and there to gather her into his arms and kiss those lips . . .

The wicket gate clicked as the watchman came out to let Vasya into the building. 'Until tomorrow then!' shouted Vladimir. 'See you at the co-operative, don't forget, will you! The meeting starts at two on the dot. We do things the American way there!'

He tipped his hat and took his leave with a deep bow. Vasya turned at the gate and hesitated, as though waiting for someone. Then the gate slammed shut and she was alone in the darkened yard. Instantly the whole thing seemed like a mere escapade and she was overcome by feelings of anxiety and melancholy. Something suddenly made her feel wretched and angry, and she was painfully aware of how insignificant she was, how dispensable . . .

Vasya sat in the compartment, her woollen scarf tucked under her head as a pillow. She wasn't asleep, but she was dreaming, about her love. Like being in the cinema, reel after reel, image after image, happiness and misery, everything that she'd lived through with Volodka came before her. These recollections were in some way so pleasant that even the memory of past miseries were enjoyable. So things had sometimes been unhappy, but they were so much better now, she told herself, settling down more comfortably on her seat. The train rocked on, soothing her, and Vasilisa recalled the co-operative meeting.

It had been noisy and restless; the bakers were an assertive bunch. Vladimir was their chairman, the only person capable of restraining them, and although he had his work cut out, he always managed to control them. The veins on his forehead would swell from the strain. He didn't notice when Vasya came in and sat unobtrusively at the back, watching.

They passed a resolution of no confidence in the Provisional

Government, demanding that the workers take the co-operative into their own hands, and then proceeded to elect their management board. All shareholders, members of the bourgeoisie and the Duma were disqualified and lost their deposits. Thenceforth the co-operative was not to be one of the city co-operatives, but instead a group of bakers and industrial workers collaborating on a new project.

But the Mensheviks weren't just going to sit and watch this happen, they'd sent some of their minions along to the meeting to intervene. The meeting was just about to break up – it only remained for the managers to convene – when suddenly a Menshevik commissar, the chief authority in the city and one of Kerensky's henchmen, apeared at the door. He was followed by a group of Menshevik and Socialist Revolutionary leaders. When Vladimir spotted them, a sly look came into his eyes.

'Comrades, I declare this meeting closed,' he announced. 'It only remains for us to install the managers of the new revolutionary bakers' co-operative. Tomorrow there'll be a general meeting for the consideration of other business, but for the moment we can all go home.'

He spoke in calm, assured tones and the audience rose noisily to its feet.

'Hold on a minute, hold on, comrades,' called the commissar irritably. 'Don't close the meeting yet if you please.'

'But you're too late I'm afraid, Mr Commissar, the meeting's already closed. If you wish to acquaint yourself with our resolutions please do so by all means; here they are. We were going to send a delegation to negotiate with you, but since you've come here in person now, so much the better. It's time you learnt that proper revolutionary conduct demands that officials should come to workers' organizations for their information.'

Vladimir stood there unperturbed, sorting out his papers, but under their thick lashes his eyes had a mischievous expression. The hall rang with cries of 'Hear hear! That's right!' and a lot of people were laughing. The commissar started to protest and went up to Vladimir, talking excitedly and nervously. But Vladimir, not at all put out, just looked amused. He spoke in a loud, clear voice, and his answers to the commissar could be heard all over the hall. The audience guffawed and applauded Vladimir, crowing with pleasure when he invited the commissar to a party to celebrate the passing of the co-operative from the bourgeoisie into the hands of the bakers.

'Good for the American !' they shouted. 'He's a sharp one !'

The commissar eventually left, having achieved nothing, threatening to resort to force.

'You just try,' Vladimir snapped at him, his eyes flashing, and the hall resounded with his words.

'You just try, just try !' they all shouted. The atmosphere in the hall had become so menacing that the commissar and his Mensheviks were forced to slip out through the side door, but the noise in the hall persisted for a long time.

The meeting of the management board was postponed until that evening so that people could get something to eat. They had been at the meeting since that morning and they were all exhausted. Vasya was moving towards the exit with the others, when, suddenly, there was Vladimir, looking unruffled and smiling, quite unlike everyone else in his clean blue jacket. But today he no longer looked to Vasya like an aristocrat, today she felt that he really was one of them. He *must* be a Bolshevik ! He'd been so brave, he would obviously stop at nothing. She could imagine him courageously facing bullets – even if he did wear a starched collar !

Vasya was seized with a sudden desire to place her hand trustingly in Vladimir's large hand. Here was a man with whom she felt she could spend her life, happily and confidently. But what could she mean to someone like Vladimir? She saw herself through his eyes and sighed. He was so handsome, he'd seen such a lot, he'd been in America. What was she? Just a plain little thing, a simpleton who'd seen nothing beyond her own provincial town. How could he take her seriously? And he hadn't even noticed her today !

Vladimir's voice broke into her thoughts.

'Good day to you, Comrade Vasilisa ! Well, we managed to get the gentleman commissar into a proper sweat, didn't we? That's taught him a lesson; I'm sure he won't be turning up here again. From now on we'll send them our resolutions just for their information.'

Vladimir was literally glowing with excitement over the affair, and Vasya found his mood infectious. They talked and laughed together happily, and if Vladimir hadn't been dragged away by his friends they would have stayed talking in the passage much longer, discussing the commissar and the resolutions that had been passed.

'Well, there's nothing for it, I'm afraid I must go now, I shall have to leave you, comrade Vasilisa,' he said, and she heard the regret in his voice. She trembled with joy and raised her brown eyes to him. Vladimir immediately stopped what he was doing and looked into them as if looking into her heart. She felt as though he were drowning in her eyes.

'Stop hanging around there, Vladimir! You're holding us up and we're up to our eyes in work!'

'Coming!' he shouted to his friends, and squeezing Vasya's hand he quickly went off. Vasya left too and wandered round the town not knowing where she was going, seeing nothing, neither people nor streets, only Vladimir. Nothing like this had ever happened in her life before . . .

Then they began to meet more often. One frosty winter evening they were leaving a session of the soviet together. The sky was bright, and fresh white snow lay on the ground, on the roofs and fences and enveloped the trees in its feathery flakes. The October days were over, and power was firmly in the hands of the soviets. The Mensheviks and the right wing Socialist Revolutionaries had been ousted, though the internationalists remained as a problem. One group now dominated – the Bolsheviks. Their power was increasing steadily and the workers were behind them to a man. Only the bourgeoisie, the priests and the officers opposed them now, and the soviets gave *them* no quarter at all. The waves of revolution hadn't yet subsided, and life was far from being back to normal. Red Guards patrolled the streets in the towns, and here and there was the occasional skirmish. But nevertheless it did look as though the hardest struggles might almost be over.

Vasilisa and Vladimir were talking about the days when they'd seized power in the town. It had been Vladimir's bakers who'd saved the day. They were tough and loyal and Vladimir was justifiably proud of them. It was thanks to them that he'd been elected to the soviet.

They walked side by side along the quiet streets. Every so often a Red Guard would stop them and ask for the password. Vladimir, like them, was wearing a red armband and a fur hat, for he had joined the Red Guards. He'd been under fire too, and Vasya had seen his sleeve with the bullet hole on the shoulder.

Though they were seeing a great deal of each other, there never seemed enough time for them to talk together properly. Now, without having arranged to do so, they'd just left the meeting together, and immediately both of them felt at ease. They had so much to tell each other, like two old friends. And then, all of a sudden, they would stop talking, immediately sensing a strong bond between them.

They passed Vasya's house without even noticing, and before they knew it they were wandering through the outskirts of the town. Stopping in amazement, they began to laugh. Where on earth were they? Then they stood very still, both gazing up at the sky and the blazing stars. How beautiful it all was! At that moment they felt young and very happy.

Vasya said, 'In the country where I grew up we never had a clock, so we learnt to tell the time by the stars. My father knew every star, and he always knew the right time.'

Then Vladimir began to tell her about his childhood. He came from a very large family of poor peasant stock who'd always had to scrape along. Vladimir longed to go to school, but the school was too far away, so he persuaded the priest's daughter to let him feed her geese, and in return she taught him to read and write. Vladimir's voice became more and more tender and wistful as he reminisced about the country, and the fields and copses near his parents' home. Just look at him! thought Vasya fondly, and from that moment he became even dearer to her.

He told her how he'd gone to America as an adolescent, determined to make a place for himself there. After two years on a cargo ship, he'd worked as a docker, and was eventually blacklisted for joining a strike. So he'd been forced to leave that state, and life had been tough. He'd been hungry, taken any job that came his way. First he'd been a cleaner in a smart hotel – she should have seen all those flashy people! And as for the women, decked out in their tulle dresses, their diamonds and their silk . . . !

Then he'd worked for a while as a doorkeeper at a fashion house. This had paid well, but he was only hired because he was the right height and build and the braided uniform suited him. The job bored him stiff, and he could barely contain his rage at the sight of all those wealthy customers. He'd got a job as a chauffeur, driving a rich cotton merchant hundreds of miles across America in his luxurious limousine. But this too soon bored him – it was nothing but wage slavery, just like all the other jobs he'd had. However, this businessman had encouraged him to work his way into the cotton business; he'd become a clerk, started taking courses in accountancy. And then, in February 1917, revolution had broken out in Russia. He'd immediately dropped everything and gone straight back.

But, he said, America had been a different world. He'd liked a lot of things about it. For instance, the businessman had stood up for him, even bailed him out, when, as a member of a proscribed organization, he'd been sent to prison after a brush with the police. He'd been impressed with such loyalty.

They walked on and on, along street after street, and Vasya listened to Vladimir talk. There was no stopping him! He wanted to tell Vasya his entire life story. Once again they came to the gate of Vasya's house.

'Do you think I could come in and have some tea with you, Vasilisa?' asked Vladimir. 'My throat is quite dry, and anyway I don't feel sleepy yet.'

Vasya hesitated : the friend with whom she lived was sure to be in bed. But it didn't matter. They would wake her up and all three have tea together – that would be even jollier. Why shouldn't she invite her 'American' in. She couldn't bear to leave him at this moment.

They went in, and Vladimir helped her put on the samovar. 'One should always give ladies a hand,' he said. 'That was one thing they took for granted in America.' They sat down to their tea, joking and teasing Vasilisa's friend whom they'd dragged out of bed, and who was sitting there blinking sleepily. Vasilisa was supremely happy.

Vladimir started to talk about America again, about all the beautiful women in silk stockings who arrived at the fashion house in their cars, while he held the door open for them in his braided uniform and his feathered cocked hat. Once a woman had slipped him a note proposing an assignation, but he hadn't gone. He didn't like those females with their petty intrigues. Another woman had given him a rose. As Vasya listened to these stories she began to feel smaller and less and less attractive – all the joy drained from her heart. She frowned. 'So I suppose you were in love with all those beautiful women you met?' she asked in a toneless voice, and immediately she was furious with herself for voicing such a stupid question.

Vladimir looked closely at her and shook his head.

'All my life, Vasilisa Dementevna, I have been keeping my heart and my love pure. The girl I fall in love with will have to be pure too. They were nothing but whores, those women, no better than a bunch of streetwalkers.'

The joy had flooded back into her heart – and there it froze. So he was only going to fall in love with a virgin, was he? Well, *she* was not a virgin! First there'd been that brief love affair with Petya Razgulov who worked in the machine department. But then he'd been called away to the Front. Then there'd been the Party organizer, and they had even considered getting married. But he had to leave too, and when he stopped writing she eventually forgot him . . .

Did Vladimir really mean it when he said he could only love a virgin? Vasya looked at him intently, trying to follow what he was saying, but by now she was in such a state of panic that she could no longer make head nor tail of anything.

He assumed he must have been boring her with his stories, and abruptly breaking off what he was saying, stood up to leave. He took his leave of her hastily and rather coldly, and Vasya's eyes filled with tears. She longed to throw her arms around his neck, but did he really want her? She sobbed all that night, vowing that she'd avoid the 'American' from then on. What was the point of ever meeting him again, what could she mean to him, if he was only interested in falling in love with a virgin?

But although Vasya might have intended to avoid the 'American', they were actually brought even more closely together soon afterwards. At a committee meeting to appoint a new mayor, a dispute arose; some people proposed Vladimir, but others wouldn't hear of him, in particular the secretary of the Party who wouldn't be budged. The whole town was up in arms about the 'American' as it was, he said, riding about in his cab just like some Tsarist local governor, doffing his hat in a lordly fashion at all and sundry. Ordinary people considered him a public menace; he wouldn't accept Party discipline, and there'd been more than one complaint about him recently for not observing the Party decrees in the co-operative.

Vasya defended Vladimir hotly at this meeting, though she certainly felt he was foolish to put on his swaggering airs. She was upset that they should still refer to him as an anarchist. It was so stupid to distrust him – as a worker he was a match for any Bolshevik! Stepan Alexeevich supported Vladimir too, and they put the matter to the vote. There were seven against him, six for – so that was that.

When Vladimir was told of the committee's decision, he flew into a rage, and began cursing the Bolsheviks. How could they distrust him when he'd worked heart and soul for the revolution? 'You constitutionalists, you centralists!' he yelled. 'You just want to establish your own police state!' He went on and on in this fashion, warning them about America, where people were ordered around and forbidden to do anything, and where the international movement was continually harassed. All this talk alarmed the committee even more, and they demanded that Vladimir submit to their decision.

But the feud continued and became increasingly bitter, with Vasya tormenting herself, defending Vladimir and arguing until she was quite hoarse. Then a new case was presented to the soviet : once again Vladimir's co-operative had failed to carry out a particular order.

Vladimir, on facing the soviet, just kept repeating the same thing over and over again : 'I don't recognize these police measures! Each department must make its own rules, and as for discipline, I don't give a damn for your discipline! We didn't make the revolution, shed our blood, drive out the bourgeoisie just to go and hang ourselves in a new noose. Who are all these commanders who've suddenly appeared from out of the blue, to order us around? Anyone would think *we* didn't know how to give orders!'

There had been fierce arguments, shouted threats. 'If you won't take orders we'll have to expel you from the soviet,' warned the chairman.

'You just try doing that!' shouted Vladimir, his eyes flashing. 'My bakers are real fighters. If I summon them from the militia, who will you have left to defend you? You'll just be crushed under the heel of the bourgeoisie, because that's what you're heading for. This isn't a soviet, it's a branch of the Tsarist police force!'

This remark stabbed Vasya to the quick. Why did he have to say that? Vladimir stood his ground, white in the face, and continued to defend himself, everyone around him getting more and more agitated.

'Arrest him!' they shouted. 'Expel him! Chuck him out, lazy good-for-nothing!'

It was Stepan Alexeevich who saved the situation. He suggested that Vladimir go into another room, leaving the soviet to discuss the whole affair without him there. Vladimir left, and Vasya with him.

She was angry with him for having given vent to such idiotic diatribes; and when he'd proved himself by his dedication to the soviet too! But then, could someone really be judged on those impulsive remarks? Why couldn't they judge him by his actions? Everyone knew how Vladimir defended the soviets, and that if it hadn't been for him it was quite likely that the soviets wouldn't have supported the Bolsheviks in October. It was he who'd disarmed the officers, it was he who'd forced the mayor to flee the town and brought the mayor's supporters onto the streets, telling them, 'Well, get on with it then! You can shovel the snow off the streets.'

Could they really expel him from the soviet merely for his irascible temper? Vasya was dreadfully upset as she went into the room behind the rostrum. Vladimir was sitting at the table plunged in gloom, his head propped on his arm. He glanced up at her, his eyes burning with resentment. He looked so distraught and anxious – suddenly Vasya saw him as a hurt child, small and vulnerable. She vowed to stop at nothing to protect him.

'So our constitutionalists have taken fright,' began Vladimir jauntily. 'Do you suppose it was my threats that scared them? But . . .'

He faltered. Vasya's expression was one of sympathy and reproach.

'You were wrong you know, Vladimir Ivanovich, and now you've only yourself to blame. Whatever possessed you to say all that? Don't you see that for them it can only mean one thing – that you're opposing the soviet?'

'And I shall continue to oppose it as long as it acts like the Tsarist police force,' insisted Vladimir obstinately.

'How can you say such things? You know you don't believe a word of it!'

Vasya moved closer to him; at this moment she felt very much older than him. She gazed at him affectionately and seriously. Vladimir looked into her eyes but didn't say anything.

'Come on now, admit it, you lost your temper.'

Vladimir hung his head. 'The whole thing's a mess. They're

45

furious with me.' Again he looked into Vasya's eyes like a child apologizing to his mother.

'There's nothing to be done about it, it's hopeless,' he said with a gesture of despair. Vasya's heart was filled with such pain and tenderness for this man, who had become so very dear to her. She put her hand on his head and stroked it gently.

'Please don't lose heart, Vladimir Ivanovich, you mustn't despair. That would never do for an anarchist! You must just have faith in yourself, Vladimir, and not allow people to insult you.'

Vasya was standing over Vladimir, stroking his head. He laid it trustingly on her breast.

'I've had a hard life, you know, I've taken a lot of knocks in my time. I imagined that in the revolution we'd all be able to work together like true friends, but I suppose it's not going to be like that after all.'

'Everything's going to be all right,' Vasya said. 'We just have to learn to trust one another if we're going to work together.'

'No, things won't be all right. Don't you see, I just can't get on with people.'

'But you'll learn, I'm sure of it.'

Vasya lifted Vladimir's face to hers, gazing into his eyes as if to inspire him with her confidence. But his eyes were filled only with anxiety and unhappiness. She leant over him and began to kiss his hair gently.

'You must try and put things right now. You'll just have to apologize, tell them that you lost your temper and that they misunderstood you.'

'All right,' Vladimir agreed humbly, looking at her as though for support. Then moving suddenly towards her, he grasped her in his arms and pressed her violently to him, kissing her passionately.

Vasya ran back to the rostrum and went straight up to Stepan Alexeevich. She had to save Vladimir Ivanovich.

The incident was finally settled, but hostility towards Vladimir lingered on and two camps began to emerge within the soviet. It really did look as if the old days of friendly co-operation were over . . .

Riding along in the now dark train, Vasya longed to be able to curb these memories, but they would keep crowding into her head. She wanted to remember precisely how their love affair had started. It had been shortly after that incident in the soviet. Vladimir had begun to walk her home regularly, they started seeking each other's company, and when they were on their own they soon began to be on informal 'ty' terms with each other.

On one occasion when the girl sharing Vasya's flat was out, he had seized her in his arms. His kisses had been so passionate – even now she could remember those kisses. But she'd struggled free of him and looked him straight in the eyes.

'No, Volodya, please don't. I don't want us to deceive each other.'

He looked at her, shocked and bewildered.

'But why should I want to deceive you, Vasya? Don't you realize – I fell in love with you the moment I saw you?'

'No, it's not that, Volodya, there's something else. Yes, I do believe you but I . . . No, please stop, you see, you told me once that you'd only fall in love with a girl who was a virgin, and, well, I'm not a virgin, Volodya, I've already had lovers . . .'

She was trembling as she spoke, terrified that she might lose all this new happiness.

But he interrupted her.

'Do you suppose I care about your old boy friends? You belong to me now, Vasya, and as far as I'm concerned, you are the sweetest, purest person in the whole world. So you do love me, Vasya? You really do love me? I can't believe that you're mine, mine, and nobody else's! Now don't you dare even mention any of your old boy friends to me again, do you hear? Don't tell me about them, I don't want to know! All I care about is that now you belong to me . . . !'

And so they had become lovers.

It was dark now in the compartment. The other woman was lying down and the entire compartment was pervaded with the flowery scent of her toilet water. Vasilisa was lying on the upper berth, trying to sleep. But try as she might, sleep would not come; memories of her past with Volodya were too vivid. And somewhere at the back of her mind was the feeling that the past was truly over, the happiness of four years ago was really just a memory. She couldn't imagine why she should feel this so acutely, when both their lives still stretched ahead of them. She just felt, for some reason she couldn't quite grasp, that their love had changed – she felt too that she herself had changed . . .

She lay there brooding in the dark, hands clasped behind her head. There hadn't been much time to think over the past three years. She now realized that she'd been so busy working all that time that there were a great many things she actually hadn't properly thought about, things she'd somehow managed to push out of her mind; all Volodya's disagreements with the Party, for instance, those squabbles with the departments. In the very early days there had been much less of that, and he'd been quite different. Of course there had been arguments, and he often crossed swords with the authorities, but Vasya had always been able to make him see reason, for he trusted her judgement and would take her advice.

When the White offensive had been launched, for instance, and the town was threatened, Vladimir immediately set off for the Front. Vasya hadn't tried to prevent him going, but did insist that he join the Party first. After much blustering and argument he'd eventually joined. He became a Bolshevik, and then left.

They didn't write to each other much. He would pay her flying visits for a day or two, and then they wouldn't see each other for weeks, even months, at a time. This was unavoidable, and indeed they didn't even have time to miss each other too much.

Then, out of the blue, Vasilisa learnt from the committee that Vladimir was up on a charge. She couldn't imagine what he had done. He was working in the provisions department, and apparently had been muddling his accounts; there was even a suspicion that he'd been pilfering.

Vasya was furious when she heard this. 'It's all lies!' she'd said. 'I don't believe a word of it! Nothing but petty lies and slander!' Nevertheless, it was obviously serious, and she'd rushed round dementedly making enquiries. He hadn't actually been arrested but he had been suspended from his job. She'd begged Stepan Alexeevich to give her a pass to take parcels to the Front, and three days later she'd gone there. That had been her first visit to Volodya.

* III *

The journey had been beset with obstacles – delays and disconnected trains all the way. First she found that she didn't have the required documents, then the goods compartment was disconnected. She worried herself sick. What if his case had already come before the court? It was then that Vasya realized how very much she loved Vladimir, how precious he was to her. Everyone else believed that as an anarchist he was capable of acting despicably, but somehow the more other people distrusted him, the more stubbornly she leapt to his defence. Nobody knew his mind like she did! He was such a gentle soul, as gentle as a woman – it was only his manner that was rude and inflexible. Vasya knew that with kindness and affection he could be persuaded to behave himself. He was embittered, it was true; after all, a worker's life was never exactly a bed of roses!

When she'd eventually arrived she went straight to the army headquarters, and after a great deal of trouble had found out where Vladimir's quarters were. She'd had to drag herself through pouring rain to the other side of town, although luckily someone had offered to show her the way and carry her parcels. She was tired, shivering with cold, but also overjoyed to find that they hadn't completed their investigations, and there was still no hard evidence against him. Opinion in the department seemed divided, and there were a lot of rumours and denunciations flying around.

Vasya had been greatly disturbed by their spiteful smirks when she'd openly announced herself as Vladimir's wife; they seemed to be concealing something from her. She was determined to investigate every detail of the case, and then see Comrade Toporkov, who had come from the Party Central Committee and knew Vladimir's work record. How could they harass and persecute him like this when there were all those Mensheviks and Socialist Revolutionaries, the real enemies, that they weren't bothering about! Why should an anarchist be treated worse than they were?

Vasilisa and her companions arrived at the little wooden house where Vladimir was quartered. The lights were on but the porch door was bolted. Her companion banged on the door. No reply. By now, Vasya's stockings were soaked through and already she was anticipating not so much her joy at seeing Volodya as the relief of getting into a warm room and changing her dress and stockings. For five days she'd been sitting in a heated goods van and had had almost no sleep.

'Let's knock on the window,' suggested her companion. Breaking a twig off a birch tree they started rapping on the window. The curtain jerked back, and Vasya caught a glimpse of Vladimir's head. He seemed to be in his nightshirt, peering out into the darkness. Then a woman's head bobbed up over his shoulder and rapidly disappeared from view. A sickening, agonizing sensation paralyzed Vasya.

Her companion shouted, 'Open up, comrade! I've brought your wife to see you!' The curtain was hastily drawn again, concealing Volodya and the woman from sight, and Vasya went back to the porch to wait for the door to be opened. What was taking him so long? Vasya thought he'd never come.

Eventually the door was flung open and she suddenly found herself in Volodya's arms.

'You've come at last, my darling! Oh, Vasya, my dearest friend!' he said, embracing and kissing her with tears of joy in his eyes.

'Just take these parcels will you? What am I supposed to do with them?' Vasya's companion reminded her sullenly.

'Yes – let's go into the house and have something to eat. My poor love, you must be so wet and cold,' Volodya said.

Inside it was bright and clean, with a bedroom and dining room – and there, sitting at a table, was a nurse with a white kerchief on her head and a red armband. She was extremely pretty and Vasilisa felt another stab of pain. Volodya introduced them to each other.

'This is nurse Varvara and this is my wife, Vasilisa Dementevna.' The two women shook hands and stared pointedly at each other, both trying to read the other's thoughts. Vladimir bustled round.

'Come on, Vasya, take off your coat. You're the mistress here now. Just look how well I live, a great deal better than your cubby-hole of a room. Here, give me your coat. How wet it is – we'll have to hang it over the stove.'

The nurse remained where she was. 'Well, Vladimir Ivanovich,' she said finally, 'we'll have to sort things out tomorrow. I wouldn't want to interfere in your family happiness now.'

She shook hands with Vasya and Vladimir and went out, accompanied by the man who had come with Vasya. Then Vladimir picked Vasya up in his arms and carried her round the room, hugging and kissing her. He was obviously overjoyed to see her, and Vasya felt easier in her mind, ashamed of her previous suspicions. But between kisses she couldn't help blurting out, 'Who was that nurse?' throwing back her head as she did so in order to be able to look Vladimir in the eyes.

'The nurse? Oh, she just came over to see me about getting provisions for the hospital. We have to speed up deliveries, but there are delays everywhere. It's not actually my responsibility, but all the same they rely on me. The least thing, and they all come running to me.'

Then he began telling her about his case. He put Vasya down and they went into the bedroom, and once again she was overcome by the same stabbing anxiety; the bed had been made hurriedly, the blankets hastily flung on top. She glanced at Vladimir, who was pacing around the room with one hand behind his back – a familiar habit of his which she loved – telling her about his case, how it had all started and how it was progressing. Ignoring her own anxieties, Vasya listened to his account and felt mortified for him; it was obviously based on nothing but recriminations and envy. Her Volodya was honest, she knew he was!

She got some dry stockings out of her suitcase, but she had no shoes to change into. Noticing this, Vladimir exclaimed, 'Just look at the woman! She hasn't even got a spare pair of shoes! I know, I'll get you some nice leather, and our cobbler will make my darling a pair of shoes. Let me take them off for you. Oh, how wet they are!'

He took off her shoes, threw her stockings onto the floor, and held Vasya's cold feet in his warm hands.

'Darling Volodka, you silly thing,' she said, laughing. She felt utterly happy. He loved her, and nothing else mattered!

They drank tea, chatting and discussing Vladimir's case. He was completely open with her and told her about all the times he'd been insolent, lost his temper, hadn't carried out instructions, wanted to have his own way, wouldn't take orders. He told her how he'd made the mistake of getting mixed up with various crooks in his job, but as for the charge of pilfering, surely Vasya couldn't believe him capable of such a thing? He stood in front of her, breathing rapidly, seething with rage.

'How could you even suspect such a thing, you of all people, Vasya . . . ?'

'It's not that Volodya, believe me. I'm just worried about the state of your accounts. They must be investigating them very carefully at the moment.'

'There's absolutely no need to worry about the state of my

accounts. The people who've cooked up this whole business won't find anything wrong with them. They're an open book. I didn't study accountancy for nothing, you know.'

Vasilisa was very relieved. She'd only have to see his comrades and negotiate with them, explaining the facts of the case.

'You're so clever, darling. Thank goodness you've come,' said Volodya. 'You know, I didn't even dare to hope you would. I know how busy you are. "She'll have no time for her husband," I thought to myself, no time for her Volodka!'

'But my sweetheart, if only you knew! I never have a moment's peace when I'm away from you. You're constantly on my mind, and I worry in case anything bad has happened to you!'

'Vasya, you're my guardian angel,' he said very gravely, kissing her. Pensive and rather mournful for a moment, he said 'I may not be worthy of you, but I love you more than anything in the whole world. You must believe me, I love you and only you, and nothing else is worth anything.'

Vasya was surprised at how tense and uneasy he seemed, and didn't really understand what he was saying.

It was time to go to bed. Vasya started straightening the bedclothes and threw back the blankets. Suddenly she stood stock still. There on the sheet was a spot of blood and a woman's bloodstained sanitary towel.

'Volodya! What's this?' – she groaned – 'tell me, Volodya!'
Vladimir hurled the towel furiously to the floor.

'Damn that housekeeper! She must have been having a lie-in again without telling me. Look, she's stained the bed!' he jerked the sheet off the bed onto the floor.

'Vladimir!' Vasya cried, her wide eyes saying more than any words could express. Vladimir looked into them and was reduced to silence.

'Volodya! Please tell me what's going on!'
Volodya collapsed onto the bed, wringing his hands.

'Everything's ruined now, completely ruined. But I swear to you, Vasya, you are the woman I love!'

'How *could* you! How *could* you do this to us?'

'Vasya, I'm a young man. I've been alone for months. They play up to me. But I hate the lot of them! The whole damn bunch of them! Brazen whores and clinging sluts!'

He stretched out his hands to her. Tears were pouring down his cheeks, dropping onto her hands.

'Vasya, please try to understand, otherwise I'm done for. My life is so hard. Please. Take pity on me.'

It was just like the episode so long ago at the soviet. Leaning over him Vasya kissed his head, and once again her heart ached with love and pity for this man who was really such a child at heart. If she didn't understand and take pity on him, who would? He was surrounded by hostile people only too ready to hurl stones at him. He had hurt her feelings so terribly, yet was that reason enough to leave him now, of all times? How could she? He desperately needed her to protect him, like a mother, from life's blows. After all, her love wouldn't be worth much if she walked out on him just because of one personal humiliation! Vasya's mind raced as she stood bending over him, stroking his hair.

Then, a knock at the door, a loud insistent knock which they both instantly understood. They embraced hurriedly, kissed passionately and went into the hall.

The preliminary investigations were over. It had been decided to arrest Vladimir. The ground began to sway under Vasya's feet, but he acted very calmly, collecting his things, telling Vasya where to find the appropriate documents, whom to cite as witnesses, from whom to take evidence, and so on. Then they led him away . . .

Vasya would never in her whole life forget that night, although many years had passed since then. She'd never experienced anything quite so devastating. Her heart was literally torn apart by those two great griefs – the ageless grief of the woman betrayed and the grief of a true friend and companion who has seen her loved one wronged, grief for human malevolence, grief for injustice . . .

After Vladimir had been led off, Vasya rushed around the bedroom like a woman half demented; all she could think about was that there, in that very room, on this very bed, Vladimir had kissed, caressed, made love to another woman! A beautiful woman with pouting lips and full breasts. Maybe he even loved this woman? Yes, maybe he'd lied to her, just to spare her feelings!

Vasilisa needed the truth! Why on this day of all days did they have to take her Vladimir away from her? She could have found out everything, if only he'd been there to answer all her questions. If only he'd been there, he could have comforted her, rescued her from this morbid torment . . .

Then, torn apart as she was by grief, she was seized with sudden rage against him. How dare he? He would never have slept with that woman if he'd loved *her*, and if he didn't love her why couldn't he just say so and be done with it, instead of driving her mad with a lot of lies. She stormed around the room now in utter panic, saved only by a new thought, which came to her with a sudden painful clarity: what if his case actually was well substantiated? What if they'd arrested him for good reason? What if he really had been mixed up with those scoundrels, and was having to answer for it?

Her jealousy, her anger, disappeared, the nurse with the full red lips vanished from her mind, and now there was only a numbing anguished fear for Vladimir, a sickening, burning sense of shame for him. He'd been publicly disgraced, arrested – and by his own comrades too! What was her own jealous outrage, compared to this outrage against the man she loved? And a new grief seized her, for she felt that even in revolution there was no truth, no justice.

All weariness went, and she felt as though her body didn't belong to her. All that remained was a heart lacerated by the claws of her tormenting thoughts. She sat up all through that night, and by daybreak she had firmly resolved to defend Vladimir, to save him from public disgrace. She would prove to the whole world that her husband was an honourable person, that he had been wronged, slandered, insulted.

Then early that morning a Red Army soldier arrived with a note from Vladimir.

My sweet wife, my dearest beloved friend, Vasya, I don't care what happens to me now, nor to the case. It's one thought that's driving me mad – the thought of losing you. Vasya, you must please believe me! I can't live without you! If you don't love me any more, don't defend me, and they can shoot me for all I care.

> Yours, and only yours, Volodya.

PS It's you I love, nobody else but you. You may not believe that, but I'd swear it even in the face of death.

A second postscript read: 'I've never held your past against you, so please try to understand me now and forgive me. I belong to you, Vasya, body and soul.'

Vasya read the note, then she re-read it and began to feel slightly easier in her mind. Of course, he was quite right! He'd never once blamed her for not being a virgin when they'd started living together. And as for men, well what could you expect! How could he help it if some slut had been playing up to him? After all, she couldn't reasonably expect him to take a vow of chastity. She read through the note one more time, kissed it, folded it neatly and put it away in her purse. Now it was time to get down to business and bail Volodya out.

In the days that followed, she dashed around in a frenzy of activity; at every step she confronted bureaucracy and apathy, and there were times when she felt like giving up. But she would rally, put a brave face on it and once more enter the fray. She didn't intend to be defeated by lies, or let a pack of informers and conspirators get the better of her Volodya.

Then she won a major victory. Comrade Torporkov himself was persuaded to take the matter up, and after reviewing the case thoroughly he proposed that it be dropped, since the charges weren't adequately substantiated. Instead two men called Sviridov and Malchenko were to be arrested.

But the morning after this news, Vasya was confined to her bed with an attack of typhus. By evening she could no longer recognize anyone, even Volodya, who had just returned. Later, she was to recall her illness as a suffocating nightmare. Towards evening, she'd opened her eyes, and, looking around her, had seen an unfamiliar room, with bottles of medicine on the table and a nurse in a kerchief sitting by her bed, an elderly, stern-looking woman. Vasya stared at her, distressed that she should have a nurse with her and enraged by the woman's white kerchief. She couldn't imagine what she could be doing here.

'Are you thirsty?' the nurse asked, leaning over her and offering her a drink. Vasya drank thirstily and then immediately lost consciousness again. In her comatose state she imagined that Volodya was leaning over her, arranging her pillows. She half awoke.

Then once more she lost consciousness. And this time she dreamt – or was it real? – that two shadows glided into her room, no, not shadows but women, only these weren't real women . . . One was white, the other grey, and they whirled about the room in what one moment seemed like a kind of dance, the next a test of strength. Vasya was aware that these figures represented Life and Death, and that they had come to fight over her. She was utterly terrified. She wanted to cry out loud. But try as she might, she couldn't, for she had lost her voice, and this increased her terror. Her heart pounded as though about to burst . . .

Then, rat-a-tat! There was firing on the street! She managed to open her eyes. The night light was burning, smoking faintly. It was the middle of the night, and she was all alone. She could hear the sound of mice scratching. They seemed to be scrabbling around under the floor boards, getting closer and closer to her bed. Vasya was seized with terror that they would hop on to the bed and run all over her, and she wouldn't have the strength to get them off.

In a weak voice she called out: 'Volodya! Volodya!'

Immediately he was by her side, leaning over her, looking anxiously into her eyes. 'Vasya my love, what is it? What's wrong, my darling?'

'Volodya, is that you? Are you still alive? I'm not just imagining it?' She stretched out her weak arm to touch his head.

'I'm alive all right, sweetheart. I'm right here beside you. Now what are you crying about? What's happened to my Vasyuk? Did you have a nightmare? Are you feeling feverish?'

He kissed her hands tenderly, stroking her damp cropped head. 'No, it wasn't a dream, it's those mice scratching over there,' she said sheepishly with a weak smile.

'Mice!' laughed Volodya. 'Well, now my Vasya is a proper heroine! She's even become afraid of mice! I told the nurse that you weren't to be left on your own. I'm so relieved that I got home when I did!'

Vasya wanted to ask him where he'd been, but was so utterly exhausted that she had no strength to talk. Besides, the feeling of weakness was so pleasurable, so soothing; and best of all, she had her beloved Vladimir sitting there beside her. She grasped his hand weakly and clung to it.

'So you're alive,' she whispered, smiling.

'Of course I'm alive,' Volodya laughed, gently kissing her head. Vasya opened her eyes.

'My hair! It's gone! Did they cut it off?'

'You mustn't worry about that. My Vasya looks just like a boy now, that's what she always was really.'

Vasya smiled. She felt overwhelmed with happiness – happiness she hadn't felt since childhood. Then she dozed on and off; Volodya stayed with her, sitting beside her to make sure she slept undisturbed.

'Go to sleep now, Vasya,' he soothed her. 'There's no need for you to stay awake. When you're better you'll have time to look at me to your heart's content. If you don't sleep now you won't get better, and the doctor will blame me for being a bad nurse.'

'You won't leave me?'

'Why should I ever leave you? I'm going to sleep here beside you on the floor every night; I'll feel easier in my mind if I can see you. Tomorrow I'll be back at work.'

'Work? In the provisions department again?'

'Yes, everything's been sorted out, and those scoundrels have been arrested. My darling Vasyuk, what's to be done with you! You really mustn't talk any more now, you must sleep, otherwise I'll go away immediately.'

She linked her weak fingers more firmly with his and closed her eyes obediently. Sleep came upon her sweetly, so gently, with Volodya there beside her, worrying and watching over her so tenderly.

'Sweetheart,' she murmured.

'Go to sleep, my little tomboy.'

'I *am* going to sleep, but I do love you ...'

Volodya leaned over her tenderly and gently kissed her closed eyes. Vasya could have cried for happiness. If only she could die now! For never again would life grant her so much happiness.

Now, as she lay on her berth in the train, it somehow terrified Vasilisa to recall these thoughts. Would life really never be so good again? What about now? Wouldn't she find the same joy and happiness? She was on her way to see her Volodechka. He'd sent for her, was waiting for her, and had even sent a colleague to make sure she came immediately. Then there'd been the money for the train ticket and the dress – that *must* mean he loved her. Vasya desperately wanted to believe that they could live together happily again, but somewhere in the depths of her heart there was this nagging doubt. She just knew that something had changed. Once again she lost herself in her thoughts and memories of the past.

Their next separation had been totally unexpected. The battle front had shifted and Vladimir had been summoned to leave. Vasya was still so weak from her typhus attack that she could barely move her legs. They parted affectionately, with no mention of the incident with the nurse. Vasya had come to realize that the woman really meant very little to Volodya, no more, as he put it, 'than a glass of vodka, something to drink and forget'.

And then, when she was strong enough Vasya had returned home, back to her old room, and had immediately gone back to work.

Everything at work was just as it had been, except that something kept preying on Vasya's mind : in her heart of hearts she was plagued with doubts and anger about Volodya and that nurse of his with the pouting lips. Still, she loved Volodya deeply, and her illness and their shared anxieties seemed to have strengthened the bond between them. Previously they had been in love, but they had not actually identified with one another in this way. Now that they had both been united by unhappiness they were emotionally closer. But this love brought Vasya none of the blinding joy of her earlier love; it was deeper, perhaps more secure, but also overcast with shadows.

But then this was no time for love, these days of civil war, threats from all sides, negotiations, separations. Everyone was overworked, and Vasilisa had to deal with the refugee problem. She was appointed to the housing committee of the soviet, and it was then that she conceived her plan of setting up the communal house. It was to be run entirely on her lines, with help and funds from the soviet.

Vasya became utterly absorbed in this project. For many months it was the cornerstone of her life. Although memories of Volodya were constantly in her mind, she had no time to be miserable. Besides, he too was working. His affairs seemed to be going smoothly now, and she was confident that he was no longer throwing his weight around, and was getting on better with the central administration and the bosses.

Then suddenly, out of the blue, there was Vladimir. He just walked into her room one day, utterly unexpectedly. Apparently he'd been caught in cross-fire and wounded, during a retreat. It was nothing serious, but he needed rest, had been given sick-leave and told to go back to his wife for 'board and lodging'.

Vasya was overjoyed, but she couldn't help feeling rather apprehensive. If only he could have come at some other time ! She'd put so much energy into the past two months' work, and foresaw at least another month of hard work ahead. She had so much to do, so many commitments. There was a congress coming up soon, then there was the reorganization of the housing department and all her activities for the communal house – simply no end to her tasks. She was expected to be everywhere at once, and now

Volodya had turned up, wounded. Somehow she would have to take some time off work.

Though Vasya's joy at seeing him was clouded by these anxieties, Volodya was as happy as a child. He'd brought with him the shoes he'd promised her. 'Do try them on, Vasya. I want to see how your tiny feet will look in their new shoes,' he said excitedly.

She didn't want to hurt his feelings, though she was pressed for time – a meeting of the housing committee was due to start soon. She tried on the shoes, and suddenly she felt she was seeing her feet for the first time; it was quite true, she realized, they *were* tiny. She looked rapturously at Vladimir, dumb with gratitude.

'I'd pick you up, darling, but for my wretched arm,' said Vladimir happily. 'Oh, I love your small feet, and your brown eyes!'

He went on talking and joking, overjoyed to see her again, but Vasya was only listening with one ear; she should have been at the meeting long ago. She kept looking at the alarm clock on the chest of drawers. The minutes were ticking by and they'd be waiting impatiently for her. She began to feel angry; why should she keep people waiting like this? It was extremely bad manners for the president to be late.

It was evening when Vasya eventually returned from the meeting. She felt tired and distraught, for there'd been a number of annoying incidents, but as she climbed the stairs to her garret, her worries diminished.

Thank goodness Vladimir's here, she thought. I'll be able to tell him everything and ask him what he thinks!

But when she went into the room Vladimir was nowhere to be seen.

Where could he have gone? There were his hat and coat hanging on the peg. He must have just gone out for a while. She began to tidy up the room and make tea on the oil stove. Still no Volodya. Where on earth could he have got to? She went out into the corridor, but he wasn't there. She went back in to wait for him, growing more and more uneasy. Where *could* he be?

She went out once more into the corridor. And there was Vladimir, just coming out of the Feodoseevs' flat, taking his leave and laughing with them as if they were old friends of his. Why, for heaven's sake, had Vladimir taken it into his head to visit them? Surely she'd told him they were up to no good?

'So you're here at last, Vasya,' he greeted her back in her room.

'I've been cooped up here all day, almost hanging myself with sheer boredom. It was lucky I happened to meet Feodoseev, who dragged me off to his flat . . .'

'But you mustn't have anything to do with those people!' Vasya interrupted him. 'They're just out to make trouble, you know that!'

'Well, do you expect me to stay closeted in your tiny room just dying of boredom? If you hadn't run away and left me alone all day, I wouldn't have been forced to visit the Feodoseevs . . .'

'But surely you can see how much work I have to do? I'd have been really pleased to have come home earlier, but I simply couldn't get away.'

'Of course, your work, quite so. But what about me, Vasya? What about the time you had typhus, and all those nights I sat up with you? When I took off every minute I could to come and see how you were? *I'm* the sick one now, Vasya, I'm still feverish . . .'

Vasya was hurt by the reproach in his voice; he was offended that she'd left him all day. But it just couldn't be helped at the moment, what with the conference coming up, and all her work reorganizing the department . . .

'I can't help feeling you're not really very pleased to see me, Vasya,' said Vladimir. 'I didn't think you'd act like this when we saw each other again.'

'How can you say that! Me, not pleased? But I . . . Oh, darling, my precious sweetheart!'

She flung her arms around his neck, almost knocking over the oil stove as she did so.

'There, there, my love,' he soothed her. 'It's just that I imagined you must have stopped loving me. I even wondered if maybe you'd taken up with another man. You're so cold somehow, you seem quite indifferent to me, and even your eyes are distant and unfriendly.'

'But I'm just tired, Volodya. I don't have the energy to cope with everything.'

'Never mind, my little ruffian,' said Volodya, hugging Vasya and kissing her.

And they lived together, 'cooped up', as he put it, in her little garret room. At first everything went well, and however difficult Vasya found it to divide her time between work and husband, she did so cheerfully. Now there was someone for her to talk to about her new plans and someone to whom she could confess her failures.

Though the matter of their housekeeping bothered her. At the Front, Vladimir had become accustomed to eating in style. Vasya's housekeeping, however, was absolutely minimal; she was quite happy with a frugal soviet-style meal, with tea and a lump of sugar. For the first few days they ate the provisions that Vladimir had brought with him.

'I got hold of some basics, flour, sugar and some sausage, though I know you don't mind eating like a sparrow, and you never store any food,' he said.

But when Volodya's provisions had come to an end he'd had to start eating soviet-style meals, which he detested.

'What's this millet mush you keep feeding me as if I were a hen?' he grumbled in disgust.

'But there's nothing else to be had! I'm living on my rations.'

'Nonsense! Why, the Feodoseevs don't get any more rations than you do, but yesterday they treated me to dinner, and a good dinner it was too, with fried potatoes, herrings, onions . . .'

'But Mrs Feodoseeva has time for cooking and shopping. I have to work so hard. I can barely manage to get through all I have to do as it is.'

'Your problem is that you take on too much, and then look what happens. What *is* all this fuss about the communal house? The Feodoseevs were saying . . .'

'I know quite well what the Feodoseevs say, thank you,' said Vasya with mounting anger; it offended her greatly that Vladimir had anything to do with those people, her enemies. 'And look here, it isn't at all loyal of you to listen to their criticisms of me.'

They began to quarrel and lost their tempers. Then they both felt annoyed with themselves and patched it up. But now Vasya began to worry even more that she wasn't looking after her husband properly. After all, he had come to her sick and wounded, and now she could only give him this soviet food to eat! He *was* more attentive to her needs; after all, he'd brought her the shoes. Sometimes Vladimir refused to eat and then she worried herself sick. After swallowing a few spoonfuls of gruel he would push his plate away, saying 'I'd rather go hungry than swallow this soviet mush of yours, I just can't stomach it. Let's make some tea and get someone to give us some bread. I'll send you some flour from the Front and you can repay them with it later.'

It was obvious that they couldn't go on like that much longer;

they would just have to find some other way to cope. One day, on her way to a meeting, she realized thoughts about resolutions and policies were becoming jumbled up in her mind with preoccupations about millet gruel. What on earth could she give Volodya to eat? Given a little time she would be able to sort something out; she just needed time to think, to come up with some solution.

And then on her way to the meeting she met her cousin. Vasilisa was delighted to see her; she was just the person she needed. This cousin had a young daughter, Stesha, a lively young girl who had just left school and was now living with her parents, helping her mother with the housework. Vasilisa arranged immediately for Stesha to come and do the housework during the day, and in return for this Vasilisa would give her cousin half her rations. Vasya hurried off to her meeting much relieved. Tomorrow at least Volodya would get a proper meal.

Stesha proved to be a quick-witted girl who hit it off immediately with Volodya. Together they began to do the housework, bartering with items from their rations or getting things from the co-operative on the strength of one of Volodya's longstanding acquaintances. Vasya was content. But although Volodya no longer complained about his food, he continued to be resentful towards her.

'Your head's full of everything under the sun except me!' he said. 'It's as if I don't even exist as far as you're concerned.'

These criticisms hurt Vasya deeply. She was already painfully torn between Volodya and her work, and it was especially unfortunate that he'd come at such a hectic period. She tried to explain this to Vladimir, but he seemed not to understand.

'You've become cold, Vasya,' he frowned. 'Why, you've even forgotten how to make love.'

'But I'm just desperately tired, Volodya,' she said shamefacedly. 'I don't have any energy left.'

Volodya continued to sulk, and Vasya was forced to recognize that her behaviour towards him was simply not good enough. After all, her husband had come to see her after a long separation, and first thing in the morning she would disappear off to work! When she came home in the evening she was barely able to put one foot in front of the other; she only just managed to sink on to the bed, let alone make love! Once a terrible thing had happened: she'd fallen asleep while Volodya was making love to her. He'd taunted her about it the following morning.

'I ask you, where's the pleasure in making love to a dead body?' he joked, but he was obviously very mortified. Vasya felt miserable and guilty. No wonder he thought she'd stopped loving him! But how was she to find the strength for everything?

One day, Vasya returned home earlier than usual to find Vladimir making supper on his own.

'What's going on?' she asked. 'Where's Stesha?'

'That Stesha of yours is a hussy. I've sent her packing, and if she as much as dares to show her face here again I shall throw her head first out of the window.'

'Why, what on earth has happened? What can she have done?'

'Look, just take my word for it, will you? That girl's a little slut. I wouldn't send her packing for nothing, but it would only upset you if I told you what happened. She's a cheap, depraved little thing, and I don't want things here tainted by her presence.'

It was obviously not the time to start asking questions. Vasya realized that Stesha had made Vladimir extremely angry. Most likely the girl had stolen something; that sort of thing was quite common these days. Vladimir did value his possessions. Even though he was generous and always shared with his friends, he still had a somewhat proprietorial instinct. If someone so much as borrowed something of his he'd raise hell and hardly forgive them.

'So what are we going to do about the housekeeping now?' she asked.

'Oh, to hell with the housekeeping! I'll just do the rounds of the food stalls, and then I can look up my old friends. I'll manage.'

Shortly after this, Stesha came to see Vasilisa at the housing department to ask for her rations.

'What happened between you and Vladimir Ivanovich, Stesha?' she asked the girl. 'What have you been up to?'

'*I* haven't been up to anything!' retorted Stesha, her eyes flashing, adjusting a comb in her hair. 'Your Vladimir Ivanovich grabs hold of me, so I give him a good punch on the jaw, that's what! He was spitting blood for a long time afterwards. Teach him a lesson too!'

'Stop babbling a lot of rubbish, Stesha. Vladimir Ivanovich was just having a little joke with you, that's all!' said Vasya, trying to speak calmly as her mind suddenly clouded over.

'Funny kind of joke, I must say! He'd already managed to throw me onto the bed; it's just as well I'm so strong. Nobody's going to try anything like that on *me,* I can tell you!'

63

Vasya tried to convince Stesha that it was all a joke, a game, and that now she'd made Vladimir Ivanovich very angry with her. But Stesha just set her mouth obstinately. What a load of rubbish! Anyway, what business was it of Vasya's? She would never set foot in their flat again, and they could keep her rations!

Vasya was deeply depressed by the whole incident. She had no right to reproach Volodya, nor even to be hurt by his behaviour, for wasn't it all her fault? Hadn't she grown 'cold', and distressed her Volodechka? No wonder he thought she no longer loved him!

There was only one thing that really disturbed her, and that was that he had molested such a young girl. Stesha really was such a baby. It was a good thing she had her wits about her and was fairly experienced, otherwise who knows what might have happened? Vasilisa was plagued by niggling doubts. Should she tell Vladimir that she knew what had happened, or would it be better to say nothing about it? The problem was that she felt herself partly to blame.

As it turned out she had no chance to mention the subject to Vladimir, for their lives began to change. Vladimir started looking up old friends, members of the co-operative and former colleagues, and Vasya wouldn't see him for days on end. Volodya would still be sound asleep when she left the house first thing in the morning, and when she came back during the day he would already have left. She would return in the evening to her empty garret, feeling irritable and dispirited, not knowing whether to go to sleep, or make some tea and wait up for him. So she would heat up some supper on the oil stove, sort out her papers for the following day, and listen for the sound of his footsteps in the corridor.

Finally, tired of waiting for him she'd put out the oil stove (she had to economize), and once again busy herself with her papers, looking through reports and sorting out petitions. Occasionally she'd hear hurried footsteps on the stairs, but no, it wasn't Vladimir. Then she'd eventually go to bed alone, miserable and cold, and quickly fall asleep, dead tired. But even in her dreams she couldn't stop listening for him, waiting for her darling to come home.

Sometimes he would return in a happy cheerful mood, waking her up excitedly to hug her, and tell her all his stories, his news, his plans. Vasya would immediately feel comforted and happy, and forget all her anxieties about him. But then there were other times, times when he came home drunk, morose, maudlin, railing against himself and hurling abuse at Vasya. What sort of life was this, he would demand, cooped up, the two of them, in this miserable little garret, with no pleasures, no real happiness, and a wife who wasn't even a proper wife? It wasn't even as if they had any children . . .

Vasya found this last jibe particularly unbearable. She did not really want children, but she longed to be able to give him a child if that would make him happy. As it was, she had found that she just couldn't get pregnant. Other women she knew commiserated with her, for to them it was unimaginable that a woman could live without children. But Vasya was obviously not meant to be a mother.

After Vladimir's comment, Vasya went to see a doctor about her infertility. He had diagnosed anaemia as the cause. In order to raise Vasya's spirits after this news, Vladimir decided to take her out to the theatre. He bought the tickets, and she came home early at the agreed time. There she found Vladimir dressed up in his best clothes, preening himself in front of the mirror, looking for all the world like a 'gentleman'! Vasya teased him fondly, although she couldn't help admiring her handsome husband.

'And what about you?' he enquired anxiously. 'What are you going to wear? I hope you've got a nice party dress you can put on!'

Vasya laughed. Party dress, indeed! That sort of thing was all very well in America! They could afford to dress in style and wear a new get-up every day! As for her, she was just going to put on a clean blouse and her new shoes; that was the best she could do. Vladimir was frowning at her and looked so angry that she began to feel nervous.

'Do you seriously imagine that people in the theatre are only going to be looking at your feet then? What about the rest of you, what do you think that looks like, draped in some kind of sack?'

'But what are you so angry about, Volodya?'

'*I'm* not angry, it's you who'll be angry when you find yourself in the company of a lot of important people looking like that! Anyone would think we were living in some kind of nunnery or prison, the way you behave! No pleasures, no nice dresses, no proper home! You live in this rabbit-hutch of yours, drink nothing but water, eat slops, dress in rags . . . Why, even when I was unemployed in America I lived better than you do . . . !'

'But you know quite well that things can't be made perfect overnight. You know as well as I do that things are hard, that Russia's suffering the most terrible devastation at the moment.'

'Oh, I do wish you'd stop going on and on about the devastation! You'd do better to look to our new leaders instead! The old lot made an utter mess of things, but now that the new ones are just beginning to put things to right, people start screaming, "Do you want a return to the bourgeois life? Give us back the good old early Bolshevik days instead!" You people just don't know how to live, that's your trouble, and that's why we'll always have this chaos. I know that I for one didn't make the revolution to live this kind of life!'

'But you don't really believe we made the revolution just for our own benefit, do you?'

'Well, who did we make it for then?'

'For everybody.'

'Including the bourgeoisie, I suppose?'

'Oh, what nonsense you're talking! Obviously not! For the workers, for the proletariat . . .'

'So who are we then? Aren't we workers and proletarians?'

They continued to quarrel ferociously. Finally they left the house and walked down the street, splashing through the spring slush. Vladimir strode on ahead in silence, Vasya struggling to keep up with him.

'Volodka dear, do please slow down a little, I'm quite out of breath,' she pleaded at last, and he began to walk more slowly, still refusing to talk.

At the theatre, Vladimir met his friends, and spent the intervals with them, leaving Vasya on her own. She wished so much that she hadn't wasted her evening in this way – it was certainly no pleasure for her, and the next day there would only be twice as much work for her to do.

Soon after this episode, shortly before Vladimir was due to leave, the congress opened. Vladimir was keen to attend, although he wasn't a delegate. Many political questions were being debated at that time, and around these debates new factions were forming. Vladimir followed Vasya's line, enthusiastically joining her faction and throwing over all his old colleagues. They were inseparable, both at the congress and afterwards in the evenings. They spent all their free time at home drafting speeches, and a crowd of people from her faction would meet together in her room to draw up resolutions.

Vladimir found an old typewriter and happily accepted his role as 'girl typist'. It was immensely cheering, all working together as friends, and with such genuine unity amongst them. Of course, there would be furious arguments sometimes, when they all lost their tempers; then for no apparent reason, they'd all burst out laughing. They all loved this kind of confrontation.

Stepan Alexeevich came too. He sat there, stroking his grey beard, trimmed like an old merchant's, and keeping an affectionate eye on everyone. Vasilisa was constantly whispering in his ear. He had a high opinion of her, and once said to a friend, 'She's got a good brain, that one.' Towards Vladimir, however, he acted rather coldly, and this troubled Vasya; she didn't know what to make of it. Vladimir didn't greatly like him either.

'He's so sanctimonious, that Stepan Alexeevich of yours,' he pronounced. 'He positively reeks of incense. He's not a real fighter, just one of those typical behind-the-scenes operators!'

In the end, Vasya's faction was defeated at the conference, but they managed to pick up far more votes than they expected, and that was enough of a victory for them!

Vladimir's sick-leave was due to expire just before the end of the congress, and once more Vasya felt torn in two; on the one hand there was her husband needing her help to prepare for his journey back, and on the other there was the congress. But now she found this conflict exhilarating; she felt once again that Vladimir was no longer simply her husband but also a genuine comrade. She was proud of him too, for he had been of invaluable help to the faction, and her friends didn't want him to leave either.

The day of his departure arrived.

'Goodbye, my Vasyuk,' he said. 'My little sparrow is going to have to stay here under the eaves all on her own, and she'll have no one to moan to about all her worries. But then there'll be no one to disturb her in her work either!'

'Do you really imagine that you've disturbed my work?' said Vasya, hugging him and kissing his neck.

'But it was you who said your husband took up so much of your time, and complained about the housekeeping.'

'Please don't remind me of that! It's so much harder without you.'

She buried her head in his chest.

'You're not just my husband, you're my friend and that's why I love you so much.'

They kissed each other tenderly and said goodbye. But afterwards, hurrying back to the congress, Vasya suddenly thought to herself, 'However much I love being with him, I feel so much freer on my own. When I'm with Volodya, I have to think for two people, and work gets neglected.' Now she could immerse herself properly in her work. Work and then rest. She hadn't slept properly when her husband was there.

'Have you seen your husband off?' Stepan Alexeevich asked her when she arrived back at the congress.

'Yes, he's gone.'

'It'll be easier for you now. You were overworking with him around.'

Vasya was utterly amazed that Stepan Alexeevich should have understood this. She didn't reply, reluctant to admit such a thing, even to herself – it seemed an insult to Vladimir.

* IV *

Vasilisa was up the moment it began to grow light. The train was due to arrive that morning and she must smarten herself up so that Volodechka would be pleased with her appearance. Seven months without him, what an eternity! Vasilisa was as light-headed as the spring morning.

The nepwoman was still in bed, yawning and stretching and peering at her face in her pocket mirror, but Vasya had already washed, carefully combed her hair, and had put on her new dress. Looking at herself in the train mirror she saw only her radiant eyes, lighting up her whole face. There seemed nothing wrong with her appearance. Surely this time Vladimir would not be able to accuse her of going around in rags.

The train came to a halt at a wayside station, and Vasilisa looked out. Although it was still early in the morning the sun was already burning hot. In the north there had been only the faintest signs of spring, but here everything was bursting into flower. Even the trees, covered with clusters of white flowers a little like lilac, were unfamiliar to Vasya. Their leaves were similar to rowan, but a softer colour. They wafted a delicious sweet smell through the window.

'What kind of tree is that?' Vasya asked the conductor. 'We don't have that kind where I come from.'

'That's white acacia,' he answered. White acacia! How beautiful! The conductor picked some flowers and gave them to Vasya. They smelt wonderful, and Vasya suddenly felt so happy she wanted to cry. Everything around her seemed so interesting and beautiful, and most of all, most of all, she told herself, in only one hour I shall see my darling Volodya again.

'Shall we be arriving soon?' Vasya badgered the conductor. It seemed the train would never move again, puffing away as if stuck for ever on this siding. But eventually it started; they passed a town, a cathedral, a barracks, then suburbs and finally there they were – at the station. Vasya peered excitedly through the open window. Where was he? Where was Volodya? The next thing she knew, Volodya was rushing up to her from the other end of the carriage and she was in his arms.

'Oh, Volodka, Volodka, I can't believe it!' They kissed and embraced each other.

'Hand me your things immediately, and come and meet our secretary,' he said. 'Ivan Ivanovich, take these things, will you, and we'll go to my car. I've got a couple of horses too now, Vasya, as well as my own cow, and I'd like to start breeding pigs. We've got lots of room, a whole farm in fact, just you wait till you see it – you'll be able to live like a lady of the manor now. And my business is settling down nicely too; they've just reopened the department in Moscow . . .'

Vladimir talked on and on, eagerly telling her about his new life, his schemes, his ideas. Vasya sat there listening to him as they drove along, but though she found it all fascinating, she was anxious to tell him a bit about herself, and to find out how he'd managed without her, and whether he'd missed her and had been lonely.

They arrived at the house. There before her was an old-style private mansion with a garden; a young errand boy in a braided cap hurried up to help them out of the car.

'Let's see how you like our home, Vasya,' said Vladimir. 'It's a bit better than your rabbit hutch under the eaves, eh?'

They went in. There was a carpeted staircase and a mirror in the anteroom. Vasya took off her hat and threw off her coat and they went into the drawing room. There were sofas and carpets everywhere and a large clock in the dining room. There were still-life paintings in gilded frames on the walls and a stuffed bird hanging from a nail.

'So, do you like it?' Vladimir asked her, beaming expansively.

'Yes,' Vasya replied hesitantly, looking around her, not quite sure whether she liked it or not. It all seemed alien somehow, unfamiliar.

'And here's our bedroom!' announced Vladimir, flinging the door open. Two large windows overlooked the garden.

'Oh, look at the trees!' she said ecstatically. 'They're white acacias!' She hurried to the window, enchanted.

'Why don't you have a look at the room first? You'll have plenty of time to run around the garden. Not bad, is it, the way I've arranged it for you? Everything here I chose and arranged myself, and ever since I moved in I've been waiting for you to see it.'

'Oh, thank you, darling.' Vasya reached up to kiss Volodya, but ignoring this, he took her by the shoulders and turned her round to face a large mirror in a wardrobe.

'Look, you'll find this terribly convenient. When you get dressed you can see yourself full length in the mirror, and below it there are shelves for all your lingerie and hats and fripperies . . .'

'Really, Volodya! What sort of hats and frippery do you imagine I have! You must have found yourself a real "lady"!' Vasya laughed.

But Volodya went on, quite unabashed. 'Now look at the bed, will you? The coverlet is genuine silk. As a matter of fact I had some difficulty in getting it, as it didn't come with the house. And then there's this pink lamp you can put on at night . . .'

Vladimir conducted Vasya round the whole house, pointing out every little detail to her, delighting in it like a child – this little nest he had built for his wife. His obvious happiness made Vasya smile too, but she felt ill at ease. She couldn't deny that the rooms were stylish and beautiful, but they still felt alien to her. It was as if she'd stepped into someone else's house; there were none of the things that she actually needed, not even a table on which she could put her books and papers. The only thing that Vasya liked unreservedly were the two windows overlooking the white acacias in the garden.

'Why don't you just tidy yourself up a bit, have a wash, and then we'll go and eat,' Vladimir said, going up to the window to draw the blind.

'Oh please don't do that,' Vasya said. 'It's so lovely to be able to look out at the garden.'

'I'm afraid we can't do that. The upholstery will fade if we don't draw the blinds during the day.' And so the grey curtains, like heavy eyelids, came down over the green garden, and the grey featureless window now seemed even more alien to Vasya. She washed her hands and began combing her hair in front of the mirror.

'What's that you've got on?' asked Volodya suddenly. 'Is that the dress you had made out of the material I sent you?'

'Yes, this is the material,' Vasya replied, eagerly waiting for him to compliment her.

'Well, come on now, show yourself off properly,' he said, turning her this way and that. But she saw from his face that he didn't like it.

'What on earth made you have these pleats at the hips? You've got such a slender figure, just right for the latest fashions. Where did you get this monstrosity from?'

Vasya stood there dumbfounded, blushing guiltily and blinking. 'Monstrosity? But Grusha said this was the latest fashion!'

'A fat lot your Grusha knows! All she's done is botched up a perfectly nice piece of material! You look like a priest's wife in it! You'd better just throw the dress away and go back to your plain skirts, you look more yourself in them anyway. Like this you look like a peahen!'

Without appearing to notice Vasya's mortified face, Volodya strode off into the dining room to speed up supper. Feverishly Vasya flung off Grusha's creation and hurriedly got herself into her old skirt and belted blouse. She felt utterly wretched. Two miserable tears rolled down her cheeks onto her blouse. They dried at once, but in her eyes there remained an expression of cold resentment.

Maria Semenovna, the servant, a stout, middle-aged woman, presented herself to Vasya during dinner. Vasya shook hands with her.

'That was quite unnecessary,' Vladimir said sharply, the moment Maria Semenovna had gone out of the room. 'Please remember in future that you are the mistress of the house, otherwise there'll be no end of bother and complaints.'

Vasya regarded her husband in blank amazement. 'I'm afraid I simply don't understand what you mean,' she said. Vladimir changed the subject, and started urging Vasya to eat. But she felt too wretched to think about food.

'You'll love the tablecloth I've bought, it's pure Morozov linen, with serviettes to match. I didn't order it to be laid because it's so expensive to have laundered.'

'Where did you get all these things from?' Vasya asked Vladimir rather sternly. 'I hope you haven't laid in great stocks of them!'

'What an idea!' he laughed. 'Do you know how much something like that costs nowadays? Millions of rubles! Do you imagine that on my director's salary I can buy a lot of luxuries like that? As a director I get these things with the house, and it was a good thing I arrived when I did, because I was able to get hold of all those fittings through various departments and on the strength of some acquaintances of mine. Of course they've put a stop to all that, and you'd never get these things now. It's cash down or nothing these days! There are one or two things, of course, that I did buy with my own money, like that cupboard in the bedroom with the mirror, and the silk quilt, and the lamp in the drawing room . . .'

Vladimir slowly enumerated all these objects with evident satisfaction, but Vasya's face became increasingly cold, her eyes occasionally expressing intense hostility.

'And how much have all these delightful luxuries cost you, may I ask?' Her voice trembled with restrained rage. Vladimir noticed nothing and continued to eat his cutlet and sauce, washing it down with beer.

'Well if you really want it in round figures, not forgetting the discount I got for paying in cash, it comes out at around . . .' and with an impressive pause, designed to bring home to Vasya the gravity of the matter, he named a substantial sum of money. As he did so he raised his smiling eyes to her, as if to say, Some husband, eh?

Vasya jumped up from the table and leant over him, furious.

'Why, Vasya, what is the matter?' he cried in alarm.

'Tell me this minute where you got those sums of money from! Tell me immediately, I want to know!'

'Come on, Vasya, calm down, please! Do you imagine that I came by them dishonestly? Or maybe you just don't understand the value of money? If you just calm down and work out how much I earn you'll understand.' He then told her what his monthly salary was.

'Is your salary really that big? And even so, I still don't see how you, a communist, can spend it on all these trashy trifles when you know how much poverty there is everywhere, when you know that people are starving. And what about the unemployed? Have you forgotten about them as well, now that you've become a director?'

Vasya questioned Vladimir mercilessly. 'Well, Mr Director, you'd better answer!' she said.

Vladimir wouldn't budge an inch. Instead he reasoned with her, trying to get her to change her mind. He even teased her, saying that she'd lived for so long like a sparrow that she'd forgotten the value of money. After all, there were plenty of people who earned far more than he did – and some of them really *did* flaunt their wealth.

But Vasya wouldn't be mollified by mere words. She'd really got the bit between her teeth, and wanted him to justify himself for not living like a proper communist.

Vladimir tried another tack. He explained the political aspects of the matter. He told her what the director's job entailed, and about the instructions he had received from the Party Central Committee. He was absolutely insistent that the main priority was to ensure at all costs that business flourished and profits shot up. Before attacking him, she should see for herself what he'd accomplished in one year. He'd built up the business from nothing and made it more profitable, so that it now compared well with any other government trust in the area.

Even if he did live like a 'civilized human being', as he put it, that didn't mean he had any less concern for every single one of his employees, down to the humblest stevedore. If she would only find out a bit more about it, she'd soon stop nagging him like this. He really hadn't expected it of her, his friend – it hadn't occurred to him that immediately she arrived she would side with his enemies like this. Work was difficult enough as it was. Why should he wear himself out, only to have his wife attack him and put him on trial for the way he lived?

By now Vladimir was deeply offended. He had worked himself up into a rage, his eyes smouldering with anger and resentment. How *could* she distrust him? How could she pass judgement on him like this?

Vasya began to soften as she listened to him. Maybe he was right. After all, things had changed. The main thing was that his accounts were in order, business was flourishing, and the national wealth was increasing. There could be no disagreement with him on that.

'And what if I do acquire some possessions and set up a home for myself? I'm certainly not going to live out my days in some communal house! Why should we be any worse off than American workers? You should just see how a lot of them live, with their pianos, Ford motor-cars and motor-cycles!'

Several times in the course of this conversation Maria Semenovna had peered into the room, anxious to serve the pancakes. She sighed. No sooner had they met than they started arguing! That was just how it used to be with the gentry, whom Maria Semenovna had served before the revolution. They were no better, these communists, she thought irritably – letting the pancakes get cold like this!

Next day, Vladimir took Vasya on a tour of the company, to the offices, the warehouses and the employees' living quarters. He took her into the accounting office, saying, 'Just look at our books now. You won't find anyone who keeps their accounts like this. You won't be able to accuse me of extravagance once you've seen how I've set things up here.' Then he asked the accountant to explain the principles of their book-keeping to Vasya. These were simple and precise, and had earned them special congratulations from the Central Committee, he said. Although Vasya couldn't follow it all, it was clear to her that a lot of hard work had gone into the business and that the people here loved their work. Volodya was obviously committed to the job.

He then showed her round the flats of the employees and made a special point of asking his colleagues' wives whether they were happy. He cast triumphant glances at Vasya as all of them came up with the same answer: 'Happy, I should say so! Considering the times we live in now, things just couldn't be better and it's all thanks to you, Vladimir Ivanovich, that we're living like this!'

'There you are, Vasya! And you were saying that I'd become a spendthrift! Believe me, my first concern was to do everything I could to provide for the employees. I positively exhausted myself for them at the beginning. Only then did I think a bit about myself. You see how they live? It's the same for the workers as for the clerks, they're absolutely no worse off. I struggled particularly hard for the workers, I simply couldn't have done more for them!'

'Well, all right, so you've done everything for them. But what have they done for themselves?'

'You really do have the strangest ideas sometimes, Vasya! Don't you see that they and I work together. In the old days there used to be one rule for the director and another for the workers, but it's not like that here. You're nothing but an old stick-in-the-mud, Vasya. You'd better watch out, or you'll get covered in moss!' He said this in a joking tone, but Vasya sensed how annoyed and offended he was by her remarks.

He spent the whole day taking her round the various sections of the firm until Vasya was so tired that her temples throbbed, her back hurt, and she had a stabbing pain in her side. As soon as they got home, she thought, she would go to bed and have a nice sleep. Her head was still aching from the sound of carriage wheels.

However, when they were returning to the house Volodya announced that guests would soon be arriving for lunch, and Vasya would have to receive them. The errand boy let them in, and stood around as if awaiting orders. Vladimir took out a note-book, wrote a short message, and gave it to the boy.

'Run along then, Vasya, I don't want any loitering. You're to give me the reply in person, is that understood?' Saying this, he turned to Vasilisa with an odd glance, guilty and watchful. 'Why on earth are you gaping at me like that, Vasyuk?' he said, uncertainly.

'No reason,' she replied. 'So the errand boy is also called Vasya, is he?'

'Yes, that's right, oh, so that's it! You're upset that there are two Vasyas in my house! Really, what a woman you are! I believe you're jealous! There's nothing at all to worry about, you know, there's only one Vasya in the whole world for me, you're the one I love.' He hugged Vasya affectionately, and kissed her, looking deep into her eyes. Then for the first time that day he started to caress her. Embracing, they went into the bedroom.

The guests soon arrived for lunch : Savelev, and Ivan Ivanovich, secretary of the board of directors. Savelev was a tall, corpulent man, with carefully combed, thinning hair, wearing a ring on his index-finger. His intelligent eyes had a look of cunning, and it seemed to Vasya that the smile on his clean-shaven face had a certain irony about it, as though he was an observer, as if somehow he didn't give a damn about anything so long as he did all right out of it.

When he greeted her, he raised her hand to his lips. Vasya quickly withdrew it in confusion. 'I'm not used to that,' she said.

'As you wish,' he said, 'But I'm never averse to kissing a lady's hand, you know. It's just an agreeable custom, and it certainly isn't going to make your husband jealous – not that you shouldn't be jealous, eh, Vladimir Ivanovich? Come on, admit it!' So saying, he clapped Vladimir unceremoniously on the shoulder.

Vladimir laughed. 'Vasya's a model wife, and I wouldn't dream of being jealous of her!'

'Well, she obviously doesn't take her husband as a model then!' Savelev winked at Vladimir.

'I don't think I've given any cause for believing . . .' Vladimir stammered nervously.

But Savelev interrupted him. 'That's all right. We all know you husbands! I was a husband myself once, you know. Now I just lead a bachelor life.'

Vasya didn't like Savelev at all. But Volodya began talking politics and business with him as though he was an old friend. Vasya would never have discussed politics with a speculator like that, or made jokes about the chairman of the executive committee, as they were doing. Volodya would *have* to be made to see reason on this, and put an end to the friendship.

They had wine with lunch – wine which Ivan Ivanovich had brought along in a wicker flagon. Vasya listened to the discussion, trying to grasp the main points. Apparently the company was concerned about the hold up of some large stocks which were due to rise in value but might arrive too late on the market. None of this had any real significance for her, and she felt throughout that they were somehow constantly evading the real points at issue. Her throbbing head prevented her from listening properly anyway – and her eyes were beginning to hurt. She wished fervently that lunch would soon come to an end.

At last they rose from the table, and Vladimir immediately ordered a car to take him to an important meeting – on the transport problem.

'Really, Vladimir Ivanovich, how can you go off to a meeting tonight of all nights, when your wife has only just arrived? Why don't you stay with her for a while? It's only proper, you know.' Smirking slightly, Savelev shot a sidelong glance at Vladimir.

'Impossible, I'm afraid,' said Vladimir abruptly, cutting a cigar with absorbed attention. 'I should have been only too delighted to stay here this evening if business wasn't so pressing.'

'But, you know, there's work and there's work,' persisted

Savelev undeterred. And once again this detestable speculator seemed to wink at Vladimir, as though making fun at Vasya. 'I would have put off all my work for today, if I'd been you, to spend this first evening with my wife. After all, business isn't going to disappear.'

Vladimir didn't answer, and reached irritably for his cap. 'Let's be off then, Nikanor Platonovich.' They went out, and Savelev and Ivan Ivanovich went too, leaving Vasya on her own in the huge empty house. She crossed the desolate cold rooms to her bedroom, where she stood for a while at the window, lost in thought. Then she lay down, under the silk quilt, and immediately fell asleep.

She woke with a start. It was dark and, putting on the light, she saw that it was quarter past twelve. Could she really have been asleep that long? Past midnight, and still no Volodya. Getting out of bed, she splashed her face with cold water, and went into the dining room. The table was laid for supper and the light was on. All the other rooms were dark and deserted. Going into the kitchen, she found Maria Semenovna clearing up.

'Isn't Vladimir Ivanovich back yet?' she asked.

'No, not yet,' she replied.

'Does he always come back from his meetings so late?'

'Oh, it varies.' Maria Semenovna was in a taciturn and surly mood.

'But do you always wait up for him like this? Don't you go to bed?'

'Vasya and me, we take it in turns. One day I'm on duty, the next day it's his turn.'

'Will Vladimir be having supper?'

'He only has supper if he brings guests back with him, otherwise he goes straight off to his room.'

Vasya stayed for a while, but Maria Semenovna was too busy with her work to so much as glance at her. So she went back to the bedroom and flung open the window. It was a chilly spring night with the sharp scent of acacias in the air. The frogs were croaking so loudly that at first Vasya took them to be night birds. The sky was dark, scattered with a multitude of stars.

Looking out into the darkness, Vasya gradually grew calmer. Savelev the speculator was forgotten now. Forgotten too were all the pinpricks of resentment at Volodya's tactless behaviour towards her that day. Her heart was filled with only one thought – she had come to see her darling, to help him understand the proper Party line. No wonder you're in a mess if you've got mixed up with a lot of nepmen, she would tell him. He wasn't to blame, and he obviously needed her advice, that was why he'd sent for her.

Vasya thought with pride of how Volodya had set up his business, what a really exemplary worker he was. The day's events now appeared to her in a very different light. Already she felt much more optimistic and clear-headed.

She was lost in these thoughts and didn't hear the car drawing up, and Vladimir's footsteps crossing the carpets. She started at the sound of his voice.

'Why so deep in thought, Vasya?' he asked, with a look of tender anxiety.

'So you're back at last, darling! I've been waiting such an age for you to come!' She put her arms round his neck, and Vladimir caught her up in his arms as he'd done in the early days of their marriage. Vasya was beside herself with joy. Volodya loved her, he loved as he had always done! How stupid she'd been! Why had she been so irritable all day?

They sat down and drank tea, chatting away happily. Vasya told Volodya what she felt about Savelev, arguing that it would be better for Volodya not to be friends with him any more. Volodya didn't argue with her. He freely admitted that he had no more respect for the man than she did, but that he really was an invaluable person to know. He reminded Vasya that if it hadn't been for Savelev, the business could never have been established in the first place. He had a number of long-standing connections with various people, he had the trust of merchants, and was able to put Volodya in contact with them. In fact, he, Volodya, had learnt an enormous amount from him. Although as a man he was obviously an utterly worthless crook, and a bourgeois to boot, he was absolutely irreplaceable in business. That was why, said Volodya, when the local authorities in their 'great wisdom' had arrested Savelev, he'd stood up for him. In Moscow they had a high opinion of him in fact, and had given the local authorities a good ticking-off about the matter.

'But didn't you describe him to me in your letters as a swindler and a thief?' asked Vasya anxiously.

'Well now, how shall I put it? He's our agent, you see, and of course he's got his own interests to take care of, but honestly, he's

no worse than any of the others. Besides, the others help themselves and don't work, whereas he works, and not because he has
to, but because he's conscientious. He knows his job and loves it.'

All the same Vasya made Vladimir promise not to see so much
of him in future. Work was one thing, but she saw absolutely
no reason why he should be friends with him too. After finishing
their tea they kissed and went into the bedroom. Vladimir held
Vasya's head close to him, tenderly kissing her curls. 'This little
head of yours is so precious to me,' he said thoughtfully. 'It couldn't
ever become a stranger to me, could it? I'll never have a friend
like you, Vasya. You're the only woman I love, my tough little
Vasya.'

★ V ★

Next morning when Vasya awoke it was already late, and
Vladimir had left for work. She must either have caught a cold
on the journey or was sickening for something, for she had a
stabbing pain in her side and a bad cough and fever. The weather
was mild and sunny outside, but she wrapped herself up in her
shawl and stayed in bed. Maria Semenovna came into the room,
standing by the door with her hands crossed on her large stomach,
looking at Vasya, waiting for her to speak.

'Good morning to you, Maria Semenovna,' she said.

'Good morning,' the other responded tartly. 'What will you be
ordering for lunch? Vladimir Ivanovich told me when he was
leaving that you were to order lunch. There are going to be
guests, he said.'

Vasya was very taken aback. She was used to regular soviet
meals. Maria Semenovna obviously realized that Vasya would be
utterly at sea in these matters and proposed some dishes herself.
Vasya agreed to all her suggestions, only enquiring about prices.
Everything seemed terribly expensive to her, but Maria Semenovna
merely pursed her lips. 'Well, you can't scrimp and save if you
want to eat well. You need to have plenty of money for everything, now that the communists have done away with rationing.'

'But have you got the money?' Vasya asked anxiously.

'Well, there's a bit left over from yesterday, but it won't tide us over today. The meat will be expensive, and we need more butter too.'

'Didn't Vladimir leave you any money, then?'

'He didn't leave me anything, he just said "Go and see Vasilisa Dementevna and sort it out with her".' Maria Semenovna was standing there, impassively waiting for her money. She was obviously not going to go away until she got it. Vasya was at her wits' end. She had a little money of her own but she certainly didn't want it to be frittered away on these kinds of housekeeping expenses, for that way she'd be left without a kopek for her own needs.

'I know,' Maria Semenovna suggested, 'if you have a little money of your own you could give it to me to do the shopping, lend it to me on credit as it were, and then you can ask Vladimir Ivanovich for it back. He won't refuse you.'

Of course, Vasya thought, greatly relieved. That was the answer. Why hadn't she thought of that herself! Maria Semenovna left satisfied and Vasya went into the garden, and wandered along the paths, but was soon overcome by tiredness and felt very unwell. She went back in, lay down on the bed and fell asleep over her book.

She tossed and turned in bed, her cheeks burning with a high fever, and tormented by oppressive dreams. Once she woke up, looked around, and felt angry with herself for her lethargy. She should be in town, getting down to work. How absurd to come all this way to see Vladimir, only to fall ill! But she couldn't even manage to raise her head, and as soon as she closed her eyes again, her thoughts became troubled and confused. She dozed fitfully, unable to focus her thoughts.

The next thing she knew, Maria Semenovna was standing over her.

'Vasilisa Dementevna! Vladimir Ivanovich will be coming back for lunch any minute. You'd better get yourself dressed and I'll make the bed. He doesn't like it when the rooms are in a mess.'

'Can it be that late already?' asked Vasya.

'It's five o'clock, and you haven't had anything to eat. I was going to wake you but I saw you were sound asleep, and I know how tiring these long journeys are.'

'I don't know if it's the journey, but I seem to have caught a cold and feel rather feverish.'

'Well, you'd better put on your woollen dress then, that'll keep you warm,' advised Maria Semenovna. 'You don't need this shawl.'

'No, my dress won't do. My husband doesn't like it.'

'What do you mean, it won't do? There's absolutely nothing wrong with it, though it has got all those pleats at the hips and the waist is in the wrong place. Look, that's where the waistline should be. I was a dressmaker once, so I do know a thing or two about the latest fashions. Why don't you let me cut up the skirt for you, dear, and then we'll restyle the dress. By the time we've finished, Vladimir Ivanovich won't recognize it.

'But will it be ready in time?' asked Vasya anxiously.

'No, of course not! You and I will do it togther in our own time, bit by bit. In the meantime you can put on your black skirt and the jacket from the dress, and you'll look quite smart.'

It seemed to Vasya that she stood endlessly in front of the mirror. Maria Semenovna restyled everything, pricking her all over with pins as she made her alterations. Then she got hold of a lace collar from somewhere. The final effect was good – simple and smart. Vasya decided she liked it; she wondered what Vladimir would say.

She'd only just managed to get herself dressed when Vladimir arrived with his guests, a colleague of his from the GPU and his wife. The GPU man had a natty moustache, and was dressed foppishly in yellow knee-length boots. Could this man really be a communist? Vasya was dumbfounded. She disliked him intensely. His wife seemed to her tarted up like a streetwalker, in her diaphanous dress, furs draped over one shoulder and rings sparkling on her fingers. Vladimir kissed her hand, and they exchanged pleasantries. Vasya couldn't make out a word of what they were saying – it seemed to be nothing but banal inanities. When they sat down at table, Vladimir leant across towards his guests, and when he and the woman exchanged glances his eyes positively danced with glee.

Vasya had been put beside the GPU man. She knew he was in the Party but she simply couldn't think of a word to say to him. Again, they drank wine for lunch, and Vladimir clinked glasses with the woman. She whispered something in his ear which made them both laugh; they made Vasya feel very uncomfortable.

As for the GPU man, he paid his wife absolutely no attention whatsoever, which Vasya found odd and very unpleasant. A facetious discussion started about fast-days, and the woman admitted that although she did believe in God and went to confession she didn't observe the fasts. Again, Vasya was shocked. How could a GPU comrade be married to a 'believer'. She frowned angrily, and was seized with sudden fury at Vladimir. What sort of friends did he think these were?

Just as lunch was ending, Ivan Ivanovich arrived saying that Savelev had booked a box at the theatre and invited everyone to come.

'Shall we go, Vasya?' asked Vladimir.

'What, with Savelev do you mean?' She looked Vladimir straight in the eye, but he pretended not to understand.

'Yes, that's right, we'll make up a party with Nikanor Platonovich. A new operetta's opening tonight which they say is very entertaining. You'll enjoy yourself.'

'No, I can't go,' said Vasya.

'But why not?'

'I really don't feel at all well. I think I must have caught a cold on the journey.'

'You do look a bit under the weather,' said Vladimir, glancing at her. 'Your eyes look quite hollow. Here give me your hand. Yes, it's terribly hot, of course you mustn't go. In that case of course I won't go either.'

'But why ever not? You go without me.' Then the guests joined in, entreating Vladimir to go to the theatre with them. At last he agreed. In the hall, in front of everybody, Vladimir embraced Vasya, whispering in her ear, 'You look pretty tonight, Vasya! You go to bed immediately and I'll soon be back, I won't stay to the end.' He asked Maria Semenovna to keep an eye on Vasilisa Dementevna. Then they all left.

Vasya began wandering round the rooms, once more overwhelmed by feelings of melancholy. This life was really not to her liking at all, although she couldn't have said precisely what was so wrong with it. Everything just seemed so unfamiliar somehow, she felt so alien here, completely superfluous. So what if Volodya loved her! He could hardly be bothered to take any interest in her. Just a hug and a kiss, and off he went!

She'd have understood if he'd had to go to a meeting or to work. But to the theatre, of all places! Why had he gone to the theatre without her? Surely he'd seen enough plays that winter! Vasya felt tormented by something she couldn't properly express, but it sapped her strength and left her feeling miserable and uneasy.

I'll stay here just one more week, she resolved, see how Volodya's affairs develop, and then leave.

But as soon as she'd settled this in her mind another question presented itself. Where could she go? Back to the communal house? That was impossible, since her friend Grusha was living in the garret. And then there'd be the Feodoseevs all over again, the same old squabbles. She'd have to fight for the house, and no doubt would quarrel with everybody in the process. She no longer had the energy for it, nor the confidence that she could cope with the situation.

She had nowhere to go, and this realization brought an awful gnawing anxiety. She began to feel cold; shivering, she tucked her hands into her sleeves. Back and forth she walked about the dark and empty rooms. She felt as if calamity was lurking in this unfriendly house, lying in wait for her. But that was nonsense, she scolded herself, just premonition. Communists didn't believe in premonitions! What *was* the meaning of this unendurable, blank despondency?

Vladimir came home early as he'd promised. Vasya was sitting up in bed reading and he sat down beside her, fondly asking how she was. He looked serious and worn, as though he'd just had some deeply sad experience.

'What's the matter, Volodya?' Vasya asked, surprised.

He buried his head in the pillow and said in a pitiful voice.

'Oh, Vasya, I have such a hard life, you can't imagine how hard it is! You see only one side of it, but I don't think you really want to understand me properly. If only you could see how much I've gone through this winter, you wouldn't criticize me, you'd pity me. I know your heart is really in the right place, Vasya.'

Vasya stroked Volodya's head consolingly and tried to comfort him. She felt sorry for him, but at the same time she couldn't help feeling a bit pleased too. At this moment she felt they were united – by unhappiness. It *was* difficult to be a director, she comforted him, having to give orders to workers.

Volodya just shook his head sadly. 'No, it's not that, Vasya. It's something else. There's something which plagues me and won't leave me in peace.'

'But what then? Are they planning to make trouble for you?'

Volodya didn't reply. It was as though he couldn't bring himself to tell her what was on his mind. Vasya hugged him.

'Please tell me, darling, what is it that keeps plaguing you like this?' She rested her head on his shoulder, and then suddenly moved away, staring at him. 'You absolutely reek of perfume! Since when have you been wearing perfume?'

He drew back from her in confusion. 'Perfume? I suppose it must have been when the barber shaved me today. He uses perfume.'

He got up from the bed and began to concentrate intensely on his cigarette, inhaling very slowly. A few minutes later he went out of the room, saying he still had some papers which urgently needed sorting through before tomorrow.

Vasya's cough did not improve. She still had a stabbing pain in her side and a high fever, and although she made an effort whenever Vladimir was at home, he couldn't help noticing. Her coughing apparently prevented him from sleeping, as he made a bed up for himself on the divan in the drawing room.

The days dragged on, empty and inactive. She was beset by petty domestic anxieties, for although Vladimir never gave her enough housekeeping money, he still demanded that everything be done 'in the proper style', as he put it. After Vasya had contributed her own money to the housekeeping, she found Volodya's veiled reproaches particularly disagreeable.

'But you can't already have spent all your money on the housekeeping! At this rate we'll never have enough to go round, what with you here as well as all the others to feed.' As if it was *she* who invited all those guests and then ordered three-course meals for them!

However, she couldn't really complain about Vladimir, since in all other respects he was solicitous, anxious about the state of her health. He'd called the doctor, who diagnosed exhaustion, and a slightly weak right lung, told her to lie in the sun as much as she could and to keep to a healthy diet. Vladimir urged Vasya to follow the doctor's instructions and ordered Maria Semenovna to look after Vasya properly and ensure that she ate at the proper times.

He even got hold of some cocoa for her and went off in his car to find her a folding chair in which she could sit in the sun. He really was extremely attentive. But although he came to see her the moment he returned from work, they didn't in fact see much of each other, for Vladimir was very busy. Things were hectic at work, he was closely involved in the swings of the market and all this made him preoccupied and exhausted.

One afternoon Vasya was lying in her folding chair on the lawn, basking like a lizard in the sun. She was already burnt as brown as a gypsy. She was thinking how strange it felt to be living like this, without work or worries; but it was a life without joy, more like a strange dream. She felt she might wake up at any moment and find herself in her real home, in the communal house. She remembered the housing department, her friends, Stepan Alexeevich, Grusha, even Mrs Feodoseeva. Those days had certainly been more difficult, but so much happier!

Vasya was waiting for Vladimir to return. He'd promised to come home early, and today, as every day, Vasya was determined that she and Vladimir would have a proper discussion about things and really talk honestly. But day followed day, and there was never an opportunity to talk; either there were guests, or Vladimir had to work.

At least Savelev no longer came. But there were other guests, uninteresting businessmen who lived in a different world from Vasya's. Their conversation resolved exclusively around loading and unloading, invoices and packaging, discounts and bonuses. Although Vasya recognized that these matters were vital to the present economy of the Republic, and that the economy couldn't improve unless there was some sort of barter system, she nevertheless found it very tedious to have to listen to them. If ever she mentioned Party matters to them, say, or some article by Bukharin, or reports in the newspapers about the German Communist Party, they would stop for a moment, listen to her, and then immediately resume their conversation about freighting and loading, net weight and gross weight.

Vladimir never seemed to find these conversations at all tedious, and always brightened up considerably when he was with these colleagues, arguing and consulting with them tirelessly. It was only when he was alone with Vasya that he became depressed, sighing, stroking her hand, and gazing at her with his great mournful eyes. It was as though he was imploring her to help him, apologizing to her for something, although she couldn't for the life of her imagine what could be tormenting him. After all, she hadn't heard a murmur against him recently.

So what could be making Vladimir so wretched? Could he think that she was dying? This ridiculous thought immediately cheered Vasya up. That *must* mean that he really loved her! True, he didn't spend much time with her. But then she had to admit that she hadn't made much fuss of him either, when he had come to stay with her. After all, she'd been out all day then, and had no time for her husband! She wondered if her behaviour then had made him love her less now – a thought that worried her a great deal.

As Vasya lay there she gazed at the tops of the trees, standing out against the bright blue sky, swaying gently, caressed by the summer breeze. The grasshoppers were chirping in the grass, and from the end of the garden came the sound of birds, singing as though competing with each other. Vasya stood up and walked along the overgrown path, brushing against bushes of flowering lilac. What a heavenly smell! She began to tie a bunch of blossoms together, and a bee buzzing nearby settled on the flower and spread its wings.

'Brave little bee!' Vasya laughed. 'You're not afraid of a human being, are you?'

Then all of a sudden she felt overwhelmed by a feeling of such pure joy that she caught her breath. Looking about her, the garden suddenly appeared to her in a magical light. The green grass, the luxuriant lilac bush, the little slime-covered pond with the frogs croaking out their messages – how beautiful it all was! How very beautiful! Vasya feared to move, feared that this sudden, bright, winged joy might vanish as suddenly as it had come. She felt at that moment as though she had never in her life before properly understood what it meant to be alive.

Suddenly she understood everything. To be alive was not a question of whether you were happy or unhappy, whether you worked or struggled. To be alive was to be like that bee there, circling over the lilac, like the birds carolling to each other in the boughs of the trees, like the grasshoppers chirping in the grass. *They* were alive! Why shouldn't she just stay here for ever and ever, among the lilacs? Why shouldn't people be able to live like God's creatures . . . ?

But what could she be thinking of? The very thought of the word 'God' made her angry with herself. God indeed! What could have possessed her! It must be inactivity, this leisured life she was

leading at the moment, at Vladimir's expense. At this rate she'd
be turned into a regular lady of leisure!

She turned quickly towards the house, all desire to stay in the
garden gone. But her mood of joy did not altogether leave her.

She was just going into the bedroom to put the bunch of lilacs
into a vase, when Vladimir's car drew up. He came straight in.
'They've started!' he announced. 'It's been a long time since I've
had any trouble from them; now the troublemakers have begun
their infernal tricks all over again, only this time it's much worse.
They've concocted some sort of charge against me it seems, and
I've just been summoned to appear before the Control Commission.
We'll just see who wins this time!' Vladimir was pacing around
the room, one hand behind his back – a sure sign that he was
disturbed.

'And they've managed to get something in about my anarchism!
And my lack of discipline and the devil knows what else. Here
am I, literally wearing myself out, putting the business into some
sort of shape, and instead of giving me a bit of help, all the
people from the Party committee can think of is how to put a
spanner in the works! If they're going to start harassing me again,
I'll just have to leave the Party. I mean that! And I'll leave
without having to be told either! They won't have to threaten
to expel me, or anything like that. And that's final!'

This was obviously a genuine crisis. Vasya's heart sank. So this
must be the calamity she'd been expecting. She tried to hide these
feelings, however, and console Vladimir. But he was inconsolable.

'And what about your Stepan Alexeevich! He's a fine one, I
must say! They ask him for a character reference, and, would
you believe it, he can think of nothing better to say about me
than to praise my work. For the rest, it seems he finds me
"terribly self-satisfied", as well as "morally unreliable". I ask you!
You'd think those people were priests, the way they go round
judging people not for their work or their politics but for their
"morals". I don't live "like a communist", apparently. Am I supposed to become a monk then? Anyway, do these people behave
any better themselves in their private lives? You can bet they don't.
They won't be bringing charges against the head of the Agitation
Department, even though he did leave his wife and three children
and marry some girl he fancied! That kind of behaviour's accept-
able, it seems! That's good communist morality for you. Why is it

only *me* who's expected to lie on a bed of nails? And what business of theirs is my personal life anyway?'

At this point in the tirade Vasya felt she had to disagree with him. She felt the Control Commission was quite right to say that it was unthinkable that communists should take the bourgeoisie as their model, that a communist, and a director at that, should set an example to everyone.

'But what the hell do you think I've done wrong?' Vladimir interrupted her. 'For God's sake, tell me in what way I've not been a good communist. Is it because I don't live in a pigsty? Or is it because I'm forced, like it or not, to be friendly with all kinds of riff-raff in the interests of my job? In that case, why don't you write out instructions as to who's to be admitted to the house, how many chairs we ought to have, how many pairs of trousers a communist should be allowed to own . . .'

Vladimir was almost beside himself with rage as he tore into Vasya's critcisms. Vasya, on the other hand, was glad to have this chance to tell him at long last about the doubts that had been lingering in her mind all this time. She didn't know precisely what was wrong with the way he lived, she said, she just felt deep down that he neither lived nor behaved like a proper communist. He had everything he could possibly want, and she couldn't really believe that business would suffer if the director's house had no mirrors or carpets! Neither could she believe that it was really necessary to do deals over knick-knacks and gadgets with the Savelevs of this world, nor that kissing pretty girls' hands would make the business prosper!

'So you're getting at me too!' Vladimir shouted. 'I knew it! I could just sense that you came here to judge me, not as my friend. And now you're just going along with my enemies. Well at least now I know that you despise me as much as they do! Why don't you just say so to my face instead of pretending you're on my side, and nagging away at me all the time!'

Vladimir had turned white with rage and resentment. Vasya simply couldn't understand why he should lash out at her like this, but there was no point in trying to contradict him in his present state. She only hoped that he'd take back what he said to her later.

'Vasya,' he continued, calmer now. 'I really didn't expect this from you of all people. I never thought you'd abandon me when I'm in such a mess. I've obviously misjudged everything. Anyway, it can all go to hell as far as I'm concerned now. If everything is ruined, well good luck to them, it's all the same to me.'

As he spoke, he gripped the table, tipping over the vase with the lilacs. The flowers scattered over the floor, and a bright stream of water trickled over the carpet.

'Now look what you've done!' Vasya cried. Waving his arm dismissively, Vladimir walked over to the window, where he stood for a while looking weary and disconsolate. Vasya couldn't help feeling deeply sorry for him, as she always did. His life was not an easy one, and she knew how hard it was nowadays to make the right choices about how to live.

'That's enough now, Volodya dear,' she said. 'You really must try not to get so depressed about it. It's early days yet, and your case still has to be investigated. There are no criminal charges against you, which must mean it's your old problem, breaking the rules. Wait till I've seen the Party committee myself, and found out what it's all about. Who knows, maybe everything will come out all right in the end.'

She was standing beside him with one hand on his shoulder, trying to look into his face, but Vladimir paid no attention. He remained sullen and engrossed in his thoughts. Vasya was quite alarmed by his behaviour. She felt they'd suddenly become very remote from each other. She fell silent. The joy left her heart, leaving only leaden and oppressive anxieties.

★ VI ★

Next day Vasya trudged off to the Party committee. The town was unfamiliar but she was in such a distracted state that she barely noticed her surroundings, intent only on getting there as quickly as possible. The more she'd questioned Vladimir about his case, the more disturbed she had become. The charges against him, even if they were totally unfounded, were obviously very grave, and she couldn't for the life of her imagine how the whole thing could be cleared up.

The Party committee offices were housed in an old private mansion, with the red flag flying and the familiar symbol outside the door – just like the one in her home town! Vasya suddenly felt more cheerful and realized how much she'd been missing her old comrades; she could never regard those people who came to see Vladimir as real Party people. She went in and asked the boy at the reception desk the way to the local chairman's office.

'You'll have to write down your name and business first. He may see you today, but he may make you wait till Thursday,' the boy replied. How Vasya loathed this bureaucracy! Still, there was nothing for it but to sit down at the table and fill out the form.

'Here, take this to the secretary,' said the boy, and the form was passed on to an errand boy. Turning to Vasya, he said 'Up the stairs and turn right along the corridor to the door marked "reception". You'll have to wait there.' He looked dreadfully bored. Then he suddenly brightened up as he caught sight of a young girl in a knee-length skirt and fashionable hat. 'Manka!' he shouted. 'Hey, Manka! What are you doing here?'

Manka fluttered her eyes at him, simpering. 'Just off to see some friends!' she replied. 'Why shouldn't I pay a little visit to your committee offices?'

Vasya looked at the girl, trying to sum her up, deciding finally that she must be a prostitute. A familiar uneasy feeling came over her. In the old days a girl like that would never have dropped in so brazenly to see her friends at the Party committee . . .

As Vasya walked down the long, brightly lit corridor, men and women workers dashed past her. Everybody seemed to have work to get on with, and this made Vasya feel thoroughly idle. When she entered the reception room she was asked her surname by a private secretary, a smooth-faced young man with a self-important air. Her name was checked against the register, kept by a hunchbacked girl.

'It won't be your turn for a while, as your business isn't urgent. You'll have to wait a bit,' she said, and Vasya sat down to wait with the other people. Workers with thin drawn faces and shabby jackets conferred with each other – some sort of delegation, most likely. There was a tall, well-dressed man in glasses reading a newspaper, an 'expert' by all appearances. An old working woman in a headscarf was sitting very still, sighing every so often as if praying for her sins to be forgiven. There was a healthy exuberant Red Army soldier; next to him sat an old peasant woman in a Russian coat, and next to him a priest in a cassock.

Just as Vasya was wondering what could have brought the priest there, the secretary announced 'Your turn, Father.' He let the priest into the chairman's office and then turned round to the others. 'He's a very clever man and could be extremely useful to us,' he said confidingly.

From time to time girls with short hair and shabby skirts (communists evidently) would run in; efficient and preoccupied, they brought papers to be signed or questions to ask the secretary. After conferring with him briefly in whispers, they would run out again. A stylish, aristocratic-looking lady entered the room. Although she wasn't in the Party, Vasya knew her to be the wife of a highly placed worker. She demanded to see the chairman immediately, announcing that she had a letter from a member of the Central Committee, that she'd come from Moscow and hadn't time to wait. At first the secretary was firm with her, but seeing the letter from the Central Committee he wavered. But he couldn't go against the rules, he said. As this was a 'personal matter' would she kindly wait her turn in the queue?

The 'lady manquée', as Vasya privately thought of her, was absolutely furious. She made it clear how much she despised this system, here in the provinces! In Moscow she'd have been admitted at once! In Moscow everybody fought bureaucracy, but just look at this place! Look at all those petty officials, with all the rules and regulations they thought up. She sat down with an offended air, carefully adjusting her sleeves.

Then a burly man burst into the room, with his cap on the back of his head, and his overcoat unbuttoned, an overbearing man whom Vasya immediately put down as a nepman.

'Comrade secretary, I ask you, what kind of a system is this you have here?' he demanded. 'My time is extremely valuable, every minute counts, a shipment is coming in right now, and all you can do is hold me up with all this inane pettifogging red tape of yours and make me fill out a lot of forms. Announce me this minute please. Kondrashev's the name!'

He had an air of fatuous complacency about him. You'd think he was Lenin, the way he behaves, thought Vasya, feeling all her old hatred of the bourgeoisie rising up. It was *this* man they should be arresting and putting in the dock, this arrogant fat face!

The secretary apologized. But he had his instructions. The nepman paid absolutely no attention, and continued to insist imperiously he should be admitted. In the end he got his way; the secretary went into the office to announce him. Almost immediately he came back, looking flustered. 'The comrade chairman begs you to take a seat,' he said sheepishly. 'He's seeing two other people before you, both on urgent business.'

'What the hell is the meaning of all these damned rules! Try and do business with these people, and they do nothing but make a lot of idiotic demands, and then threaten you and badmouth you as a saboteur! But we all know who the *real* saboteurs are, don't we!'

So saying, he wiped the sweat from his forehead with a handkerchief and sat down, fuming. The 'lady' eyed him approvingly, the 'expert' glanced censoriously at him from behind his newspaper. The workers, however, had remained engrossed in their business, apparently oblivious to this scene. Their turn came next.

Vasya found the wait tedious; going to the window she looked out onto the small garden where two young children were playing, chasing a dog.

'Pull Bobka's tail! He'll squeal but he won't bite! Come here, Bobka! Catch him, quick!' Their childish voices rang out.

At last Vasya's turn came and she went into the chairman's office. Behind a large desk was a small man with a goatee beard, and spectacles; his bones seemed to protrude from his thin shoulders. He glanced somewhat coldly at Vasya, and stretched out his hand to her without bothering to get up.

'Well, what can I do for you? Is it personal?' he asked in a neutral tone – she was, after all, just another petitioner.

'I've come to introduce myself to the committee,' she said. She'd decided it would be as well not to bring up Volodya's case immediately as it was obviously going to be anything but simple to talk about it. 'I arrived in town recently.'

'Yes, so I heard. Staying with us for long, are you?'

'I have two months' leave, but as I've been ill I shall most likely stay on longer.'

'Are you going to be resting or will you be taking on some work?' he asked, not looking at Vasya as he spoke but continuing to sort through his papers as if to say, Why should I make small talk with you when I'm so busy.

'I can't take on anything permanent,' Vasya replied, 'but you could use me for agitational work.'

'We may be able to use you, yes. Next week we're starting a campaign around the transition to the local budget system. I hear you're an expert on the housing question?' He glanced at Vasya again, briefly, and immersed himself once more in his papers.

'I worked for two years in the housing department,' she replied, 'and I organized a communal house.'

'Indeed! How very interesting! In that case you can show us how to make our communal houses pay.'

'I'm afraid I can't do that,' Vasya said, shaking her head. 'You see, as soon as we started becoming self-supporting the whole thing went to pieces. I think that communal houses should be more like schools, places for inspiring the communist spirit . . .'

'Look here, I really don't have the time nowadays to busy myself with such matters,' he interrupted her. 'But if you can give us some ideas on how to approach the matter – as well as a rough financial estimate – that would certainly help us reduce the state budget . . . So you think housing can be used as a method of educating people, do you? But we've got schools for that sort of thing, and universities too!'

The chairman laughed patronizingly from the heights of his wisdom. Vasya felt angry and rose abruptly to leave.

'I'll say goodbye then, comrade.'

'Yes, until we meet again,' he replied, regarding her more attentively now. She returned his glance coldly, looking him straight in the eyes.

'And if you would like to work for the agitation department, all you have to do is go along and register. Why not drop in on the women's department too? They're always short of workers there,' he suggested.

'And now that I'm here,' she said suddenly, 'I should like to ask you about Vladimir Ivanovich's case.' She looked at the chairman severely as if saying, I know this business is all your doing!

'Yes, well, er, how shall I put it?' The chairman frowned, moving his cigarette to the corner of his twisted mouth and suddenly looking rather grave. 'Look here, I've heard about you, you're obviously a Party comrade of an extremely high calibre. It really wouldn't be proper for me to discuss Vladimir Ivanovich with you.'

'But what are your accusations against him? Vladimir Ivanovich can't have done anything criminal.'

'Well, I suppose it depends what you mean by criminal, doesn't it?' he replied. 'However, I really cannot go into the case with you. You'll have to make your own enquiries at the Control Commission. And now, my respects to you, goodbye for now.'

He nodded his head at her and buried himself once more in his papers. His message was obvious – don't bother me now, I've got a lot of work to attend to.

Vasya left the chairman feeling angry and put out. Nobody would have been received like that in her home town, not even a non-Party member! She had gone there to talk to her comrades and had been made to feel like a stranger! Vladimir was right when he said they'd all turned into petty officials acting like pre-revolutionary governors. Vasya was walking along so deep in thought that she almost bumped into someone going the other way. There stood Mikhailo Pavlovich, an old friend, a worker in the machine department of the factory where Vasya had worked.

'Well I never!' he exclaimed. 'I can't believe my eyes! Bless you, Vasilisa, my dear!'

'Mikhailo Pavlovich, my dear friend!' They hugged and kissed.

'So you've come to stay with your husband, have you?'

'And what about you? What are you doing here?'

'I've come to purge the Party! I'm a member of the Control Commission now. It's a full-time job – there's always a lot of shady business going on,' he said, laughing.

He had a red beard and a kindly face and was as enthusiastic as Vasya remembered him. They excitedly exchanged news and asked each other many questions.

Mikhailo Pavlovich insisted that Vasya should come to where he was lodging. He lived in a house which used to belong to the gentry, and he had the room which had been the porter's, next to the front door. The room wasn't much to look at, just a bed with a basket beside it containing his belongings, two hard chairs and a table covered in newspapers, a few glasses and some tobacco. He'd intended to move there temporarily but had ended up staying there.

They recalled old friends and comrades, reminisced about their town, discussed which ventures had prospered and which had gone to the dogs. Then they touched on the subject of the NEP. The very term stuck in Mikhailo Pavlovich's throat and he was none too keen on the local committee chairman either.

'He's nothing but a petty upstart,' he said, 'with him it's all "me, me, me". Of course, he does work hard, he's energetic and he's certainly nobody's fool. But everything has to come from him. It's as though he wanted to see his name in lights, to show everyone who's chairman. And the workers don't like it one bit. They say "the congress decided on more democracy, but instead what have we got? Even more bureaucracy and even more respect for rank!" So much intrigue going on behind the scenes nowadays, and that means a whole lot of new factions, and then work is held up and the authority of the Party is undermined. The chairman's job ought to be to unite everybody; he's got to be impartial, like a father. But instead he harasses people.'

'Look, dear Mikhailo Pavlovich, how is the case against Vladimir going? And what are the charges against him? Are they very serious? You can tell me as a friend, you know.'

Mikhailo Pavlovich stroked his beard. After thinking a moment he told Vasya that the case itself was not worth a kopek, and that if communists were now going to be brought to trial for activities like Vladimir's, almost every one of them would have to be indicted.

The whole thing had started when Vladimir Ivanovich first arrived. He'd immediately fallen out with the chairman, who had ordered him around, and Vladimir had refused to take orders. Vladimir had said 'Your rules don't concern me. That may be the Party line but I'm not subject to you. I shall deal only with the industrial authorities. Let them be the judges of my work.'

Reports of this conflict had finally reached Moscow. The Moscow Party committee, while ostensibly supporting the chairman, took the director under their protection and so nothing came of it. It was made to seem as if both of them were right!

But inevitably there were repercussions, and once again neither of them would yield an inch. After the slightest incident, both would independently send reports to Moscow.

Finally, a delegation had to be sent from Moscow to sort the whole thing out. Resolutions were drafted in the strongest possible terms; and no sooner had they left than the fight started up again. It was then that the Control Commission had been called in to investigate the matter and Mikhailo Pavlovich had attempted to settle things peacefully. The director, he had said, was running his business on his own lines. This was considered quite proper in industry, and the Party central committee was satisfied with his work.

There were no direct charges against Vladimir, and Mikhailo Pavlovich thought it unlikely that any could be made against him. He had told the Commission that he personally knew the 'anarchist American', and had lived in the same town as him back in 1917 when they'd worked together closely. Even if he did live in rather fine style nowadays, even if his conduct was immoderate and his behaviour 'uncomradely' – well, who could claim to be innocent of such charges these days?

But the chairman and various other members of the Party commission were determined that the case should get a serious hearing, and to use this case against the director to teach other people a lesson. They didn't want the Party to go round condoning this sort of behaviour.

'But what are all these "activities" of his you keep referring to?' asked Vasya in bewilderment. 'I know he has a grand apartment, but that's not Vladimir's anyway, it's what any director would get at the state's expense.'

'I'm afraid that the case doesn't just concern his apartment. People are wondering where he got the money to set up two different establishments,' Mikhailo Pavlovich replied.

'What do you mean' "two establishments"?' asked Vasya angrily. 'Do you really suppose that Vladimir Ivanovich has been supporting me as well? What an idea! If you really want to know, I've been putting my own money into the housekeeping! And that's only because Vladimir hasn't enough of his own . . . You see, it's only for the sake of his job that he has to give all these dinners and receptions.'

Mikhailo Pavlovich listened to her with a pitying look, which made Vasya even angrier. Why *should* he pity her for standing up for her anarchist husband? She knew he hadn't approved when she'd first started living with Vladimir.

'Well, what are you gaping at me for? Don't you believe me? How could you think for one moment that I'd rob him of his money like that?'

'But it's not you we're talking about, is it, my dear?' he replied gently. 'The main problem is all those unsuitable friends of his . . .' He looked at her as though to see how she would react.

'Are you referring to Savelev by any chance?' she asked.

'Well, yes, there's Savelev of course, and there are other people too . . .'

'But Savelev no longer visits us now, and Vladimir has promised to have nothing more to do with him – apart from business, that is. And as for the others, he's promised to see them only on strictly necessary business matters. There are so many people he doesn't particularly like who live in a completely different world to ours,

but what's to be done about it? All these shareholders and technicians, they're all part of business . . .'

'Yes, quite so, dear,' murmured Mikhailo Pavlovich abstractedly,
stroking his beard.

Vasya went on to tell him about all the things she found so
difficult to come to terms with these days. People were so different
now, and so was work. She often felt terribly confused as to what
was wrong and what was right, about how communists ought
and ought not to behave . . . And she would have sat discussing all
these things with him for much longer if a friend hadn't come
round to take him to the Control Commission.

Before he left, Mikhail Pavlovich said he would introduce Vasya
to some 'regular comrades' from a factory and he would think
hard about Vladimir's case. He warned Vasya, however, that if
Vladimir went on acting as he had been doing he would be
threatened with expulsion from the Party.

Vladimir had obviously been waiting for her at the window, for
when she returned he met her on the porch.

'Back at last, Vasya my rebel! Where have you been fighting,
then? At the Party committee? So what did they have to say?'

As she spoke, he paced anxiously round the room, smoking.

'So, they're accusing me of living in two establishments, are
they? What a lot of hypocritical humbugs they are! It wouldn't be
any business of theirs if I lived in five establishments! What does
it matter so long as my accounts are in proper order, and I don't
steal the goods or take bribes?'

This talk of two establishments disturbed Vasya deeply. But
she was most emphatic about Savelev. The thing would have to
stop here and now, and if ever he came to Vladimir's office he
must be sent packing the moment they had discussed their business. Then she asked Vladimir about his workers. Was it really true
that he was rude to them and even shouted and cursed at them?

'What a lot of nonsensical rumours! What rubbish!' he shouted.
'Of course there are times when I shout at them and let them
have it, and with good reason too, let me tell you! It wouldn't
do at all to get too slack with some of those fellows, especially the
loaders – a lazy, irresponsible bunch of men they are, I can tell
you!'

Vasya didn't mention that the Party was thinking of expelling
him. Instead, she decided that she herself would instigate some

changes at home. From now on there'd be no more guests hanging around the place, they'd eat more simply, and the horse Vladimir had bought would have to be sold. What use were horses anyway, if you had a car? At this suggestion, Vladimir got very worked up, insisting what a fine horse it was, broken in to carry a lady's saddle too. It was hard to get hold of a horse like that nowadays, it was pure luck to have found it in the first place, and it hadn't been so expensive either. A horse meant capital these days!

'Capital! Really, Volodya, are you trying to set up in business as a capitalist, then? You *must* give up these expensive habits of yours, dear, if you don't want to regret it later.'

'So you think they'll expel me from the Party, do you? What has the Party come to, if it can start expelling people for their morals? Let them go ahead, I don't care! I'll just work for the state institutions!'

Vasya didn't try and contradict him. She merely insisted that from now on their life must change – they must live more modestly. Most important, he would have to break off all contact with unsuitable friends. She promised to discuss things with Mikhailo Pavlovich again, and, if need be, go to Moscow and raise the matter with Torporkov, who had helped to get him acquitted after the previous charge.

Vladimir glanced at Vasya sitting on the window-sill, so pale and skinny with her huge mournful eyes and her thin face. Throwing his cigarette on the floor, he went over to her and kissed her, pressing her face close to his.

'Vasya, sweetheart, don't leave me now, will you, my love! Please support me, tell me what I should do. I know only too well how wrong I've been, but it's you I've wronged, not them.' He put his head on her knees like a child.

'But what have you done, Volodya?'

'Oh, Vasya, do you really not understand? Don't you realize yet?'

'Well, if you mean you've betrayed yourself and your class, you needn't try and justify yourself to me.'

'Oh, Vasya, Vasya!' he sighed, moving away from her disconsolately. Then, changing the subject abruptly, he asked, 'Why isn't dinner ready yet? I'm famished. I haven't had anything to eat since this morning.'

Soon after their first meeting, Mikhailo Pavlovich had put Vasya

98

in touch with a group of women mat makers and she started going to the factory regularly to help them in their attempts to get better working conditions.

To be working once more with people was a real joy for her. It was just like going home. She also met Mikhailo Pavlovich frequently and was soon on good terms with his friends, whose opinions she found she could share. These men, without actually forming an official group, were unanimous in attacking the chairman and would have no truck with the bosses either. There was one old worker they *did* *r*espect – *he* had not lost touch with the people or started acting like a boss. They had elected him director of the steel casting industry.

Vladimir's case was still unresolved and according to Mikhailo Pavlovich some new evidence had come in – bad evidence, he warned Vasya. From now on Vladimir would have to be even more careful and avoid all dealings with Savelev, who was apparently implicated in some extremely squalid affairs. However vociferously the state institutions might protest, it was clear that the GPU wasn't going to let this man get away with it for much longer.

Vasya was distraught with anxiety for Vladimir. It all seemed so terribly unjust, especially at this time, when he was working flat out from morning to night. The minute he got home, he would sit down at his ledgers. He had received instructions from the Party centre to radically reorganize the book-keeping system of the firm. He'd called in a bank official to help him on this job, and the two of them would often pore over the files until three in the morning. He began to lose weight and sleep badly, which was hardly surprising considering the double load of problems he had to cope with. Now, on top of this new and important work, he had to put up with all this persecution and backstairs machinations. Vasya's heart bled for him, and she could feel nothing but tenderness for her poor victimized husband.

They no longer entertained guests, and Savelev's name was never so much as mentioned. Apparently he'd gone off somewhere and good riddance too! Vladimir stopped going out to the theatre or visiting friends, and just stayed at home every evening, grim and preoccupied. Vasya racked her brains for ways to distract him from his gloomy thoughts and help him reduce his heavy burden of work. It was really only at the mat factory when she was involved with the women there, that she was able to put him out of her mind.

Those women had a hard life. Their wages were low, and as there was never time to review their wage rates they were always owed an increase. The intervention on their behalf by the administration had come to nothing and Vasya was furious at the mess they'd made of things. She put pressure on the authorities and stood up for the women's interests. She also helped to put the women's union on its feet so they could then bring a case before the arbitration committee. When she was at the factory she rushed around, oblivious to everything else, completely forgetting the outside world until it was time to go home.

She'd walk back with Lisa Sorokina, the organizer, a very bright girl with whom Vasya formed a close friendship. They'd talk as they walked along, outlining their plan of action and discussing which of them should be chosen to put their case to the arbitration committee. The time passed so quickly that they often reached Vasya's house before she even noticed.

One day when she returned from a meeting, Vladimir came out to meet her. He looked a changed man, positively beaming with that special happy look of his. Hugging her, he said, 'Well, Vasyuk, you must congratulate me! I've just had a letter from Moscow and apparently they're appointing me to a new post — in other words I've been promoted! I'll be superintending a whole region from now on! I only have to stay on here another two months and then wind everything up. What fools we shall make of our Control Commission now. What *will* the chairman say, I wonder!'

'I wouldn't rejoice too soon, if I were you,' Vasya warned him, 'just in case the charges against you get in the way of your appointment.'

'Rubbish! The Control Commission definitely won't go on making trouble for me now. They obviously need me to work for them.' He was jubilant, like a child. 'Well, little rebel of mine,' he said, fondling her, 'I've got something for you to celebrate the event, a little present.' He led her into the bedroom, and there, laid out on the bed, was a length of blue silk and beside it some lawn.

'Look, this silk will make a lovely dress for you, darling, and you can smarten yourself up a bit; this grey-blue colour really suits you. And then there's this lawn for some shirts'

'Shirts! But, Volodka dear, what can you be thinking of!' exclaimed Vasya, laughing. 'Material like this for shirts?'

'This is the finest ladies' lawn,' he insisted. 'I know it's used to make underwear, but I wish you didn't have to wear those terrible hair shirts of yours – they always remind me of balloons.'

'But surely it could be made into something better than just shirts? And as for silk, well, of course it's lovely, but you shouldn't have got it. Was it for cash? How could you spend your money on a thing like that?' She shook her head, for Volodya's presents gave her no pleasure; she was made uncomfortable by his extravagance. But she hated having to hurt his feelings.

'Don't you like it then?' asked Volodya.

'It's absolutely beautiful material, it really is. But surely, Volodya, you must see that it's not my style at all.'

'But how about when we go to the theatre?'

'So that's how a director's wife is supposed to get herself up for the theatre, is it?' And the mere thought of herself dressed up in blue silk made her laugh. 'Thank you, darling, all the same, for being so kind and taking so much trouble.' Standing on tiptoe she hugged Volodya and kissed him passionately.

'You haven't forgotten how to kiss then, Vasya. I thought you didn't love your poor husband any more, turning me out of the bedroom like that and never coming up to give me even a little kiss!'

'But, Volodya, you know that neither of us have had any time – you've had so many other things on your mind.'

'So you still love me?' he asked.

'How could I ever stop loving you!'

'Do you want me to remind you how we used to make love?' he asked, and they both laughed, as though they'd met again after a long separation.

Vasya was just setting off for the factory next day when she remembered Bukharin's *ABC of Communism* which she had meant to take with her. It was on Volodya's bookshelf and she hurried back into his study to collect it. As she was opening the glass door of the cupboard, a packet fell off the shelf and the wrapping came undone. Stooping to pick it up, her heart contracted. There was a piece of blue silk identical to the one Vladimir had given her, and the same lawn too, covered with bands of open lace work.

Dimly thoughts began to stir in her mind. 'He lives in two

establishments.' Could there be some truth in it? The very idea was too terrifying to contemplate. A wave of jealous suspicion swept over her. 'He lives in two establishments . . .' He'd certainly been unpredictable recently, one moment acting like a stranger, barely recognizing her, the next being excessively affectionate towards her. As though he felt guilty about something.

She began to recall how Volodya always smelt of perfume after he'd been to the theatre, how he preened himself in front of the mirror when he was going out for the evening, suddenly remembering too that long-forgotten nurse with the pouting lips, the blood stain on the sheet.

Everything clouded over, her hands felt numb, and an indescribable pain gripped her heart. How could Volodya deceive her, his dearest friend! Her adored husband and companion, making love to another woman behind her back, when she was right here, beside him! If they'd not been living together it might have been different, for she'd never expect a man to be permanently faithful to her. But now, when she was offering him all her love, all her tenderness, everything, how could he do such a thing?

Perhaps he no longer loved her? She couldn't even entertain such an unbearable thought, and began to clutch wildly at straws for comfort. If he no longer loved her why would he treat her so affectionately and considerately? And why would he have called for her to come to him in the first place? It was impossible – they were friends and lovers who'd gone through so much together they'd become as one. Was it true? Was this yet another calamity? She could not, would not, believe it.

And yet . . . why did he spend so little time at home? Why was he always so wretchedly miserable? Why wasn't he delighted to see her any more? Why did he seize any pretext, such as her cough, to sleep on his own? Thinking about these suspicions, she wanted to cry out, but she was too appalled by them to be able to take in their full meaning. It's all lies, she told herself, lies! He loves me, he must love me! He made love to me only yesterday. Maybe the material belongs to someone else, maybe he had to deliver it to someone . . . Why had she jumped to the conclusion that this was his parcel? His name was not even on it. She must have invented the whole thing.

Now she began to feel ashamed of her distrust of him. She was no better than an old woman, keeping tabs on her husband. But despite her attempts to reassure herself, the wretched serpent of jealousy kept gnawing away and, try as she would, it wouldn't leave her alone. There *must* be a simple explanation. When Vladimir got back she'd ask him about everything, they'd talk it over together, she would give him the opportunity to explain, and then she'd find out the truth. Picking up her book, she went off to the factory. She was quite late enough as it was.

After work, she hurried home, anxious not to be late for dinner. At the factory she'd been at peace, but the minute she found herself alone on the street her jealousy began to stir again. Two separate establishments, two pieces of silk, two pieces of lawn . . . And how did Vladimir know that they made underwear like that anyway, apart from learning it from streetwalkers and ladies with money to fling around?

And then what was it he'd said about her blouses? Hair shirts that reminded him of balloons. Did he really dislike her blouses? In the old days he'd loved her in them. But then in the old days he would never have gone out like that, leaving her alone when she'd just arrived. And if he had really been going to a meeting, as he'd said, why had he primped himself in front of the mirror like that, and why had he reeked of perfume afterwards? Why did he no longer look at her with that old, special, look of joy?

She'd demand an explanation, whom he had got the material for, why he'd concealed it on his bookshelf, why he hadn't just left it lying on the table. If he tried to evade her questions or lie to her she would never forgive him. She ran up the steps onto the porch and hurriedly rang the bell. The car was parked outside – Vladimir was already back.

He would have to explain himself the moment she saw him. If he'd been deceiving her and humiliating her just the way a husband might humiliate a wife whom he didn't love . . . the very thought made her boil with agitation and rage. Oh, why was it taking so long for the door to open!

At last the bolt rattled and Maria Semenovna opened the door.

'We've guests from Moscow,' she announced. 'Six people, six mouths to feed. What a business!'

Vasya couldn't imagine who these guests could be. She heard them chatting away amicably in the drawing room. Vladimir was there playing host, and introduced them to his wife. The guests turned out to be men from the syndicate who'd brought the plans for the new work schedule. Vasya was immediately eager to hear

about the latest news from Moscow and recent political develop-
ments which were on everybody's mind.

But then she saw Maria Semenovna standing in the doorway,
beckoning furtively to her. She badly needed some help in the
kitchen; Vasya the errand boy had been sent out to get wine,
Ivan Ivanovich had gone off to fetch appetizers, while poor staid
Maria Semenovna was rushed off her feet, trying to attend to the
roast in the kitchen, and laying the table at the same time.
Vladimir had given orders that everything was to be done in style
and the table laid formally. Vasya would just have to help her.
They bustled round. Ivan Ivanovich returned – just as well, as they
needed an extra hand. All this time, Vasya was too busy to think
about the blue silk. She just wanted to be sure she didn't let
Volodya down; now that he was a director he couldn't afford to
lose face in front of the men from the syndicate. Soon the other
Vasya ran in with the wine, and Ivan Ivanovich uncorked the
bottles.

The table was eventually decked out as if for an Easter banquet,
with appetizers, wine, flowers, the Morozov napkins and the best
silver knives. They called the guests in, and Vladimir cast an
anxious eye over everything. Then he seemed to relax.

But surely he could have given Vasya just a brief glance of
gratitude for working so hard to please him? Her anxieties re-
awakened, she felt utterly dismal and rejected. She made small
talk with the guests, but all the time the blue material was on her
mind. Who could it be for? She began to look at Volodya with
new eyes – he might have been a stranger, for only a stranger could
have lied and deceived her like that or allowed this hellish serpent
to bury itself in her heart.

Vasya was kept busy all that evening, and sent the errand boy
for some extra pillows to make the guests comfortable for the
night. All the time she was arranging their beds in the study she
kept looking at that cursed bookshelf. The blue material was still
there and she still no nearer knowing who it was for. She was
exhausted.

She gave the guests their tea, but all they could talk about was
their own affairs, grades of merchandise, methods of packaging,
specifications, estimates. This was the world of business again. All
these men were former merchants, including the two communists
amongst them who were already experienced traders and had
become real 'red merchants'. Vladimir blossomed in their com-

pany. He talked proudly of his business, which had far outstripped the others and was increasing its profits every month. The merchants evidently had great respect for him, and listened attentively to everything he had to say, completely disregarding the opinions of the other bosses.

At any other time Vasya would have been happy for Vladimir, but today she just didn't care. There he was, talking away about business, business, never even a thought for her. Couldn't he see how exhausted she was, how tortured by her jealousy?

She couldn't help wondering whether, if he was capable of deceiving her, he mightn't be unscrupulous about business too. Maybe the Party committee had been right to bring him to trial. Oh, what were these syndicalists talking about now? They hadn't stopped talking all day. If they would only leave her alone with Vladimir, if she could only ask him about the material . . .

Vasya began to get ready for bed. Vladimir was going to be sleeping with her that night as the guests had taken up the other rooms. She was waiting for him, listening for his footsteps. He'd said good night to the guests and was just giving Ivan Ivanovich his orders for the next day. When she heard him approach the door her heart began to thump and her knees gave way so that she had to sit down on the bed. She was going to ask him the moment he came in.

But Vladimir was too full of himself to give her the chance. He wanted her advice on how they should reorganize the bureaucracy so as to strengthen the position of the communists and keep the bourgeois syndicalists under Party control.

'Do advise me, Vasya,' he begged her. 'You're the expert on these matters. Think about it, will you? Tomorrow I'm going to examine the new charter with them, but I'd like you to read it through beforehand and give it your undivided attention. The bourgeoisie are doing their damnedest to get their pot-bellies into the government and are encroaching on workers' power, but they haven't a hope, don' you worry. We'll get them by the short hairs. It's just a problem of organizing the bureaucracy so that it can't move an inch without the sanction of the Party and the *real* communists.'

'But how can you say that, when you're not even following Party regulations?' Vasya enquired. 'Many's the time when you said it would be no great catastrophe to be expelled from the Party, and you could survive quite well without it!'

'Never mind what I may have said in a temper,' Vladimir grinned at her, 'you know me better than that. How could I live without the Party? Do you really think I could break with it?' He began pulling off his boots, thinking aloud. 'As soon as this stupid case is behind me, Vasya, you and I will start living together properly, and you'll see what an exemplary communist I'll become once I've been transferred to this new district! No more confronting the chairman; in fact I'll soon be in the Party pantheon!'

He was happy, his eyes alight, not at all his recent bad-tempered self. 'Let's go to sleep now,' he said, and was just about to switch off the lamp when Vasya stopped him.

'No, please, wait a minute, I . . . There's something I want to ask you . . .' she stammered, propping herself up on her elbow so she could see Volodya's face better. Her heart was beating violently and her voice sounded strange. Vladimir was immediately on his guard.

'Well, get on with it, what do you want to ask me?' he said, not looking at Vasya but staring at the wall.

'I want to know why you've got that material in your book-case, that silk and lawn?'

'What silk? Oh, I suppose you mean the patterns.'

'No, I don't mean the patterns! It's the whole length of material the same as you gave me, and I want to know who it's for! Tell me, who is it for?' She watched Vladimir's face closely.

'Well, do you really want to know? D'you mean that you haven't guessed yet?'

'No.'

'Well, you see, it's like this: Ivan Ivanovich asked me to get a coupon for the material to give his fiancée. He's always plaguing me to do things. Whatever I have, he has to have too, he just apes me in everything.' He explained this simply and unhurriedly.

Vasya blushed with shame. 'Ivan Ivanovich? For his fiancée? Oh, and I thought . . .'

'What did you think?' laughed Vladimir, turning round to look at her.

'Oh, Volodya darling!' Vasya said, kissing him, feeling deeply ashamed of herself. How *could* she have harboured such thoughts against him, suspected her friend like that?

'So tell me what you thought? You're quite a little detective, I must say! You've turned into a regular interrogator!' He hugged

Vasya, but a trace of anxiety lurked in his eyes.

'Now let's get some sleep, shall we? No more kissing now. Tomorrow we have to entertain our guests and we'll never get through our business. I must get up early.'

He switched off the lamp. Vasya felt terribly relieved and was just falling asleep when the serpent stung again. Suddenly she felt very wide awake.

What did he call me a detective for? That must mean there really *is* some reason to spy on him? Vladimir was already sound asleep, but Vasya lay there wide awake, shivering, staring into the darkness. Did she believe him or not? On and on through that sleepless night this question nagged her tired brain. No answer came.

After the men from the syndicate left, Vladimir had more work than ever, reorganizing the business – as if he hadn't got enough worries already. But there were compensations.

One day Mikhailo Pavlovich invited Vasya round to his room to tell her that a special decree had come from the Party centre. Apparently, there were now no direct charges against the director, and more importantly, no more rumours about his insubordination and 'irregular behaviour'; the case had been shelved and she could now rest easy about it. Vasya breathed a deep sigh of relief – she almost succumbed to old habit and said, thank God. Mikhailo Pavlovich was pleased about the outcome too, more for Vasya's sake, since he was very fond of her and felt sorry for her.

Then Vasya suffered a great blow. When the women workers' case came before the arbitration committee, the case was decided in favour of the management. The women were irate and there was talk of taking strike action. The Mensheviks, working under the guise of non-aligned, non-Party members, also began to agitate for strike action and fuelled the women's fury. Vasya had a bad cough and a high fever, but despite this, she spent days on end at the factory, arguing furiously with the management, demanding concessions, while at the same time trying to make the women see reason.

She was so totally absorbed in her work that she quite forgot about the blue silk. Then suddenly she was jolted into remembering, and somehow from that moment the serpent couldn't be dislodged.

It all started with a dog. One day the errand boy brought a white poodle to the house, with a ribbon tied between its ears.

'Whose is that dog?' Vasya demanded. 'Where does it come from? Why have you brought it here?'

The boy replied that Vladimir had given orders for the poodle to stay in the house for the time being. It belonged to Savelev, he said, and when Savelev went away the poodle pined for him. Vladimir's sudden concern for the dog amazed Vasya. Surely he couldn't have done it simply to please Savelev? All her old hatred of Savelev returned; she was furious that Vladimir had continued his friendship with this worthless man. When Vladimir came home the poodle was all over him, as though welcoming its master. Vladimir petted it and talked to it.

'Where does this dog come from, Volodya?' asked Vasya. 'Does it belong to Savelev?'

'Indeed not,' he replied. 'It belongs to Ivan Ivanovich's fiancée. She's gone away, and Ivan Ivanovich has asked us to have it here in the meantime.'

'But the errand boy said it was Savelev's.'

'Well, he's got it wrong then. It's true, the dog has been staying in Savelev's house these last few days, and as Vasya had to fetch it from there I suppose he thought it was Savelev's.'

This explanation seemed simple enough, but it didn't ring quite true to Vasya. Once again she simply didn't know whether to believe him or not. When Ivan Ivanovich arrived, she tackled him about whom the dog belonged to, and he related all the details at great length; his fiancée had asked him to look after the dog but he'd no room for it – he didn't even have a house. So then he'd sent it to Savelev's, but there was only one servant in the house, and she often went out, locking the poodle in on its own . . . and so on and so on. Whatever the real story might be, Vasya took a distinct dislike to the animal.

Shortly after this episode, Vladimir went away for a few days, to a conference of the syndicate. Vasya thought that she would feel miserable without him, but in fact she suddenly felt freed from a dead weight of anxiety she carried around when she was with him. She stopped feeling all the unspoken resentment at the way he seemed to ignore her existence. Without him, things began to go better, for when he was there, her foolish feminine heart still craved signs of his affection, even though she realized that he was preoccupied and had his head full of other things. Alone, there was no waiting, no listening, no struggling against feelings of resentment.

She invited her friends from the factory, Lisa Sorokina and Mikhailo Pavlovich, round to dinner. She loved entertaining her friends like this. After the meal, they discussed Party matters, walked in the garden, sang songs, and everyone enjoyed themselves, especially Vasya; how different from making polite conversation in the drawing room with men like Savelev or the syndicalists! Time flew by.

Vladimir returned one morning on an early train to find her drinking tea. She jumped up to greet him, but, without kissing her, he merely took her hand and pressed it to his lips for a long time. When he looked up she saw that his eyes were filled with tears.

'What's the matter, Volodya?' she asked with a sinking heart. 'Have there been more problems?'

'No, Vasya, nothing like that; life's so hard, that's all . . . I'm sick and tired of it all.' He sat down at the table, rested his head on his hands, the tears pouring down his cheeks.

'Do tell me what's upsetting you so terribly, Volodya. Tell me, my sweetheart, it will make things easier in the end.'

'But will it really, Vasyuk?' he asked her mournfully. 'I've thought such a lot about it, I've racked my brains – you can't imagine how much I've gone through, Vasya. I don't think talking about it would make things easier; I just can't see any solution.'

These odd garbled hints made Vasya's heart miss a beat.

'Volodya, you must stop torturing me like this. What are you talking about? Tell me the truth, I beg you. I can't stand it any longer, I'm absolutely worn out with worry. I never have any peace of mind . . .' As she spoke she began gasping for breath and then started to cough.

'There now, you've started coughing. How can I talk to you now?' There was reproach and sorrow in his voice, and as she continued to cough he frowned and lit a cigarette. 'Why not drink some tea? Maybe that'll stop it.'

'I'll just take one of my lozenges,' she said. Her coughing fit subsided and she poured Vladimir some tea.

He began, in his usual matter-of-fact manner, to tell her about his problems at work. He'd been told about them by Ivan Ivanovich as soon as he'd got off the train. The loaders were causing a lot of disruption, demanding more wages for overtime and reducing their output. Because of this, the syndicate was suffering heavy losses, and now the loaders were threatening to strike if they weren't paid immediately. Vladimir thought there might even be saboteurs amongst them, inciting them : after all you couldn't keep watch on all of them. A fine state of affairs! He only had to go away for a few days to find trouble brewing in his absence. What were the other bosses doing? Apparently they didn't want to exacerbate matters! So now there'd be long drawn-out proceedings, giving extra ammunition to the chairman . . .

'Is that what made you say that life was so hard, and there was no solution? All because of the loaders?' asked Vasya suddenly.

'Yes, of course. What did you think I meant?' Vladimir puffed his cigarette, slowly stirred his tea and then went on talking about the problem, and how best to settle the matter without scandal and publicity.

But Vasya was only half listening. The old suspicions tugged at her heart. Would he *really* have cried just because he had problems with his loaders? That wasn't like the Vladimir she knew! There must be something else preying on his mind – such as the blue silk, for instance . . .

She wasn't going to give way to her feelings of jealousy now. Vladimir must really be very tired. After all, his dealings with the Control Commission had worn him down to the point where even the pettiest trifle was liable to upset him.

Yet Vasya longed for reassurance. She wanted desperately to believe that Vladimir's worries were only business worries.

★ VII ★

Vasya finally won her case at the factory. She persuaded the management to grant concessions, and afterwards the jubilant women had carried her in triumph on their shoulders. Vasya realized that but for the chairman, their case would never have been won, for she'd talked a great deal to him and had come to appreciate him as an uncompromising fellow who refused to humour the managers.

She hurried home after this victory. Nearing the house, she saw the yard filled with loaders. They were arguing heatedly amongst themselves. 'Higher pay!' some of the more vociferous were shouting. 'Otherwise we'll just down tools and stop work.

The bosses and clerks can do the loading themselves!'

Slipping unnoticed into the crowd, she listened to what they were saying and began to ask them questions. They all talked noisily, explaining their grievances to her: they were underpaid, got no overtime, and the accounts hadn't been kept properly. The men surrounded her, threatening the management and demanding that she take up their case and explain matters to her husband.

She listened to everything they had to say and continued to question them. Their complaints were only too familiar, their demands utterly reasonable. The men were beside themselves, furious with the bosses and clerks for the easy lives they lived at the expense of the loaders, who couldn't even afford enough food or clothes for their children.

Vasya realized that they needed help to make their own case heard. They'd have to put pressure on management through their union; they wouldn't get far without proper organization and concrete plans. The leaders came to an agreement with her. They decided to formulate their demands, and then if management didn't concede to them, they would go straight to the arbitration committee. She became passionately absorbed in the business, quite oblivious to her position as director's wife. She had no choice – she *had* to advise these friends who were so lacking in experience and proper leadership.

She invited the leaders into the house so they could put their demands on paper. As they passed through the reception rooms on the way to Vasya's bedroom, the men cast furtive glances at the director's furniture. It was only then that Vasya realized how irregular it was for her to have let them in, but it was too late now. The men sat down at her table and began drawing up their demands.

It was now quiet outside. The loaders had broken up into small groups, waiting, chatting and smoking. Suddenly they started murmuring – the director's car drew up and Vladimir stepped out.

'What's going on here?' Vasya heard him shout angrily. 'So you've taken it into your heads to hold meetings here, have you? Are you here to threaten me with your grievances? Well, I don't intend to discuss them with you here, do you understand? This is my private house. You'll have to go to the manager's office. And if it's about pay, then go and complain to your union, because it's nothing to do with management. They've got enough problems as it is. If you intend to strike, that's entirely your affair. If your union agrees to it then do by all means organize a strike. But get out of here this minute! I refuse to listen and that's final. We'll discuss it at the office.'

Slamming the front door behind him, he went into the house and straight to the bedroom. Opening the door he saw Vasya there, sitting at the table talking to the loaders. He froze.

'What the hell is going on here? How did you men get in? How dare you break into my house like this without my permission? Clear off! Get out this minute!'

'But, Vladimir Ivanovich,' protested the loaders, 'we didn't come in on our own . . . Your wife here . . .'

'Clear off, I said, otherwise . . .' Vladimir was white with rage, and looked as though he could barely restrain himself from going for them. But as they were moving towards the door, Vasya intervened.

'Are you quite out of your mind, Vladimir? How *dare* you? It was *I* who invited them in! Comrades, do please wait, don't leave!'

She ran up to stop them, but Vladimir caught her and squeezed her elbow so hard that she cried out in pain.

'So you invited them in, did you? And who asked you to interfere in my affairs, I should like to know? You don't have to answer to the syndicate. Why don't you run off to your mat factory if you like organizing strikes so much, you little busybody!'

'So you're trying to get rid of me, are you! I suppose if I'm on good terms with my friends here I don't protect your interests as director and I lower your bonuses!'

'Vile hypocrite!' he shouted at her.

Vasya felt as though he'd lashed her with a whip. Vile? Her, vile! They confronted each other with utter hatred, like sworn enemies. And an unutterable sadness filled her heart, a feeling of black anxiety that seemed to spell the end of all happiness.

The minute the loaders had left Vladimir went off to the manager's office, leaving Vasya sprawled across the bed, her face buried in the silk quilt, which was soaked with her tears. But crying would never resolve this grief. For Vladimir she was something vile; they'd become strangers, hostile, enemies at war.

The days that followed were grey and joyless. Vladimir stayed at home much of the time, but there seemed little point in this now that they were so estranged. They spoke to each other only when they absolutely had to, and both went their separate ways. When Vasya fell ill again it was Ivan Ivanovich who sent for the doctor, who told her to get more rest. Vladimir and Ivan Ivanovich were wholly preoccupied with their work for the accounts department. They'd sit up until late at night in the study, emerge only to eat, both of them taciturn and bad-tempered.

Lisa Sorokina came round to see Vasya bringing her news from the factory and messages of love and sympathy from all the women there. But Vasya was too unhappy about her quarrel with Vladimir to care much about her illness. She knew that neither of them could ever forget that confrontation over the loaders, neither in their heart of hearts would ever forgive the other.

Vasya considered going back to her home town. She felt so homesick but then she was without a home. She certainly couldn't stay with her parents, for they'd just moan about their lives and curse the Bolsheviks. There was nowhere for her to go. She wrote to Grusha asking her to find a room for her, and to Stepan Alexeevich begging him to find her some Party work in a factory : she was determined to leave as soon as she heard from them. What was the point of her staying now that nobody needed her any more? Vladimir would be perfectly capable of surviving without her.

The days dragged on, melancholy and interminable.

By now it was midsummer and in the garden the cherries had ripened and the plums were turning dark blue. Delicate white lilies were in bloom, swaying on tall slender stems. But none of these things any longer gave Vasya any pleasure as she wandered about the garden. She remembered how happy she'd been that spring when she lay outside in her folding chair, and then felt even more wretched. She'd felt like an entirely different person then, more innocent, more trusting. She'd lost something she couldn't understand or put a name to; she only knew that she'd lost it for ever.

Occasionally Vladimir would come to the study window, anxiously peering at Vasya as she paced listlessly around the garden. He'd stand there, frowning for a while and then disappear back to his business with Ivan Ivanovich. Vasya would sigh with disappointment. She always hoped he might come out into the garden to see her, but he never did. He had no time for her; his business was obviously more important than her unhappiness.

One morning Vasya was awakened by a rustling sound and she

saw Vladimir looking through his cupboard for something.

'What are you doing up at this hour of the morning, Volodya?'

'I'm just going to meet a consignment of goods off the train,' he replied.

'On your own?' she asked.

'Yes, I have to do the stock-taking,' he said. As she looked at him struggling to put on a new tie in front of the mirror all her old affection for him flooded back.

'Come here, Volodya, let me help you with it,' she said, and he went over to her obediently and sat on the bed while she knotted his tie. They looked at one another and embraced silently.

'Oh my love, Vasyuk darling, it's so painful to be such strangers. It can't go on like this, can it?' he asked sadly, and drew her curly head towards him.

'Do you imagine it isn't painful for me too? Life is hardly worth living like this.'

'Why have we fallen out so badly, Vasya?'

'I don't know, something terrible has come between us . . . !'

'Oh no, Vasya!' he interrupted her. 'Nothing can ever seriously come between us. I belong to you.'

'So you still love me?'

'Silly thing!' he said, kissing her. 'Look, let's put an end to our quarrelling now! It's all so stupid and it makes us both so unhappy. I just couldn't endure the thought of losing you, Vasya, you know I couldn't live without you. Suppose we just stop bickering from now on?'

'All right, but only if you stop ordering me around!'

'And only if *you* stop inciting the loaders against me!' They both laughed.

'Go back to sleep now, Vasya. You know you'll be sick again today if you don't sleep properly. I'll be back in an hour or two.' He tucked her up, kissed her eyes and went out of the room, leaving Vasya feeling so relieved and happy she fell at once into a deep and blissful sleep. All old happiness had returned, all her fears gone.

Vladimir didn't return directly from the unloading, but telephoned to say he had to go to the office and would be back for lunch. Vasya was feeling a lot better that day but decided not to go to the factory. Instead, she helped Maria Semenovna with the housework and the two of them gave the house a thorough cleaning.

Just before lunch the telephone rang and Vasya went to answer it.

'Hello, is Vladimir Ivanovich there?' asked a female voice.

'No, not yet. Who's speaking?'

'I'm calling from the office.'

'Then why are you calling him at home? He should be at the office himself at the moment.'

'No, he's not at the office, he's already left. Sorry to have troubled you,' said the woman.

Vasya knew that voice! She knew it and disliked it. She remembered then that this woman had rung several times when Vasya had first arrived. Then the calls had suddenly stopped.

Vasya immediately went to ask Ivan Ivanovich who it was making all these calls to Vladimir from the office – and during working hours. Ivan Ivanovich said it must be one of the secretaries. Why should one of the secretaries call him? Once more the familiar doubts overwhelmed her and the wretched serpent stirred.

Vladimir brought back two colleagues for lunch. They could talk of nothing but the morning's deliveries, though Vladimir did find the time to ask Vasya how she was feeling and whether she'd been sunbathing as the doctor had told her.

'No, I haven't been sunbathing,' said Vasya icily, and then almost before she realized it she blurted out, 'That lady phoned again, you know, the one who's always calling you from the office.'

'A lady? Who can that be, I wonder?' said Vladimir, wide-eyed with astonishment. 'From the office, you said? Then it must have been Shelgunova – a lady indeed! She's a respectable housewife with children, I'll have you know! You've seen her, Vasya, that fat woman with the warty face.' He spoke quite naturally, but Vasya's anxieties were not so easily allayed. It all rang false to her.

After lunch the two managers took their leave, and Vasya happily contemplated the prospect of spending the rest of the day with Vladimir. If he was with her she'd find the consolation which their conversation this morning had promised. But no sooner had he seen the managers off than the telephone rang jarringly from the study. Vladimir answered it hurriedly.

'Yes, yes, it's me,' he said curtly . . .

'But I told you not to call me . . .'

'Yes, of course, if family circumstances permit,' he grinned . . .

'No, not on any account, I forbid it categorically, once and for all . . . All right, all right,' he yielded. 'But only very briefly, mind. Goodbye.'

Vasya stood in the next room listening. Who could he be talking to? Who was he promising to see 'very briefly'? Who could he 'forbid' like that?

Vladimir came out of the study and went into the bedroom, ignoring Vasya and walking straight past her. Vasya followed him. He was standing in front of the mirror combing his hair.

'Who were you talking to on the telephone, Volodya?' she asked.

'Savelev,' he answered.

'So he's back, is he?'

'Yes, he came back this morning.'

'Did you meet him?'

'Would you mind telling me what all this is about? Is it some sort of interrogation? You know perfectly well that the deliveries came in this morning.' He spoke irritably.

'And so you're intending to go and see him? Did you promise to go?'

'Yes, I am going to see him.'

Neither of them spoke. Vasya's heart was pounding as though it would burst, but she no longer cared about anything. This agony of doubt was unendurable. She went up to Volodya, taking his hand and saying affectionately, 'Volodya, please, I'm begging you not to go! Please don't start everything all over again.'

'All what over again, what are you talking about?' he asked.

'You know quite well what I mean – associating with that seedy racketeer. I've got it on good authority that the main charge against you is your unsuitable friendships . . .'

'Oh so you're going to start that up again, are you? Parroting what the Party bosses keep screaming at me? Do you want to wear me down, all of you? Break my will so you can tie me to your apron strings?' Vladimir snatched his hand furiously from hers.

'Stop, Vladimir, stop! What can you mean – I don't want to tie you to my apron strings! Be reasonable! It's you we're talking about, not me. You mustn't dig your own grave in this way. You've got quite enough enemies as it is, and now you have to start up your old friendship with Savelev again!'

'What's Savelev got to do with it?'

'But isn't it Savelev you're going to see?' Vasya looked at him, faltering.

'Yes, of course. But what of it? It's just a business visit, can't you understand? I can't get out of it now.'

'But I don't believe you!' she said vehemently. 'I'm sure you can put it off until tomorrow. Just phone the office and tell them . . .'

'Oh, Vasya, what a baby you are!' he said, relenting a little. 'All right, if you really want to know, the fact of the matter is that Savelev wasn't calling on business. We settled our business at the office. It's just that there's a small party of close friends at his house and he was inviting me round for a hand of cards. I haven't set foot out of the house for almost a month now, stuck here working all the time. You must allow me some free time occasionally, Vasya. I'm still young, I want to live a little. You can't expect me always to live like a hermit.'

'Yes, I do understand that, Volodya,' said Vasya dejectedly. 'Of course you're right, dear; and I don't want to stop you having a good time. But I do beg you not to start up again with Savelev – he's a crook and a menace and you know it. You don't even respect him. What does he mean to you anyway? The word will be out that Vladimir Ivanovich is friends with Savelev again, and then what will you do? Volodya darling, I implore you not to go there today. You can phone him back and refuse . . .'

'Oh, this is all utterly preposterous!' he said impatiently. 'If the chairman really wants to spend his time bringing court cases based on people's friendships then he's more of a garbage heap than a chairman if you ask me. And you, Vasya, you're exaggerating the whole thing ridiculously . . .'

'But what about *me*? What if I don't want you to go there, Volodya? I know that he doesn't like me, and I'm sure he invited you just to spite me. I heard you telling him on the telephone that you couldn't come because of "family circumstances", and you both laughed. Oh, Volodya,' she said desperately, 'it makes me so terribly unhappy when you laugh at me like that, and especially with someone like Savelev . . . you know I'd never forbid you to go.'

'But that's exactly what you are doing now!'

'If that's what you think, why don't you just go then! Just go and see him, but remember one thing, that's all!' she said, her eyes flashing. 'Remember there's a limit to what I can stand. I've helped you out of trouble, I've suffered for you, I've always defended you, and I've had enough. Go, if that's what you want to do, but I know what I mean to do . . .' Her voice broke.

'Look here, I'm absolutely fed up with these hysterical female outbursts of yours!' he said, losing his temper at last. 'What *has* got into you? What do you want of me?'

'Oh, Volodya,' she began to cry, 'I've hardly ever asked you for anything, but now I'm imploring you to stay, for your sake and for mine!'

'Oh my God! Females! All the same! Every single damned one of you! I've had enough of it!' He pushed past Vasya, went quickly into the hall, banging the front door as he went out. The car engine started up.

Vasya howled like an animal in pain.

★ VIII ★

'Lisa, I need your help. Could you put me up? I've left him for good.' Vasya's voice was breaking but her eyes were dry. Her misery went too deep for tears.

'So you've left him! And about time too! We were all amazed that you stuck it out for so long.'

'What's so unbearable is we've become completely estranged, Lisa,' said Vasya.

'Well, I must say I'd be surprised if you hadn't. Whatever made you love him in the first place?'

Vasya said nothing. Then she started explaining what she felt. She still couldn't quite believe what had happened, she only knew she couldn't forgive or forget that final insult. The first time she'd been prepared to forgive him. But now she felt as though he'd trampled on her dead body, and she just couldn't understand the reason for it. Surely it wasn't simply so that he could go off for a game of cards with a scoundrel like Savelev and his bunch of seedy cronies?

For all Vladimir cared, she could die of unhappiness, just as long as *he* was having a good time. Was that supposed to be love? How could her friend and comrade, a communist too, behave like that? Vasya rambled on incoherently. Lisa found it hard to picture what had happened between them, let alone how Savelev came into it.

'But don't you see, Lisa, it's this Savelev who's the cause of it all. Vladimir was going to see him . . .'

'You don't really believe that he was going to see Savelev, do you?' Lisa interrupted her.

'Well, who else could it be? Do you suppose it wasn't Savelev then?'

'It's not a question of "supposing"!' expostulated Lisa. 'My God, the whole town knows about it, and it's only you who seem to be blind to what's happening! Either that, or you deliberately won't see and don't want to understand!'

'See what, Lisa? Tell me!'

'The fact that your dear Vladimir has got himself a girl friend!'

'A girl friend!' Vasya couldn't take this in immediately, and stared at Lisa, wide-eyed not with fear or grief but with pure amazement. 'Did you say a girl friend? But who is she?'

'She's not one of us, she's not a worker. She's a secretary.'

'So you know her?'

'Well, I've seen her – the whole town knows her.'

'How?'

'Because of the way she flaunts her fancy clothes, that's why our friends are so angry with your Vladimir. But did it never occur to you, after all that Mikhailo Pavlovich told you about those friends of his? Just look at you! You're not usually an idiot, but I must say you seem to have behaved like a proper idiot in this business!'

But it was something else that really bothered Vasya at that moment. 'Does he love her?'

'Well, you never know about things like that. But I suppose he must if he's been carrying on with her for all these months. Everyone thought that when you came he'd put a stop to the affair, but not a bit of it! He still goes on visiting her in her flat, in his fancy motor-car.'

'So she has her own flat, does she?'

'Oh yes, and it's smarter than your house, too!' said Lisa.

So this was what they meant by the two establishments! Now Vasya understood everything. Except one thing. Why had Volodya lied to her and tortured her like that?

'But what did you expect? Did you expect him to bring his woman to see you? Or ask your permission to go and see her? It was up to *you* to see what was happening, but you didn't because you were a fool, and now you've only got yourself to blame!'

'Please, Lisa. You don't need to keep reminding me that I've acted like a fool! Anyway, that's not the important thing. What's important is whether he really does love her or whether it's, well, you know, just one of those things.'

'What do you mean "one of those things"? He must love her if he spends all his money on her, and gives her those expensive presents . . .'

'Do you think so? I'm not sure. You see . . .'

'Look, you don't really think he still loves you, do you? Vasya, my dear, you honestly must stop deceiving yourself, it'll only make the whole thing more painful. Obviously he cares for you because you're his wife and a dear friend too. But as for loving you, believe me, Vasya, he stopped loving you long ago.'

'I just don't believe you!' Vasya shook her head vehemently.

Annoyed by what she saw as Vasya's foolishness, Lisa began to describe Volodya's girl friend to her in deliberately flattering terms. She was incredibly beautiful, incredibly well dressed. She always wore silk and was surrounded by a crowd of admirers vying for her favours, amongst whom was Savelev, a close friend of hers. They all spent wild evenings together, and rumour had it that Vladimir went halves with Savelev over her keep. Vasya found the idea of Vladimir being part of that world unbearably painful. Could he really love this whore? She couldn't believe it. Whatever people said, she didn't believe it! It just didn't make any sense.

'Well, if you don't want to believe it, that's your business!' retorted Lisa angrily. 'But ask anyone you like, and they'll all tell you the same thing. She used to be a clerk, Savelev's personal secretary, then she started to "visit" the directors and God knows who else, for extra money. There are rumours that Ivan Ivanovich and some of the managers visit her. But however much of a prostitute she may be, she doesn't actually have a ticket – and she can thank the Soviet government for that!'

'But Vladimir would never love a woman like that!' Vasya protested.

'What makes you think that? Men are quite capable of loving women exactly like that, especially men like your Vladimir. As far as he's concerned, the more depraved they are the more he likes them . . .'

'Stop it, Lisa, at once! How dare you say such a thing! You don't even know him! What makes you think you have the right to judge him like that!'

'But why do you defend him when he humiliates you in front of the whole town? It's a different story as far as she's concerned, believe you me! He'd stand by her through thick and thin, I can tell you!

'What do you mean, humiliates me? You've invented it all! Anyway, what business is it of mine how Vladimir behaves? I'm not responsible for him! You don't seem to understand, Lisa, it's not *that* I care about, it's something completely different . . .'

'Yes, I know, you care that he's stopped loving you.'

'No, it's not that either, really, although of course that's a terribly painful thing to have to face. The main thing is that I know what I feel but somehow I just can't express it any more, and I don't know how that's happened. We used to be so very close, before Vladimir started concealing things and lying to me. And then he started being afraid of me. Me, of all people – it seems impossible! Did he imagine that I'd stand in his way or interfere in his love affair? Surely he couldn't have thought any such thing. I can't make any sense of it. He can't really love that woman so much . . .'

'Well, she's certainly spread enough scandal about the whole thing,' said Lisa with a gesture of impatience. 'There's no way of making you see sense, Vasya. You're obviously still terribly besotted with your Volodka. "Beat me, trample on me, I don't mind, I'm just your meek and humble wife." That may be all right for you but it definitely wouldn't be for me. I'd pay him back for everything he'd done to me, if I were you.'

Vasya refrained from arguing, but the more mercilessly Lisa condemned Vladimir, the more adamantly she defended him. She wanted to convince Lisa that she didn't blame him for having a girl friend and possibly even for loving another woman, but for concealing it all from her, as he would from a complete stranger. Nor was he treating her just as a stranger either, but as a person whom he couldn't trust. It was as if he feared that as his wife she would insist on her conjugal rights!

'That's exactly what you *should* do!' shouted Lisa. 'And you must do it! How dare he degrade you like that! You absolutely must leave him. He's not good enough for you, Vasya, he's not worth your little finger!'

Vasya argued with her hotly. It was always the same. However much she might criticize Vladimir herself, whenever anyone else attacked him she rushed to his defence and was furious that people should misunderstand him. *She* was the only person who understood her 'American'. It was only when she mentioned the word 'American' that she began to cry. Memories of the Vladimir she had loved, the man who had led the co-operative and defended the soviets, flooded back, and she was overcome with misery. She clung on to Lisa, sobbing. Thoughts of Vladimir the director disappeared. All she felt was an unbearable nostalgia for the Vladimir she'd fallen in love with.

'Oh, it's all so terrible, Lisenka, I just can't help it!'

'I know, my darling, my precious. Do you know, the same thing happened to me last year, and it's given me the strength to face anything. It will pass, dearest, it really will pass.'

Lisa stroked Vasya's head and comforted her friend as best she could. Then she put her in her own bed, and made up a bed for herself on some chairs. She'd had an exhausting day and was soon sound asleep.

But Vasya couldn't sleep. She tossed and turned, sitting up, lying down again, racked by anxieties and obsessive chaotic thoughts which tormented her and tore her apart . . . There was that terrible night when she'd discovered the blood stain in the bed and they'd come to arrest Vladimir. But it was no longer jealousy which obsessed her now, but the idea that Vladimir had not trusted her – she could forgive him anything but that. The heart has laws of its own but she couldn't for the life of her grasp why he'd had so little faith in her that he couldn't even tell her that he loved another woman.

It was really so simple! He'd been living on his own for months, after all, and just started having an affair. After all, he was a passionate man. She remembered Steshka. She supposed he must have slept with her once, and that was that. But then this woman was obviously not going to let go of him so easily. Lisa said that she was putting pressure on him – so she couldn't really love him, she must surely be taking advantage of him. Vasya knew how clever and cunning that kind of woman could be. She was obviously not going to let go of someone like Vladimir, however much he might wish to break it off.

She remembered again how miserable he'd been recently, and how unpredictable – affectionate and then suddenly distant towards her, for no apparent reason. Now she realized how dreadfully tormented he must have been. What torture it must have been for him! To have lived with someone he loved when all the time this ruthless woman was sharpening her claws behind his back!

Vasya remembered all those times when Vladimir seemed on the point of asking her to forgive him for something and then had suddenly stopped short. . . . Like that morning when the trouble with the loaders had started. Vasya had felt apprehensive at the time, and then, by some twist of fate, she'd started coughing and Vladimir had changed the subject. Was this because he took pity on her? And if so, did that mean he loved her?

Then Vasya recalled the pieces of blue silk, identical for both his women, and realized there was no reason at all to suppose that he loved her. He was merely saying, 'Here, this is for you, because you're my wife even if you're repellent to me! I bought my beautiful mistress a present but I didn't forget you! Just take your silk and shut up!'

Damn him! Damn him! Vasya clenched her fists, overcome with a desire to strike Vladimir then and there. The venomous coils of jealousy engulfed her, and she felt suffocated by misery.

She could find no peace of mind. Had he really gone to Savelev's yesterday? But then she remembered – Savelev was neither here nor there, apart from acting as Vladimir's alibi, a 'cover' so that nobody would be any wiser about what was really going on. If Savelev really had been the cause of everything, she would never have forgiven Vladimir. 'I don't care whether you forgive me or not, I'm going to get my own way in this. Go on, die of grief, I want everything I can get, and I wouldn't sacrifice one single kopek for you, because you're repellent to me . . .' If he'd really trampled on her feelings like that yesterday just for that gang of racketeers and their idiotic card games she'd never have forgiven him.

It was yesterday's events which had made her so wretchedly unhappy, and which had made her leave him. If she'd known then that he had a girl friend and was going through all the agonies of being in love, she might have controlled her rage. She'd have cried, certainly, and would have been terribly distressed, of course, but she would have *understood*.

She might have understood about his girl friend, but would she actually have forgiven him? She'd forgiven him about Steshka, who was a friend after all. Would she have grown to like the white poodle, to finally put that damned blue silk out of her mind? But this wasn't the time to be thinking about these things. The only thing that was really important was whether they could live together as true friends, concealing nothing from one another. At one time they had gone hand in hand together into battle, but now they were going such separate ways, what remained to hold them together? Their hearts? But what if Vladimir took his heart from her, what was left then? Nothing. There was no reconciliation possible, nothing but misery. Nobody in the world had ever known such misery . . .

The next morning Lisa had just left for work when Maria Semenovna came in, her head covered in a lace kerchief. It was a hot summer's day, and she was out of breath and very red in the face.

'Good day to you, Vasilisa Dementevna,' she said. 'I've brought a letter from your husband. He told me to take a cab and get here as quickly as I could, but where can you find a cab nowadays I'd like to know? I'm all out of breath!'

It was a government envelope – Vasya tore it open with fingers that were so numb she could hardly make them obey her. She began to read . . .

Vasya! What has happened? What are you doing to me?
Why do you torture me so cruelly? Do you want this scandal
to spread through the whole district and give my enemies more
ammunition against me? Do you want to destroy me utterly?
You said you were my friend. How can you side with my
enemies like this? You're tearing me apart! I just can't live like
this any longer. If you've decided you don't love me any more
then tell me honestly, but don't attack me behind my back like
this. You know I love you – people may gossip about me, but it's
nothing but a fleeting foolishness of mine. Listen to me! I wasn't
at Savelev's yesterday, but I swear I didn't betray you where I
was, for wherever I am, my heart will always be with you. This is
so unbearable, Vasya, I beg you to have pity on me and come
home so that I can look into your sweet eyes and tell you
everything, the whole truth. If you're a true friend to me I
know that you'll come. If you don't then it's goodbye. Just believe
me when I say I won't be able to live without you.

Your heartbroken Volodya.

Vasya read the letter twice and her heart was filled with such a sweet joy that tears rushed to her eyes. 'Fleeting,' he'd said, 'I love only you!' Then suddenly she was filled with rage. As if *she* had 'torn him apart', indeed! So *she* was expected to take pity on him, was she? And would he take pity on her, and stop tearing her apart? Her tears dried and she set her pale lips. 'So he's unhappy! He thinks he's unhappy, when he's just spent the night in another woman's arms and given her blue silk material . . . !'

All pity for him disappeared now. Yesterday she'd begged him so desperately to stay, her words, her eyes, beseeching him, but he'd just pushed her away, shouted those typical male insults – and gone off!

And now he was writing 'I love only you!' What a lot of rubbish! He didn't love her at all! And if he did, a fine sort of love that was, nothing but insults and scenes and anxiety. She could do without that kind of love! And then why had he written 'Goodbye, just believe me when I say I won't be able to live without you . . .' What did he mean by that? Why, it meant absolutely nothing, it was an empty threat, calculated to arouse her pity and make her come running to him like a fool. Vasya read his letter for a third time.

Meanwhile Maria Semenovna sat there, placid and indifferent, wiping the sweat from her face and fanning herself with her handkerchief.

'Vladimir Ivanovich returned the moment you left,' she said. 'He asked where you were and I said "How should I know?" Then he went into his study and sat down to his papers. After a bit he telephoned Ivan Ivanovich, asking him to come over, and they sat in his study for a while. Around midnight he came into the kitchen and asked me whether you'd come back yet, and when I said no he went out again. Well, when he'd seen Ivan Ivanovich off he went into the bedroom and then he must have seen your note, I suppose, because I could hear him sobbing, just destroying himself with grief he was, like a child. Then he was pacing around all night, and he wouldn't drink his tea this morning. "I don't want anything," he said "just go and find Vasilisa Dementevna for me. Go round to all her friends until you've found her, and don't you dare show your face in this house again until you have".'

These words made Vasya's heart ache, but now her old feelings of tenderness for Vladimir merely irritated her and filled her with hopelessness. So he'd spent the night alone, waiting for her, long-ing for her, sobbing for her, and then he'd called for her. She longed to be with him, and she was tortured by jealousy. It was obvious that the bond between them was not irrevocably broken and they still felt very deeply about each other. But why prolong this agony? Why should she go back merely to explain and understand, and go through the same things with him again?

'So what did Vladimir Ivanovich do when you'd left him? Did he go to the office?' she asked Maria Semenovna.

'When I left him? Well, he phoned his girl friend at once, most likely to tell her how miserable he was, or maybe how happy he was, you never know with men, do you? As long as there's no scandal they don't care about anything . . .'

So – he'd phoned his girl friend that very morning! After writing that letter to Vasya! Maybe Lisa was right, after all, and he only wanted to hold on to Vasya to avoid scandal. If she hadn't been his wife he would have let her go her own way. Now he had called for her just so that he could lord it over her once again. This time she'd had enough! She would somehow have to control her foolish heart, for she was not going to him, she was not going to walk blindly into his trap. She felt faint.

'Tell Vladimir, will you, that there's no reply for him, that's all. Now please go as quickly as you can, go on!'

'Well, I can't go any quicker than my legs will carry me, can I?' grumbled Maria Semenovna. 'Besides, you're acting much too hastily. I'd give it more thought, Vasilisa Dementevna, if I were you. Of course he's wronged you, of course you are his wife, but you've wronged him too, you know. You should never have left that young husband of yours on his own for months at a time! And you know what a wonderful husband Vladimir Ivanovich is to you in many ways – he always takes such good care of you. Didn't he get you cocoa when you were sick? Didn't he tell me to buy you fresh eggs? He takes better care of you than you do of yourself, and he'd never refuse you anything. And as for the other women . . . well, which man isn't guilty of something on the side, I'd like to know? *You're* his wife, *you're* the one he respects, and as for the other one, well he just gives her money and presents and that's all there is to it!'

Maria Semenovna would never understand. She'd never understand that if Vladimir wasn't a true friend any longer, she could no longer trust him, and if there was no trust between them, they couldn't go on living together.

'Why don't you wait till this evening, Vasilisa Dementevna? I can go home now and tell your husband you're thinking things over and you'll send him an answer this evening. That would be much more sensible. Otherwise I'll have to tell him that you decided all in a rush, just spat the words out and told me to be off. When you're upset like this, you can make mistakes that you live to regret, and then you'll be really sorry.'

'No, Maria Semenovna, please don't try to make me change my mind. I meant what I said, I'm not going to go back to him, ever again. It's all over.' Her lips trembled and large tears fell down her thin cheeks.

'Well, it's up to you. I've given you my advice, but it's still up to you to decide.'

Maria Semenovna left, and Vasya longed to howl like an animal, a long anguished howl that the whole street would hear. It was all over and she was not going back. Goodbye, Volodya, goodbye, my darling! She stretched out her thin arms to Volodya, longing for him with all her heart, the tears pouring down her pale cheeks, all the while the cold light of reason telling her, 'Stop, that's enough. You're not going back to him. It's over, it's the end.' She cried for a long time, then burying her head in Lisa's pillow she fell asleep, exhausted.

She was woken abruptly by a loud hooting and she heard a car draw up outside the window. Who could it be? She leapt up. Maybe Vladimir had come to see her! Trembling with hope and joy she ran to the shutters and hastily flung them open. But it was Vasya the errand boy standing at the door.

'There's been a terrible disaster, Vasilisa Dementevna,' he said breathlessly. 'Vladimir Ivanovich has gone and poisoned himself!'

'What! What did you say!' Vasya rushed towards him, seizing him by the hand. 'Is he dead?'

'No, not yet. He's still alive, but he's raving terribly and in great pain. He's calling for you, and they sent me to fetch you in the car.'

Vasya rushed to the car, just as she was, without putting on a coat. Her teeth were chattering and she was shivering. She had killed her beloved! She'd destroyed him, she'd failed him, let him down when he'd called for her, called from the depths of his heart! Vasya's eyes were large, stupefied, not so much with grief as with something that she was as powerless to control as death itself.

Vasya the errand boy didn't notice her expression and began a brisk account of everything that had happened. He was thrilled by this new drama! Apparently Vladimir had left for the office that morning, stayed there an hour and then returned home. He'd gone into his study and Vasya, who was sweeping the yard outside, had seen him go to the cupboard with the chemical phials used for testing colours. Later Vasya had gone into the hall and heard a terrible moaning. He went into the study and there had found Vladimir Ivanovich lying on the couch. His eyes were rolled upwards, his mouth was open and there was foam on his lips. Vasya thought he was dead.

Then there was chaos. Vasya had run out to get the doctor, who was just sitting down to his dinner. Vasya shouted, 'Look, a man is dying, you'll have plenty of time to eat your dinner later.' Then Vasya was sent to the chemist and Ivan Ivanovich had come to the house. Everyone was rushing all over the place – there was total confusion.

Vasya tried to listen as he chattered on, but she couldn't concentrate. She felt at that moment as though she'd ceased to exist. Now Volodya and his suffering was the only reality, and she felt her identity merge with his. If Volodya did not survive, her life too would be over, and there would stretch before her only the void, emptier than the grave.

★ IX ★

Vasya went into the hall just as Ivan Ivanovich was seeing a doctor out. She stopped him. 'Is he alive?'

'Well, we're doing all we can, of course, but we can't really say anything definite until the morning,' said the doctor

She tiptoed towards the bedroom, the groans getting louder and louder as she approached. In her agonized state she felt as though she was Vladimir and these groans were hers.

Everything was unusually untidy in the bedroom. The carpet had been rolled up, the bed had been shifted – but where was Volodya? Then she saw a large white object on the couch. His face was grey, his eyes closed and the groaning had stopped. Oh no! Surely he wasn't dead!

'Volodya! Volodya!' she gasped.

The doctor turned on her with an angry look. 'Shh! I beg you, no hysterics, please !' He was fussing over Vladimir, assisted by a nurse in a white cap. They looked serious and severe and refused to allow Vasya near him. Volodya opened his eyes and drew several rapid breaths. He was alive !

'Doctor,' Vasya whispered, 'please tell me the truth. Is there any hope?'

'As long as the heart continues to function there is always hope,' snapped the doctor.

What did that mean, she wondered, 'as long as the heart continues to function'? And what if it didn't. But she daren't question the doctor again. He and the nurse were now lifting Vladimir's head and pouring something into his mouth. He started to groan again, spasmodic, animal groans, and as Vasya listened in her numbed, blank state, she felt that she could endure no more.

It grew dark and the night light was put on in the bedroom. More doctors arrived, and after conferring together they sent the errand boy off to the health department to get a permit for some special kind of medicine. Vasya was still not allowed to sit by Vladimir and now he'd stopped calling for her. One moment he seemed to drift into a coma, the next he would start groaning again, excruciating groans. It seemed to Vasya as though with each groan the life was going out of his body, as though his spirit was fighting with his body, his body refusing to release the spirit. She felt useless, merely getting under the doctors' feet, unable to do anything to help.

Then a thought struck her with a terrible force. Rumours about this must already be circulating. People would be saying, 'Just fancy, a communist trying to kill himself like that ! I wonder what he did it for !' And then the whole story would come out. She must think of some plausible explanation immediately.

She thought fast – he'd eaten some poisonous mushrooms ! Yes, he'd eaten them at lunch, and now he was at death's door ! She remembered staying with her grandmother in the country where exactly that had happened. A tailor had come from town to stay with his brother and had picked some poisonous mushrooms; he'd cooked them, eaten them, and died.

Vasya made a series of telephone calls. First she called Mikhailo Pavlovich, intimating that when she saw him she'd explain things in more detail, but she just wanted to tell him about this terrible disaster; Vladimir Ivanovich had eaten some poisonous mushrooms and was now close to death. Then she called the chairman, and a few other friends. After that, she alerted Ivan Ivanovich to the story, asking him to explain it to the managers and the clerks.

Vasilisa spent a long time rehearsing Maria Semenovna and Vasya the errand boy in what to say. The errand boy was shrewd and knowing about the whole thing; he sniffed disdainfully and shrugged his shoulders, but finally agreed to the explanation. What a fuss! Still, what did it matter to him? Let it be mushrooms for all he cared, it was all one to him!

Maria Semenovna, however, just crossed her hands on her stomach, pursed her lips, and refused to go along with the story. She was deeply hurt. 'How can you poison yourself like that with mushrooms!' she objected. 'Now everyone will be saying "What can that cook have been thinking of?" '

But Vasya insisted, telling her that everyone else had already been given this explanation for the illness.

'As you wish. But it's a stupid thing to have thought of. Anything but mushrooms! Who in their right mind would have cooked him poisonous mushrooms!'

Vasya left the kitchen. Maria Semenovna remained very flustered and stirred the food angrily. 'They've created scandal after scandal, confusion after confusion, and now they want *me* to take the blame! They've made a hash of things that even the devil himself wouldn't touch, and now, God bless my soul, it's me who has to clear it all up for them! Maria Semenovna's the culprit, they'll say. As if I didn't know a poisonous mushroom from a good one. As if I'd ever put such a thing on his plate! Twenty years now I've been at the stove, and I'm no ordinary cook or a kitchen maid doing a cooking job. Why, I've got a whole drawer full of recommendations. General Gololubov's late wife was ever such an important lady, but she never called me anything but Maria Semenovna! And then there were the Pokatilovs, millionaires they were, they gave me a gold watch and chain for Christmas, just on account of the sauces I made . . . And now I come here and what do I find? "Maria Semenovna's put poison mushrooms in the director's food!" I never thought I'd live to be insulted like this, when I've served him and done my best for him. I've always been sorry for that Vasilisa too, and more than once in her presence I've held my tongue about her husband's sweetheart . . . And that's all you get by way of gratitude! Why it's downright scandalous! And them supposed to be communists too!'

'What's getting you so steamed up, Maria Semenovna?' interrupted Vasya the errand boy, in a blasé tone, stirring the soup with gusto. 'As if it mattered what we have to tell folks! They'll never keep it quiet anyway, and you won't have to take the blame. It's just to avoid scandal that they invented all that about the mushrooms. Anyway, I like it! A regular mix-up and no mistake, quite a tragedy, just like the cinema! It's really comical!'

'Well you might find it comical, you stupid boy, a man is in there dying and all you can say is how comical it is! What's going to become of you all? Nobody has any respect for life now, the slightest thing and they shoot a man down, bang! like that! You don't even care about your own life. Mark my words, it's all because you've abandoned the Lord!'

'Now don't start going on at me about God,' said Vasya impatiently. 'I may not be a communist, but God I don't believe in.'

'And a very bad thing too, young man, if you ask me. Anyway, why are you lounging around wagging that foolish tongue of yours instead of getting on with your work? You can help me clear the plates away. Oh those devilish doctors! Look at all these plates they've used! They keep asking for tea and refreshments but it won't make any difference, they still can't do anything. It will all be as God ordains. I said as much to that hussy who waits on Vladimir Ivanovich's sweetheart. I'd just started to serve the doctor's dinner when she slips in through the back entrance, swishing her skirts and rustling her lawn apron. She had a bow like a white butterfly tied round her head. "My mistress sent me to ask about the state of Vladimir Ivanovich's health" she says. So I say, "As for his health, he may at any moment surrender his soul to the Lord, since the Lord punishes each and every one of us for our sins. And you can tell that brazen hussy you serve that she'd do better to go to church and repent. For by heaven, it's been her and no one else who's been the ruin of that man!" '

Maria Semenovna might be taciturn with Vasilisa, but with anyone who would listen there was no stopping her!

In the days that followed, the house was crowded with Vladimir's colleagues who dropped in to visit him, and with doctors who held lengthy consultations. Lisa came and sat up night after night with Vasya to prevent her brooding wretchedly about Volodya's state. Lisa felt that she was to blame for having turned Vasya against Vladimir, and this was unbearable to her.

'But it wasn't you, Lisa,' Vasya reassured her. 'It was I who set myself against him. It was only when I faced the possibility that he might die that I realized there was nobody in the whole world who was more precious to me! How could I possibly live without him now, when it was I who was the cause of all this . . . ?'

Next morning it was very quiet in the house, and Vasya was sitting alone at Vladimir's bedside, resting her head on his arm. She was wondering what would happen if Vladimir died, leaving her nothing to live for? What would the revolution or the Party mean to her? The Party needed people who had no crime on their conscience, but for her there would always be the knowledge that she had killed Vladimir. And for nothing but female jealousy!

Of course, if Volodya had been secretly involved in fraudulent deals with Savelev and his cronies, undermining the country, then she would have been vindicated, but as it was, she'd forced her friend to try and kill himself just because of another woman.

And what a staunch friend he had proved to be too! She'd thought that he no longer loved her! How could she have thought that when he'd gone to this terrible extreme of trying to kill himself for her? He must feel that life without her had no joy to offer him. And despite her unhappiness, this realization made her want to cry tears not of bitterness, but of gentle repentance.

She looked at Volodya and whispered tenderly, 'Will you ever forgive me, my darling? Will you ever forgive me for what I did to you, my precious?'

Vladimir stirred, tossing his head restlessly. 'Water, water,' he murmured.

'Here you are, my love, drink this,' and she raised his head carefully from the pillow as the nurse had shown her, and helped him drink. He opened his eyes and looked at her without appearing to see her.

'Are you feeling a little better, Volodechka?' Vasya asked, leaning over him solicitously.

He didn't reply, just blinked his eyes. Then in a weak voice he asked, 'Is Ivan Ivanovich here?'

'No, he's gone home. Why, do you need him?' He nodded.

'Telephone him and ask him to come over,' he said.

'But the doctor said you weren't to work,' she said gently. An expression of impatience and suffering crossed his face.

'Please don't nag me now. Just call him . . .' And he closed his eyes again.

Vasya's heart missed a beat. Why had he said, 'don't nag me

now'? So he hadn't forgiven her for causing him this suffering. She duly called Ivan Ivanovich and when he arrived Vladimir asked her to leave the room as he wished to be alone with him. Vasya went out into the garden.

The sun no longer caressed her as it had that spring. It was so hot that it scorched her head, shoulders, and arms. A bush of crimson roses had burst into blossom and the dahlias were in full flower. The garden was rampantly overgrown, honeysuckle intertwined with lilac and laced with ivy. In this heat the sky was the colour of molten silver. Vasya began to pace along the scorched paths. Vladimir would never forgive her. If only she'd come to him that morning when he'd called for her, none of this would have happened. But now she'd lost him for ever! She'd lost not only her husband and lover but her dearest friend. He would never trust her again, never again seek her support . . .

Vasya leant against the acacia tree – the same tree which that spring had blossomed so profusely, and closed her eyes. If only she'd poisoned herself. If only she were dead . . .

Then she heard Ivan Ivanovich shouting, 'Vasilisa Dementevna! Vladimir Ivanovich is calling for you!' He started up the car and Vasya wondered where he could be going – maybe to take a message to Vladimir's girl friend. Not that Vasya cared any more, for it was all over.

The summer sun was unbearably hot. Inside, the blinds had been drawn and Vladimir was dozing. Vasya knelt at the head of his bed and kept away the flies. 'Let him sleep and rest,' she thought. 'He's suffered enough.'

Maria Semenovna had gone off shopping and Vasya the errand boy was also out somewhere; Vasya and Vladimir were alone in the house. She was glad to be alone with him like this, for she felt for the first time as though he belonged to her – and to nobody else. As she looked at him lying there so helpless and weak she longed for him to understand, to see into her heart and sense how passionately she loved him. How chilling it was always to be craving for his affection, when he was always so taciturn and sullen with her, when he never even noticed her. She only had to arrange his pillows not quite to his liking for him to say irritably, 'You're as bad as the nurse! Why can't you arrange them properly!' Of course, that sort of thing was to be expected from an invalid, but she still wished he wouldn't be like that with her.

Was it possible that he would never forgive her, that this cold, estranged existence of theirs would drag on and on. She looked at Vladimir's sweet familiar face with those wonderful eyelashes which she had fallen in love with the moment she first saw him. He'd fallen in love with her plait, but her plait was gone! It was like something out of a fairy-story. She'd bewitched her lover with her plait and when the plait was cut off her lover had left her . . .

How they had loved each other in 1917! And afterwards too: she remembered that night during the White attack when they'd both gone out to arrest the conspirators. 'They may kill me, Vasya,' he'd said, 'but you must promise not to let that stop you doing what you have to do. There'll be plenty of time for crying later.'

'And the same goes for you too, Volodya' she'd replied. 'Let's both swear to each other that we will go on, whatever happens.'

They'd clasped hands, gazed into each other's eyes, and then set about their business. It had been a frosty night, and the footsteps of their detachment crunched in the hard snow.

At the memory of past happiness, tears of nostalgia poured down her cheeks. So far she hadn't cried once over this catastrophe, she had tried desperately to put a brave face on it, forgetting about her own feelings, but now she was crying for the old days.

'Why, Vasya, Vasya, whatever is the matter?' Volodya raised his head from the pillow and looked at Vasya – not with the cold eyes of a stranger, but with his old affectionate look, compassionate and sad. 'Tell me what's the matter, Vasyuk, why are you crying, my poor little one?' He laid his hand tenderly on her curly head.

'Volodya darling, my precious Volodya, will you ever forgive me for what I did?'

'Silly Vasya, what have I to forgive you for? Please stop crying like that and we'll talk about it. Sit here, closer to me, that's right. It's so much harder for both of us if we don't talk, isn't it, Vasya?'

'But I'm afraid you'll only upset yourself, my darling. Suppose we leave it till later?'

'No, we won't be able to say what we want to say to each other later. It will relieve my mind to talk about it. I was in agony, Vasya, and that was why I tried to kill myself, and even now that I have the will to live again, I still can't see any way out of it.'

'But surely we can find some way out of it together, Volodya, I can't have become so remote to you that we can't do it together!'

'So you know everything, Vasya?'

She nodded. 'Yes, I know all about it.'

'And you understand why I've been so depressed and anxious, and you just kept carping on at me about all sorts of ridiculous things, and nagging me about Savelev . . .'

'Yes, Volodya, I know.'

'And there was another thing you were wrong about too. You thought that I loved her, but I never loved her, Vasya. It's you I love, my guardian angel, my dearest and most faithful friend. She was something completely different, call it infatuation if you like, anything but love. And you were jealous of her, you were suspicious and you spied on me.'

'But I never did that, Volodya!' remonstrated Vasya.

'What do you mean? Don't you remember the whole incident with the material? Don't you remember how you kept badgering me about why I smelt of perfume or where Savelev was living? You just wanted evidence for your suspicions.'

'Yes, but I didn't spy on you, Volodya, that's not true. I was being driven mad by my fears. And I did try to drive them out of my head because I didn't want to lose my trust in you.'

'Well, your fears aside, you were jealous all the same, admit it. You never said so outright, you just made life unbearable by harassing me. What more is there to say? We were both to blame.'

Neither of them said anything for a while. Then in a wretched voice Vasya asked, 'Volodya, is our life together always going to be like this?'

'I don't know, Vasya, I just don't know what to do about it. I'm at the end of my tether.'

There was another long silence.

'Volodya, don't you think you might really be happier with her?' Vasya said at last, cautiously, amazed that it caused her so little pain to ask the question.

'Oh Vasya, Vasya! Why don't you trust me? I was prepared to kill myself when I realized I'd lost you! Isn't that proof enough for you that it's you I love?' His voice, his eyes were filled with reproach, and Vasya's heart began to tremble for joy and her brown eyes shone with sudden happiness. 'Volodya darling, my husband!' Pressing herself against his body, she put her arms around his neck and sought his lips.

'No, Vasya, not now, calm yourself, Vasyuk! You see how weak I am still, I can't even kiss you yet.' He smiled and stroked her hair, but his expression was one of deep sadness. It seemed there was no way through the barrier that separated them, no way through the impenetrable thicket of estrangement between them.

* X *

Vladimir eventually went back to work. That morning, after he had left the house for the office, Vasya couldn't help feeling happy to be free again. She hurried off to the Party committee. From there she was going on to the mat factory, where Lisa needed her help in preparing for a trade union conference.

Vasya was smiling as she hurried to the committee. She felt as though suddenly released from a cage, and all was well with the world. It had been a long time since she had seen her friends, and they had obviously missed her. She was much valued by them, for she was efficient, responsive to the problems of others, and never made a fuss.

They put her to work annotating texts, preparing material and speeches. The time literally flew by. Before she knew it, it was eight o'clock. Vladimir must be getting tired of waiting for her and she was worried that, without her there, he wouldn't eat what the doctor had ordered.

She walked back with Lisa, and they discussed the news from Moscow that a friend had just brought back. There were many things going on in the Party at that time which perplexed them, and Lisa for one was not in agreement with the new line. She sided with the men from the factory who were putting up their own candidates for the forthcoming Party congress; this was clearly going to involve another battle with the chairman.

Vasya felt envious of Lisa, for although she went to the factory she was never able to take any real part in anything. She was beginning to feel like a mere fellow-traveller.

'Well, that's because you've turned into a director's wife,' Lisa retorted. 'You'd get involved again soon enough if you lived on your own.'

Vasya sighed. She didn't need Lisa to remind her of this, but it wasn't the time to be thinking of such things. As soon as Vladimir was recovered she'd leave him and go back to her home town.

'Oh, no you won't,' said Lisa. 'You'll never leave him! You're absolutely tied hand and foot to your Vladimir Ivanovich. In fact, you're nothing but a meek and humble little wife!'

Vasya said nothing. What could she say? She knew full well that Lisa was right, but after everything that had happened, she could hardly complain. Volodya was alive and out of pain, that was all she cared about now.

When she got home Volodya was not there. 'Where is Vladimir Ivanovich?' she asked Maria Semenovna. 'Isn't he home yet?'

'Yes, he came home at three and waited for you. He waited and waited, and then as you didn't come he had lunch with Ivan Ivanovich, and now they've both gone off in the car,' said Maria Semenovna. 'Oh, and there's a note for you on the table.'

Vasya grabbed the note and began to read:

Dearest Vasya,

We agreed that from now on we'd have no more secrets and you said you'd always understand. It's absolutely essential that I go to her tonight. I'll tell you the reasons later, and I know you'll understand. Please remember what we agreed together and don't be upset.

Love, Volodya.

Her hands slumped to her side. Not again! Nothing had changed! But then why had she ever imagined it would? After all, she'd known all along that Ivan Ivanovich's role had been to flit between Volodya and the woman, to act as their go-between, and Volodya was only quite honourably doing what she'd asked him, telling her the truth. So why did the old agony rise up again, why was she overcome with anger again, just as if he was deceiving her?

Maria Semenovna was laying the table. 'Are you going to eat something?' she asked, glancing disapprovingly at Vasya. 'Or are you up to your old tricks again? I don't know, first it's one of you not eating, then it's the other, and never a thought about all the cooking! And then it's more quarrels and tears, until you end up driving each other into the grave! You can do as you please, Vasilisa Dementevna, and be as angry with me as you like, but I'm going to tell you the truth. You're no wife to Vladimir Ivanovich! Just look at you, eating your heart out over his letter and then crying just because he's gone to see his mistress! What

I say is that you've brought it on yourself. Why, the man's only just up from his death bed – he poisoned himself because of you! And the moment he's out of the door, off you run! Of course, if you had a job to go to, that would be another matter because you'd have to go to work. But no, all you do is hang around those meetings of yours, trying to put some sense into a lot of stupid women. If you ask me, you should start putting your own house in order before you go off teaching other folk, because I can tell you I'm ashamed to be a servant of yours! This is no home, it's nothing but a slum!' So saying, Maria Semenovna disappeared into the kitchen, slamming the door angrily behind her.

She reappeared a few minutes later, more benevolent now, carrying an omelette and a glass of cocoa for Vasya.

'There now, Vasilisa Dementevna dear, have something to eat and stop tiring your brain with all that thinking.'

Sitting down beside Vasya at the table, she began to reminisce about a similar occurrence in the house of General Gololubov's late wife, only this had all revolved around the French governess. After it was all over, the General and his wife had been reconciled and lived together on excellent terms until his wife's death.

Vasya was only half listening as Maria Semenovna rambled on. She didn't interrupt, however, because during Vladimir's illness the two had become allies. Maria Semenovna had been sorry for Vasya, and Vasya shared Maria Semenovna's irritation with the doctors, the specialists, Vladimir's colleagues – all of them bourgeois to a man!

So Vasya was obliged to listen to Maria Semenovna's interminable anecdotes about the Pokatilovs, who were millionaires, and about how the General's late wife had doted on her . . . Despite her bad temper, Maria Semenovna was a good soul. But Vasya longed to be left alone, to think and make sense of things.

'Thank you so much for the meal, Maria Semenovna,' she said at last. 'I really must go and sort out my papers.'

'Is that all you're eating then? I wouldn't have cooked so much if I'd known. You'll do yourself in, Vasilisa Dementevna, you really will, if you go on like this, it won't do at all. If you want to know what I think, Vladimir Ivanovich's girl friend isn't worth a kopek. She's not worth your little finger!'

That was exactly what Lisa had said. 'Why, what makes you think that, Maria Semenovna?' Vasya asked. 'Everybody says how lovely she is.'

'What have her looks got to do with it? All powdered and painted she is, like a clown!' And she's only got one thing on her mind, frippery and how to squeeze as much as you can out of men.'

'Do you know her then? Have you seen her?'

'Oh, you can't help knowing her! Many's the night she's spent here, before you came, that is. Little baggage! And gives herself airs too, you have to heat up water for her in the night and it's all "Give me this, fetch me that!" She acts the lady, says she was born into the gentry. It's all a lie! The real gentry weren't like that, they were always polite and said please and thank you to the servants. That hussy does nothing but order people around, "Give it to me, do this, take that". I don't know . . .'

'What's her name?' Vasya interrupted.

'Her name's Nina Konstantinovna, and she's got some fancy surname too which I can't remember, but everyone in town just calls her Nina Konstantinovna.'

'I should really like to see her, just once,' mused Vasya, turning Volodya's letter over in her hands.

'Well, that can be managed easily enough!' said Maria Semenovna. 'She takes a walk in the park every day when there's music at the bandstand. We can go tomorrow, and you'll be able to see our princess for yourself. There used to be plenty of women of that sort gadding about the streets of Moscow, I can tell you!'

'So she goes to hear the music, does she? Well, suppose we do go then, Maria Semenovna. I might feel easier in my mind once I've had a look at her.'

Maria Semenovna shook her head dubiously, but there was no dissuading Vasya now, and besides, she too was curious to see a confrontation between the two rivals.

Vasya left the room and began to pace round the dark empty house. Darkness was more consoling to her anxious mind. Everything had seemed fine that morning. Volodya had been better and had gone back to work. Vasya had started work again and had decided she was definitely going back to her home town, for she was now clear that she no longer wanted to be the 'director's wife'. She'd felt so much easier in her mind since she and Vladimir had spoken honestly to each other.

Yet here she was again, feeling all the old pangs of uncertainty. How could she be obsessed by jealousy when Vladimir had kept his side of the agreement, and had told her the truth as a friend?

Why was she so wretched? It must be her fault for wanting too much. She should never have assumed so blithely that Vladimir would just come back to her, and break with the other woman. Her misery revolved round this, and, whatever she told herself, she realized that she was hoping desperately that he would do just that.

It all came back to the same thing. Once again Vladimir was spending the evening with the other woman, leaving Vasya alone in the house. Had he no feelings for her? She no longer understood anything. She had no idea whether he loved her his friend, or the other woman, his beautiful mistress. He might say that he loved Vasya at this moment, but his actions contradicted his words, and her misgivings were becoming intolerably oppressive.

It would be better to accept that he no longer loved her, and just leave. But how *could* she leave him? She might realize, too late, that once again she'd been mistaken. He might even try and kill himself again . . . It was out of the question to leave him now. Besides, it would be very hard to be apart from him in her present anxious state. It would be easier to cope with the situation if she was with him. All she knew was that she still loved Vladimir, and that if she hadn't loved him so deeply she wouldn't be suffering so terribly.

Yet, however much she loved him, she seemed to understand him less and less. It was as if they were walking through a forest along two paths which diverged more and more the deeper they went in. However much she loved him, she still found herself condemning him for his behaviour.

Why had he become involved with a woman like that in the first place? It would have been much less shameful if she'd been 'one of them', a good comrade and a communist, but this woman seemed like a real old-style lady! And even Volodya had admitted that she was 'different', a pampered lady. According to the description he had once given her, she evidently had no sympathy for the Bolsheviks or the communists and yearned for a return to 'old times'.

Apparently she had lived in luxury, and her family had had seventeen house servants. She'd had her own horse, broken in to carry a lady's saddle. When the revolution came, her father had joined the Whites. Her mother had died at this time and her brother became a White officer and was killed in action. Left on her own, she looked for work and as she knew several foreign languages she was able to get a job as a secretary at the manager's office. That was where she and Volodya got to know one another.

She'd fallen in love with him and started writing to him – Vasya wasn't there at that time. Volodya was desperately lonely and so they'd embarked on a love affair. News of it soon spread around the office and people began to look censoriously at Nina Konstantinovna. She couldn't bear it, and eventually left her job. It was then that Savelev had taken her on as his secretary . . .

Vasya paced up and down the room as she remembered the exchange they'd had . . .

'Just his secretary?' Vasya had asked before she could stop herself. Her impulse to irritate Volodya was as strong as her desire to find out about the woman.

'Where did you pick up that vile piece of gossip!' shouted Vladimir, his face red with rage. 'Aren't you ashamed of yourself, Vasya, repeating such filth! I must say I thought better of you! I never imagined that you'd start acting like some old woman and dragging someone into the gutter. How could you say such things, Vasya?'

He had then explained that Savelev was acting as a sort of guardian to Nina Konstantinovna. He'd been a family friend and when Nina Konstantinovna had lost her family he'd taken care of her, given her advice and money. It was he who had got her the job at the manager's office, and when she'd left there, he'd once more come to her rescue. She had nowhere to live and nowhere to go and she couldn't possibly move in with Vladimir. When Savelev had proposed that she move into his house she'd refused, saying that she'd rather go on the streets. Eventually Savelev had found a self-contained flat where he could set up his office and he suggested that Nina Konstantinovna should live there. He'd merely acted as her guardian, in her best interests.

It infuriated Vasya to hear Volodya refer so lovingly to the woman, and she couldn't prevent herself from saying, 'and I bet he makes passes at her too'. She never realized that Volodya could be so terribly gullible. Vasya didn't trust the woman an inch – *everybody* said she was just a whore.

Vladimir had once more lost his temper. 'Lies! Lies and gossip!' he yelled. 'What makes you so eager to wallow in all this squalid scandalmongering? If you want to know the truth about her, ask *me*! Nina Konstantinovna has eyes for nobody but me. I'm the man she loves! She's a lovely woman and Savelev is not the only man to make passes at her. And what of it! There's Makletsov, you know, the man from the Foreign Trade Department – he's offered her diamonds and every luxury that money can buy, but Nina just shows him the door. Of course, I'm not denying that Savelev may not be completely indifferent to her, and his love for her may not be purely paternal, but Nina's utterly repelled by him, physically I mean. I assure you there could never be anything between those two, it's completely inconceivable. I know Nina too well . . .'

It was obviously himself he was trying to convince. She realized this only too well, but what was even more distressing to her was that Savelev should be embroiled in everything Volodya did. She'd obviously had good reason to take an instant dislike to the man, and it was with good reason that the Control Commission had warned Vladimir to keep away from him.

'Anyway,' she said, 'whether or not Savelev is involved in all this is really neither here nor there. What matters is that there's a lot of gossip going round, and the general opinion seems to be that you and he go halves in keeping this girl friend of yours.'

'Well, you can just go and spit in the eye of anyone who even dares to suggest such a thing!' said Vladimir. 'I wouldn't expect you to understand this, Vasya, but my main misery about the whole thing is that when I first slept with Nina she was a virgin, nobody else had touched her . . .'

This statement pierced Vasya's heart like a fine needle. She recalled that night in 1917, when they were drinking tea in Vasya's room and he'd said 'I shall only give my heart to a woman who is still a virgin'. Then she remembered him stroking her hair after they'd made love, saying 'There's no purer person in the world than you, my Vasya.'

'A virgin! What a lot of rubbish!' she snapped irritably. 'What are you babbling about, Vladimir Do you really mean to say that people's purity lies in their virginity? Because if so, I'm afraid you've started thinking like a dyed-in-the-wool conservative!' She was really furious now.

'But, Vasya, you must realize that it's not I who think like that, it's her. You see, for her, it's the most terrible misfortune to have slept with me without being married first! Now she regards herself as a "fallen woman", and that just breaks her heart. Can't you grasp that, Vasya? You can't possibly imagine the agony she suffers.

She doesn't think like us proletarians, you see, and according to her the first man to sleep with her should be the one to marry her.'

'Why on earth didn't you tell me all this in the first place then? What's to stop you marrying her? I certainly wouldn't want to stand in your way!'

'Oh, Vasya, Vasya, an intelligent person like you, but just a peasant when it comes to matters of love! How could I marry her, Vasya? We're utterly incompatible! We're completely unalike in every single way! I don't really love her, only I do feel pity for her. How could I marry her, tell me that?'

Only a feeling of pity! Did he really mean that? Vasya began to tremble with happiness, she wanted so desperately to believe this.

'But why do you go on seeing her if there's no real love or understanding between you, and it brings you both so much unhappiness?' she asked.

'Do you think I could just abandon her then, Vasya? Things aren't so simple. I have to consider what will become of her if I leave her? Who knows, she might allow Savelev to keep her, or become a prostitute.'

'Why does she have to be kept? Why can't she go out and find herself a job?'

'Easier said than done these days! You try finding a job nowadays, with people being made redundant all over the place! And I don't know what kind of a job she could do anyway. It would never do for Nina to get an ordinary factory job.'

Vasya had longed to shout 'And why not a factory job? What's so special about her then?' But she had to consider Vladimir's feelings, for he was still far from well, and the doctor had warned her not to excite him. The conversation had been upsetting enough for him as it was.

But now, as she kept her lonely vigil in the dark house, Vasya keenly regretted that she hadn't shouted out the truth and told Vladimir what she thought of the woman's fraudulent tricks.

She simply didn't believe Nina Konstantinovna's repeated assurances that she loved Vladimir. She was obviously leading him on so as to get the most out of two men. It wasn't because she was a whore that Vasya detested her, but because she was obviously so unscrupulous. Whores could be a lot better than society ladies. There was curly haired Zinka, for one – she'd eventually been shot by the Whites, but just as she was dying she managed to shout 'Long live the Soviet government! Long live the revolution!' She'd been a real prostitute all right, but as soon as the revolution had broken out she seemed to take on a new lease of life. She started working for the political police with passionate enthusiasm, taking on the most perilous and punitive assignments.

Now if Vladimir had fallen in love with a woman like that, of course Vasya would have understood! But Nina was a lady, a bourgeois, a class enemy, and a ruthless woman who was leading Vladimir on to suit her own purposes. What could be her hold on him? The strength of her position obviously lay in his pity for her. 'I'm so weak and helpless and I was a virgin . . . !' Yes, thought Vasya, you've been a virgin ever since you left a white mark with that spotless virginity of yours! Why, surely all that 'virginity' must have gone to those men who've been giving you presents for it! And yet Vladimir still actually believes you and feels sorry for you! Vasya was utterly beside herself with rage at the woman . . .

Maria Semenovna's querulous voice broke into her thoughts. 'Vasilisa Dementevna! Holy Mother of God! Are you going to pace up and down like that much longer? You'd do better to save your strength, my dear, because you're going to need it for all those meetings of yours! Now be a good girl and go to sleep, and don't sit up waiting for that husband of yours. There's no reason why you should have to let him in if he's been off with another woman; I can make up a bed for him in the drawing room.'

Vasya hugged her and felt even more miserable. It seemed that everyone felt sorry for her except the man she loved, her husband and supposedly her best friend. He was sorry only for that cunning creature who clung to him like a snake . . .

Vasya lay in bed, her eyes wide open, oppressed by a great weight of misery which kept sleep away. It seemed that a long, long time passed before Vladimir strode in and turned on the light. 'Vasyuk, are you asleep?' he said.

'No, I'm not asleep.'

'So you're angry with me, eh, Vasyuk?' Sitting on the bed, he tried to kiss her, but she turned her face away.

'Ah, so you *are* angry then! Just as I thought. And what about our agreement? I told you everything, because you begged me to, and now it seems I'd have done better to lie.' Vasya did not reply. 'Now look, it would never do for us to start all those arguments and recriminations again, would it? What are you so angry about? Is it just because I've visited Nina? Can't you understand, Vasya? All this time you and I have been together, but she's been alone! Don't you realize she's been worrying herself sick about me too? She's suffered as well, you know.'

Vasya felt like crying out 'I don't give a damn if she has!' but she bit her lip and said nothing, her heart pounding.

'And you needn't imagine that anything happened between us tonight, Vasyuk,' he went on. 'Because I wasn't alone with her. Savelev was there, and Ivan Ivanovich came soon afterwards. We had to talk things over. Do you know why I went to see her today? It was to say goodbye to her for good . . . Why are you gawping at me like that? Don't you believe me? Ask Ivan Ivanovich, he'll tell you. I told him to come and help with the unpleasant task of moving Nina Konstantinovna and clearing out her apartment.'

'So where's she going?' asked Vasya dully.

'To Moscow. Savelev will be going with her. He has some relatives there who Nina can stay with while she looks for a job. It'll make things much easier for everybody this way.'

Vasya said nothing, but her expression was one of utter incredulity. Why this sudden change? What could have happened? He couldn't have discovered all of a sudden that he didn't love the woman?

'Let's not start talking about love,' he said hastily. 'That's really rather beside the point at the moment. The point is that even Nina has realized things can't go on like this – in fact it was her decision to go to Moscow. It's been on her mind for some time. That morning when you ran away from your Volodka, Nina phoned me and said she couldn't live like this any longer, that I must choose between you, otherwise she'd leave for Moscow.'

'Oh, now I see everything! So that was why you poisoned yourself! One of us had already gone and the other was threatening to go if you didn't marry her! Oh, what a fool, what a dumb fool I've been! Now I understand everything! It was because you were afraid of losing her! I thought it was because of *me* that you tried to kill yourself!' Vasya broke down in hysterical laughter.

'Now you're distorting everything, Vasya! How can you be so cruel! My old Vasyuk was never like that,' Vladimir said sadly, getting up from the bed. 'We're obviously getting nowhere, and I did so want to clear everything up, so there wouldn't be any more secrets between us. It seems that the more honest we try to be, the worse things become. You're like a different person, spiteful and unkind.'

'Oh no, Volodya, no, wait a moment! Don't go, please!' Vasya's voice was breaking, for she felt in despair. 'Let's talk about it if we must. So why *are* you sending her to Moscow, when it's her you love and not me! You'd have stayed with me today if it was really me you loved, but it's her you care about, it's her you pity!'

'Vasya, Vasya, you're still being very unfair! If only you knew how much Nina has suffered, she's only young, just a child really; she has no friends and everyone slings mud at her, and all for what, Vasya? Just because she had the misfortune to fall in love with me! You're so different. Vasya, you've got the Party, and you've got your friends. She's got nobody but me. I'm her only protector, her only support.' Vladimir was pacing round the room, one hand behind his back.

It was then that he told Vasya about the time Nina had become pregnant by him. All his dreams fulfilled! A child! His child! What joy and what misery!

'Well, where is the child then?' Vasya was dumbfounded.

'Do you imagine that Nina could have had the child, with all the scandal, and your unhappiness? We wanted to spare you that. It nearly broke her heart, of course – it almost killed her to make the decision, but for your sake, Vasya, we decided between us that we'd arrange for her to have an abortion.'

For *her* sake? He'd come to this arrangement with a completely unknown woman, he and this unknown woman had decided between them to 'spare' Vasya, as though she was some kind of enemy, not somebody to be trusted? It was this Nina woman, not Vasya, he had gone to in his unhappiness. He *must* be closer to Nina; Nina, not Vasya, was quite obviously his friend and lover.

'It was on the day you arrived that I discovered Nina was pregnant,' he said. 'Now do you realize why I was so anguished, Vasya?' She nodded in silence. Vladimir said that to avoid gossip, Nina had left for another town where Savelev had made the arrangements for an abortion. The operation hadn't been completely successful and there were complications; Vladimir had had to visit her there.

'Was that the time when the loaders first went on strike?' she asked.

'Yes, about then I suppose.'

'I see.' So that was why he'd cried when he was sitting at the table, because of Nina, nothing to do with the loaders at all!

'And tell me, did she come back that morning when Savelev arrived?' Vasya continued.

'Yes.'

'Yes, I thought so.'

Neither of them said anything. The cruel words hovered in the air between them. If they spoke them, they'd be sorry of course, but by then it would be too late, their love would be damaged, mutilated like a face disfigured by smallpox, no consolation, no joy . . .

'Vasya!' Vladimir broke into the oppressive silence. 'Why do we put ourselves through this hell? Who's to blame? I swear I was only trying to do everything I possibly could to spare your feelings.'

'But if only you'd really trusted me as a friend, you wouldn't have needed to spare my feelings,' she said.

Vladimir sat down beside her and took her hand. 'But, Vasya, I do know you're my friend – don't you see it makes it all the more difficult,' and he put his head on her shoulder as he had in the old days. Vasya stroked his familiar head with a mixture of grief and joy. Despite everything he was still here beside her, and maybe he even still loved her.

'Volodya,' she began cautiously, 'do you think it might have been better if I'd left rather than her?'

'Oh, Vasya, please don't start that up again, don't plague me like this. Support me, don't let me do the wrong thing again. I've opened my heart to you as a friend and told you everything, so now you must stop this talk about leaving me.'

'But I'm only thinking of you, Volodya. If you really loved her . . .'

'What's love got to do with this. Vasya! Love is one thing, but I can't for the life of me understand why you think Nina and I could have anything in common. She's not a comrade and she could never be a true friend, like you are. I'm just sorry for her, and worried about what will happen to her if I walk out on her and break it off for good. I still feel responsible for the woman, can't you understand? She was a virgin!'

'Oh, Volodya, you're just being ridiculous! How on earth can you consider yourself responsible for her? She isn't a child, she knew quite well what she was doing. Anyway, who cares about their precious virginity any more nowadays?'

'Well, that's how the proletariat thinks, of course, but Nina's different, she's not like that. For her it's a terrible thing to have on her conscience . . .'

'Exactly. That's why I said I should be the one to leave, and then you can go ahead and marry her!'

'Please, Vasya, not again, I beg you! Stop testing my feelings like this! Anyway, it's too late now, everything's been settled. Nina Konstantinovna is to leave for Moscow on Thursday, and that will be the end of it. We'll be able to forget the whole thing and start again.' He said this so calmly and resolutely that Vasya almost believed him. 'Vasya darling, just be patient for a few more days and meanwhile please don't let's exhaust ourselves. When she leaves, you and I will begin to live as we always have before. I wouldn't be surprised if things weren't even better from now on, now that we've gone through so much together.' He embraced her and kissed her eyes.

'I'd like to sleep with you tonight, Vasya, may I? I'm so tired and my head is spinning.' He lay down beside her, and resting his head on her shoulder, he fell asleep.

But Vasya could not sleep. If he'd really loved her he would have sensed what she was feeling and made some gesture of affection towards her. And as she looked at his familiar head, she realized how alien were the thoughts inside it. His lovely lashes concealed expressions of such tenderness, but she knew that his tenderness was not for her. His lips, his kisses, aroused another woman's passion. She pushed his head off her shoulder – he was a stranger to her!

'Why are you teasing your Volya-Sunny?' Vladimir murmured sleepily. Whoever called him by that name? It certainly wasn't her! Even in his sleep he couldn't distinguish between this other woman and herself!

She looked furiously at her sleeping husband – her husband? Her dear friend? The man she'd loved in the days when they'd fought together for the revolution. Now he was an utter stranger. Vasya felt cold and alone, mocked and tormented by the serpent of jealousy.

* XI *

It was an enervatingly hot summer. The relentless sky had sent no rain to wash the dusty trees or water the wilting grass. The town park was dusty and withered. The band was playing, but few people were around. Some children were romping near the bandstand and groups of Red Army soldiers were sitting about or promenading with women on their arms. On a bench in the shade, a surpliced priest sat leaning on his crozier, deep in thought, and beside him sat a nanny with a toddler. Vasya and Maria Semenovna sat down next to them. It was an inconspicuous place from which they would be able to see everything and wait for Nina Konstantinovna to appear.

'I just hope we see our princess today,' said Maria Semenovna. 'She generally comes here whenever the band plays, to show off her latest outfit. The ladies come here specially to see the latest fashion. They know that whatever it is, Nina Konstantinova will be wearing it.' Vasya listened absentmindedly. She longed to see what Nina Konstantinova looked like, but she had a terrible feeling that when she saw her she would become distraught.

'Look!' she clutched at Maria Semenovna. 'That woman in pink, the one just sitting down on that bench to the right of the bandstand, is that her?'

'What can you be thinking of! That's not Nina Konstantinovna! You'll pick her out at once! Like a mannequin, she is, dressed up to the nines!'

They sat there watching, but still Nina did not appear. Then, just as they were on the point of giving up and going home, Nina Konstantinova suddenly appeared from the other end of the park. She paused beside the bandstand, chatting to Savelev and two young men, completely oblivious to the way everyone was gaping at her. So here she was at last! She wore a thin white dress which enveloped her body in soft folds and clearly exposed her breasts, long sand-coloured gloves, and a matching hat tilted over her eyes so that Vasya couldn't see her face properly. All she could see were her lips, bright crimson, as though smeared with blood.

'Why, look at her lips! They're just like blood!' she exclaimed.

'That's lipstick,' Maria Semenovna explained sagely. 'And you ought to see her eyes too, all smudged with soot! I'd just like to get a cloth and scrub all that mess off her face, *then* we'd see what she really looked like! Hah! Even I'd be a beauty for you if they primped me up like that!'

Nina Konstantinova was leaning on a white lace parasol and kicking it with the heel of her white slipper. She laughed and tossed her head, and the two young men laughed with her.

Savelev stood aside all this time, tracing patterns in the sand with his cane, looking bored.

'But I can't see her face with that hat on!' protested Vasya.

'Well, why don't we walk past them?' suggested Maria Semenovna. 'Then you can get a proper look at our princess. But I wouldn't look too closely if I were you, there's not much to look at. When I was in the service of General Gololubov's late wife I saw plenty of real ladies and beauties, I can tell you, and she certainly doesn't match up to them!'

But Vasya was obsessed by a morbid sense of curiosity. She just had to understand what it was that made Volodya love a woman like this. Just as they were getting up to walk towards her, Nina shook hands with the young men and said goodbye, loudly enough for Vasya to catch the words, 'See you again soon in Moscow, then!' She turned towards the park gate, followed by Savelev.

'Shall we catch them up, Vasilisa Dementevna?' whispered Maria Semenovna. 'No, better not. It's different for her highness, but people know you, and there'd only be a lot of gossip!'

Vasya slowed down without taking her eyes off Nina for a second. She was tall and stately and swung her shoulders as she walked, but as she got further from the bandstand her head began to droop and Vasya thought she must be crying. Savelev leant over and began to remonstrate with her, but she shook her head as if to say no. Then she raised a yellow gloved hand to her face to wipe away a tear. So she really was crying! She must have come here to say her final farewell to the music!

What if she did love Volodya, after all, and wasn't merely taking advantage of him. These thoughts increased Vasya's uneasiness for even now that she'd seen Nina Konstantinova she didn't feel any happier. Her jealousy had left her, now it was something quite different, a sort of compassion for the woman was dimly surfacing in her mind. Why was Nina crying? Why had she come to hear the music? Was she saying goodbye once and for all to past happiness? Vasya was annoyed with herself for allowing these new feelings to prey on her mind. As if she didn't have enough worries of her own! A fine state of affairs, breaking her heart because this woman was having to leave her Volodya!

Shortly after this episode in the park Nina Konstantinova left for Moscow. Two weeks passed. Vasya felt all she had to do was to start enjoying life again. Nina had gone and Vladimir was all hers. Now she knew that she really was more important to him than Nina, who had been a passing affair. She began to smile and laugh more, and her cough improved. She attended the Party committee regularly and Vladimir absorbed himself in work, reorganizing the business on the lines laid down by the syndicate. As soon as he'd wound up these affairs he and Vasya would be able to leave for Moscow and thence Vladimir would be transferred to a new district. At the moment he seemed happy to immerse himself in his work, and everything seemed to be going well . . .

And yet the old happiness they'd known before was gone. There seemed to be nothing they could do about it. Vladimir was not exactly unkind, but he found it hard to control his temper, and would fly into sudden rages with Vasya. Once it was because she returned late for lunch from the Party committee. He'd shouted at her for keeping the guests waiting. Did she expect them to sit down and eat before their hostess arrived? Another time he'd lost his temper because his collars were dirty. At this point Vasya lost her temper too. Why should she be responsible for them, she demanded? He could take care of himself perfectly well, and ask Maria Semenovna to do them! This row left them on particularly bad terms. And all because of some stupid collars!

One day Vasya came home in the pouring rain. She'd left her fur hat at the Party committee room to save it from getting wet. Instead, she'd tied a handkerchief round her head. Vladimir frowned when he saw her. 'What a fright!' he said. 'You should just look at yourself! Your shoes are worn at the heels, you're skirt's spattered with mud, and that handkerchief on your head makes you look just like a peasant woman! You look a complete frump!'

Vasya retorted furiously, 'Well, we can't all deck ourselves out like mannequins, can we? And I'm certainly not going to go batting my eyes at Savelev!' Vladimir shot her a furious glance and although he said nothing, Vasya felt that he longed to strike her, and had barely managed to restrain himself.

Things just weren't working out as they should have done. They both wanted so badly to be friends again, but the least thing would make them lose their tempers. And then Vladimir was always having fantasies about his new job and how they'd set up house and arrange their domestic affairs, all of which Vasya found very tedious. What was the point of having your own house? Where was the pleasure in it? It would have been quite different if they'd been establishing a communal house, but Vladimir disagreed violently with her on this and attacked her 'conservatism'.

Then Vasya would talk to him about how, in her Marxist study group, they were debating whether history was created by economics alone or by ideologies. She became terribly excited as she struggled to explain everything they'd been discussing. But he found it boring. It was nothing but a diversion for him. The real thing was how to make business more profitable . . . And then another argument would start.

Gradually they found that they had less and less to talk about or do when they were alone together, and sometimes they'd telephone Ivan Ivanovich and ask him to come over, for they felt more at ease in his presence. Vasya was still waiting for a letter from her home town, but the days came and went, and she heard nothing, either from Grusha or Stepan Alexeevich. What could they be doing? She would never have admitted it, but in her heart of hearts she longed for them to ask her to come back, although she still wasn't sure whether she would go or not.

Then at last a letter did come, a registered letter from Stepan Alexeevich. It was brief and to the point: he wanted Vasya to take over a new work scheme, laid down by the Central Committee, in a group of textile factories. These factories were just outside town and she'd be able to live there. He would await her reply.

Vasya's heart began to beat faster as she thought about the prospect of going back to her friends. After all, what sort of a life was it here, without a proper job or real happiness, only constant anxieties? She felt tied hand and foot – like the jackdaw her brother Kolka had caught in the forest when they were children. He'd tied its wings with thread to prevent it flying away, and it would strut around the floor, opening its beak wide, looking at the windows with its intelligent black eyes, and trying to flap its wings. After a few desperate attempts, flapping and cawing, it would pick its way across the floor, resigned never to fly again.

If Vasya's wings had been tied by the joys of love, that would have been different. But it was her wretched fears which held her back, her anxiety lest something should happen to Vladimir again, her sense of gratitude to him for staying with her and sending off his mistress. The threads that bound her to him were fine but they were fast, and tied so artfully that even Vasya herself had never noticed before how they trapped her.

'Vasilisa Dementevna!' Maria Semenovna's voice broke into her thoughts abruptly. 'We're out of beer! We should tell Vladimir Ivanovich to make sure they send some round from the brewery. What if guests arrive unexpectedly for dinner! Then it'll be me who has to dash round and rustle some up from nowhere, I suppose!' She looked at Vasya closely, one of her disapproving looks. 'Just look at yourself, Vasilisa Dementevna! You do nothing but sulk all day! And what is it now, might I ask? God be praised is what I say, the mannequin's gone off to Moscow and you've got your Vladimir Ivanovich with you from now on. Does he so much as stir one step from the door, unless it's to go to work? No! So why are you always such a misery? Husbands don't like that, you know! They like their wives to be cheerful and brighten up the home so that when they get back from work they can forget all their worries. They ought to be able to look forward to a bit of peace at the end of the day, after all . . .'

Vasya smiled as she listened to these well-worn views, and thought, Who knows, maybe she's right! Maybe I should try and pull myself together and become the old Vasya again, like I was in 1918. We did work hard in those days, and yet we still managed to have a lot of fun. How would it be if she went to see Vladimir in his office this minute! She would surprise him, arrive unannounced, and tell him about the job. She'd laugh as she told him that she couldn't possibly part from her Volodya, and she was going to refuse. Then he'd realize how much she loved her darling Volodya, and he'd be so overjoyed he would hug her and kiss her eyes!

He'll call me his own Vasya like he used to, she thought excitedly as she picked out a white blouse to wear and tied a dark blue scarf around her neck. Carefully putting on her hat in front of the mirror, she arranged her curls. Today she was going to make herself pretty for Volodya, today she was taking him a very special present – her letter to Stepan Alexeevich refusing his offer of work! Today she decided to go with Volodya to the new district, and take up work there.

Arriving at the office, she went straight to the director's room. It was empty. The director was at a meeting, so Vasya sat down to wait, glancing through some Moscow newspapers, smiling to herself. She was going to show Volodya how grateful she was for everything – for loving her more than anyone else, and sending his mistress away!

The mail arrived and was put on the director's table. They were mostly business letters, and Vasya began to sort through them in case there was anything for her. Suddenly her heart started pounding and she caught her breath. An oblong pink envelope addressed with minute and elegant handwriting – it could only be from Nina Konstantinovna!

So it was not over. All the old deceptions were continuing as before . . . She felt as though she was falling, everything spun before her . . . She must have staggered forward, for the next thing she knew she'd knocked an ashtray off the table and broken it. That oblong pink envelope seemed to control her destiny. In a flash the letter was in her pocket. This would be the end of all lies.

At that moment, Vladimir entered the room with some managers.

'Hello there, Vasya,' he said in surprise. 'What are you doing here? Have you come on business or is it a social call?'

'There's no more beer in the house, we'll have to order some more from the brewery,' she replied flatly.

'Look at my Vasya! Turning into quite a little housewife, aren't you? I won't be recognizing my old Vasya soon!' he laughed, evidently well pleased with her.

Laugh on! she thought, you don't know how I hate all the chains you've put on my freedom! I'm going to break them and expose every single one of your lies!

'Is that all you came about, Vasya? You have to be leaving now, do you?'

Vasya nodded dumbly; she was shaking so much she was barely able to control herself.

Unable to wait until she got home, she went to the park and sat down on a bench. Frantically tearing open the pink envelope, she began to read.

My darling Sunny-Volodya, my sweetheart, my tormenter, my master. One more day, and not a word from you. This is the third day and I haven't had even a line from you. Have you forgotten about me? Have you stopped loving your Egyptian monkey, your own capricious Nina? I don't believe it! But still I can't help being afraid when you're with her, and I'm all alone.

I'm afraid because I know how she bosses you around, and how much influence she has on you. She'll try and convince you that our love is a 'sin against communism', that we should

'abstain' in true communist fashion, deny ourselves everything
that gives us pleasure, and only love each other on Saturdays.
I'm afraid of her, because I know her power over you. But
my God! I'm not even taking you away from her – I'm asking
so little of you! She's recognized by the whole world as your
wife, and you're with her all the time for ever and ever, while
all I ask is a few hours of your time because I love you so much.
Please take pity on me, for if you don't, nobody else will, nobody
else in the world!

I wake up in the middle of the night, terrified that you've
stopped loving me and are about to leave me, terrified at what
would happen to me then . . . I'm too terrified even to think
about it. You know how Nikanor Platonovich watches me like
a spider, and however much he plays the papa, you and I know
what he's after! He'd be overjoyed if you left me, because then
I'd be completely alone, helpless and defenceless against him!
He'd be delighted if that happened! There are days when I loathe
him so much that I'd rather go on the streets, anything, just so
long as I don't have to feel so completely at his mercy all the
time!

Volya, my darling, Volya, I love you so insanely. Do you
think this nightmare will end some day, and you'll come and
rescue your Ninka? Won't you take pity on your 'monkey'?
Don't you ever think about me? You are so cruel to me, so
unkind. I know that at this very moment you are kissing that
other woman – it's her you love, I know it! It breaks my heart
to think about it! I want you so much, my passionate insatiable
Volodya! Don't you long to kiss me and hold me in your arms?
I can't bear it – I want to put my soft arms around you, my
breasts ache for you to caress them. I can't endure much more
of this, Volya. I can't live without you. Why, oh why did you
send me away to Moscow?

This can't go on. When you move to the new district you
must find me a small house with a garden, where you'll be
able to visit me when it grows dark, and I'll show you that there
is nothing, nothing in the whole world better or more important
than a love like ours.

When will you come to Moscow? And will *she* be coming
with you? Why can't you just take one week off and we could be
together! Just think of it – one whole week to ourselves!

Nikanor Platonovich tells me that in the new district you're going to be given a sweet detached house, with a dining room done out in gothic style. He says there's no lamp, and I've already found a heavenly chandelier for it. It's on the expensive side, but it's absolutely exquisite and I know you'll love it.

I've babbled on quite enough. This letter's going to be so long you won't have anywhere to hide it!

I may joke, but I feel like crying all the time. Will you ever understand how wretched I am? Oh, why won't life allow us to be happy together? But don't worry, you're the boss, I'll stop grumbling. I think I'm a little bit wiser now after everything I've suffered. You must do as you think best. I'll do anything you say, but one thing I won't let you take away from me – your kisses, your love and your pity for your poor, lonely confused little Nina.

Moscow, Ostozhenka Street 18, Apartment 7 (not 17 as you wrote last time – it was only by luck that I got your letter!)

I belong to you, from my lips to my toes,

your own Nina.

There was a PS in the margin. 'Just think, I'm so happy, I found that powder I was looking for, L'Origan Coty!'

Vasya read Nina's letter very slowly, lingering over each word, reading not only with her eyes but with her whole heart. When she finally finished, she put the letter on her knees and gazed at the dry dusty grass at her feet where a bee was buzzing angrily. It flew amongst the blades, darting off irritably and then returned again to rummage in the same patch of grass.

In the spring, when the lilac had been in flower, the bees had been buzzing so cheerfully. But this one was bad-tempered, as if the summer had deceived it. Suddenly Vasya realized that her thoughts were on the bee, not the letter. She felt no particular unhappiness, just a dull sensation of utter indifference.

Gradually the serpent set to work again; yes, Nina's words had stung her. 'Smooth arms, soft lips . . .' The serpent's vile tongue lashed her heart with the words, and she struggled against the unbearable pain. Surely there must be some corner of her heart which wasn't filled with this poison!

Slowly, painstakingly, she folded the letter and put it back in its envelope. She got up, went past the bandstand and walked towards the gate. There was no music playing today, no people, no music. Now Vasya finally knew who it was that Volodya loved.

She went through the wicket-gate of the dusty park, out onto the street rumbling with traffic. For her, the park had become a graveyard, for she'd just been to a funeral – the burial of her happiness.

* XII *

When Vasya finally got home she found Vladimir back earlier than usual. He was cheerful and full of his good news; the long-awaited letter had come from the Central Committee, confirming his new appointment. He'd have to leave for Moscow immediately.

'Moscow?' said Vasya. 'I see. Well, I'm going away too, but not to Moscow. I'm going back to my home town.' She spoke with apparent calm but her feelings were in chaos as she thought of Nina's oblong pink envelope in her pocket. But Volodya didn't seem to notice Vasya's drawn face, nor the sparks of anger in her eyes. He obviously had no idea what she was planning. She went into the bedroom to pack her suitcase.

'Are you planning to visit your relatives then? Excellent idea! We can meet in Moscow, unless you'd rather go straight to the new place.' Hope had momentarily flooded her heart, her last hope – that he would protest and prevent her from going. Now even that hope had finally been shattered.

'I'm not going with you at all. I've been asked to go back home to work, and I'll be staying there, not just temporarily but for good. I've had enough of this, I've been suffocating in this cage of yours for too long, and now I'm tired of playing the director's wife. You must find yourself a wife who appreciates that kind of life . . .'

The words almost choked her, but she went on talking, on and on, falling over her words in her haste to get everything out. She wouldn't be deceived in this way any more, she said. She was glad that finally the whole affair was over. All the time she'd been living surrounded by those bourgeois syndicate men, she'd been pining to get back to her work, and had only endured it for Vladimir's sake. She was deeply sad that she was no longer necessary to him, that their love and friendship were over, but she could no longer simply act as his wife, his hostess and his cover, just so that he could say 'I live with a communist, and I keep another woman in a secret house for my pleasure'.

How cleverly they'd planned everything between them, Vladimir and Nina! There was only one thing they'd forgotten, and that was whether Vasya was prepared to agree to such a disgusting life! Vasya's eyes were green with rage and she started to gasp for words.

Vladimir shook his head angrily. 'Vasya! I really can't believe you mean all this. I don't even recognize you in this mood! Why can't you understand – if I've concealed anything from you it's only been to protect you!'

'Thanks a lot, but I really don't need your pity! I'm quite strong enough to take the truth. Do you really imagine that your love for me is the only thing in my life? Well, you can put your love for me right back where you found it, and let me tell you something – it's been nothing but one long torment for me. I want to leave you just as soon as I can and get out of here. And I don't want to know what you do with yourself after that either. Fall in love with whoever you want, sleep with them, lie to people, deceive them, become a general director, be a traitor to communism for all I care, it's all the same to me!'

'But, Vasya, Vasya, what about our friendship? And your promise to understand everything?'

'Our friendship? What of it? Where has it gone? Where is it, tell me that! I don't believe anything you say any more, Vladimir, you've killed my confidence in you. Did you imagine that I'd have stopped you if you'd just come to me and said "Vasya, it's terrible, I know, but something very sad has happened – I've fallen in love with someone else?" Did you think I'd have blamed you, or stood in the way of your happiness? No, Vladimir, you forgot that I wasn't just your wife but your friend, and that's why I'm so hurt, can't you understand that? That's why I shall never forgive you, as long as I live . . .' The tears began to run down her cheeks, and brushing them off with her sleeve she turned away from Vladimir.

'I had such confidence in you as a friend, but you just trampled on it. How can two people go on living together when one of them no longer has trust in the other? No, this has to be the end of our life together, our happiness together is over . . .'

Her heart was aching and she shook with emotion as she turned away from Vladimir again and sat down on the bed, crumpling the silk eiderdown in her hands, her eyes full of tears. Vladimir sat down beside her and grasped her shoulders.

'Vasya, how can you say you've become a stranger to me, that you don't love me any more? How can that be true? Why would you be so terribly upset over all this if you no longer loved me? Have you tried to consider my feelings? Don't you believe that I still love you? Please try to understand me. I do love Nina, yes, but that's completely different. My love for you is much deeper, it's much more real. Without you I'm nothing, I'd have nowhere to go. Whatever I tried to do without you I'd always be wondering what you'd say about it. You're my guiding star! I need you, Vasya!'

'You really can only think about yourself, can't you?' said Vasya sadly. 'But what about me? This life is stifling me, Vladimir! I can accept the fact that you have a mistress, but what I can't bear is that we're no longer friends.'

'Do you really think I don't feel the same way? But can you tell me how it happened? I don't understand anything any more. We miss each other when we're apart, but when we're together we just irritate each other. You tell me that it wasn't like that in the past, but then we never spent much time with each other before, did we? We never had a settled family life – we were always too busy working, and we could only pay each other fleeting visits. I know, why don't we try living like that again, Vasya? Would you like that? We could both do what we wanted, and as soon as we got bored with each other we could just separate. How would you like that? Then my Vasya would be her tough little self again, the Vasya I love so much, and we wouldn't have to lie to each other any more. We can't just break it off like this, Vasya, it would be dreadfully painful to separate completely. Please be kind to me, Vasya!' He laid his head on her knees, burying his face in her lap. Neither of them said anything.

In the quietness, both of them began to feel the warm sensation of desire, and little sparks of their old passion, so long buried under the ashes of insults and suspicion, began to kindle slowly.

'Vasya darling!' Vladimir's strong arms embraced Vasya, and drew her down to him, overwhelming her with kisses. Vasya gave herself up totally to this sweet forgotten passion. At this moment she knew that he loved her undividedly, he loved her as he'd always loved her. Now Volodya was betraying his Nina not only with his body but with his mind and his feelings, and this knowledge brought Vasya a kind of ruthless happiness quite new to her. It was painful and pleasurable. So let him betray Nina like this!

Strange morbid days followed. The spark of their passion, smouldering so long like an extinguished bonfire, was fanned by a gust of autumn wind. It flamed up wildly and spread, licking their charred wounds and seeking out the corners in their hearts which had not been scarred yet by its flame.

Vladimir was tender, Vasya was submissively affectionate. It was almost as though they had fallen in love again. They assured one another that they could never live apart, and at night they'd lie holding each other tightly, terrified of losing one another. Vladimir would kiss Vasya's eyes and Vasya would clutch his dear face to her. They had never before loved one another so passionately, but now there was a sense of sweet nostalgia and bitter happiness about it : both knew that finding one another again was their own way of burying their love and happiness.

One moment Vasya would be smiling and joking, the next she would collapse into tears. And while Vladimir caressed her and they looked into each other's eyes, she could read in his an expression of the utmost sadness. They seemed to be wordlessly saying goodbye to her. And so as not to have to see them and his tears, to kill the unbearable sadness, she would put her thin arms around his neck and seek his lips. He would press her to his heart and fondle her, seeking her body insatiably until she was beside herself with ecstasy and they both finally fell asleep in exhaustion.

Strange morbid days, suffocating and dark . . . No real happiness now, none of the winged joy which is born of love.

* XIII *

So they agreed that Vasya would go and work in her home town for the time being, and when Vladimir had settled into the new town they'd meet. Where they were to meet was not specified, and the question of separation was not mentioned. On the surface everything seemed simple and clear, so reasonable, above all so honest. The one thing that Vasya didn't tell him was that she'd stolen Nina's letter; she'd hidden it away and was keeping it. She felt she still needed it.

However, she did insist that Vladimir send Nina a telegram to say that he'd be arriving in Moscow alone. She couldn't have explained why she did this, when it cost her so much, it was just something she had to do. Vladimir stalled for a while, looking suspicious and apprehensive, but he did finally agree and afterwards he was even more affectionate and passionate towards her.

Vasya no longer cared. It seemed right that they drink the last remaining drops of their happiness together, for these combined the intoxication of passion with the sweet grief of separation. She became brisk and cheerful – it was a long time since Volodya had seen her like that.

'I feel as though I've cast off a skin that didn't fit me. I wasn't much good as a director's wife, was I? You need a completely different kind of wife! I'm no good for you, I'll never make a nepwoman!' Vasya joked.

'I don't know who you are any more,' admitted Volodya. 'All I know is that you're the old tough Vasya, and I wouldn't give that up even if five Party committees needed you! In time, maybe yes, but at the moment there's absolutely no reason why we should separate.'

Vasya laughed. So be it. Why shouldn't they meet for short visits from now on, not as husband and wife but as free agents and friends? Vladimir agreed that this would make things much easier between them, but he still insisted that he couldn't exist without Vasya beside him. 'I have so few friends in the world, Vasya, especially at the moment when everything is going to the dogs, and everybody's out for what they can get. You and I are such old and true friends, aren't we, Vasya?'

They could talk now as if the barrier between them had been broken down. And the old obsessions seemed to have left Vasya. But then, just as she was feeling at peace, feelings of jealousy would suddenly stir. Vladimir would sometimes become very distant, for no apparent reason, and start talking about Nina. It was evident that he thought about her a great deal.

She was so well educated, he said, she could chatter away in French with a Frenchman, in German with a German, she'd been to an institute . . .

'If she's so well educated, why can't she find work, then? Or is she used to living off other people? She's a parasite through and through – although that's what a mistress is for, I suppose.' Vasya realized she shouldn't talk like this, but she wanted to take out some of her pain on Volodya.

'Vasya, why do you say things like that? It's so unkind. It's some other Vasilisa Dementevna talking, not the Vasya I admire.'

But hurt and ashamed though she felt, she couldn't stop herself goading him again and again until he finally lost his temper and she would realize what she was doing. 'Darling, please try not to be angry with me, forgive me for being so unkind. You know how much I love you; if I didn't, the whole thing wouldn't torment me so.'

Then they would reach out to each other and drown everything in suffocating kisses, the intoxication of their love-making. No need to think or suffer, forget everything, cheat the harsh and unbearable truth . . .

Some days later, having said her farewells to the people on the Party committee, Vasya went home to pack. She had to see to everything, collect boxes and suitcases, baste and straw in which to wrap things. She asked Maria Semenovna how to pack things so that they wouldn't get broken or damaged on the journey to the director's new home.

'Why are you making such a fuss about it?' Maria Semenovna fretted. 'I don't know why you're taking the trouble, now that you've made up your mind to go back to your own town. You mark my words, the minute you've gone, his girl friend will come through the door to take your place. Why should you take all this trouble and work yourself to death for her benefit!'

But her words made absolutely no impression on Vasya. She no longer felt that it was as Volodya's wife that she was helping him. Indeed, if she *had* been his wife she couldn't have done it at all, but would have attacked him for his bourgeois ways. Now that he was going his way and she was going hers there was no reason not to help him, just as any friend would offer to help another. For she no longer bore him any grudge, and if he wanted to trail all this junk behind him and overload the public transport system with his boxes of crockery, as well as suitcases full of silk clothes, that was his affair. She certainly wouldn't have landed herself with all this luggage, but why shouldn't she help him with the packing of it, now that it no longer mattered to her?

When Volodya saw her doing this he was amazed. No need for her suddenly to be such a conscientious housewife, he said, when there was Ivan Ivanovich or the managers to do it. And anyway, who would arrange all these things in his new house, he asked, if she didn't come soon?

'Well, what use is Nina Konstantinovna, then? Or doesn't she like to dirty her lovely white hands? Perhaps she's too much of a lady for that. I suppose all she has to do is to see that everything is done to her liking, make sure her meals are served on silver salvers, and generally enjoy the fruits of other people's hard work and money . . .'

Immediately she was furious with herself for hurting Volodya and once more couldn't imagine what had got into her. Volodya looked at her reproachfully, and she flung her arms round him.

'Oh, darling, I hate myself for being so cruel to you; it's only because I love you so much. Don't be angry with me, darling, it was only a joke!' And she buried her face in his jacket, stifling the tears that welled up in her throat. She did still love him! She loved him dreadfully, suffered for him, was terrified of losing him, living without him.

'My poor sweetheart,' he soothed her. 'Dear little Vasyuk, I know you so well, that's why I love you and shall never be able to tear myself away from you. For me there's no other Vasya in the whole world and I shall never have another friend like you . . .' Once again that bitter heady passion enveloped them and they stifled their pain in suffocating embraces.

'Leave a corner in your heart for your old anarchist lover won't you?'

'If you'll remember your tough Vasyuk – and our past happiness'.

Strange and intoxicating, those last days together, suffocating and dark.

⋆ XIV ⋆

Vasya knocked on the door of her garret where Grusha now lived. They'd told her downstairs that Grusha was back from work, but the door was locked. Where could she be? Could she be asleep? Then turning round she saw her, hurrying along the corridor carrying a teapot and some hot water.

'Grusha!'

'Vasilisa, my precious! When did you arrive? Well I never, fancy seeing you!' Grusha put the teapot down on the floor and the two friends hugged each other delightedly. 'Come in, make yourself at home, remember it's your garret and it's all thanks to you that I'm living here. Let me just open the door. There've been a lot of robberies in this house, you know, and I have to lock up even when I fetch water. Mr Furazhin had his autumn coat stolen the other day, straight off the hook where it was hanging, and it was almost new too. We alerted the whole house and called in the militia, but they couldn't find anything. Well, Vasya, you're back in your old home, so why not take off your coat and have a wash after your journey? I was just going to make some tea. Would you like a bite to eat? There are some eggs, bread and a few apples . . .'

Home? Grusha had said this was her 'home'. Would Vasya ever really have a home? Looking round her, it was certainly the same familiar garret, but it was no longer Vasya's. There was a treddle sewing-machine and a dressmaker's dummy in the corner, scraps of material scattered around, patterns and pieces of thread on the floor. The walls were bare; gone were the pictures of Marx and Lenin and the group of communards which she'd put up when they'd celebrated the anniversary of the revolution. Now there was just a faded red paper fan and beside it a tattered postcard depicting an Easter egg and an archaic inscription in gold letters: Christ is Risen! There was an ikon in the corner too.

Grusha wasn't in the Party. She believed in God, observed fast-days, even though she supported the soviets and was friendly with a number of communists. She'd once had a fiancé who'd fought with the Whites and she didn't know whether he was alive or not. If he'd been killed, it could only have been by the Red Army, and that was why Grusha was unwilling to become a communist; she wanted to treasure the memory of her fiancé. 'He would curse me from the other world if I joined you,' was what she said.

At first Vasya hadn't been able to understand how Grusha could love a White soldier, but now she knew differently, now she knew that feelings often seemed to have laws of their own. She and Vladimir had gone their separate ways, but as for their love, that was still very much alive, and it gave her no peace of mind.

Grusha was overjoyed to see Vasya and kept plying her with questions. Why on earth hadn't Vasya put on some weight, with all that money her husband had? She'd come back looking as scraggy as when she'd left, even skinnier!

Vasya could say nothing. She'd somehow imagined that when she saw Grusha again she'd hug her and sob out all her troubles to her, but now that Grusha was actually there, reticence overcame her and she just couldn't find the right words. How could she begin to describe what she was going through?

People in the building soon heard about Vasya's arrival. The old tenants were happy that she had come back, the new ones curious to see what she looked like. The housing committee representative glowered; he hoped she wasn't going to go ferreting around in his administrative affairs again.

But it was the children from the children's club who were the first to come running into Grusha's room, and straight away the eldest one approached Vasya with a complaint; apparently under the NEP the children's club had been closed, and the authorities had said that it couldn't be re-purchased from the State, since according to them, the premises were needed for something else. Where were the schoolchildren to prepare their lessons now? Their botanical collections had all been removed and their library distributed amongst other clubs or sold.

Vasya simply couldn't imagine how this could have happened and immediately began to work out how to deal with it. She'd have to go this very day to the housing department. The NEP was all very well, but how dare they lay so much as a finger on something the workers themselves had organized through their own efforts! 'I'm going to fight this,' she said. 'Don't you worry now, children, I shall defend your rights. I'm not going to let them get away with this, even if it means going to Moscow!'

The older children laughed. They'd been confident that Vasya would defend them, and here she was, going off to fight for them! She'd always been known as a fighter, and it was true!

After this the older residents came to greet her, each one of them eagerly telling Vasya their problems and stories. She listened as carefully as she always had, and questioned each of them closely, giving advice and comfort. Before long, there was such a crowd of people gathered in the garret that there was hardly room to breathe.

'Listen, please friends, couldn't you all wait a bit!' implored Grusha. 'You haven't even let her have a bite to eat after her journey, and the poor creature's quite worn out. You might think of all those nights she's been travelling, instead of plaguing her with your demands!'

'No, Grusha,' Vasya said, 'please don't stop them, I'm not a bit tired. Now what were you just beginning to tell me, Timofey Tomofeyevich? Oh yes, about your taxes. I don't understand, it's not as if you're a landlord or a director . . . ?' As she said the word, Volodya came into her mind, and for a moment she felt the old pain again. But it was immediately submerged by other people's worries; she had no time to think . . .

One by one, her old friends left and Vasya tidied herself up to go to the Party committee. She was so anxious to get matters moving immediately that she didn't notice how tired she was. As she buttoned up her blouse she listened to Grusha's news : so-and-so had got married, so-and-so had left the Party, so-and-so had been elected to the soviet . . .

Suddenly, Mrs Feodeseeva's voice resounded through the corridor. 'Where is she, our little darling, our precious guardian angel, Vasilisa Dementevna?' Before she knew it, the woman had flung herself at Vasya, hugging her, drooling over her, soaking her with tears. 'Oh, I've been waiting so long for you to come back, my angel. You're my only hope now. I said to myself, as soon as she's back, our guardian angel, she'll sort things out. Once she's back he won't dare insult his lawful wife like this, the wretch, he'll be ashamed to turn this building into a cesspool – him and that slut of his. Our Vasya will take pity on me, having to struggle on alone with my poor litttle ones. She'll bring him to justice, and then he'll have to do what the Party says. You're my last hope, my pet.'

Vasya was usually quick to grasp other people's problems, but she was completely at a loss to know what Mrs Feodoseeva was talking about. Certainly she'd changed beyond recognition. Before, she'd been a strong, large-bosomed woman, now she looked old, yellow and haggard.

She proceeded to tell Vasya her story. Apparently Feodoseev had embarked on an affair with an 'unbaptized little Jewess' named Dora, had left his wife for her, and was now disgracing his wife throughout the entire neighbourhood. He was shamelessly renouncing his own children and spending all his money on his girl friend. ' "Take me in", he says to her. "My family can die in a ditch for all I care, but don't leave me, pockmarked wretch that I am!" '

'What can Dora see in him, the little fool!' spat Mrs Feodoseeva. 'Why, he's not even a proper man! Ugh! Rat-faced little shrimp! Eight years I've put up with him and kissed his poxy face for the sake of our children. "However ugly you are, Vasilevich", I told myself, "it's fate that has bound us together and the church that wedded us, so I'll just have to put up with you." I always found him revolting, the way he crawled over me with his kisses, but still I endured it and never so much as looked at another man. I thought at least he'd be grateful – to think I wasted my youth on that pockmarked shrimp! And now see what happens! As soon as I lose my looks he starts chasing after little girls, and he's hooked up with this Jewess of his and is making an exhibition of himself throughout the neighbourhood . . .'

Mrs Feodoseeva was sobbing, and as Vasya listened, her heart flooded with emotion. Her own grief was reflected in Mrs Feodoseeva's; it was infinitely depressing to experience her old feelings of outrage in this way.

She suddenly felt weary and drained of all energy. She no longer had any desire to go to the Party committee, all she wanted was to bury her head in a pillow and hide her face. But Mrs Feodoseeva went on sobbing, kissing her shoulders, imploring her 'wise Vasilisa' to make her husband see sense, and to defend the interests of her children by threatening him with a Party trial.

But as soon as Vasya arrived at the Party committee, she forgot about everything else. There she felt as though nothing but the Party mattered. She argued with them heatedly and made enquiries about the children's library. It was such an absorbing task that her spirits soared, and later her friends walked her home; they had so much to discuss, and she felt so happy and full of energy that she flew up the stairs to her little garret. It was only then she realized how tired she really was.

While Grusha was bustling around making supper, Vasya lay on the bed, and at once fell into a deep sleep. Looking at her lying there, Grusha didn't know whether to wake her or not; Vasya looked so worn out that she decided to let her sleep on. She undressed her like a child, took off her shoes, and covered her with a blanket. Then she draped a shawl round the lamp and sat down to do her buttonholes.

Suddenly there was a knock at the door. Who the devil could that be? Grusha wondered, angry at being disturbed. She opened the door, and there stood Feodoseeva's husband.

'What do you want?' she asked him.

'I've come to see Vasilisa Dementevna. Is she in?'

'Have you all taken leave of your senses! Here's someone just arrived after a long journey, worn out after all those sleepless nights, and all people can do is besiege her, like a pack of starving dogs after a bone! Vasilisa Dementevna is asleep!'

Grusha stood at the door haranguing poor Feodoseev, who insisted on being let in. Grusha refused, and he finally agreed to come back the next day. She slammed the door in his face. Dirty little creep! What about his lawful wife and his three children, while Dora there showed off that big belly of hers! Let him clear up that mess for himself! Grusha disapproved of Feodoseev, and had no sympathy for Dora, taking up with a married man like that, as if there weren't enough single men around! Grusha had never been able to forget her fiancé, and now she was 'keeping herself pure'. She applied this strict moral code to everyone.

⋆ XV ⋆

When Vasya woke she felt clear-headed and much calmer. An autumn sun danced through the window and tinged the sewing-machine with gold. Grusha was heating up a flat iron on the oil-stove, preparing to put the finishing touches to a dress.

'Who's that dress for?' Vasya asked.

'For the secretary of the executive committee, it's her name day,' Grusha replied.

'Really? Do people celebrate their name days nowadays then?'

'I should say they do! And more splendidly than under the gentry too! You should just see the huge tables full of food, wine, vodka . . .' Grusha's iron started hissing and she had to stop talking.

Vasya snuggled down into the familiar narrow bed. She'd slept with Volodya on this bed. How had there ever been room! Lately even in a large bed they'd felt so cramped and got in each other's way. It had been different in the old days . . .

Her heart was filled with a melancholy which again threatened to destroy her peace of mind. But gradually she felt quite calm and reconciled again, like a garden after a violent storm. Maybe the worst torment was over.

Grusha suddenly recollected the arrangement she'd made with Feodoseev.

'Let him come in then,' said Vasya. But she felt reluctant, and rather annoyed that she had to get involved with the Feodoseevs again. Why should it be those mischief-makers, of all people, who'd suffered the same disaster as she had? She asked Grusha about Dora.

'Why, don't you remember her?' Grusha asked in surprise. 'She's that dark, pretty girl. She once did a tambourine dance at the Komsomol celebration.'

Vasya remembered liking her. She was on the Higher Education Commission, and was working amongst the tanners. She was clever, still very young, and she sang well. Poor Mrs Feodoseeva! What a contrast!

Grusha didn't agree with Vasya about Dora at all. 'You have to follow the rules,' she said. 'If the communists tolerate husbands behaving like that, every man would be free to leave his wife and children and run off with younger girls.' She'd heard that they were preparing a case against Dora in the Party.

'That must be Mrs Feodoseeva's doing then,' said Vasya coming to Dora's defence. 'What a repulsive woman she is! There's no law on earth to compel a man to go on living with a wife he doesn't love! You can't make Feodoseev sleep with his wife by force of law. Anyway, she's a trouble-maker, and loathes him!' Vasya got very worked up, and gave vent to her deep hatred of Mrs Feodoseeva.

But as she argued about Mrs Feodoseeva she was thinking all the time of Vladimir, and as she defended Dora she was seeing a white lace parasol and Nina's red lips . . .

Grusha was amazed that Vasya should be so caught up in the Feodoseevs's affairs. 'You'd think they were your closest friends!' she said. 'And to think of the way you used to complain to me about them, and all the problems they caused you! I'd strongly advise you not to get mixed up in this scandal, though it's up to you, of course. Two dogs can fight it out between themselves, so let them sort it out between them . . .'

But Vasya insisted that if they did get up some charge against Dora, she would defend her. Did Mrs Feodoseeva really, in all honesty, imagine that being his legal wife gave her such rights? Because if she did she was wrong, there were other rights too and no laws could ever apply to the rulings of the heart. There was no human being strong enough to go against them, for everyone had their own special needs.

Grusha was ironing the hem of the secretary's dress. She glanced up and peered at Vasya, as if trying to read her thoughts. Vasya frowned. Why did Grusha have to stare at her like that? Wasn't she right? What rules did Grusha want to see imposed on the workings of the heart?

'Who can say?' said Grusha. 'Of course, people's feelings are what count, you're not human without feelings. But just now when I was looking at you, Vasya, I saw how much you were suffering, and how full of resentment you were. And when you were standing up for Feodoseev like that I could have sworn you were thinking about your husband and trying to find excuses for him. That's the only way I can explain it.'

Vasya looked down without replying, and Grusha asked no more questions. She took the dress off the ironing board, shook it, and pulled out the loose threads. It was ready.

'Have you finished?' Vasya enquired, her thoughts far away.

'Yes, that's it now.'

'Well, Grusha, I'd better be off to the Party committee. If Mr Feodoseev should come, tell him to wait, will you?'

'All right,' sighed Grusha.

So a new active phase began in Vasya's life. Before she left for her job at the textile factory she had to consult Stepan Alexeevich, study her instructions and spend several evenings at sessions with skilled workers. Time flew and Vasya was too busy to think much about her feelings. Then there were the Feodoseevs' problems to sort out, and Dora too. In the end, they'd all three come to her with their worries and she couldn't get rid of them.

Feodoseev told her his version of the story. He'd got to know Dora Abramovna through the higher education department. He'd been singing in a choir, and Dora Abramovna had taken a liking to his bass voice and suggested he should take some music lessons; she was a trained musician herself. She'd introduced him to the department, and things had just developed from there.

When his wife got wind of the affair, all hell was let loose. Feodoseev was furious with his wife for her scandal-mongering and for setting Dora Abramovna's friends against her. She was spreading lies that Dora Abramovna was fleecing him for money, and was living off Feodoseev's earnings. In fact it was the other way round. Dora wouldn't take a brass kopek off him, and what was more, she was genuinely concerned about his family, and would willingly have given them her last kopek. She'd always been interested in children, and it was she who had got places for the younger ones in a kindergarten, and got exercise-books and textbooks for the elder child, who was at school. And of course she did all this in such a way that his wife would never know about it.

It was Dora who'd fitted Feodoseev out with a tie and shirt for concerts – but out of sheer spite people were putting the whole thing in a completely different light. Feodoseev's heart bled for Dora. It didn't matter about his reputation, she was the one he was concerned about. What if she had difficulties with the Party, just because of him? It was all his wife's fault for standing in their way . . .

All the time Feodoseev was talking, Vasya was thinking about Vladimir and Nina. This was how they must have tortured themselves as they looked for solutions to their situation. They must have been angry with Vasya in exactly this way for standing between them and their happiness! Feodoseeva should get out of the way. She should stop clinging to the past, preventing present happiness. It was useless anyway, for happiness has its own momentum.

But then, Vasya thought, who was she to talk? Wasn't she still standing in the way, clinging to a past happiness? Feodoseev so obviously adored Dora. He only had to mention her name and he suddenly became a gentler person. Vladimir too changed whenever he mentioned Nina's name . . .

'Dora Abramovna has a heart of gold,' he was saying. 'Everyone in the union thinks highly of her, and the non-Party members can't believe that the Party is considering bringing a case against her. Some of them are positively pleased about it. They say she can come over to their side, that they'll stick by her loyally.'

No sooner had Feodoseev gone than Mrs. Feodoseeva waylaid Vasya, kissing her, ingratiating herself and entreating Vasya to take her side. Vasya disliked the woman greatly at that moment, and angrily shook her away; from that moment on Feodoseeva inveighed against the entire household, pouring abuse indiscriminately on the three of them, Dora, her husband and Vasya.

Vasya arranged to meet Dora at the Party committtee. They found themselves a secluded corner in a room full of typists, working away. The clatter of the typewriters made it easy for them to talk without being overheard.

Dora was wrapped in a shawl to conceal her pregnant stomach. It was she who started talking, not about herself, but about Feodoseev.

She was very concerned about him, she said, she valued him and thought very highly of his talent. He had a remarkable voice – every bit as good as Shalyapin's, it just needed training. That was partly why Dora was pressing him to leave his family and marry her. Then he could throw in his job at the cobbler's workshop and concentrate properly on his singing.

But although Dora lavished praise on Feodoseev, she also complained about his indecisiveness. When he was with her, he was prepared to do anything. No sooner was it all agreed and settled that he would leave his wife and get a divorce, than he'd get home and all of it would go by the board. He just couldn't face it; and they would have to start all over again. Dora had been struggling like this for months, and still he hadn't moved one inch.

A feeling of unease came over Vasya as she listened to Dora. Nina must have talked just like that about Vladimir!

For Dora, the conventions of marriage and divorce were quite superfluous – 'just a lot of mumbo-jumbo' as she said. She was all for free unions, but Mrs Feodoseeva would never leave them in peace unless they actually registered at the Commisariat. So Dora got herself pregnant, to force Feodoseev to get a divorce. She wasn't afraid of becoming a mother, and could manage perfectly well without a husband if she had to.

Had Nina done that too, Vasya wondered? Had she got pregnant to force Vladimir to get a divorce?

As Dora went on talking and pleading for Vasya's sympathy, Vasya became immersed in her own thoughts. Dora saw only the good in Feodoseev. That must be how Nina loved Vladimir; but Vasya was incapable of loving like that. She knew and loved Vladimir's bad sides too. Loving him meant suffering for the bad things about him, wanting to help him to change; maybe this was what had hurt Volodya so much.

'Why does his wife have to cling to him like that?' Dora was asking angrily. 'Did they ever love one another? If so, it must have been a long time ago, because they have absolutely nothing in common now. Does she really know him and appreciate him? Does she really understand his needs?'

It's just the same! thought Vasya. It was like that between me and Vladimir, him not knowing what I wanted and me not knowing what he was thinking. That was why our lives went their separate ways.

'He's a complete stranger to Mrs Feodoseeva, they're different in every way. Their tastes are different, their aspirations are different. She's only clinging to him because he's her husband. She doesn't need him as a person at all; he's not necessary to her,' said Dora.

And asking herself these same questions, Vasya knew, clearly, that she didn't *need* Vladimir as he was now.

'What kind of love is it anyway?' persisted Dora. 'They can't agree on anything, there's nothing but quarrelling and they both go their own ways, with no friendship or trust between them.'

Yes, yes, agreed Vasya silently. No friendship or trust!

'But Feodoseev and I understand each other without having to speak – our minds work so similarly,' said Dora.

That must be how Vladimir and Nina loved one another! There were so many things which Vasya was only slowly beginning to understand, so many new feelings . . .

Although Vasya had much urgent Party work to do before she left for her new job, she didn't neglect the Feodoseevs, and bustled round trying to speed up their divorce, getting Feodoseev reconciled with his friends, exonerating Dora in the eyes of the Party. For some reason that she couldn't have defined, she felt this to be very important indeed.

Vasya was hurrying home from the Party committee. She was to leave for the textile factory next day and her mind was filled with how she would reorganize the work there, carry out the Party's instructions, and how she would make contact with the non-Party members too. For now that the non-Party members' attitudes were often so similar to the communists', they could be firmly relied on. She trusted them to examine facts for themselves and to question everything, for these people didn't take anything simply on trust. She would allocate their jobs to them before she started worrying about their political views.

As Vasya's mind went over these preoccupying questions, her old grief was forgotten. She was no longer conscious of having lost her husband and friend, nor could she even recall very clearly the events of the summer, when she'd been the director's wife.

As she hurried along she realized that she'd not eaten anything since that morning, but the very thought of food made her want to vomit and her head started spinning. What day was it? Could she be ill, or could she be . . . ? There was an unformulated question mark in her mind. Wasn't this the third month that she'd gone without a period? She really ought to go and see her doctor friend, Maria Andreevna, who lived in a nearby street. They'd worked together at one time organizing crêches for communal houses. Maria Andreevna would be able to examine Vasya and tell her whether she was too sick to leave.

Vasya turned into the street, went up to a white door and rang the bell. Maria Andreevna came to the door, delighted to see Vasya.

'What have you come to see me about? Is it on business or do you want some advice?'

Vasya was suddenly overcome with embarrassment and blushed. Maria Andreevna gave her a sharp look, then took her by the arm.

'Come, let's go into my surgery and I'll examine you,' she said. She questioned Vasya about her appetite, her periods and her dizziness, but it was if she knew all the answers in advance. Then she examined her. Vasya didn't enjoy this at all, and felt very awkward; she'd never been examined by a woman doctor before. When she was made to lie on the examination couch she was panic-stricken.

After it was over and she was putting on her clothes again, her hands trembled so much that she was barely able to do up her buttons. Maria Andreevna was standing by the sink in her white coat, carefully washing her hands in soap and water. 'Well, Vasilisa my dear,' she said, breaking the silence. 'I don't know whether to congratulate you or console you, but there's no doubt about it, you're pregnant.'

'Pregnant?' gasped Vasya. Then, involuntarily, the thought of a baby brought a smile to her lips.

'So what do you intend to do?' continued the doctor briskly, drying her hands on an embroidered towel. 'Are you going back to your husband?'

'My husband? Oh no!' Vasya shook her head vehemently. 'No, I'll never go back to him, we've separated for good.'

'So you've separated, have you? Well, it wasn't a very good time for this to happen, was it? How do you think you'll cope, my

dear? Maybe things can still be put right between you, eh? How
are you going to manage all on your own with a child? You're
not so strong either.'

'But I won't be alone,' Vasya interrupted her. 'Tomorrow I'm
leaving for the textile factory. There's a very good cell of workers
there, most of them women, and between us we'll arrange a
crêche. Yes, and I meant to ask you, how did you manage to
re-purchase your crêche from the state? Would you give me some
advice on that?'

So they began to discuss crêches, and subsidies, and dues and the
salaries of professional workers . . . Vasya quite forgot about her
news and it was only as they were saying goodbye that Maria
Andreevna reminded her.

'Now Vasya, you won't overwork, will you? Remember you're
not strong, I can't help worrying about you.'

She gave Vasya lots of advice, telling her the 'do's' and 'don'ts',
which Vasya carefully memorized for the baby's sake.

She walked back along the street, smiling. A baby! How wonderful! She'd be a model mother! After all, it should be possible
to bring up a child in true communist fashion. There was no
reason for women to set up with husbands, in families if it merely
tied them to the cooking and domestic chores. They'd get a
crêche going, and re-purchase a children's hostel. It would be a
demonstration of childrearing to everyone. And as she began to
think about it, Vladimir vanished from her thoughts as though
he had no connection with the baby . . .

When Vasya got home she immediately started packing. Suddenly she came across a box containing Volodya's old letters and
a photograph of him. On top of it was the oblong pink envelope,
Nina Konstantinova's letter. Vasya looked at it, and turned it
over. She knew it would only stir up old and painful associations
and she'd feel chilled by Volodya's lies and deceits, and her own
jealousy. Nevertheless she took the letter and sat down near the
window to read it once more. The light was already fading.

Unfolding the familiar piece of paper, she began to read, line
by line. She felt no melancholy now. The serpent had lost its
venom, and her heart was at peace. Wholly unexpectedly, a feeling
of compassion stirred. She wept for Nina Konstantinova, for the
outraged misery and pain of this poor woman. She remembered
how Nina had wiped away her tears with the tips of her fingers as
she'd left the bandstand. Why should she have had to suffer like

that? What terrible anguish she must have endured! She'd been pregnant too, and had had to get rid of her child. Vasya went to the table, piled Grusha's dressmaking patterns to one side, set some ink in front of her and started writing.

Dear Nina Konstantinovna,

I don't know who you are. I've only seen you once, and on that occasion, quite frankly, I didn't take a great liking to you. But when you left the bandstand and started to cry, I felt I truly understood how unhappy you were and I felt so sorry for you. I've just read again your letter to Vladimir Ivanovich, which I'm returning to you as I was wrong to steal it from him. But I think it's served its purpose well, so please don't be too angry with me.

I've given a lot of thought to your letter, and now that I've re-read it I realize that I don't feel anger or resentment towards you any more. I realize how very much you must have suffered on my account. I've said this to Vladimir and now I'll say it to you; let's stop playing hide and seek with each other.

You must marry Vladimir Ivanovich and become his lawful wife. You're more suited to each other, I'm sure, then we were. I cannot be his wife any longer because our tastes have changed. We're quite different now, quite separate. I don't understand what he thinks any more, and he doesn't understand me. Our life together gives us nothing but misery – it would have been like that even without you. We separated not because you took Vladimir away from me, but because his heart no longer had any love in it for me.

I shall live now as I lived before I was with Vladimir. He's all you have in the world, you have nothing else to live for, and that's always the case when two people really love one another. Vladimir Ivanovich and I had a common-law marriage, so there'll be no need for a divorce. I have no grudge against you, and if I'd known before how deeply you loved each other I would have taken this step long ago. Tell Vladimir Ivanovich that I'm not angry with him and that I shall remain his friend as I have always been. If the need should ever arise, I should be very happy to help you in any way. I used to feel a deep hostility towards you but now that I think I understand things, I'm only sorry about all the tears you must have wept, all your suffering and anxieties.

As one sister to another, I want you to be happy. Give my
regards to Vladimir, and tell him from me to look after his
young wife! I'll give you my new address in case you need it,
and if and when you should write to me, I shall reply. We're not
enemies, you and I. We never intended to cause each other so
much pain.

I wish you much happiness.

Yours, Vasilisa Malygina.

She wrote the address neatly, and putting both letters into an
envelope, she licked it and stuck it down.

It was only then that she finally grasped that this was the end.
No more pain, no more tormenting serpent, no more of the old
gnawing nostalgia. No more Volodya the 'American'. Now he was
just plain Vladimir Ivanovich. When she thought about Vladimir
she saw Nina, and when she thought about Nina she saw Vladimir
there beside her. They'd become as one person for her, inseparable
and indivisible. As one person, they could bring her no more unhappiness.

The old passion had spent itself, burnt itself to ashes, and she
felt at peace with herself. Her mind was calm and clear after the
storm.

* XVI *

She remained standing at the window, admiring the sunset, stormy,
overcast with purple gold-edged clouds. Crows were wheeling
overhead, cawing as they looked for a place to roost, and the air
smelt of dead leaves, mushrooms and damp autumn earth. It was
a sweet, childhood smell, far from the stale enervating air of
Vladimir's house. She breathed deeply, eagerly drinking it in, and
leaning out of the window, she caught sight of Grusha in the yard
below, taking her washing off the line for the night. 'Hey, Grusha!'
Vasya called. 'Come up quickly! I've got some good news to tell
you!'

'I'm just coming!' replied Grusha. When she came in, she threw
the washing on to the bed. 'Well, what's the news then? Have you
got a letter? Is that it?'

'I didn't actually get a letter, but I've just written one, and guess who to.'

'It must be Vladimir Ivanovich,' said Grusha.

'Wrong! Not him but his girl friend, or rather his future wife, Nina Konstantinovna.'

'What did you do that for?' asked Grusha, startled.

'Well, you see, Grusha,' Vasya explained, 'I read a letter that Nina wrote to Vladimir, and I began to feel so sorry for her. She's suffered so much on my account. She even got rid of her baby just because of me, and she ate her heart out. Such needless suffering! We aren't rivals or enemies. If she'd taken Vladimir away from me without loving him, just to get money out of him, of course I would never have forgiven her – I would have hated her. But now that I know about her, why should I hate her? She loves Vladimir Ivanovich deeply, far more than I do; that gives her the right to marry him. Apart from Vladimir, she has nothing to live for – that's what she wrote. "Without you I'm lost," she said. And is Vladimir necessary to me in that way? I've thought about it all so much, Grusha, and I've realized that it's not him I'm wretched about. It would be different if Volodya the American were to come back, but he no longer exists for me. So why should I go on torturing poor Nina, and stand between them. I don't really want to share my life with a director.'

'I agree a director's not for you,' said Grusha firmly. 'It's bad the way so many bosses lose touch with the people and become directors. But we don't have to be too sad about it, Vasilisa; after all, look how many of the old comrades are still with us! And you should see the non-Party members too! I tell you, you'll find more real proletarian communists amongst them now than in the Party itself.'

'Yes, that's true. But although we're gaining strength every day, what about that bunch who long ago traded in their class loyalties for lamps and silk eiderdowns! We just don't talk the same language, that's why I've been asking myself why I should harass Nina and cling to Vladimir when he's neither properly married to me nor really free of me. What good does it do me? It was time to call an end to it, without recriminations. We've all suffered quite enough as it is. It was something I couldn't grasp when I'd just left him, and I kept waiting and hoping for something, I didn't quite know what. I really thought that if Vladimir left me for another woman I'd die without him, and I was in a daze of misery when I first arrived here. I just couldn't see what to do. But as soon as I got back to work on the Party committee there were other people's problems to worry about and the pain gradually went. And now, believe it or not, I honestly don't feel jealous or unhappy any longer. I feel quite calm about it.'

'Well, praise the Lord for that!' said Grusha, hastily crossing herself and glancing at the ikon in the corner. 'So it wasn't for nothing I've been praying all these nights on my knees to the blessed virgin. I begged her to pity a woman in distress and heal our poor Vasilisa!'

Vasya smiled. 'Really, you're incorrigible, Grusha! Do you still believe in those ikons of yours? But you're right all the same, I'm properly healed now. These past months I've been going around in such a state I quite forgot who I was, I forgot the Party and everything was a complete fog. But now I'm better I think how good life is to me and everything seems new and exciting. No more Vladimir now, just the Party. I remember this was how I felt after I'd had typhus and was starting to get better.'

'I only hope you don't fall ill again when that husband of yours starts writing you remorseful letters,' said Grusha.

'No, Grusha,' Vasya shook her head pensively. 'That's not going to happen. I feel as though I've been through a sort of personal revolution. All the grief and reproaches have been removed. We were all three of us fighting each other in a kind of cursed magic circle, and all trying to get out of it. We hated each other and would have gone on hating each other if we hadn't managed to escape. It was when I began to understand how Nina was feeling that I saw my way out of it. I didn't have anything to forgive her for – I was sorry for her, as I would be for my sister. Both of us, as women, went through the same things; she suffered no less than I did, and through no fault of hers, but just because our lives had all become so pointless. As soon as I began to sympathize with her I felt so much better, Grusha.'

'Well, I'm not surprised,' said Grusha. 'That means you definitely don't love him any more, because love always brings unhappiness. As soon as love allows you a glimpse of happiness, grief slips into its shadow. So when there's no more grief left, that can only mean that love is over!'

'That can't be true, Grusha, you must be wrong,' Vasya shook her head. 'I haven't stopped loving Vladimir, he's still very dear to me, it's just that my love for him has changed. There's no more of that old resentment and hatred. I'm glad we once loved each other and were happy together. Why should I be angry with him? Whose fault is it if he doesn't love me now? I'm glad about the past; Vladimir and Nina are like a dear brother and sister to me now. Believe me, Grusha, I mean it! We've been happy, now it's their turn. Everyone has a right to it, as long as it doesn't involve lies and deceit.'

'That's all very true, what you say about deceiving, but it's beyond me how you can think of Nina as a sister! You're becoming quite a philosopher, Vasilisa! You'd better not overdo your philosophizing, or you'll start overdoing the communism too! Of course it's best to forgive Vladimir for Nina, forgive and forget, out of heart out of mind. But there's no need for you to *love* them! You'd do better to keep your love and sympathy for the working people – they really need you now. They're losing confidence, they need spirit and hope, not a lot of Party dogma. Believe me, Vasilisa, I always know what's happening. I may not be in the Party, but I see everything that's going on, and I understand communism just as well as you do.'

'Of course, Grusha, you're one of us, everyone knows that. But how can you go on believing in those ikons of yours? Now, don't be cross with me, stop frowning at me like that! I take it back! I don't want us to argue, because today is a very special day! In fact I feel quite reckless, I'm so happy! And you'll never guess what finally cured me!'

'I simply can't imagine!'

'It was the Feodoseevs!'

'How amazing! Well, in that case I wish them well and I'll forgive that vile Mrs Feodoseeva all her sins!'

They both laughed. 'But I still haven't told you the main news, Grusha,' Vasya went on. 'I've been to the doctor and I'm having a baby!'

'Pregnant!' Grusha clapped her hands excitedly, then spoke more gravely. 'But Vasya, how could you have let your husband touch you? You can't bring up a child without a father! Or do you intend to have an abortion, as everyone seems to be doing these days.'

'Why should I have an abortion? I'm perfectly capable of bringing up a child myself. What do I need a husband for? It's all those fairy stories about fathers! Look at Mrs Feodoseeva, she's got three to look after now Feodoseev has gone off with Dora!'

'But how are you going to raise a child all on your own?'

'What do you mean, all on my own? Everything will be arranged perfectly, and we'll set up a crêche. In fact, I thought of asking you to help us run the crêche. I know how you love children. And soon there'll be a new baby, for all of us!'

'A communist baby!'

'Precisely so!' They both laughed.

'I really must get on with my packing now, Grusha. The train is leaving early tomorrow morning. Tomorrow I'll be starting work and organizing my life properly. Stepan Alexeevich has given me his blessing. I'm so glad to be starting work again, Grusha, you just can't imagine how well I feel!'

She caught Grusha's hands and they whirled around the room like a couple of children, almost knocking over the tailor's dummy, and giggling so loudly that people in the yard below could hear them. 'We must live, Grusha!' shouted Vasya.

Live and work, work and fight, live and love life, like the bees in the lilac, like the birds at the bottom of the garden, like the crickets in the grass!

Three Generations

One morning in the office, amongst a pile of business and personal letters, I came across a thick envelope which caught my attention. Deciding that it must be an article, I opened it immediately. It turned out to be a letter, several pages long. I looked for the signature and was surprised to see that it was from Olga Veselovskaya.

I knew comrade Olga Sergeevna Veselovskaya to be an extremely responsible worker who had an administrative job in one of the major sections of soviet industry. She was not the least bit interested in working amongst women, so I couldn't imagine why she should be writing me this interminably long letter. I glanced at the envelope, and it was only then that I saw the large inscription written in red pencil: 'Strictly Personal'.

For the women who write to me, 'Personal' generally indicates some family crisis. Could it be that same Olga Sergeevna who was caught up in some family drama? It seemed impossible.

There was some urgent current business awaiting my attention and so I couldn't read it immediately, but the long letter and the image of Olga Sergeevna kept coming into my mind.

I remembered my business meetings with her, that dry restrained manner she had with people, and her quite extraordinary, renowned 'unwomanly' efficiency. I recalled that she had a husband, a good man who had once been a worker, a man with a pleasant open face who was generally liked, but much less highly thought of than his wife. He worked under her in the same department, and was younger than her. They were both conscientious people, and whenever I had seen them together their relationship had seemed exceptionally harmonious.

I remembered him saying once, 'Why are you still arguing? Didn't you hear Olga Sergeevna's opinion on the matter?' For him, she obviously represented the highest authority. Then I remembered how Olga Sergeevna's face had changed, losing its rather remote expression and becoming suddenly human, when they had told her once at a conference that her husband had been taken ill (for he was sickly). It was possible that her crisis had to do with his illness, but surely she wouldn't have written at such length about that . . .

I was still working in my office when evening approached, and it was only then that I got around to reading the letter. It began :

I am in a complete quandary. In all the forty-three years of my life I have never been in such a ridiculous position. I'm really in a quandary.

You know me only as a worker, you know my reputation too for being rather pedantic and heavy-handed. So it may be rather difficult for you to imagine that I, at my age, am experiencing a specifically 'female' crisis. And a very commonplace crisis it is too, all the more galling and painful for being so trite and of such music-hall banality.

But I feel that its triteness is only in its superficial aspects, not in its essence. I feel the whole thing is a direct result of the conflict between our everyday life and our political ideas in Russia at the moment; along with everything that is so splendid, there is much that is petty and mean, oppressive and rotten.

At times it sickens me to have to face the things I'm writing to you about, and the very idea that these are not isolated occurrences induces in me a feeling of disgust. But at other times I feel that I am the one who is wrong and that part of me is talking like someone of the old school; maybe my daughter Zhenya and my husband, Ryabkov, are right in pointing out that I still have strong bourgeois prejudices, that I really am distorting the whole picture.

Please help me to get to the bottom of it. I don't know who is right, them or me. If I am wrong, and am indeed merely expressing attitudes instilled in me by my upbringing, then help me to understand things in the light of the new morality.

The letter broke off at this point, and Olga Sergeevna continued her narrative on the next page, in steadier handwriting.

I would like to have come to the point immediately, to tell you the essence of my emotional crisis, but if I recount only the facts without telling you anything of my previous life you would get a distorted picture of things. You might see only the superficial events, without realizing that these are not the real cause of my suffering, which is far more profound and complicated. The facts I can understand, but as for the motives behind them . . .

In short, I'm going to ask you to bear with me and read my letter all the way through. And please remember that I am writing to you as a friend who is looking to you for support.

There were a few blots on the letter, which then resumed on the next page.

Do you remember my mother? She was alive until recently, and to the end was running her mobile library in the province of N. She worked there for the Department of Popular Education. I don't really need to describe my mother to you, as you knew her personally.

Yes, I had known Maria Stepanovna Olshevich and still remembered her well as a typical humanitarian of the 90s, a publisher of popular scientific works, a translator and tireless worker for popular enlightenment. She carried much authority with the liberals of the day, and even the underground activists respected her in their way. She'd in fact given a great deal of financial assistance to the underground, and her circle of acquaintances was large and varied.

Politically she had been closer to the Populists, but she'd never taken an active part in politics. Her passion was for books, libraries and the enlightenment of the peasantry and impoverished city dwellers. All the local organizations, soviet, professional, and Party had come to her funeral a few months ago.

A tall woman, slim and erect, with a lovely tilt to her head and a fine expressive face, she had always inspired a kind of deferential respect, even of fear. She had a dry, clear voice, and spoke briefly and to the point, a cigarette constantly in her mouth. She dressed simply and never followed fashion; but she had the beautiful, well-cared-for hands of a lady, and on her fourth finger she wore a thick gold ring set with a dark ruby.

Olga Sergeevna continued :

But what you may not have known is that when my mother was young she too had an emotional crisis. After it was over she developed a rigid moral code in matters of love, and deep down she mercilessly condemned anyone who did not adhere to this code – even despised them. My mother was a good person, and progressive in her attitudes, but in matters that concerned sexual morality she was severe and pitiless.

The disagreements between my mother and myself were not based on political differences, as you might suppose, but specifically on our differing interpretations of the 'necessary' and the 'possible' as far as my personal crises were concerned.

My mother married a soldier, for love, and against her parents' wishes. She lived the provincial life of a regimental officer's lady, and, according to her, was quite happy with this for some time. She had two sons, was regarded as a model wife and mother, and her husband idolized her.

But gradually she began to feel oppressed by this passive and rather prosperous life. You know what an inexhaustible source of energy my mother was. She had received a good education, at least for those days, she had read a lot, been abroad and corresponded with Tolstoy. I'm sure you can imagine that a regimental commander could not really satisfy her needs.

Fate willed her to meet the *zemstvo* doctor, Sergei Ivanovich Veselovsky. Sergei Ivanovich, my father, was a character straight out of Chekhov, with all the same vague idealism. He was a man constantly aspiring to something, to the unknown, with a fondness for eating and good living, greatly perplexed when faced with evil and injustice. He was handsome and robust, read the same books as my mother, talked emotionally about the peasants and the *zemstvo,* grieved for the 'unenlightened peasantry' and had platonic dreams of establishing libraries, schools and general enlightenment throughout Russia.

It all turned out as one might have expected. One hot summer evening when the regimental commander was away on army manoeuvres, my mother found herself in the arms of my future father. A book, *Mobile Libraries in New Zealand,* lay beside them unread, and was buried in the grass . . .

My father was apparently not too anxious to regard the poetic idyll of that summer evening as an event which warranted any radical change in his life. He valued his freedom, and moreover he had at the time a housekeeper, a young peasant widow. But my mother, as I've already told you, had her own special rules on sexual morality, and as she told me later, she never tried to resist her love for my father since, for her, love had more rights than had conjugal obligations. Love for her was something great and sacred, she was incapable of toying with emotions and would have considered this ignoble. In Sergei Ivanovich, my mother found, to use her own words, everything that her heart, soul and mind were seeking – a man she loved passionately, a person she respected, and a friend with whom she could embark on work, hand in hand, on the great task of enlightenment.

It only remained for her to annul her union with the colonel. She remained impervious to the prospect of scandal; she knew clearly that she wanted to build a new life, and, more importantly, one she had freely chosen. She asked Sergei Ivanovich to meet her one morning; they met in the lime grove, where, to the chirruping of crickets, she read him her brief resolute letter to her husband – a letter which concealed nothing and which asked him for a divorce.

Sergei Ivanovich was seriously taken aback by this. He had not anticipated such a swift reaction. I think he mumbled something to the effect that my mother should guard her reputation, and even spoke to her of her maternal obligations to her sons. But my mother, although quite flabbergasted by his words, was inexorable, and as at that time she was enchantingly pretty and my father was still in amorous mood, the conversation ended in more kisses, which strengthened my mother's resolve to bring everything into the open immediately.

But it didn't prove easy. The poor colonel, who was passionately in love with my mother, was utterly demented with grief and anger. One moment he would hurl reproaches at his wife, threatening to kill her, himself and the scoundrel of a doctor; the next moment he would lapse into a penitent mood and implore his wife to stay, even if only as a mother and housekeeper.

My mother felt very sorry for him, but her love for her hero with the compatible soul was more powerful than her pity, and, convinced that no argument would prevail on her husband, she collected her things, her money and her papers, kissed her sons, and left the colonel without so much as a word of farewell.

For a long time the province resounded with this scandal. The liberals sided with my mother and regarded the act of leaving her soldier husband for a *zemstvo* doctor as some kind of protest against the régime. Somebody even dedicated some

verses to her in the local newspaper, and somebody else
proposed a toast at a *zemstvo* dinner to those heroic women
who cross the threshold of conventional marriage to join those
toiling for the welfare of the people . . .

Mother began to live quite openly with Sergei Ivanovich.
And immediately she set about realizing her cherished scheme
– one about which my Chekhovian hero of a father also waxed
lyrical – that of establishing a mobile library. The scheme
demanded an enormous amount of effort and energy, for of
course these were the most savage years of the Reaction, after
the assassination of Alexander II.

But with characteristic persistence, my mother confronted
the *zemstvo* leaders as well as the local governors, travelled
to St Petersburg, established sympathetic contacts, argued her
case and stood her ground. But just when the scheme was close
to realization, my mother was arrested, along with the poor
perplexed and frightened Sergei Ivanovich, and they were
sent into exile – not a very remote place. It was there that I was
born.

My mother lost none of her old fighting spirit even in exile,
where she formed a self-education circle, taught, laid the basis
for libraries and generally spread enlightenment.

My father languished, put on weight and went to seed.
But on their return from exile he found he had gained himself
a reputation as a revolutionary, and he fell in with the *zemstvo*
activists. My mother meanwhile busied herself with renewed
enthusiasm in spreading enlightenment throughout the district,
and for a while my parents' life seems to have followed a
well-defined and untroubled path.

But then an unpleasant little incident cropped up; my
mother caught her balding but still attractive husband making a
totally unambiguous proposition to the farm girl, Arisha.
Father tried to make excuses, but the situation proved to be
more serious than he had imagined; Arisha was pregnant.

Without any lengthy discussions, my mother immediately
packed her things and, taking me with her, moved to the
district capital, leaving my father a business-like letter without
any reproaches or complaints.

She insisted, amongst other things, that he provide for
Arisha's child, and that he curb his consumption of alcohol,
of which he was becoming increasingly fond.

All these details I learnt from my mother much later, she hoping that by being frank about herself she could persuade me onto the path of duty.

I well remember mother's enormous self-control in bearing her grief at that time. Not once did I see her in tears, even though according to her she never stopped loving Sergei Ivanovich, and was faithful to him for the rest of her life. In the district capital she set about organizing a publishing house which brought out popular scientific books and which bore her name. I was with her constantly. From my earliest childhood I was part of her circle of people involved in revolutionary ideas and activities, and as an adolescent I was already reading the underground press and was quite familiar with 'illegals' and 'illegal' activities. We lived very modestly, even ascetically. Our home was always dominated by an atmosphere of work, with ideas and new plans constantly hovering in the air. I was not even sixteen when I was first arrested, something which made my mother very proud.

But it was at that point that our ideological paths began to diverge. I joined the Marxists while she remained a Populist. Working in the ranks of the revolutionary movement, I got to know an active and subsequently prominent member of the Union of Struggle. He was much older than I, and politically experienced. It was under his influence that I became a Marxist, and later a staunch Bolshevik.

We became sexually involved, although we refused, on principle, to get married. My mother tut-tutted at first, saying that I was much too young, that I should have waited, and that I must have some of my father's traits, which did not augur well for constancy in love. But eventually she became reconciled to the situation, and we moved in with her and continued our work. However, as the man I was living with was an 'illegal', we all ended up being arrested. Mother was defended by her friends, but I went into exile with my 'husband'.

I'm afraid you must be bored with this interminable preamble, but without it you won't be able to make any sense of my present dilemma. You must remember and understand that I am the daughter and pupil of Maria Stepanovna herself! And no amount of logic will obliterate those things which you absorb in childhood and assimilate in youth. So please have a little patience and go on reading my letter, for I'm coming now to the crisis of the second generation!

I managed to escape from exile, although my 'husband' had to stay behind. I found my way to St Petersburg, where, in order to cover my tracks, some friends found me accommodation as a governess in the house of a prosperous engineer called M.

The house was furnished lavishly – they lived comfortably. People who came to the house were interested in politics in the same way as they were interested in the Arts theatre or the paintings of Vrubel, that fashionable and decadent painter of the nineteenth century. For them, politics was merely an entertaining subject for drawing room conversation, although in his student days M had been a Marxist.

I was totally unfamiliar with this world, which I found remote and deeply alien to me. It was during my first evening there that I confronted my host (on the question of Bernsteinism, as far as I can remember) with a passionate enthusiasm that was wholly inappropriate to the atmosphere of the drawing room. And then I spent the entire night tormented and infuriated by my own lack of restraint.

I was particularly incensed for some reason by M's ironic tender glances at me. There was something about the man that irritated me the moment I had set eyes on him. But although he struck me as an utterly unsympathetic and unprincipled character, nevertheless I wanted passionately to convince him that it was we Marxists who were right; I wanted to make him change his mind.

His wife was a fragile doll of a woman, dressed up in lace and furs, who had somehow managed to produce five sturdy children. She followed her husband everywhere, watching him with adoring eyes, laughingly assuring people that despite all the rules, she found the longer she lived with him the more in love with him she was!

I was exasperated by this atmosphere of cosiness, this rather too ostentatious family happiness. M's consideration for his pretty wife, and his perpetual anxieties about her health drove me to fury, and I would deliberately make spiteful and insulting remarks about prosperous liberals, smug petit-bourgeois lives and philistine crassness. I would talk about life in exile, and reduce the nervous Lydia Andreevna, M's wife, to hysterical tears.

'Why did you do that?' M would reproach me afterwards, with a look of sad, tender reproof.

I sometimes fancied that I hated them both so much that I was even prepared to let drop some sort of careless remark, so that police intervention might disrupt their blissful serenity. But I could not move out of their house, for it served not only as refuge for me but also as a convenient conspiratorial meeting place. Whenever I mentioned to my comrades the possibility of moving, they would get angry, and simply couldn't understand my reasons for wanting to do so.

'Why do you have anything to do with them if you feel that way,' they would say. 'You should just keep out of their way.'

But that was quite inconceivable. Although I was aware how much I loathed M's handsome self-satisfied figure, his slightly guttural voice and his careless gait, I would nevertheless be on edge if I did not see him for a day or two. I was mortified that I should be so superfluous, such a stranger in their home, and the slightest negligence towards me on his part caused me acute misery.

But every time we did meet we would inevitably get into an argument, arguing until we were quite hoarse, shouting and cursing at one another, so that an observer might have supposed that we really hated each other. But then sometimes in the middle of one of these arguments our eyes would meet, and these glances had their own special vocabulary, one which I was afraid to understand or interpret . . .

Then, on one occasion, when Party business had kept me out of town longer than I had anticipated, I did not return until late at night. M opened the door to me.

'So you've come back at last!' he said. 'I'd already lost all hope that you would.' And before I knew it I found myself in his arms, overwhelmed by his violent kisses.

It was strange. I wasn't at all surprised by this and had long been expecting it to happen.

At dawn I went back to my room and he spent the rest of the night in his study where he always slept whenever he had to work late.

The following evening there were guests, and we began arguing again, passionately, implacably. Once again it seemed that we were enemies. But when the guests had left, M proposed that I take a ride with him to the islands (it was

spring, and a white St Petersburg night). His wife insisted
laughingly that I go with him – it struck her as rather amusing,
and she would never have deigned to be jealous of me.

My life was gradually becoming very complicated. It was a
difficult time for the Party, and I was up to my eyes in work
and political anxieties. Like a coward, I kept putting off the
moment when I would have to bring matters to a head with M.
I excused myself by saying that I had no time, and waited for
the imminent departure of M's wife to the south with the
children. And do you know, however unlikely this might seem
to you, it was at this time that I began to think especially
lovingly of my friend and husband in exile, and took active steps
to get him released?

If you had asked me then whom I loved I would
unhesitatingly have replied my husband, my friend. But if that
had been conditional on leaving M, then I would sooner have
died. M was a stranger to me, and yet oddly similar too. I hated
the way he looked at me, I hated his habits and his lifestyle,
but as a person I loved him desperately, for all his weaknesses
and imperfections, for all those qualities which were so
opposed to everything I valued and loved in people. Our love
brought neither of us any happiness, yet neither of us could
contemplate parting.

I was amazed, and still am, by what it was that attracted me
to M. Even in those days I was not at all pretty, I had no idea
how to dress well, and no desire to either; I was austere and
'unfeminine'. Yet I knew that M loved me in a way that he
had never loved his pretty and adoring wife.

We spent the summer alone in the house together, a strange
and agonizing summer, full of conflicting emotions for both of us.
Neither of us had a moment's happiness, yet neither was afraid
to reveal to the other how unhappy we were, and in some
strange way this brought us closer together.

Then as autumn approached I discovered that I was pregnant.
Maybe I should have terminated the pregnancy, but neither
of us would have entertained such an idea. I left for my
mother's . . .

Olga Sergeevna's letter broke off at this point. It had obviously
been written at different times. It continued, in shaky pencilled
handwriting, on an office form.

Immediately I arrived at my mother's, I told her everything.
I told her of my misery, my duplicity and the feelings which, in
their different ways, were tormenting me and M as well : and
of his love both for me and for his wife.

When mother had heard me out she sat for a long time in her
bedroom in silence, lost in thought and puffing at a cigarette.

Then, next morning, she came into my room, and sitting
down on the bed, announced firmly : 'It's quite clear that you
love M. The first thing you must do is to write to Konstantin !'
(That was my husband).

'But what am I going to write to him?'

'What an absurd question ! Why, that you're in love with
someone else of course. You can't leave him with any illusions
about the situation, and any thought of sparing his feelings
would be quite misplaced – it would only create more misery
later on.'

'But I don't want to spare his feelings. I love Konstantin,
I've never stopped loving him.'

'How could you have fallen in love with another man if
you hadn't stopped loving him?' asked my mother, greatly
perplexed. 'You're talking a lot of nonsense.'

'No, it's not nonsense at all. It's exactly that which is causing
all this misery.'

I attempted to explain to mother once again the two emotions
which I felt simultaneously – my deep love for Konstantin,
my emotional rapport with him, and my wild attraction for M,
whom as a person I could neither love nor respect. But
mother simply didn't understand.

'Well, if it's only a physical attraction that you feel for M,
and it's Konstantin whom you love and respect, then you'd
better pull yourself together and leave M.'

'But that's the problem, mother. It's not just physical attraction
I feel for M, it's love too, a different kind of love. If someone
told me that M was in danger, I'd give my life to save him,
but if I was told to die for Konstantin I'd refuse. And yet it's
Konstantin I love and need emotionally, and without him my
life would be cold and empty, whereas I just don't love and
respect M in that way.'

'What a lot of rubbish !' said my mother angrily. But she was
rapidly becoming confused, first demanding that I write
immediately to Konstantin and break with him, then telling me

to leave M. I felt for the first time in my life that I'd made a mistake in going to her for support. Our chief disagreement lay in my mother's insistence that I break with one or other of them, whereas I instinctively wanted to keep both Konstantin and M. This decision seemed to me the more correct one, more humane and more appropriate to the underlying truth of the situation.

The outcome of it all was that I wrote to Konstantin telling him everything, not only the facts of the situation, but my anxieties about it as well, my doubts and my divided feelings. At first I got only a brief reply from him in which he said that he would have to assimilate things and come to terms with the situation before he could reply properly. But even these few lines were filled with a warmth that immediately told me that Konstantin, unlike my mother, would understand.

And indeed Konstantin did finally understand. Far away from me, in his place of exile, he lived through all my anxieties, my conflicting emotions, and came to accept me as I was. He resigned himself to the inevitable and managed to assert his claims on that part of me which still reached out to him and could not live without him. As far as I was concerned the matter had been partially resolved.

But my mother was still waiting for some decision to be made. She found it galling that I should receive letters from M (in her name!) as well as letters from Konstantin, and that both made me happy.

It was at this point that she began to tell me about her own 'crisis of the heart', to try and force me to make some decision. She was distressed by what she saw as my cowardice and lack of will-power.

'In every other way you are so strong, so persistent and fearless. I simply cannot understand why love should make you so cowardly. I wonder if you inherited that from your father?' my mother mused aloud. She just could not accept that a decision had already been made – everything had been brought out into the open and we were all trying to accept each other as we were.

'So what about M's wife then? Are you going to tell her everything too, and make her "accept" the situation too?'

'No, I'm afraid that she doesn't really come into this, and we can't tell her anything. But you see, M has never been at all emotionally close to her. He loved her, and still does, as he would some fragile toy, and his love for me has robbed her of nothing.'

At this, mother lost her temper and told me that we were nothing but crass philistines, that these four-way marriages might well flourish in ultra-decadent Paris, but that sooner or later I was going to have to choose.

In the spring my baby was born, a little girl. M came to stay with us and those few weeks in mother's house were possibly the happiest of my life. It was strange the way that mother and M immediately established a much warmer relationship than had ever existed between her and Konstantin. By the time M had left, my mother had decided quite positively that the choice was obvious : I had to stay with the father of my child.

But strangely enough, the more mother took M's side, the more sharply I became aware of how deeply lonely I was without Konstantin. It was as if mother and M were in one camp and Konstantin and I were in the other. I suppose that ideologically this was indeed the case – my mother, the humanitarian and Populist, was on the same side as the representative of the liberal bourgeoisie, while Konstantin and I were in the camp of the proletariat.

Then another arrest and another period of exile effectively postponed the whole issue. My little girl lived with her grandmother and I continued to write both to M and Konstantin, until eventually Konstantin and I had the good fortune to meet in exile.

To my mother's horror we started living with each other again, and we did so without dramatics or scenes of forgiveness. We lived with each other quite naturally and happily, as two people who are emotionally at one with each other. It was then that my mother in her heart of hearts began to reject me, writing me letters filled with reproaches, sadness and the most profound resentment, taking M's side, saying that I was destroying the man I loved out of a sense of mere compassion.

M for his part delivered several ultimatums to me and then abruptly broke off all relations, and I remained with Konstantin.

The springtime of liberalism came around, with banquets held under the benevolent eye of Svyatopolk-Mirsky. We returned from exile, and fate once more brought me to St Petersburg. A meeting with M was inevitable, and I will not conceal from you the fact that I greatly desired and actively sought such a meeting.

When we did meet it was as if we had never parted. Everything started again, all the agony, all the joy, all the doubts, our feelings of mutual isolation and the power of our mutual attraction.

But I feared the power of our feelings all the more now that M, carried away by this renewed outburst of passion, was prepared to leave his wife, insisting that we make public our liaison and get married. More than ever before I felt how emotionally alien we were from each other. The political struggle was flaring up and the parties were now more sharply divided than ever, clearly defining their positions. What had been a merely theoretical argument three years ago now became a vital platform for action. M had not even progressed as far as a liberationist position, and we were literally speaking different languages.

I despised myself every time we met and pined desperately when we were apart, while M hated my work, despised the Bolsheviks and longed to possess me 'for ever and always'. I loathed the petit-bourgeois in him, attacked him for his bourgeois liberalism, but lacked the strength to tear him from my heart. There was something strangely maternal about my feelings for him at that time – I was sorry for him, I always felt that he was maligning himself, that I had to help him understand himself, and that I could not just abandon him at the political crossroads . . .

This agony went on for several months, until unexpectedly Konstantin arrived. This time my confession caused him great pain, and his feelings of jealousy were only too evident. Nevertheless, we started living together, as 'friends'. This was more than M could endure, and he flew into a towering rage, refusing to believe that we weren't sleeping together, demanding that I leave Konstantin, and all but leaving his wife himself. In short, every day brought some new painful incident.

Eventually something absolutely absurd occurred. M burst into our flat, yelling obscenities at Konstantin and demanding that I leave with him there and then, otherwise everything would be over between us.

I didn't go. We parted as enemies. Konstantin and I had an unbearably difficult time after that; he saw that I was unhappy because of his own jealous feelings, but he was unable to help me. For the first and only time in my life (although at the moment I'm experiencing something rather similar) I could not devote myself to my work. Everything was submerged beneath my unhappiness.

At this point my mother arrived, summoned by M's despairing letters. She came with my daughter, and with her own uncompromising demand that I stop prevaricating and come to a decision.

'But I made up my mind long ago, mother,' I protested.

'Well, in that case, stop living with him then' (she meant Konstantin). 'You say that you are no longer his wife and I believe you, but why all the pretence? Why are you torturing M like this?

'No mother, you're wrong, I'm going to stay with Konstantin.'

But she just closed her ears to this. She knew from M's letters of the events of the past months. I had written to her too, describing my hesitations and anxieties.

'You love M,' she repeated stubbornly, 'and love has its own laws. You're just cluttering them up with a lot of idiotic intellectual logic. You mustn't break your heart, you must be courageous in your love and break down all obstacles, even your political differences with him. You can make a Marxist out of M. He loves you so much that he'd do anything for you, and besides, you're much stronger than he is.'

But mother's advice only had the opposite effect on me, and I now felt even more acutely that I must not and could not join my life with M's. I knew now that this would mean utter spiritual bankruptcy. Mother arranged a meeting with M and tried to reconcile us, in the presence of our child, but with all the hypocrisy and misery of this meeting, it came to nothing.

Then 1905 was upon us – that historic year – and events swept everybody up so inexorably that people's private lives retreated into insignificance. My petty griefs were submerged in the ocean of historical events as the revolution raged about us. I left for south Russia, Konstantin went abroad and mother hurried off to her estate in the provinces. M stayed on to lead one of the liberal 'unions'.

We worked and hoped, we fretted and argued. We struggled. And then the Reaction set in, once more leaving us with no time to think about ourselves.

In the autumn of 1908, I met M again, quite by chance, in a god-forsaken little factory town. The post-1905 Reaction had intensified and the revolution was now crushed. M had put aside all his temporary radicalism of 1905 and had speedily risen in the world of industrial finance. He had become an important person, whose arrival in any town would be noted in the provincial newspapers.

I knew he was in the same town, and the knowledge troubled me, as it had done in the old days, and prevented me from getting on with my work. I avoided him and didn't want another meeting with him.

But then the police got on to me. My friends warned me that I should get away immediately and find some safe refuge, if only until morning, not so much for myself personally as for the papers which I had on me and which I didn't want to destroy. A cunning idea occurred to me. Why should I not go to M's place? I would certainly be in no danger in his factory flat, where he was living as a guest of honour.

And so I went to him. A footman announced my arrival (I used my old surname), and M came out. He looked genuinely pleased to see me. But when we were alone and I told him my reason for coming, he was visibly shaken. His look now changed to one of obvious hostility and lost all traces of his old affection for me. As we stood looking at each other like two complete strangers, both of us must have been wondering in amazement how it was that once we had loved each other so passionately, suffered so intensely, nearly died without each other. I felt that this was some distant relative of M's standing in front of me, not M himself. In his appearance there was some remote resemblance to the man I had once loved, but in general he now appeared to me as some totally uninteresting stranger.

I bitterly regretted having come, but I decided to go through with it for the sake of the documents, however much my bourgeois self cursed and shrunk from the task. He could be useful to me, and besides, it might make him lose a bit of weight! He, for his part, gave me courteously to understand how exceedingly inconvenient my presence there was for him, whilst I pretended not to understand what he was talking about and even invoked the rights of our old friendship.

So he was left with no alternative but to let me stay the

night. My God, I can well imagine how badly M slept that night!
I slept excellently, however, utterly unaffected by the
knowledge that sleeping (or more likely not sleeping) two rooms
from mine was the man whose footsteps, whose laughter,
whose fleeting glances had never failed in the past to induce in
me a burning wave of passion, whose presence I had always
sensed even from the other end of the house.

It was that night that I finally realized that our love was
dead and buried. All that was left behind was emptiness and our
little girl, about whom M had not even asked. Next day we
took leave of each other coldly, without expressing any desire
to see each other again. The past was buried and forgotten.

But the curious and incomprehensible thing was that shortly
afterwards I met Konstantin, whom I had not seen for a very
long time. We had been working in different parts of Russia.
And do you know, I suddenly felt quite extraordinarily remote
from him too, and began to regard him in a totally new light.
It was as though everything we had experienced in those
hectic years of the first revolution had left its mark, and had
completely obliterated all traces of our old familiar selves.
We now disagreed in our interpretation of events, our approach
to the tasks of the moment, and we differed even in our vision
of the future.

Konstantin had had a difficult time, and had fallen out with
the Party. There had been troubles of a semi-personal, semi-
political nature, which had left marks of bitterness and
pessimism. He no longer argued with his old passionate faith
in the revolution, and was convinced that for many years to
come there would be an inevitable period of stagnation. With a
passion coloured by his own feelings of personal resentment,
he pointed out all our mistakes. He had now adopted a
position of cautious watchfulness, and both his words and
gestures were those of a man grown weary in battle, who,
without admitting it to himself, was unconsciously withdrawing
from the political movement to find himself some calm refuge.

I, on the other hand, was filled with renewed energy, for
unlike him I had been stirred and inspired by the revolution.
I felt I had matured emotionally and had grown stronger, and
that now I would truly be able to work to the limits of my
ability. Though Konstantin and I were affectionate when we
met, and we planned to work together once more, it was not

long before I realized how fundamentally estranged and remote
we had become. When the opportunity presented itself to me
to go abroad (illegally of course) I resolved to go to pursue
my chemistry studies, which had been interrupted by Party work.

I never met Konstantin again, and he gradually moved away
from us altogether. When the war broke out he became a
defensist, and worked as a teacher in a secondary school. He
actively sabotaged the power of the soviets, and as far as I
know he died while participating in one of the White Guard
conspiracies.

M managed to leave the country just in time to avoid the
'punishing hand of the proletariat'. but for me both these men
had long been dead by that time, and their fates no longer
much concerned me.

But you must be wondering as you read this unconscionably
long autobiography of mine, where on earth the crisis is in all
this. These are all past experiences, long buried in oblivion.
What exactly is her problem? – you must be thinking.

I felt that if you were to understand my present unhappiness
you ought to know a little about what sort of person I was.
My story should show you, if nothing else, that my female
instincts are no less strong than anyone else's, and that I do have
some understanding of the complexities of the human heart.
But for all my tolerance, I am utterly unable to deal with the
situation which has just arisen with my daughter.

As I mentioned before, I occasionally console myself with the
thought that, just as my mother, Maria Stepanovna, was
unable to understand me so I do not understand Zhenya. But
in general the whole business strikes me as so fundamentally
trite and prurient that I just sink into a complete state of
lethargy. Please help me to make sense of it, even be critical of
me if necessary. For the problem may simply be that I am
behind the times, and the new style of our lives has bred a new
psychology which is unfamiliar to me.

I cannot write any more today. If you don't mind, I think
I'll come and see you. Now that you know something of my
past, I shall more easily be able to describe the problem
simply and concisely. Will you ring me and tell me when you'll
be on your own? Late evenings are best for me. I shall await
your call. Comradely gretings to you,

from Olga Sergeevna

A few days later, Olga Sergeevna came to see me at the agreed time, late in the evening. I noticed immediately how drawn she looked and the troubled expression in her eyes. But it was with a new interest that I looked at this modestly dressed woman, with neatly arranged hair, who was always so quietly self-possessed. There was an undeniable charm about her, the charm of a fully integrated personality. Nevertheless, looking at her as we discussed recent political matters, I just couldn't reconcile the image of this highly placed worker and industrial organizer with the woman who had written me her confession.

'But now let's talk about my problem, shall we,' said Olga Sergeevna, interrupting herself in that dry clear voice of hers which reminded me of her mother's compelling voice. 'The problem is my daughter, Zhenya. I'd like you to have a word with her. It may well be that there is something I just don't understand, and that this is just the inevitable crisis between the generations.

'But it may be something else; possibly Zhenya really has been corrupted by the abnormal conditions of her upbringing. Even as a very little girl she was being carted from one place to another, with her grandmother, with me, with friends. Over the past few years she's lived in a factory, fully involved in factory life, she's gone to work at the Front, taken part in the recent production drive, and naturally she's experienced many things which in the past girls of her age would only have heard about. Perhaps this is all as it should be, and one just has to face it, but on the other hand . . .

'Oh if only you knew how utterly confused I've been these last few weeks – I just don't know what's right and what's wrong! It used to make me so happy that Zhenya was so unprejudiced and that she faced up to life so boldly; she could extricate herself from any sort of practical difficulty, she was not intellectually equivocal, she was honest to the point of naïvety, it often seemed to me, and now suddenly . . .

'Well, briefly the facts are these. You know that when I was studying abroad I met Comrade Ryabkov whom I nursed back to health in Davos. Since that time we have been living as man and wife. Of course, I'm considerably older than he is, and you might say he was my pupil, but in all these seven years together we've been very happy. When we returned together in 1917 we both helped to establish the power of the soviets.

'You know what a sunny disposition Comrade Ryabkov has –

he's a true proletarian by temperament and a totally uncompromising person by nature. I don't need to tell you what kind of a worker he is either, everybody knows about that. I thought there was no cloud in our relationship and that everything was happy and simple between us.

'Last year when we settled in Moscow I decided Zhenya should live with us. She's a Party worker as you know, although she's only just twenty. She's a tireless, passionate girl – just like her grandmother. And she has a good reputation in her district.

'You know our housing allocation; one room for three people. We're cramped but that's unavoidable in the present circumstances, and besides we're very rarely at home, especially me. I am frequently out of town visiting factories. When, after such a long separation, Zhenya did move in with us, she immediately established a close relationship with us. It was exceptionally friendly. I didn't feel at all like her mother, and just being with her made me feel young. Her energy, her laughter, and her youthful self-confidence were so infectious.

'Comrade Ryabkov got on with her splendidly too, and I was delighted, as I had feared that they wouldn't take to each other. But Zhenya and Andrei became excellent comrades, and I would send them off together to the theatre, or to meetings and public conferences. We lived together, amicably and harmoniously, and what pleased me most of all was that Andrei became so much more cheerful and fell ill less often.

'That was all fine until . . . until something happened which changed everything . . .'

Olga Sergeevna broke off suddenly, as if it was too painful for her to continue. I waited, while Olga Sergeevna looked over my shoulder out of the window.

'Well, Olga Sergeevna,' I said at last, 'I would suspect that what happened is distressing but inevitable – Zhenya and Comrade Ryabkov slept together. But, come on, what's so dreadful and sordid about that? You really must try to understand that sort of thing.'

'Oh, but it's not that! It's not that at all!' Olga Sergeevna interrupted me hastily. 'No, it's just that afterwards I felt I could suddenly see into his and Zhenya's minds . . .'

'And what did you see there?'

'Oh, it was a kind of heartlessness which I found utterly incomprehensible, a calm confidence in their own rights in the matter

– there was something cold and rational about it, a kind of cynicism. You see, there's no love involved, no passion or regrets, nor any desire to end the situation. It's as if everything is just as it should be, and it's only me who doesn't understand and is behind the times.

'Sometimes their behaviour strikes me as the most utterly contemptible moral laxity and incomprehensible promiscuity, but then I'm assailed by doubts and wonder if it really is me who is behind the times. After all, my mother didn't understand my emotional crisis. And so that's why I'm asking you to help me to make sense of things.'

Olga Sergeevna then told me that her daughter had come to see her at work and had asked her mother for a ten minute interview because, as she said, 'there's no other way of getting hold of you, mother.'

Very calmly, and without preamble, she had informed her mother that she had all the symptoms of being pregnant. Olga Sergeevna had been utterly aghast at this, and involuntarily exclaimed 'But by whom?'

'I don't know,' Zhenya had replied. Her mother had concluded that she did not want to tell her, but something about this news had devastated her.

Zhenya asked her mother's advice on how to arrange an abortion (the new abortion law had just come into effect), and wanted the papers to take to the appropriate department. She didn't want a baby, she didn't have time for one.

Olga Sergeevna hadn't told her husband of Zhenya's news, as she regarded this as Zhenya's personal affair, and she could always tell him herself if she wanted to. But there was something, some unconscious anxiety about the whole thing, which preyed on Olga Sergeevna's mind. Doubts began to stir in her, and details of their life together started taking on a wholly different light.

Olga Sergeevna despised herself for these thoughts and tried to drive them from her mind, but they persisted and prevented her from getting on with her work. And they persisted so obstinately that one evening in the middle of a conference she pretended to be unwell, went home – and there she had found her daughter and her husband in each other's arms.

'You know, it wasn't so much the facts of the case which stunned me at the time, it was what happened afterwards. Andrei simply grabbed his hat and walked out, and when I blurted out to

Zhenya "But why did you tell me that you didn't know by whom you were pregnant?" she replied quite calmly: "I'll say again what I said then – I don't know whose baby it is. It might be Andrei and it might be the other one." '

' "What do you mean, the other one?" '

' "Well, these past few months I've been involved with another man, nobody you know." '

'Can you understand how flabbergasted I was at this news? Zhenya then told me that even when she was taking parcels to the Front she was already having sexual relationships. But the thing I found most bewildering and shocking was that she declared quite openly that she did not love anyone and had never done so.'

' "But why did you sleep with men then? Is it because you're really so attracted to them physically? You're still so young, why, it's not normal at your age!" '

' "How can I put it, mother? For a long time I was really just physically attracted to men, as you probably understand the term anyway. That is, until I met this other man, the one I've been involved with over the past few months, although it's all over now. But I liked the men I slept with, and they liked me. That way it's simple, and it doesn't tie you to anything.

"I can't understand what you're so upset about, mother. It would be different if I was prostituting myself or being raped. But this is something I do quite voluntarily, of my own free will. We stay together as long as we get on with each other, and when we no longer do, we just part company and nobody gets hurt. Of course, I'm going to lose two or three weeks' work because of this abortion, which is a pity, but that's my own fault and next time I'll take the proper precautions."

When Olga Sergeevna asked her how, after everything she'd said, she could have two relationships at the same time, and why she should want to anyway, since she did not love anyone, Zhenya replied that it had been a coincidence. The other man attracted her emotionally, but treated her like a baby, and refused to take her seriously, which had infuriated her. It was her feelings of outrage that had led her to take up with Andrei, whom she felt to be a kindred spirit, and whom she loved as a friend and with whom she always felt happy and comfortable.

'And do they know about each other?' Olga Sergeevna had asked her.

'Yes, of course. I don't see that I have anything to conceal from them. They don't have to sleep with me if they don't like it. I have my own life to live and Andrei doesn't mind,' she had replied. 'Oh, the other man got angry about it and started to give me ultimatums, but of course he came round in the end. Anyway, I've left him now. I lost interest in him, he was so crude, I really don't like that sort of person.'

Olga Sergeevna had then tried to point out how unacceptable this frivolous attitude to sexual relationships was – frivolous about life, and about people in general.

But Zhenya had argued back, saying 'Look, mother, you say that my behaviour is shabby, that you shouldn't sleep with people you don't love, and that my cynicism is driving you to despair. But just tell me honestly, if I was a boy, your twenty-year-old son, who had been at the Front and had generally led an independent life, would you be so horrified to hear that he had been sleeping with women he liked? I don't mean with prostitutes he'd bought, or with little girls he'd seduced, because I agree that *is* shabby, but with women he liked and who liked him too. Would that really horrify you so much? Admit it, it wouldn't, would it? So why are you in such a state of despair about what you describe as my immorality? I assure you, I'm exactly the same sort of person, and I'm perfectly well aware of my obligations and my responsibilities to the Party.

'But I don't understand what the Party, the revolution, the devastation of the country, the White Guard, and everything else you've been talking about have to do with the fact that I sleep with Andrei and with someone else at the same time? I couldn't possibly have a baby, I know that. It would be terribly wrong at this time, when there are so many political problems. I'm quite well aware of that, and at the moment I certainly don't intend to be a mother. But as for everything else .·. .'

'But what about me, Zhenya?' cried Olga Sergeevna. 'Did you never consider how *I* might react to your relationship with Andrei?'

'But how can it make any difference to you?' Zhenya objected. 'It was you who wanted us to be close to each other, and you were so pleased that we were friends. Where are the boundaries of intimacy? Why is it all right for us to experience things together, enjoy ourselves together, but not sleep together? It's not as if we've taken anything from you – Andrei still worships you as he has always worshipped you, and I certainly haven't robbed you of one iota of his love for you. Anyway, what does it matter to you? It's all the same to you, you never have the time for that sort of thing.

'Besides, Mother, do you really want to tie Andrei to your apron strings so that he can't have a life of his own without you knowing about it? That really would be a terribly possessive attitude. It must be grandmother's bourgeois upbringing coming out in you! Anyway, you're being so unfair! In your day you lived your own life, so why shouldn't Andrei now?'

What had upset and angered Olga Sergeevna most of all was that neither her daughter nor her husband had shown any signs of remorse, just saw everything as quite natural, simple and not worth discussing. It was only with the greatest condescension to her, as someone who didn't really understand things, that Andrei and Zhenya had laboriously made a few superficial remarks about how sorry they were that everything had worked out like this, and regretting that they had made life so unpleasant for her.

But she had been only too painfully aware that neither Zhenya nor her gentle sincere Andrei truly considered themselves to be in the wrong. Both of them constantly repeated variations on the theme that nothing had changed, and that she was viewing the whole thing quite needlessly in these tragic dimensions. Nobody, they assured her, wanted to cause her any pain or unhappiness, but if it was really upsetting her so much they would both agree to call it a day, although they couldn't imagine what difference that was going to make.

It was because she was plunged in this chaos of ideas and emotions that Olga Sergeevna had decided to ask for my advice and for some clarification of the matter. Was this nothing more than wanton promiscuity, unchecked by any sort of moral standards? Or was it some quite new phenomenon created by new life styles? Was this in fact the new morality? We discussed these questions at great length.

'What I find most painful about the whole thing,' said Olga Sergeevna, wearily leaning on her shapely arm in a gesture which reminded me of Maria Stepanovna, 'is that they're so totally cold and rational, like two old people with no emotions left. I could understand it if Zhenya loved Andrei and he loved her, and even if it did make me unhappy (because I do love Andrei very much, you know) I wouldn't have this unpleasant taste in my mouth, this feeling of physical nausea. To put it quite bluntly, I have grown very hostile towards Andrei and Zhenya – I cannot understand how they could have treated me so unscrupulously, with so little regard for my feelings and reactions. Do you know, it's shaken my faith as to whether these two people are capable of loving at all. They both keep telling me that they love me, but what do they mean by love when they cause me so much unhappiness and inflict it casually too, without any qualms or remorse. I really think they must be emotionally deficient in some way. I don't understand either of them.

'Once I couldn't help reproaching Zhenya, and she just retorted; "Well, didn't you conceal your relationship with my father from his wife? Didn't you lie too?" But then surely that's the whole point – there's an enormous difference there that Zhenya can't grasp and won't understand. First of all, I never loved M's wife, who was like a total stranger to me. I never had any deep feelings for her and I only spared her the truth for humane reasons. Secondly, I loved M, loved him passionately, no less than his wife did, if not more. Our feelings gave us both equal rights over him, and my justification then was the power of my love for him and the suffering he caused me.

'But in this case, you see, there's nothing – no love, no suffering, nor remorse, nothing. Only a sort of icy self-confidence and an insistence on their right to seize happiness however and wherever they may find it. That's what I find so dreadful, the fact that they seem to lack any warmth or kindness, even the most rudimentary sensitivity to others! And yet they call themselves communists!'

I couldn't help laughing at this somewhat illogical conclusion; and Olga Sergeevna also smiled shamefacedly, admitting that this conclusion did not really follow from her previous accusations.

When at last we said goodbye, we agreed that I should see Zhenya within a day or so.

It was two days later, in the morning, that Zhenya came to see me – she worked in her district all day and in the evenings. She was a slender girl, very tall, with a lively face and a small head that reminded me of her grandmother's. She looked rather pale and had dark circles under her eyes. Her hand when I shook it was cold and damp, and she'd obviously not yet fully recovered from her operation. She had a simple direct manner, and started to speak at once.

'I expect the main thing that surprises you is that I sleep with men just because I like them, before I've had time to fall in love with them. But don't you see, you have to have *leisure* in order to fall in love – I've read enough novels to know just how much time and energy it takes to fall in love and I just don't have the time. At the moment we've got a really enormous load of work on our hands in our district. Come to that, have we ever had any spare time over these last few years? We're constantly in a rush and our heads are always full of other things.

'Of course, sometimes you have periods when you're less busy and then you suddenly realize that you like someone. But as for falling in love, there's no time for that! Just as soon as you've grown really fond of each other he'll be called to the Front or shoved off to some other town. Or else you have so much work to do that you forget all about him. That's why you cherish the few hours when you *can* be together, and then you both enjoy it. It doesn't commit you to anything, and the only thing I'm always afraid of is catching some venereal disease. But actually if you look someone straight in the eye and ask him whether he's got it or not, he'll never lie to you. There was one man who liked me very much, I think he even loved me, and when I asked him it was terribly hard for him to admit it and I could see how upset he was. But in the end we didn't sleep together, and he knew I would never have forgiven him if we had.'

Zhenya had lovely wide-open eyes, and she gave an impression of utter directness and honesty.

'But tell me, Comrade Zhenya,' I said. 'If you can tell me that, how is that you did not tell your mother everything immediately? Why did you conceal your relationship with Andrei from her all those months?'

'Well, I didn't think it concerned her, that's why. If I had fallen in love with Andrei and he had loved me, then of course I would have told her all about it, and I would probably just have gone out of her life. I wouldn't want to do anything to make her unhappy. But it wasn't as if there was anything that could possibly have robbed her of Andrei's affections! Why doesn't she understand that! If it hadn't been me it would only have been somebody else, and she really can't tie Andrei to her apron strings, or prevent him seeing anyone else or getting involved with other women, can she? I simply can't understand her!

'She's not at all upset by the fact that I'm friends with Andrei, that he talks to me more than to her, and that he's closer to me emotionally. But as far as she's concerned, the fact that I slept with him means that I'm taking Andrei away from her. But mother has no time to sleep with him – it's true, she just hasn't the time! Anyway, Andrei is nearer my age than mother's, we share the same tastes, and really the whole thing is so natural . . .'

'But maybe, without really being aware of it, you actually have fallen in love with Andrei?' I interrupted her.

Zhenya shook her head. 'I don't know what you mean by love, but my feelings for him aren't anything like what I understand love to be. If you love a person, then you want to be together all the time, you want to sacrifice everything for his sake, you think about him, you worry about him. But if you suggested that I set up permanently with Andrei, I'd say thanks a lot, but no. Oh, he's a pleasant person, and it's nice to be with him because he's so frail and so cheerful about it, as mother probably told you. But I get bored if I have to spend too much time with him, and then I prefer Abrasha. Not that I love him either, I never did, although Abrasha did have some sort of hold over me. I used to be at his beck and call and there was nothing I could do about it!'

Zhenya frowned and thought for a bit. Then she suddenly brightened again. 'The thing that upsets mother so much is that I don't love any of them and that she sees it as "immoral" and abnormal for someone of my age to be sleeping with men I don't love. But I think mother is wrong, and that things are much simpler and better this way. I remember how, when I was a child, mother was always rushing between Konstantin and my father, eating her heart out and tormenting herself over the whole thing. Everyone suffered, Konstantin and my grandmother too. Why, even now I can hear my grandmother's voice ordering my mother to make some decision. "Stop being such a coward," she used to say, "You must make your choice and come to a decision."

'But mother was quite unable to decide, since she loved both of them and they both loved her. They were all so unhappy and made each other so wretched that they eventually started hating one another, and finally parted as enemies.

'As for me, I don't part with anyone as an enemy – when I stop liking them that means it's over, and that's all there is to it. Whenever someone starts to act jealously I always remember how wretched mother was and how jealous Konstantin and my father were of each other, and I tell myself that I wouldn't go through that for anything. I don't belong to anybody, and they'll just have to accept that!

'But do you really mean to say that you've never loved anyone, and don't love anyone now?' I asked her. 'Quite apart from anything else, I doubt whether your definition of love is terribly plausible. It sounds as if you've got it out of books!'

'But what makes you think that I don't love anyone?' said Zhenya in honest amazement. 'What I said was that I didn't feel any love for the men I slept with. I certainly didn't say that I didn't love anyone . . .'

'Would you mind if I asked who you do love, then?' I said.

'Who do I love? Why, my mother, more than anyone else in the whole world. There is nobody like my mother – in some ways she's more important to me than Lenin. Anyway, she is completely special, and I couldn't exist without her. Her happiness means more to me than anything else . . .'

'And yet you've put paid to your mother's happiness and almost broken her heart. How do you reconcile that with what you've just said?'

'Look,' replied Zhenya thoughtfully, 'if I'd thought for one moment, if I'd known that Mother would take it this way and that it would make her so miserable, I expect – no, I'm *sure* – I would never have done it. But I really imagined that she was above that sort of thing and that she saw things in the same way as Andrei and I did, and wouldn't pay much attention to it all. Now I realize how wrong I was, I feel terribly sad, much sadder than she realizes . . .'

For the first time during our conversation the tears welled up in Zhenya's eyes. Much embarrassed, she wiped them away with the tips of her fingers, trying not to let me see them.

'I would give my life for Mother, and those aren't just empty words, that's how I feel about her. She herself can tell you how much I suffered when we thought that she had caught typhus. But do you know what I find so especially painful now? I'm very, very sad for Mother, and furious with myself for being so foolish and for being unable to understand, anticipate, or even guess that the whole business would affect her like this. I can't think of anything now that I wouldn't give for this not to have happened. But despite all this, deep down I still feel that mother is wrong and that Andrei and I are right. There must be some other interpretation of the whole thing which will make it all clear and simple and stop everyone being so unhappy. Then we'll all be able to continue as friends and no one will despise anyone.

'You see, however deeply I love mother, I feel for the first time in my life that she is terribly wrong, and that . . . Oh, that's what is so painful for me! I'd always considered mother to be utterly infallible, and now that's been shaken and I've lost all the old faith that mother was above everything and everybody and that she understood everything. It's dreadfully painful – I don't want to stop loving or trusting her, because how could I ever believe in other people if I did that? Oh, you can't imagine how unhappy all this has made me, and not for the reasons that my mother thinks either. It's all so sad . . .'

Zhenya no longer tried to conceal the large tears that ran down her cheeks and fell onto her frayed black skirt.

We talked about how best to resolve the situation. Zhenya had already decided to move into a hostel with some of her girl friends, and would be going there in a few days' time. She was only anxious as to how her mother and Andrei would cope without her constantly being there, for the whole tedious business of seeing to the provisions rested on her.

'I'm quite sure that mother won't eat properly,' she said disconsolately. 'If someone isn't there to take care of her and push food at her she'll go the whole day without eating. And Andrei's just as bad. I can't imagine how they're going to manage without me, they're both as helpless as children. Of course I can call on them and do everything I can, but it won't be the same. I'm busy too, you know. Everything is so much simpler when you all live together.'

She sighed, and went on talking about her mother and Andrei in a sober, maternal voice, as though she was dealing with children.

When it was time to say goodbye, I said 'I'm so glad that I shall be able to reassure your mother now about everything, and tell her how much you love her. What upset her particularly was the idea that you were incapable of strong, healthy emotions, and that you were too rational about things.'

Zhenya smiled. 'Well, she can rest easy about that, because I'm quite sure I'll get myself into some stupid scrape again because of men! I'm not her daughter and my grandmother's grand-daughter for nothing, after all! Anyway, there are people whom I love now, whom I love very much, other people besides mother. There's Lenin, for instance – don't smile, I mean it! I love him far more than all the men I like and have slept with. I'm always beside myself for several days whenever I know I'm going to see him and hear him talk – I'd give my life for him too!

'And there's Comrade Gerasim, do you know him? He's our district secretary. Now there's a man for you! I love him too, I truly love him and even if he's not always correct I'll always submit to him because I know that his intentions are good. Do you remember when there was that scandal about him last year? I didn't sleep for nights, and what a fight we put up for him! I mobilized the entire district to support him. Yes, I love Gerasim,' Zhenya concluded with conviction, as if trying to vindicate herself and her feelings.

'Well, I must be running off now. We've got some urgent local work to do, and now that I've been elected secretary of our cell,' (she said this with some pride) 'there's even more work to do. Oh, how good life would be if only mother could understand and accept things.' She sighed again, a deep childish sigh.

'I'll get in touch with mother. Please, do try to convince her that Andrei is all hers, that I need him about as much as I need this table here. Do you think she'll understand and go on loving me? I'm so terrified of losing her love – I couldn't live without mother, without her love. It's so awful that this whole business is affecting her work too. Say what you like, I never want to fall in love like mother did! How would you ever find the time to work?'

It was on this note that Zhenya disappeared out of the door. I remained sitting where I was, wondering who was right, whose view would be taken up by the new generation, this emerging class grappling with these new ideas and feelings.

Behind the door I could hear Zhenya's youthful laugh and her cheerful voice, saying 'Well, friends, I'll see you this evening! You mustn't delay me now, I'm late as it is, and we have so much work to do!'

Sisters

She had come to see me, as did many other women, for advice and moral support. I had already met her in passing at delegates' conferences. She had a lovely face, with rather melancholy, though observant, eyes.

'I've come to see you because I've nowhere to go,' she announced. 'I've been without a roof over my head for three weeks, I've no money, nothing to live on. You must find me a job, otherwise there's nothing for it but to go on the streets!'

'But how has this happened,' I asked. 'You used to work, didn't you? Surely you had a job? Or did you get the sack?'

'Yes, I used to work in a despatch office, but I got the sack over two months ago. It was because of my child. She was ill, you see, which meant I had to miss work. I managed to avoid the sack three times, but finally in August I lost my job. Within two weeks of that my child died, but by then they wouldn't take me back.'

She hung her head, and I realized that she was concealing tears. 'But why did they sack you?' I asked her. 'Weren't you working satisfactorily?'

'Oh no, it wasn't that, I'm a good worker. They just thought I had no reason to work since my husband makes a good living. He's working at the moment for a government trust company where he's got an important post; he's an executive.'

'So why did you say you have no money and no roof over your head? Have you separated?'

'No, we haven't officially separated. I've just left him and haven't gone back. And I'm not going to either, whatever happens!'

Now she could no longer check her tears. 'Oh, I'm so sorry! I haven't cried once all this time, I just couldn't, but now . . . when you meet someone who's sympathetic it's more difficult not to . . . But if I just tell you what's happened then you'll understand.'

She had met her husband in 1917, at the height of the revolution. He was a typesetter at the time, and she was working in the despatch office of a large publishing house. They were both supporters of the Bolsheviks. Both were committed to the same passionate faith, the same desire to overthrow the power of the exploiters, to build a new and just world. They shared a love of books and were eager to educate themselves. They were caught up in the whirlwind of revolution.

In those October days, at their posts and in the heat of battle, amidst the thunder of bullets, they had opened up their hearts to one another. However, there had been no time to formalize their liaison and they each continued to live their own lives, meeting only irregularly in the intervals between work. But these meetings had been full of joy and happiness, for in those days they had been true friends. Within a year she was expecting a baby, they had registered their marriage and started to live together. Her baby had not kept her away from work for long, and she had set up a crèche in the district. Work, after all, was far more important than family matters. Her husband had grumbled occasionally, and with reason too, for she did neglect the housework, but then he was never at home either. When she was elected as a delegate to a conference he was very proud of her.

'I hope you won't sulk when your lunch is cold!' she'd said.

'Who cares about my lunch! Just as long as it's not your love for me that grows cold! I'm proud of you – everyone will see you up there with the people!'

They'd both joked about it, and it had seemed that nothing could destroy their love for one another. They were not just man and wife, but true friends, both working for the same goal with no care for themselves, concerned only with their work. Their child too was a source of great happiness to them, and was healthy and lively.

But at some point this had changed. Perhaps it was when her husband had been taken on at the trust company. At first they'd been overjoyed, although life was tough for them. Then suddenly the crèche closed down, and she was at her wits' end as to what to do with their child while she was working. Her husband took pride in the fact that he could now support his family properly, and suggested she stop work. But she was very reluctant to do this – she'd grown used to talking to her friends at work, and enjoyed the work itself. Besides, she was far too independent to give it up; she'd after all been earning her living since she left school.

So she decided to stay at work. At first there was no great problem about this. Things seemed in some ways easier for them; they moved into a new flat, with two rooms and a kitchen, and a girl came in to look after their child. Local political work took her out of the house even more than before, and her husband was also very busy, virtually only coming home to sleep.

On one occasion he had to go away on an assignment for the company, and spent three months away with some nepmen. When he returned she immediately sensed something about him that grated on her; he seemed like a stranger to her. He didn't listen to her stories and barely looked at her. He'd taken to wearing stylish clothes and even started using perfume. He no longer spent any more time than he had to at home.

That was the beginning of everything . . . He'd never been a drinking man, not even on holiday. But then in the old days of the revolution, rushed off their feet, it would never have occurred to them to drink. Now this had changed.

The first occasion when he came home drunk she'd been worried for him rather than for herself. She thought it would damage his reputation. Next morning she started remonstrating with him, but he sat there drinking his tea in total silence. Then, without a word in reply, he left the house. She was miserable, but comforted herself with the thought that he was probably too ashamed to discuss it.

Three days later he came home drunk again. She was now very distressed. Perhaps she would have to accompany him on his evening jaunts in future, to prevent this. It was an unpleasant prospect. He was a sweet man, but this was just disgusting! Next morning she was anxious to have a talk with him, but no sooner had she started speaking than he turned on her with a look filled with such loathing that she felt shattered, the words froze on her lips. He saw her as his enemy!

He began increasingly to come home drunk. One day she could endure it no longer, and decided to stay at home in order to confront him. She waited until he was sober, and started appealing to him, saying everything she'd been bottling up – that they couldn't live like this, that they couldn't continue to be friends if there was only one thing which kept them together, sharing the same bed. She poured out her feelings about his drunkenness, she warned him, threatened him, tried to shame him, and she cried . . .

He heard her out, and began trying to justify himself. She didn't understand, he said. He was obliged to keep company with the nepmen, it was expected of him, there was no other way to do business. Then, after thinking for a moment, he told her that this sort of life wasn't to his liking at all. He begged her not to distress herself, and admitted that she was right.

When it was time for him to leave, he came up to her, held her head and looked into her eyes, kissing her as he always used to do.

Her mind at rest, she went happily to work that day. But before the week was out her husband again came home drunk. On this occasion, when she tried to protest, he banged the table, saying 'It's none of your business! Everyone lives like this! And if you don't like it, nobody's keeping you here!'

So saying, he left the house, and all that day she felt as if a stone was weighing down her heart. Had he really stopped loving her? Should she leave him? That evening, however, he came home unexpectedly early. He was sober, apologetic and humble. They spent the whole evening talking and once more relations between them became easier. She came to understand how difficult it was to exercise restraint in the sort of company he kept. Those people just threw their money around, and it was very awkward to let them outdo him. He told her a great deal about the nepmen, about their wives and their women, about how they did business and how difficult it was to detect the real proletarians amongst all those sharks. You always had to be on your guard with them, he said.

She was very depressed by what he told her, more depressed than she'd ever been in the whole course of the revolution. It was at this point that she discovered that she was to be made redundant. Her anxieties were now very serious. But when she told her husband, he was quite unperturbed by the news, saying that it might even be for the best. She could spend more time at home and attend properly to the housework. 'At the moment, our flat looks like nothing on earth,' he said. 'We certainly couldn't entertain a respectable guest here.'

Amazed by his attitude, she began to protest, but he merely said, 'Well, that's your affair, I'm not standing in your way. You can work if you want to.' And he went out.

She was very disturbed that her husband had so misunderstood her, and apparently taken offence, but she nevertheless decided to stand up for herself. She went to see her comrades at work and argued with them that they should give her her job back. They were finally persuaded to keep her on for the time being. But as soon as she'd settled that problem, her daughter fell ill.

'One night I was sitting with my sick child feeling dreadfully lonely and troubled when the doorbell rang,' she said. 'I went to open it, assuming it would be my husband, glad that he was back and that at least I'd be able to share my unhappiness with him – at least if he was sober! But when I opened the door, I just couldn't believe my eyes. Who was this creature with him? A young woman with rouge on her cheeks, evidently rather drunk.

' "Now be a nice wife and let me in,' he said. 'I've brought a girl friend round. Don't take offence, I'm no worse than anyone else! We two are going to have some fun and you're not to interfere!" '

'I realized how drunk he was – he could barely stand upright – but my knees were trembling. I let them into the dining room where my husband usually spent the night these days, on the sofa, and I went straight back to my daughter.

'I locked myself in and just sat there, completely stunned with misery. I didn't really feel angry with him – what can you expect from someone who's so drunk? I just felt terribly hurt; what was more, I could hear everything that was going on in the next room. If I hadn't had to attend to my sick daughter I would have blocked my ears to it. Fortunately they soon quietened down – they were drunk enough as it was. In the early hours of the morning I heard my husband take the woman to the door, and then he went back to sleep. As for me, I didn't go to bed at all, and just sat there thinking.

'That evening my husband once again came home earlier than usual. We had not seen each other all day, and I deliberately greeted him coldly, and avoided looking at him. He began to sort through his papers. Neither of us said a word, but I saw that he was looking closely at me. Let him! I thought. Most likely he'll pretend now to be sorry and ask me to forgive him, so he can just go on doing the same thing. I'm not taking any more of this, I thought, I'm going to leave him!

'But oh, how my heart was aching! I had once loved him, and there was no point in pretending that I didn't love him still. But now it was all over, and I felt just as though he had died – or worse. At least my feelings for him would have survived if he had died . . .

'When he saw me putting on my coat as I got ready to leave, he suddenly exploded with rage. He grabbed my arm with such force that he bruised it, and tore off my coat, hurling it to the floor.

' "Why have you suddenly taken it into your head to throw a fit of female hysterics? Where do you think you're going? What do you want of me? You'll never find another husband like me! I feed you, dress you, you want for nothing – don't you dare criticize me! I have to live this way if I'm going to do business!" '

'He talked on and on. There was no stopping him; it was as if the dam had burst and he wouldn't let me get in a word edgewise. At one moment he would be shouting, venting his rage on me, then on himself; the next he would be justifying himself, and arguing as though his life depended on it. I saw before me a man tormenting himself, and I became so wretched for him that I gradually forgot how unhappy I was. I tried to soothe him and reassure him that things weren't so bad. I told him that the nepmen were to blame, not him . . .

'That evening, we made it up once again, but I still felt very bitter when he said that I shouldn't be so angry and resentful at him. How could I have made demands on him when he was so drunk, he asked? I begged him not to drink any more. "It's not your bringing home a prostitute that I resent, it's the fact that you let yourself get into such a horrible state," I said. He promised to behave more carefully and to avoid his old companions, but I still felt resentful. It was true of course that you shouldn't make demands of someone who's drunk, and maybe he really didn't remember anything that happened, but nonetheless from that day something painful nagged away at my heart.

'I was constantly tormented by the thought that if he'd loved me as he had done in the days of the revolution he would never have gone looking for another woman. I remembered how in those days one of my friends had pursued him – she was much prettier than I, but he had never so much as glanced at her! Why couldn't he tell me openly if he no longer loved me? Once I tried to broach this with him, but he just lost his temper, shouting that I was bothering him with my female inanities again, at a time when he was up to his eyes in work and didn't give a damn for women, including me! Then he left the house, leaving me even more depressed.

'Then the possibility of my losing my job came up again. My

little girl had been ill all this time, and I'd been missing work. I pleaded with them once again, and eventually prevailed upon them to defer my dismissal for the time being. I don't really know what it was I was hoping for, but I just kept stalling. Now, more than ever before, I was terrified of becoming dependent on my husband. Life with him was increasingly difficult, and we were gradually becoming complete strangers to one another. We lived in the same flat, and yet knew absolutely nothing about the other's life. He did ocasionally look in on our little girl, and I gave up my local work in order to be able to spend more time with her. During this period my husband drank less and always came home sober, but he totally ignored me. We slept apart – I would spend nights with my daughter while he slept on the sofa. Every so often he would come to me during the night, but there was no pleasure in it and it only made things more difficult afterwards, because I would feel all the old unhappiness with one more anxiety added to it. He would hold me in his arms, but he never asked me how I was feeling or anything about my life at all.

'So that was how we lived together, both of us going our own ways, neither of us asking questions of the other. He certainly had his anxieties, and I had mine – and it stayed that way. Then the final blow struck – our little girl died. A few days earlier I had been sacked.

'I thought that now we shared the same grief my husband might start thinking a little more about me. But not a bit of it! Even this tragedy didn't help to bring us closer. He didn't even go to his own daughter's funeral – he had to go to an urgent meeting instead. From then on I stayed at home, unemployed and unpaid.

'Of course, there was plenty to be done in the district. But as for making a living, that was more difficult. In any case, it would have been tactless for me to demand a salary with so many unemployed people around; everybody knew that my husband was an executive and highly placed. How could I possibly ask for a salary? It made me very unhappy to be supported by my husband, especially at that time, but there was nothing I could do about it. I just endured it, hoping, and waiting for something to happen.

'How foolish we women are! You see, I realized that all my husband's old feelings for me had gone, and that I felt more bitterness and resentment than love for him now, but I kept thinking that this would pass! I imagined that he could love me again, and everything would be all right. And so I waited, waking up every morning with this hope, hurrying home after working in the district just in case my husband had come home early, alone. But if he was at home, he might just as well not have been; he didn't pay any attention to me at all, and would just busy himself with his work. Either that, or his nepmen friends would come round. Nonetheless, I still went on hoping and waiting! That is, until the last incident . . . After that I left him for good, and I haven't been back.

'It was about midnight and I'd just got back from a meeting. I wanted some tea and I put on the samovar. My husband wasn't back yet, and I wasn't really expecting him. Then I heard the front door open – that meant he'd come back (he had his own door key so as not to wake me when he came home). I was attending to the samovar when I remembered that an important packet had come for him and was lying in my room. Leaving the samovar, I took it in to him. When I saw him, I felt exactly as I had on the other occasion – I just couldn't grasp who this woman with him could be. There was my husband and beside him a tall slender woman. They both turned to face me, and when my husband's eyes met mine I saw immediately that he was sober. That made it even more intolerable! So utterly intolerable that I felt like screaming out loud.

'The woman looked very upset too. Somehow I managed to put that packet on the table calmly, saying "Here's an urgent packet for you", and then left the room. But as soon as I was on my own I began to tremble feverishly all over. As I was afraid that they would hear me in the next room, I lay down on the bed, covering my head with a blanket, doing my best to hear, feel and know nothing. But thoughts kept crowding into my head, tormenting thoughts . . .

'I could hear them whispering and they didn't sleep. The woman's voice was louder than my husband's, and she seemed to be berating him. Maybe she was his girl friend, I thought, and he had deceived her and not told her he was married. Maybe at that very moment he was renouncing me!

'I went through agony. I had been bitter, certainly, that time when he'd been drunk and brought home a prostitute, but it hadn't caused me anything like the same misery. Now I realized once and for all that he did not love me! He didn't even love me as a sister or a friend – if he had, he would surely have spared me this! And what sort of women were they anyway! Street girls, prostitutes! This girl must certainly be one of them. Only a woman like that would have come home with him for the night! All of a sudden I was overcome with such a violent fit of rage that I was quite prepared to throw her out of the house with my own hands.

'I went on torturing myself in this way until dawn, and didn't manage to close my eyes once. It was quiet in the next room. Then suddenly I heard cautious footsteps in the corridor. It sounded as if someone was stealing out of the room and I knew that it must be her. I heard her open the kitchen door. What could she be wanting in there? I waited and listened. Everything was quiet suddenly, so I sprang up and went into the kitchen. There she was, sitting on a stool near the window, her head bent, crying bitterly. Her beautiful long hair covered her like a shroud. She looked up at me with such grief in her eyes that I became afraid. I went up to her, and she got up to speak to me.

' "I am so sorry that I came to your house," she said. "I never knew that he wasn't living alone. Oh, this is all so hard for me . . ."

'I couldn't understand. She couldn't be a prostitute, I thought, she must be his girl friend. I don't know what made me speak, but I blurted out "Do you love him then?"

'She gazed at me in utter amazement. "We met for the first time yesterday. He promised to pay well, and I just don't care who it is nowadays, so long as he pays . . ."

'I don't remember now how we got started, but soon she was telling me everything about herself. Three months earlier she'd been made redundant; she had sold everything, done without food and without a roof over her head for a while. She'd been very distressed because she could no longer send money to her old mother, who had written to tell her that she too was dying of hunger. Two weeks ago she had gone on the streets, where she had immediately struck lucky. She'd made a good friend, and now she had clothes and food and could send her mother money too.

'As she talked, she was wringing her hands. "I've got a certificate, you know, and I had a good education. I'm still very young, too – I'm only nineteen. I just can't believe that I'm going to end up on a garbage heap like this!" '

'You may not believe this, but as I listened to her talk I was overwhelmed by feelings of pity for her. And then it suddenly dawned on me that if I hadn't had a husband, I would have been in the same position as her, with no job and nowhere to live!

That previous night, lying on my bed, I had been in such a state of agony, I was literally seething with rage about her; now suddenly my rage turned against my husband. How dare he exploit this woman's desperation! And him a conscientious, highly placed worker! Instead of trying to help an unemployed friend, he just bought her, bought her body for his own pleasure! This struck me as so disgusting that I immediately thought that I couldn't go on living with such a man!

'She talked to me a great deal more, and then together we lit the stove and made some coffee. My husband was still asleep. Then she hurriedly got ready to leave.

' "Did he pay you?" I asked her.

'She blushed, insisting that she wouldn't dream of accepting any money after everything we'd said to each other. She absolutely could not do that. I realized that she was anxious to leave before my husband woke up, and I didn't try to stop her.

'It may seem strange to you, but I was sad when she had to go. She was such a young creature, so unhappy and alone. I got dressed and accompanied her out. We walked together for a while, and then sat down in a square and began talking again. I told her my problems, I still had my redundancy pay which I'd saved, and which I begged her to accept. For a long time she refused to take it, and only finally accepted on condition that I promised to come to her if ever I was in need. And that was how we parted, as sisters.

'My old feelings for my husband had finally died, suddenly. There was no resentment, no pain left now. It was as though I'd buried him. When I got home he tried to make excuses for what had happened. I didn't try and contradict him. I didn't cry, and didn't reproach him. Next day I moved in with a friend. I've been looking for three weeks and I don't expect anything to turn up.

'A few days ago I realized that it was becoming inconvenient for my friend to have me staying there any longer, and so I went to see the girl my husband had brought home. It turned out that she'd left the previous day to go into hospital, and so I began roaming around, without work, money or anywhere to sleep. It seems as though I'm destined for the same fate as her . . .'

In my companion's eyes I saw so many questions and doubts – doubts about life itself. They expressed the horror, the misery and the anguish of women without work and without a home, facing the inexorable enemy of unemployment. It was the expression of a woman on her own, challenging an outmoded way of life . . . After she had left, the look haunted me. It demanded an answer from us, action, work, struggle . . .

Afterword

SHEILA ROWBOTHAM

In these moving love stories Kollontai pursues themes from her non-fiction writing – particularly those from *Communism and the Family* and *The New Morality and the Working Class*. She was concerned with the complicated connections between personal life and political ideas, and was convinced that relations between the sexes must be freed from the restraints imposed by women's economic dependence on men.

Yet she tried always to examine the gap between the official surface of things and the actuality within – and would not rest content with the easy formula that changes in the mode of production and the external structures of work relations under communism would automatically create a new freedom and equality between the sexes.

Though completely opposed to those feminists who thought there could be women's emancipation within capitalism, she also fought continually inside the Bolshevik Party against the kind of complacency which failed to take sexual relations and the positive creation of a new culture of daily life seriously. She wanted complete equality between the sexes, realizing that this necessitated big changes in the structure of the family, the organization of domestic work and the economic position of women.

Convinced of the need for all these changes, she also indicates in her non-fiction writing that she hoped for an inner transformation – for a 'new eros under communism', a love which extended throughout humanity. Kollontai is more optimistic about emotional love between her women characters than passionate sexual love between men and women. Indeed, the conflict between passion and freedom appears in her writing almost as a natural tension. And in addition Kollontai realized that there was more than the ideal future to consider; there was the immediate – and difficult – present. The past haunted this present, and the peculiar circumstances of 'socialism in one country'. Civil war, scarcity and reconstruction restricted the emergence of the new culture of which she conceived.

223

Kollontai shows how the state of the Soviet economy in the New Economic Policy period helped maintain old-style relationships between men and women. Free unions became a cover for male irresponsibility, and women were left with the children. Communal housing turned into overcrowded barracks. The material problems facing the country fed the conservatism of the vast majority of women – for them, new freedom also meant insecurity, and perhaps better the devil you knew . . . It is clear in these stories how much Kollontai felt it necessary to struggle against this conservatism.

Her characters experience conflict between their desire to create new forms of personal relationships and the need to subordinate their personal feelings to the revolutionary cause. The grandmother in 'Three Generations' believes in 'the great love' and defies convention to follow her ideal, with painful consequences. Her daughter Olga Sergeevna appears on the surface quite removed from the inner turmoils of physical passion – a responsible, competent Party cadre: the reality is, however, quite different. Vasilisa Malygina sees changes in living as a form of learning; political education is not just a matter of new ideas, but of creating a culture of everyday life. She struggles with a recalcitrant co-operative household, and against being overwhelmed by sexual longing for her husband. These sexual feelings conflict with her dislike of her role of the passive, director's wife, and with her political beliefs; and she finally breaks with her love, deciding to bring up her child 'in the communist fashion'. Vladimir, her husband, on the other hand, falls easily into a traditional bourgeois pattern of masculinity. He is, in the final resort, ready to accept the divisions of wife and mistress, respecting one, desiring the other, one belonging to his public world, the other the object of his passion. His desire for Vasilisa is diminished by his unease with her political principles, by which he feels criticized, and this affects their whole relationship. Absorbed in his work, he is also able to cut himself off from his feelings.

In all three of these stories the relationships between women are close ones. Vasilisa Malygina overcomes her jealousy for her beautiful rival and is able to see the other woman's vulnerability – expressed in the remarkable letter to her. In 'Three Generations', Olga Sergeevna's daughter affirms her love for her mother despite their very different views on sexuality. 'Sisters' is a story of the growth of solidarity between a prostitute and a deserted wife.

At the time *Love of Worker Bees* was written, sexuality was a subject of great controversy in many countries. The conservative elements saw the feminist movements, easier divorce, freer relationships between the sexes as part of a process of disintegration; for liberals these events represented an evolution towards progress. Marxists frequently dismissed sexuality as peripheral, seeing it as subject simply to changes in the external structures of social relations.

Kollontai was conscious always of a more complex dialectic. In her stories she describes economic and social circumstances *and* inner patterns of feelings. She was aware of an unevenness in the relation between new social forms and sexual passion – an unevenness which bore the weight of centuries of oppression. Here Kollontai is straining towards an alternative culture of communism, which would transform all human relationships. Though the context for such a culture has completely changed, and we face a very different political situation, the problems that Alexandra Kollontai so intensely describes persist. If the setting and some of the assumptions seem strange to us, *Love of Worker Bees* still has an immediate relevance.

Glossary

Names Russians have a first ('Christian') name, a patronymic and a surname. The customary mode of address is first name plus patronymic, thus, Vasilisa Dementevna, Maria Semenovna. There are more intimate abbreviations of first names which have subtly affectionate, patronizing or friendly overtones. So for instance Vasilisa becomes Vasya, Vasyuk, and Vladimir becomes Volodya, Volodka, Volodechka, Volya.

Meals The main meal, lunch, at this period was usually eaten between 3.00 and 5.00 in the afternoon. There would be a light meal before going to bed.

Name days In the atheist Soviet Union people nevertheless still celebrated their saints' days.

Names, events, groups before and after the Revolution are listed chronologically.

BEFORE THE REVOLUTION

Emancipation of the serfs After the Crimean War, the return of demobilized soldiers to the impoverished countryside exacerbated thousands of peasants' revolts, which finally forced Alexander II to emancipate the serfs in 1861.

Zemstvo Introduced after Emancipation as the elected provincial authority. Though without any real executive powers, it came under much police pressure at the end of the nineteenth century, as *zemstvo* liberals took up more radical positions. By 1905 it had already become officially representative of conservative public opinion.

Populism Populists (active around 1860–95) believed Russia could achieve revolution (bypassing capitalism) by strengthening the

226

peasant commune, regarded as the embryo of socialism. Populists travelled to the countryside to learn from the peasants and to urge them to seize land.

Mobile libraries Used by Populists to take books to the peasants.

Socialist Revolutionaries (SRS) various Populist groups joined together in the 1890s to form this party, which believed that the revolution would be achieved by the peasants rather than the urban workers. They carried out many terrorist attacks against local governors in the period 1901–5. In February 1917, the SRS rose to high government positions, and after October 1917 they struggled against the Bolsheviks, splitting off from the pro-Bolshevik left SR group.

Union of Struggle for the Liberation of the Working Class Underground illegal Marxist organization founded in St Petersburg in 1895 by Lenin and Martov with the aim of training factory workers, theoretically and practically, to prepare them for their role as the nucleus of a new centralized revolutionary party.

The 'Reaction' These stories mention two periods when revolutionary activities provoked extreme reactionary measures against the entire Russian population – after the assassination of Alexander II in 1881, and the period following the 1905 revolution.

Svyatopolk-Mirsky Minister of the Interior from 1904. It was thought his liberal reputation would ensure a period of reforms, but it was he who was responsible for ordering soldiers to shoot down workers in St Petersburg in the peaceful demonstration on 9 January 1905.

Bolsheviks and Mensheviks. The Russian Social Democratic Party split decisively into two groups in 1903. Lenin and the Bolsheviks as they called themselves, wanted a small party of dedicated revolutionaries, while Martov and the Mensheviks wanted a party open to all who accepted its programme and was willing to obey its leadership. The February 1917 revolution was largely set off by Mensheviks while Lenin was in exile, and between February and October 1917 the antagonism between them was at its most acute. It was when (thanks largely to Trotsky) the Military Revolutionary Committee of the Petrograd Soviet joined the Bolsheviks that soldiers were able to seize power for the Bolsheviks on 25 October 1917, and installed the new government.

Soviets Emerged in the 1905 revolution as councils elected by strike committees to co-ordinate and supervise their demands. The first and most important soviet was the St Petersburg one, but soviets rapidly spread throughout all the major towns of Russia. Trotsky, who was close to the Mensheviks in the 1905 period, led the St Petersburg soviet, in which members of the various socialist parties predominated. By February 1917, soviets in all towns were known as 'soviets of the workers' and 'soldiers' deputies'. The creation of the new Petrograd soviet and the assumption of power by the Provisional government happened within days of each other and inaugurated a period of dual power, in which the soviet constantly undermined the latter's authority, especially in the army.

When Lenin returned to Russia in April 1917 demanding 'All Power to the Soviets', he meant the Bolsheviks in the soviets, as well as the soviets themselves as a rudimentary form of self-management. Since then, Bolsheviks and soviets have often been referred to interchangeably.

By September 1917, the Bolsheviks already had a majority in various soviets, including Petrograd, and could use the Military Revolutionary Committee of the Petrograd soviet as the co-ordinating centre of the October revolution. By the early 1920s the soviets had evolved into local one-party bodies of the Bolsheviks, and Stalin was later to describe them as 'transmission belts from the Party to the masses'.

Duma The State Duma was set up after the 1905 revolution by the Tsar as a weak parliamentary body for discussing legislation. The peasantry was heavily represented, and there were a few members of the urban working-class. Nevertheless, the Social Democrats were able to use the Duma as a forum for criticizing the government.

Provisional Government; February revolution February 1917 the Tsar decreed the dissolution of the Duma, at which the Duma's Provisional Committee was set up with the intention of reforming rather than abolishing the monarchy. After negotiations with the (largely Menshevik) Petrograd Soviet, the Provisional Committee announced the formation of a new Provisional government, and the Tsar was forced to abdicate.

'Liberationist position' ie a member of the Union of Liberation, a liberal landowning organization working within the Duma for a

programme of universal suffrage and a variety of social reforms. In October 1905 it was assimilated into the Constitutional Democratic Party.

Eduard Bernstein The German Social Democrat economist who attacked Marxism's economic foundations, arguing that the path of reform and steady economic pressure from the trade unions would achieve more for the working class than a proletarian revolution.

'Defensist position' The Mensheviks were divided in their attitude to the First World War. One group, the Defensists, took the patriotic line of most of the European social democrat parties in supporting the war, while the Internationalists, like the Bolsheviks, saw the war as the prelude to the coming international revolution.

AFTER THE REVOLUTION

'October Days' The days in October 1917 when the Bolsheviks took power.

Civil War Many anti-Bolshevik groups joined forces to fight the authority of the new government. A White Army was formed out of these groups, to fight the powerful Red Army created in 1918 by Trotsky, and under his leadership. The Bolshevik government was under constant threat from the fighting, which continued from 1918 until 1921 when the Western armies propping up the White forces were eventually withdrawn.

Industrial Front The economic crisis created by the civil war necessitated the organization of workers into labour armies and the militarization of labour.

New Economic Policy (NEP, hence nepman and nepwoman) Introduced by Lenin at the 10th Party Congress in 1921, after the Bolshevik civil war victory. The economic and political alliance of the proletariat (urban working class) and the peasantry, threatened during the civil war by economic pressures and grain requisitions, was to be safeguarded by granting peasants relatively free use of the land and its products. NEP's main aim was to 'increase at all costs the quantity of output', to expand large-scale industry, and thus provide the economic basis for the dictatorship of the proletariat. Although the 'commanding heights' of the economy remained under state control, private enterprise was selectively authorized and so was born the 'nepman'.

'One-man' management of industry; was the manner in which many Party members described this selective private control of the economy.

'Nepman' These were the new managers, directors, 'red' merchants all of whom prospered under the new economy. Many bourgeois industrialists and technical specialists who had flourished before the revolution had considerable control over small enterprises under the NEP.

'Nepwomen' These were the wives of nepmen, or women who kept company with these men. (The term is, needless to say, a derogatory one.)

Trust companies Small private enterprises were encouraged under the NEP to combine into units called trusts, whose fixed capital was in state hands.

Syndicates Trusts could combine into larger groups called syndicates.

Red Guards Armed Bolshevik detachments before the revolution, encouraged and funded by the Bolsheviks during the Provisional government.

Co-operatives Established after the emancipation of the serfs, they accompanied the growth of numerous small business enterprises. Co-operatives set up direct channels to the sources of supply, and many of them became rich and politically powerful after the revolution.

GPU September 1917 saw the establishment of the 'Cheka', the Commission for the Struggle against Sabotage and the Counter-revolution. In 1922 it was replaced by the Government Political Administration (GPU), the political police force. Today it comes under the KGB.

Central Committee of the Bolshevik Party Elected by Party congresses as the executive arm of the Party, instructed by the Party rules to direct the whole work of the Party in the intervals between congresses. Under Lenin, the Central Committee was an important decision-making body.

Party membership Because the Bolsheviks initially defined themselves by their illegal underground activities, there was little fear that the Party would attract unsuitable opportunist members. For most people, the dangers and difficulties of membership in the civil war period did not provide much incentive to join, although as early as 1919 the open-door policy was threatening the Party with an influx of careerists. Recruitment constantly alternated with 'sifting out', and Party membership fluctuated. It was, however, in the 20s, a predominantly male party (only 7½ per cent of its members were women in 1922, most of them politically inexperienced and without formal education).

Apropos of Vladimir's threatened expulsion in 'Vasilisa Malygina', it is interesting to note that of the members expelled in the early 30s, most were expelled for political 'passivity', about a quarter for 'bourgeois life style', drunkenness or careerism, and a small number for bribery and corruption.

Komsomol The youth organization of the Party. Its initially loose connection with Bolsheviks strengthened in 1919; the Komsomol reached its peak of activity in the civil war, but membership dropped sharply after 1921.

Central Control Commission Set up by the Party Central Committee to direct the Party purges (which hadn't yet acquired the sinister connotations they had under Stalin).

House of Motherhood Kollontai wanted to see buildings all over Russia where women could go and learn about birth control, childbirth and child care.

Prostitutes Prostitution was legal in Tsarist Russia, and prostitutes had to carry 'yellow tickets' instead of passports, and work in registered houses. Prostitution decreased sharply after the revolution only to rise again with the rise in women's unemployment under the NEP.

The 'New Morality' The ambiguous connotations of this phrase reveal much both of people's optimism and their fears about the way in which their private sexual lives suddenly became so public after the revolution. It was used optimistically by those who wel-

comed the benefits of the humane marriage laws and divorce legislation, and the legalizing of abortion. It was used derisively by
many people in the Party for whom it meant free love and
frivolous promiscuity. It is significant that, in 'Vasilisa Malygina',
the fact that Vasilisa's marriage to Vladimir was a common-law
one was considered unimportant.